W9-BKR-914

TWO DAYS GONE

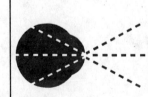

This Large Print Book carries the
Seal of Approval of N.A.V.H.

A RYAN DEMARCO MYSTERY

TWO DAYS GONE

RANDALL SILVIS

THORNDIKE PRESS
A part of Gale, Cengage Learning

GALE
CENGAGE Learning·

Farmington Hills, Mich • San Francisco • New York • Waterville, Maine
Meriden, Conn • Mason, Ohio • Chicago

GALE
CENGAGE Learning

LIBRARY OF CONGRESS CATALOGING-IN-PUBLICATION DATA

Names: Silvis, Randall, 1950– author.
Title: Two days gone / Randall Silvis.
Description: Large print edition. | Waterville, Maine : Thorndike Press Large Print, 2017. | Series: Ryan Demarco mystery | Series: Thorndike Press large print mystery
Identifiers: LCCN 2016055495| ISBN 9781410497871 (hardback) | ISBN 1410497879 (hardcover)
Subjects: LCSH: Murder—Investigation—Fiction. | Large type books. | Psychological fiction. | BISAC: FICTION / Mystery & Detective / General. | GSAFD: Mystery fiction.
Classification: LCC PS3569.I47235 T96 2017b | DDC 813/.54—dc23
LC record available at https://lccn.loc.gov/2016055495

Published in 2017 by arrangement with Sourcebooks, Inc.

Printed in Mexico
1 2 3 4 5 6 7 21 20 19 18 17

FOR MY SONS,
BRET AND NATHAN,
HEART OF MY SOUL,
SOUL OF MY HEART

■ ■ ■ ■

DESIRE

■ ■ ■ ■

ONE

The waters of Lake Wilhelm are dark and chilled. In some places, the lake is deep enough to swallow a house. In others, a body could lie just beneath the surface, tangled in the morass of weeds and water plants, and remain unseen, just another shadowy form, a captive feast for the catfish and crappie and the monster bass that will nibble away at it until the bones fall asunder and bury themselves in the silty floor.

In late October, the Arctic Express begins to whisper southeastward across the Canadian plains, driving the surface of Lake Erie into white-tipped breakers that pound the first cold breaths of winter into northwestern Pennsylvania. From now until April, sunny days are few and the spume-strewn beaches of Presque Isle empty but for misanthropic stragglers, summer shops boarded shut, golf courses as still as cemeteries, marinas stripped to their bonework of bare, splintered boards. For the next six months, the air will be gray and pricked with rain or blasted with wind-driven snow. A season of surliness prevails.

Sergeant Ryan DeMarco of the Pennsylvania State Police, Troop D, Mercer County headquarters, has seen this season come and go too many times. He has seen the surliness descend into despair, the despair to acts of desperation, or, worse yet, to deliberately malicious acts, to behavior that shows no regard for the fragility of flesh, a contempt for all consequences.

He knows that on the dozen or so campuses between Erie and Pittsburgh, college students still young enough to envision a happy future will bundle up against the biting chill, but even their youthful souls will suffer the effects of this season of gray. By November, they will have grown annoyed with their roommates, exasperated with professors, and will miss home for the first time since September. Home is warm and bright and where the holidays are waiting. But here in Pennsylvania's farthest northern reach, Lake Wilhelm stretches like a bony finger down a glacier-scoured valley, its waters dark with pine resin, its shores thick on all sides with two thousand acres of trees and brush and hanging vines, dense with damp shadows and nocturnal things, with bear and wildcat and coyote, with hawks that scream in the night.

In these woods too, or near them, a murderer now hides, a man gone mad in the blink of an eye.

The college students are anxious to go home now, home to Thanksgiving and Christmas and Hanukah, to warmth and love and light. Home to where men so respected and adored do not suddenly butcher their families and escape into the woods.

The knowledge that there is a murderer in one's midst will stagger any community, large or small. But when that murderer is one of your own, when you have trusted the education of your sons and daughters to him, when you have seen his smiling face in every bookstore in town, watched him chatting with Robin Roberts on *Good Morning America,* felt both pride and envy in his sudden acclaim, now your chest is always heavy and you cannot seem to catch your breath. Maybe you claimed, last spring, that you played high school football with Tom Huston. Maybe you dated him half a lifetime ago, tasted his kiss, felt the heave and tremor of your bodies as you lay in the lush green of the end zone one steamy August night when love was raw and new. Last spring, you were quick to claim an old intimacy with him, so eager to catch some of his sudden, shimmering light. Now you want only to huddle indoors. You sit and stare at the window, confused by your own pale reflection.

Now Claire O'Patchen Huston, one of the prettiest women in town, quietly elegant in a way no local woman could ever hope to be, lies on a table in a room at the Pennsylvania State Police forensics lab in Erie. There is the wide gape of a slash across her throat, an obscene slit that runs from the edge of her jawline to the opposite clavicle.

Thomas Jr., twelve years old, he with the quickest smile and the fastest feet in sixth grade, the boy who made all the high school coaches wet their lips in anticipation, shares the chilly room with his mother. The knife that took him in his sleep laid its path low across his throat, a quick, silencing sweep with an upward turn.

As for his sister, Alyssa, there are a few fourth grade girls who, a week ago, would have described her as a snob, but her best friends knew her as shy, uncertain yet of how to wear and carry and contain her burgeoning beauty. She appears to have sat up at the last instant, for the blood that spurted from her throat sprayed not only across the pillow, but also well below it, spilled down over her chest before she fell back onto her side. Did she understand the message of that gurgling gush of breath in her final moments of consciousness? Did she, as blood soaked into the faded pink flannel of her pajama shirt, lift her gaze to her father's eyes as he leaned away from her bed?

And little David Ryan Huston, asleep on his back in his crib — what dreams danced through his toddler's brain in its last quivers of sentience? Did his father first pause to listen to the susurrus breath? Did he calm himself with its sibilance? The blade on its initial thrust missed the toddler's heart and slid along the still-soft sternum. The second thrust found the pulsing muscle and nearly sliced it in half.

The perfect family. The perfect house. The perfect life. All gone now. Snap your fingers five times, that's how long it took. Five soft taps on the door. Five steel-edged scrapes across the tender flesh of night.

Two

DeMarco took the call at home just a few minutes after kickoff on Sunday afternoon. He was halfway through his first bottle of Corona. The Browns, after only four plays, had already driven inside the red zone. Pittsburgh's Steel Curtain appeared made of aluminum foil. DeMarco was settling in for an afternoon of mumbling and cursing when the call came in from Trooper Lipinski, who was working the desk at the State Police barracks.

The bodies of the Huston family had been discovered approximately twenty minutes earlier. Claire's mother and father had driven up from nearby Oniontown, just as they did every Sunday through the fall and early winter, "to watch the Steelers beat themselves," as Ed O'Patchen liked to say that season. The O'Patchens went up the walk and onto the covered porch as they always had, Ed lugging two six-packs of

14

Pabst Blue Ribbon, Rosemary cradling her Crock-Pot of cheese and sausage dip. As always, they walked inside without knocking. Rosemary went searching for the silent family upstairs while Ed tried to figure out how to work the remote on the new widescreen Sony.

The Browns scored while DeMarco was taking the call. He saw no more of the game.

Later that day, DeMarco and three other troopers began interviewing the Hustons' neighbors up and down Mayfield Road. Not a single resident along the tree-lined street had anything negative to say about the family, and none were aware of any financial or other marital problems between Thomas and Claire. All were stunned, most were grief-stricken.

Two residents, however, a homemaker and an elderly man, reported that they had seen a man who might or might not have been Thomas Huston walking through the neighborhood in the weak light of false dawn. "Kind of shuffling along," the homemaker said. "Looking confused," said the elderly man.

Both witnesses had been standing close to their own homes while keeping an eye on their dogs as they sniffed through dewy yards and saw the man from the rear as he was walking away from them. The woman hadn't yet put in her contact lenses and saw the man as "Just a shape, you know? Just the shape of a man." The elderly gentleman, who saw the man at a nearer distance, reported that the man who might have been Huston stopped twice, paused with his head down, and once turned fully around to look back down the street. The elderly gentleman asked from two houses away, "You lost?" But the man in question did not respond, and eventually he continued moving away again.

Four women traveling north on Interstate 79 at around eight thirty Sunday morning, on their way to breakfast at Bob Evans and then a day of shopping at the Millcreek Mall, telephoned 911 at around ten that morning to report passing a man as he leaned over the low concrete bridge abutment where the highway spans a spindly extension of Lake Wilhelm. He was staring into the dark water, they said. They agreed with the other witnesses as to what Huston was wearing: khaki trousers, a dark blue knit shirt, brown belt, and brown loafers or moccasins. They could not agree as to whether the man looked as if he were about to jump into the water or if perhaps he were watching something as it fell and disappeared beneath the surface. Only one woman claimed to have seen the object in his hand before it disappeared into the lake. "It was shiny," she said. "Like a knife. But a big knife." They would have called sooner but had come up from New Castle and weren't aware of the tragedy until a salesclerk mentioned it to one of them.

In the chill of the following morning, just two days before Halloween, a gray mist hung over the lake, clinging to the water like a spirit reluctant to tear itself free from the memory of flesh. DeMarco stood next to the same bridge abutment where Huston had paused the day before. Two dozen men and women from the criminal investigation units of Troops D and E huddled close on either side — primarily troopers from the two county stations affected by the apparent homicide in Mercer County and consequent search for the primary suspect in Crawford County. All wore blaze-orange plastic vests over black jackets. Four of the troopers knelt beside their search dogs, keeping the leashes snug for now. The dogs, all of mixed breed, were certified in tracking, search and rescue, and cadaver identification.

DeMarco's eyes stung from the morning's cold. A thin pool of dampness lay in his left lower lid, blurring his vision. The left eye was DeMarco's weak eye, the one he had injured long ago. It watered up at the slightest provocation these days — from a gust of wind, a blast of air-conditioning, an invisible speck of dust — and no matter how often he blinked, he could not whisk away that tiny pool of dampness that warped a corner of the world behind a rain-streaked window. Sometimes the eye would water for no reason at all, most frequently in the stillness of a new morning when he sat in his dark house with the television on, a glass of tepid Jack in his hand. Now, there on the low bridge, his eyes felt heavy from a lack of sleep. But that was nothing new either; his eyes always felt heavy.

Along the entire length of the bridge, and for some distance on either side — a total of two hundred yards or so — the right lane of the two northbound lanes of Interstate 79 had been blocked off to traffic with orange cones and yellow flashing lights. The passing lane, however, was still open, so DeMarco's voice as he spoke to the troopers frequently rose to a shout to carry above the rumbling approach and passage of a vehicle.

"If he managed to get ahold of a tarp or a blanket of some kind," DeMarco said, "he can last out there for two weeks or so. He might still be carrying the murder weapon with him. You should assume that he is. And according to the lab, it's no piddling little switchblade. Think machete, Bowie knife, maybe even a decorative sword of some kind. Where he might be headed or what might be going through that brain of his is anybody's guess, so *do not attempt to apprehend.* You are here to assist in the tracking of a suspect in a multiple homicide. Tracking is the full extent of your job. Any other action you engage in had best be warranted."

An eighteen-wheeler roared over the bridge now; the vibration rattled up through DeMarco's boots and into his knees. "Under no circumstances should you lose visual contact with the trooper nearest you. You see anything, and I mean anything, you radio it in to me. You see tracks, you call me. You find a recent campfire, you call me. You see Huston, you back off immediately and call me. Do not approach. The order to close in and apprehend will come from me and me alone. Also, be aware that there are field officers from the Game Commission stationed all around the perimeter of these woods to keep the public out, but that doesn't mean one or two of them won't slip past and come sneaking up on us. Therefore, you *will* exercise all due restraint."

Now DeMarco gazed out across the tannic water, squinted into the wisps of rising fog, and wondered what else he needed to say. Should he mention the uneasiness he had felt in his gut all morning, the sense of being slightly off balance, as if the floor were canted, ever since the moment the day before when he had walked into the Huston home? Should he attempt to describe the peculiar ache of grief that buffeted him like a bruising wind each time he considered Huston's smallest victim, the toddler with whom DeMarco shared a name? Should he tell them he had read all of Huston's novels, that autographed first editions stood side by side in the armoire his wife had left behind, one of them personally inscribed to De-Marco, all sharing the top shelf with his other prized first editions, nearly all of them gifts from Laraine, including the jewels of his collection, Umberto Eco's *The Name of the Rose* and J. M. Synge's *Riders to the Sea*?

Should he tell them of the three lunches he had shared with Thomas Huston, the fondness and admiration he felt for the man — the growing sense, and hope, for the first time in far too many years, that here, perhaps, was a friend?

Would any of that information do anybody any good, least of all himself?

"If all he's got are the clothes on his back," DeMarco told them, "he's not going to last long out there. He's probably cold and wet and hungry by now. So let's just get in there and do our job, all right?"

A red-winged blackbird flitted past De-Marco, so close that, had he been quick enough, he could have reached out and grabbed it, could have caught it in his hand. The bird stiffened its wings and glided low over the water. It rested on the tip of a reed at the water's edge. The reed swayed back and forth under the bird's weight — so gracefully, DeMarco thought, *like water.*

He became aware then, as if it had materialized out of nowhere, of the roar of a panel truck as it crossed the bridge. The rumble sent a chill through him, a frisson of fear. Strangely, his wife came to mind, and he hoped she was all right, hoped that whatever stranger she had taken to her bed the night before had been kind to her, tender, and had not given her what she craved. He turned his back to the vehicle, but its wake of cold air blasted over him. He wiped the dampness from the corner of his eye.

The troopers were watching him, waiting. Their stillness angered him. But he bit down hard on his anger. It was an old anger, he knew, and misdirected. "All right, let's get to it!" he shouted. "I want Thomas Huston sitting in the back of my vehicle, alive and well and cuffed, by the time the sun goes down on this fine October day."

THREE

On a low hillock nearly a hundred yards back from the water, in a shallow cave beneath an overhanging rock, a depression only five feet wide, two feet high, and maybe three feet deep, behind three boughs of spruce he had broken off and dragged to the cave at dusk the night before, Thomas Huston lay curled tight, his knees drawn close to his chest. Through the fragrant needles, he watched a thin light seeping into the forest. He knew that if he stretched his legs, numb from lack of movement, both feet tingling, a chill would rattle through him, cutting all the way to the bone. Then he would have to crawl out of his burrow, climb to his feet like a human being, try to make some sense of the world. This, he did not want to do. He did not feel capable of either the necessary decisions or the action. He believed that if he moved, he would probably start vomiting again, and there was nothing left in his stomach to expel. There was only blood and bile, the viscera itself, though he felt himself to be eviscerated already, as hollowed out as the four Cornish game hens he had made for dinner on Saturday night, the last meal he had prepared; those four tiny carcasses he had rinsed in cold water, patted dry, stuffed with bread crumbs and mushrooms spiced with sage and basil and thyme. No, he would not mind dry heaving if it resulted in unconsciousness, if he could annihilate all sentience through dry heaving, send himself into oblivion. He had only to let one of the four horrible images float to the surface of his mind and a pain like none he had ever experienced would seize him and double him up again, twist him into a rigid knot of agony whose only release, short-lived and painful itself, would be an animallike scream.

Think about dinner, he told himself, *the last time you had anything to eat. Go back to where it started. Think it all through.*

The four naked little birds lay lined up on a cutting board, their chests split open. A handful of stuffing. Slip it inside, work it in snugly. The scents of sweet basil and chopped onion. The heat rising from the oven. In the living room, sitting cross-legged

24

around the coffee table, Claire and Tommy and Lissie played Monopoly. Tommy was the real estate baron; he snapped up every property he could get his hands on. And little Davy, sweet, tireless Davy — time after time after time after time, he pulled the string on his Barnyard See'n Say. The cow says *Moo!* The rooster says *Cock-a-doodle-doo!*

Yes, that was real. Saturday night was real. But the rest of it . . . How could it be?

Fricatives, he thought. *Affricates. Diphthongs.*

Those were the words he had turned over in his mind that night, first during dinner, then later, in bed with his wife. He had intended to write them down, add them to the list he was compiling for his protagonist. His protagonist was a logophile, a man who liked words for their sounds more than their meanings, a man who would walk around saying "fricatives" just for the pleasure of it. The words had come to Huston while he was thinking about his protagonist, trying to envision and create a nuanced portrait of him. As often happened when Huston got into the head of a character, words would come to him as if straight from the character's mouth, words that Huston might have no conscious understanding of, no clear

25

idea as to their meaning. He would hear the words and write them down and, as he had meant to do on Saturday night, would later look up their meanings to be certain he had used the words correctly. Invariably, he would discover that he had, and what a pleasing discovery it would be, this mystery of creation, this sense of story as a gift from somewhere else.

But on Saturday night, he had not had an opportunity to reassure himself as to the precise meanings of the new words his protagonist had given him. Now the protagonist was silent, and now Huston was numb with cold and hunger and disbelief, a man in a cave in a situation that could only be fictional, was too horrific to be believed.

The story had changed. No computer, no pen. No ink, no paper.

"Fricatives," Huston whispered to the tangerine light as it bled through the spruce bows. "Affricates. Diphthongs."

A click inside his head. A screen shot filling his field of vision. He winced and pulled away, turned his face to the dirt. Image as pain. Memory a thrust and stab, a thousand synchronized blades.

His mind felt like a junkyard choked full of disparate parts. Like a huge jigsaw puzzle somebody had kicked all over the room.

Here's a piece of blue sky. Here's a piece with the corner of an eye in it. Is this a bird's wing? Is this brown grass or a strand of silky hair?

Any minute now, he kept telling himself, any minute now, he would manage to push himself up and out of this nightmare. "Wake up!" he scolded himself again and this time shook his head so hard that a pain stabbed into his left eye, sent a surge of nausea tumbling through his stomach. "Wake up, for Chrissakes!"

He remembered going online after dinner, checking the *Times*'s website. And there it was, there it had been, *The Desperate Summer,* still number eight after seven weeks. *That* was real. "Is it better than Steinbeck's *The Winter of Our Discontent*?" Michiko Kakutani had written. "I think it is."

He had the actual clipping in a folder in his file cabinet, kept all his clippings there, sometimes took the folder out and read through the clippings just to remind himself that they were real, that he wasn't dreaming his good fortune. Yes, they were real. Words made real in pulped wood, cotton rag, and ink. Wholly and tangibly real.

The dog says *Woof!*

The duck says *Quack!*

Then he saw little Davy again, the baby

27

asleep. He closed his eyes and again heard the baby's breath, that sweet whisper of life, the rise and fall of the little chest. He felt the knife heavy in his own hand. But was it his hand? How could it have been? *Is this a dagger which I see before me, The handle toward my hand?* Who was it that had said that? It was Macbeth, right? Half-mad Macbeth. *Art thou not, fatal vision, sensible To feeling as to sight? or art thou but A dagger of the mind . . . ?*

Art thou?

"Art thou?" Huston asked. His body tightened in a spasm of grief, clenched in upon itself, and a stifled moan worked its way up from his chest, a moan as taut as stretched sinew, as sharp as honed steel.

"Please, God," Thomas Huston groaned into the dirt. "Please, please, please, God. *Please just let me wake up.*"

FOUR

The previous summer, a Friday in July. De-Marco had spent the morning at a hearing in the courthouse, where he had testified that a drug-addled wife beater had taken two shots at him, then had thrown down his handgun and invited DeMarco into the house for a glass of iced tea. The man claimed he had never aimed to shoot De-Marco or anybody else, and DeMarco admitted that the nearest of the two bullets had knocked the lid off a garbage can some six and a half feet to his left.

The judge asked, "Are you saying that you never felt your life was in peril?"

"I feel like my life is in peril every time I climb out of bed," DeMarco answered. "Doesn't everybody?"

The wife beater was ordered to complete eight weeks of rehab, after which he would serve 120 days for reckless endangerment.

Now, at a few minutes after eleven, De-

Marco returned to the barracks with two cups of convenience store coffee — one black, for him, and a hazelnut cappuccino, for his station commander. As usual, De-Marco had to suppress a smile when he walked into the office and found Sergeant Kyle Bowen there behind the long mahogany desk, looking very serious, very busy, and very young.

DeMarco handed him the coffee. "I see it's bring-your-son-to-work-day again. Daddy taking a pee break?"

Bowen peeled the lid off the cardboard cup and sniffed. "What is this, hazelnut?"

"It's what you always drink, isn't it?"

"I'm going to write it down and pin it to your jacket, I swear. Mocha is fine. Vanilla is fine. Plain French roast with two creams and one sugar is fine. Anything is fine except hazelnut. Why do you keep doing this to me?"

"You're too young to drink coffee. It will stunt your growth."

Bowen pushed the cup to the outer edge of his desk. "So what did he get?"

"Two months rehab, four months to contemplate the error of his ways."

"Jesus. Another victory for the criminally insane."

"But job security for us," DeMarco said.

Bowen shook his head, tore a sheet of paper off his notepad, and handed it to De-Marco. "How about laying this on Jenny's desk on your way past?"

"She's out again?"

"Fourth time in two weeks."

"Preggers for sure."

"No doubt."

"When are you going to tell your wife?"

"Here's an idea: go get some work done."

DeMarco smiled and brought the sheet of paper close enough to read. "T. Huston?" he said. "Thomas Huston?"

"Did I invite you to read that?"

"You didn't invite me not to."

"Don't read it. It's for Jenny, not you."

"Info request," DeMarco read. "T. Huston. Writer." He lowered the paper and looked at Bowen. "What kind of info is he looking for?"

"The kind Jenny provides."

"Is this his home number or the university?"

"You are not public relations. You got nothing to do, go grab a radar gun."

DeMarco folded the paper and slipped it into his jacket pocket. "I need a break from the criminals. You ever read this guy? Or are you still working your way through the Hardy Boys?"

"Let Jenny do her job, would you, please? And you do yours."

"This guy writes dark stuff. Seriously dark. Jenny's all puppies and roses. I'll take this one."

Bowen sat back straight in his chair, put both hands on the edge of his desk. "You know, I don't mind the coffee pranks and the other abuse, but don't you think you should maybe just once do what I ask you to do?"

DeMarco rubbed his cheek. "You familiar with an old song by Johnny Cash? 'A Boy Named Sue'? You're my Sue."

"So you're trying to toughen me up, is that it?"

"You can thank me when you make lieutenant."

Bowen leaned forward and brought his hands together, rubbed a thumb across the palm of his other hand. "Is it because of my dad?"

"Hey, your dad's a good man. He did what he had to do. And he made the right decision. How is the old goat anyway? Still shuffleboard champ of Tampa–Saint Pete?"

"He says when you were my age, you were ramrod straight. Eye of the tiger and all that. But afterward . . . it was almost like you wanted to get demoted."

32

DeMarco gazed at the ceiling and made a popping sound with his lips. Then he looked down at Bowen again. "Are we done reminiscing here?" He patted his jacket pocket. "Some of us adults have work to do."

"Go," Bowen told him and waved him away. "Just go."

DeMarco reached for the cup. "Thanks for the coffee."

FIVE

DeMarco first met Huston at a place called Dino's, a small, narrow brick building shaped like a diner, its six booths all lined up against the long window overlooking busy State Street. "I don't often get down this way," Huston told him. "It's closer for us to go to Erie for everything. But I like it here. I like the feel of it."

DeMarco nodded, smiled, sipped his sweet tea. He had recognized Huston from the photos on his book jackets. None showed the writer in a coat and tie, yet DeMarco was still pleasantly surprised by the day's growth of stubble on Huston's cheeks, the washed-out jeans and dark blue T-shirt. Except for his six-foot height, he reminded DeMarco of a young Jack Kerouac.

Huston took off his navy-blue baseball cap and laid it on the seat, then finger combed his hair while he considered the sandwich board behind the counter. "What's good here?" he asked.

"When I come, it's for the eggplant parm or the junkyard dogs."

"So how about we split the twelve-inch eggplant parm and an order of four dogs? They have iced coffee here?"

"I'm sure they can pour some of yesterday's over ice for you, no problem."

"That's how I make it at home," Huston said.

DeMarco leaned back against the booth and allowed himself to relax. He had dealt with academics before and had found most of them either socially dysfunctional or condescending. But here was a respected professor from a private, very expensive college, a critically acclaimed novelist, big-screen handsome, still young — DeMarco felt both envy and a sudden, unexpected fondness for the man.

"So who are the Tigers?" he asked.

"Excuse me?"

"The baseball cap. Those aren't Detroit's colors."

"My boy's Little League team last year. I was an assistant coach."

"Was?"

"They moved him up to PONY League this year. I could've helped out again, but Claire, my wife, she thought it was time I

35

take a step back, you know? Time to let him be his own man for a change."

DeMarco read the look on Huston's face. "Not easy to do, huh?"

"Fathers and sons, you know? It's hard to be a spectator."

This time, it was Huston's turn to read the subtle change in the other man's eyes. "You have children, Officer? Is that the proper way to address you, by the way? Or do you prefer 'Trooper'? 'Sergeant'?"

"Ryan will do. And no, no children."

"Ryan is my baby's middle name. David Ryan Huston."

"Good name," DeMarco said.

Huston nodded toward the gold band on DeMarco's left hand. "You're married, though."

"Separated."

"Sorry, man."

"Hey. Life," DeMarco said. He looked down at the table, squared up the paper place mat.

Huston did not allow the awkward moment to linger. "So what's it like being an officer of the law?"

"It's great. You get to see humanity at its worst day in and day out. What's it like being a professor?"

Huston smiled. "You know how many

academics it takes to change a lightbulb?"

"How many?"

"Four to form a committee, two to write a report, one to file a grievance with the union, and one to ask the secretary to call the janitor."

DeMarco smiled.

"Don't get me wrong," Huston said. "I love my students. And I get a lot from them. Their passion, you know? That fire in the belly."

DeMarco started to nod but then stopped himself. What did he know about passion? The fire in his belly had been snuffed a long time ago. "So your new book," he said, "this one you're working on. It's about the state police?"

"A trooper is one of the main characters, yeah."

"One of the good guys?"

"Good guys, bad guys . . . it's all fairly ambiguous, you know?"

"It's been fairly ambiguous in all of your novels, seems to me."

"So you're a reader."

"Got into the habit when I first met my wife. She's an English teacher. She kind of insisted that if I wanted to date her, I had to broaden my literary horizons."

"Thank God for the annealing effect of

women," Huston said. "So then, are you familiar with Nabokov's *Lolita*?"

"Heard of it but haven't read it. Isn't it about an older man's involvement with a young girl?"

"Right. And there's this character named Quilty, the narrator's nemesis. I'm thinking of making him a state trooper."

The server appeared at their table then, a thin Asian girl in a crisp, white uniform. Huston gave their order and engaged her in pleasant conversation for another minute or so. When she walked away, he turned to see DeMarco smiling.

"I wasn't flirting with her," Huston said.

"I know. You didn't look at her butt when she left."

"Did you?"

"It's a very fine butt."

Huston grinned. "You're not what I expected in a policeman."

"You're not what I expected in a pompous ass," DeMarco said. "So anyway, back to this guy in your book who's based on me. He's extremely good-looking, right? Sort of a George Clooney type."

"Not a bad choice," Huston said. "Clooney is quite convincing at playing bumblers."

"Wait a minute. My character is a bumbler?"

"In Nabokov's novel, yes. He's rigid. He's obsessed. He's a moralizer who refuses to see the immorality of his own actions."

"Tell you what," DeMarco said. "It's probably better to just leave me out of the story. That way I won't have to arrest you for something."

They met on three more occasions that summer. At the second meeting, again at Dino's, Huston quizzed DeMarco on the hierarchy of authority in the state police organization, who did what, the types of firearms they carried, under what conditions the state police assisted or overrode the local police. But he also talked at length about his own life, his wife and three children, all obviously adored.

Then there was a pause. And Huston told him, quietly, "You know about my parents probably."

DeMarco nodded. The bungled robbery of the Hustons' hardware store, the blast that tore out his mother's throat. His father's suicide two weeks later from an overdose of his antidepressant. The horrific images that still haunted Thomas, the memories that sometimes overwhelmed him.

DeMarco found himself so moved by the intimacy of that conversation that he nearly dragged out his own ghosts and demons for examination, thought that if he chose now, after all these years, to finally speak about that almost hallucinatory happiness of the early years of marriage and fatherhood, then the sudden violent extinguishment of it, his anger and too-aggressive behavior and the subsequent demotion, that here was a man who would understand. Unfortunately, he could bring himself to speak only elliptically of Ryan Jr. and to say of Laraine, "She left me not long after that."

Huston's hand slid across the table as if to reach out to DeMarco, but it stopped short, and Huston said only, "Fuck, man. Jesus. I'm so sorry."

DeMarco nodded, but he was looking away now, watching the traffic go by outside, and he was relieved when Huston asked nothing more, and grateful when the server walked by and Huston told her, "We're ready for the check now."

For their third meeting, in August, De-Marco was invited to a barbecue at Huston's home. He met Huston's beautiful wife and three beautiful children, was given a tour of the lovely Victorian, and spent the rest of that dulcet evening conscious of and resenting the heavy ache of envy deep in his chest.

The envy reached its crescendo near dusk, with Huston and DeMarco seated side by side on lawn chairs, both relaxed, both watching the other guests. DeMarco was watching Tommy with one of his friends, the boys taking turns mugging with a Wiffle bat, tongues stuck in their cheeks like wads of tobacco, maybe imitating a parent or coach from Little League practice. The scene made DeMarco smile, and when he said to Huston, "He looks just like you," he hadn't meant it to sound as wistful as it did.

But Huston obviously heard the underlying ache in the words — his eyes said that he had heard it — and he smiled too, and then both men remained silent for quite a while, two fathers smiling together at one son, both men painfully aware of the son who wasn't there.

And it was during those silent moments that DeMarco understood the true difference between Huston and himself. It had nothing to do with money or position. Both were solitary men in their own way, though DeMarco lived alone and Huston did not. Both had several complicated relationships with others. But Huston conducted all of his relationships from a solid center, from within the stabilizing orbit of his family, always venturing out from and returning to family, with his every action and reaction synchronized with family first, family last, family always, whereas DeMarco, on the other hand, had no center. He ventured out to the other relationships from emptiness, and to emptiness he returned. Every action synchronized with nothing. Emptiness first, emptiness last, emptiness always.

Their final meeting took place the next morning, when Huston showed up at De-Marco's door. He stood there grinning, holding a book in one hand, a cardboard carton in the other.

DeMarco said, "Do I smell chili dogs?"

"Ever try them for breakfast?"

"I've always wanted to. C'mon in."

Huston handed him the carton, and De-Marco nodded toward the novel. "You going to read to me while I eat?"

"I'm going to eat while you eat." He laid the book atop a small lamp table against the wall.

DeMarco read the cover. *"The Desperate Summer?"*

"I know you've already read it, or at least pretended to. But this is a first edition. I inscribed it for you. From what I hear, they're going for about a thousand per right now."

"Thank you," DeMarco said. "I'll put it up on eBay first thing tomorrow."

Huston grinned and slapped him on the arm. "What's a good breakfast drink with chili dogs?"

"There's a pitcher of iced tea in the fridge. I'll get the glasses and napkins."

They sat on the back porch, side by side on the edge above the steps, the carton of chili dogs between them. They ate the first dogs in silence. Halfway through his second one, Huston nodded at the overgrown yard. "Who's your lawn boy?" he asked.

"I ordered a goat from Amazon but it hasn't arrived yet."

Huston chuckled. "I like the path, though. If you need any help someday . . ."

"Yeah, well . . ." DeMarco finished his last hot dog, wiped his mouth with a napkin, took a sip of iced tea. "It's sort of a project in limbo."

"Waiting for more bricks?"

And that was enough, after ten seconds of silence, to open him up. It started with, "I haven't worked on it since Laraine walked out. Same with the studio apartment I started in the garage out there."

"That little barn across the alley?"

He nodded.

"She left you after your baby died?"

43

"A week after the funeral, my first day back to work. I came home and she was gone. Left her wedding ring on the kitchen counter."

After that, DeMarco recounted the accident that took baby Ryan's life and finished with, "She lives by herself now, up in Erie. Mostly by herself. I still see her once in a while but . . . She'll let me in, but she won't say a single word to me. I can talk myself blue, and she won't say a single word."

More silence passed. "You still wear your ring," Huston said.

"Neither one of us has ever filed. Never even mentioned it."

"So there's still hope."

The silence continued for a long time after that. Finally, DeMarco pushed himself to his feet. "You're right about this yard. I need to break out the lawn mower."

Now Huston stood. "Personally, I like the natural look."

DeMarco smiled. He stared at the path awhile longer, then turned to Huston. "Thanks for the dogs and the book. Thanks for stopping by."

DeMarco turned to face the porch, then bent down to fill his hands with the pitcher and empty glasses. "Just leave the carton there," he said. "I keep my garbage can out in the garage."

Huston leaned closer and, with the heel of his fist, laid a soft punch on DeMarco's arm. "Don't be a stranger," he said.

"A stranger what?"

Huston smiled, then turned and crossed along the side of the house, out to the sidewalk and his car.

Only after DeMarco had washed out the pitcher and glasses and had crumpled up the hot dog carton and mashed it into the overflowing trash container under his sink did he retrieve Huston's novel. He opened it to the title page.

To my new good friend Ryan DeMarco, Huston had written in blue ink, *this small token of appreciation — not for the information you provided, which I could have found on the Internet, but for the pleasure of your company. May that sadness in your eyes soon melt away, my brother, and may our supply of junkyard dogs never diminish.*

And now it was October, almost Halloween. Huston's latest published book had been an international bestseller since the middle of September. The beautiful family now all lay on cold steel tables beneath cold white sheets. Huston was out there somewhere in the dark, tangled woods, and De-

45

Marco had no stomach now for junkyard dogs or anything else.

SIX

The troopers had been in the woods for less than an hour when DeMarco received the radio call. He had moved ahead of the others but stayed close enough that, if he looked over his shoulder, he could see the four canine units stretched out behind him in a line, each unit some twenty yards from the next. In the strengthening but still slant and broken light, the dogs moved as briskly as their leashes would allow, damp noses to the leaf-matted ground, their muscled bodies carving tight zigzagging paths. None of them had yet found the scent they wanted. Each trooper carried a plastic bag containing an article of Huston's clothing, and, from time to time, a dog would pull up short, lift its nose, and sniff the air, scanning from side to side and finally gazing up at its handler. The trooper would then hold the plastic bag open and allow the dog to poke its muzzle inside, freshen its memory

47

with the unique scent of Thomas Huston, and soon the dog would lower its nose to the ground and pull forward again.

Behind these canine units came the other troopers, an uneven line as wide as two football fields. Their orange vests flashed like huge fireflies flitting through the gray woods.

Mutant fireflies, DeMarco told himself. Drawn here not by love, but by Huston's rage and madness.

He breathed in the scent of the woods as he walked, a damp and heavy fragrance, adumbrated and autumnal, the perfume of decay yet somehow fecund and sweet. De-Marco was a man who loved the dark woods, loved the stillness punctuated only by the chirp of birds, the chittering of a squirrel. He loved the thumping flight of a whitetail as it crashed through the brush. The explosive wing flutter of a flushed grouse. The distant warbling gobble of an amorous turkey.

The crackle of his radio, on the other hand, was as startling as a bee in his ear. "Got a cave over here, Sergeant. Looks like he might have spent the night in it. Left flank, about a hundred yards from the lake-shore."

DeMarco sent the canine units ahead of

him, ordered the other troopers to hold their positions. By the time he arrived at the shallow cave, the dogs were straining at their leashes, wanting to leap forward, whining with their eagerness to pursue the quarry.

"Keep those animals still," DeMarco told the handlers.

He knelt outside the depression, shined a flashlight beam inside.

"These pine branches were broken off, probably used to cover up the opening," Trooper Morgan told him. Morgan was a slender man of medium height, long jawed and taciturn. He smiled frequently but infrequently spoke. "You can see over here where they were dragged along the ground."

DeMarco imagined what it must have been like for a man six feet tall to lay huddled in that tiny space. The earthen walls were indented with a hundred heel marks, half-moons gouged into the soil. De-Marco put his fingers to one of the heel marks. *He rolled and turned and pushed at these walls through the longest night of his life.* But the soil was cold. Huston had fled at least an hour earlier, leaving nothing behind but a damp depression filled with his scent. It was enough to make the dogs crazy, make saliva drip from their black gums, make their long tongues flap. But the sight of that hole filled DeMarco with grief. *A brilliant man reduced to a beast.*

DeMarco pulled away from the cave and stood, flicked off the flashlight. He looked at the dogs. "Let's get 'em moving," he said.

Two and a half hours later, legs weary, DeMarco and the four canine units paused along the edge of an unpaved road overlooking a swamp. On the photocopied map DeMarco carried, this area was labeled *Cranberry Bog,* but to DeMarco's eyes, it was nothing more than a vast, wet morass of thorny bushes and vines. "There's no way he went through this mess," DeMarco said aloud, though only to himself.

Three of the dogs sat panting beside their handlers; the fourth lay at his handler's feet, chin in the dirt. DeMarco thought the posture of the dogs reflected dejection, maybe even embarrassment. Ten minutes earlier, Huston's trail had intersected with the dirt road and, initially, had turned south. But after only thirty yards or so, the dogs had come to a halt, retreated, found the scent again, then sniffed their way northwest along the same road only to lose the trail at the edge of the swamp.

And DeMarco said, "He changed his mind."

One of the troopers asked, "You think he's

headed home?"

Another trooper said, "That wouldn't be very smart, would it, Sarge?"

DeMarco offered no reply. The dogs were idle, the troopers at a loss.

Three of the troopers moved close together not far behind DeMarco. Only Trooper Morgan was from the Mercer County station, DeMarco's station, and only he did not participate in the conversation.

"You don't think he waded or swam across that bog, do you?"

"It would be a good way to put the dogs off."

"Yeah, but Christ, that water can't be more than fifty degrees this time of year."

"It would take him, what, twenty, thirty minutes to wade across? He'd have hypothermia in ten."

"You say 'wade' like you know how deep it is."

"It's a cranberry bog, for Chrissakes. How deep can it be?"

"So you're an expert on cranberry bogs?"

"I know they aren't very deep."

"Then how deep are they, genius?"

"I'd say three to five feet. Somewhere in that range."

"So wade on out there and let's see."

DeMarco flashed a look of annoyance at the trooper from his station. DeMarco and Morgan had known each other for seven years, had worked together many times. Morgan turned to the others now and said, "Keep it quiet, guys."

"Why bother?" one of them asked. "If he was anywhere near here, the dogs would know it."

Morgan faced the man who had spoken. "Quiet," he said again.

Overhead, the droning whir of a helicopter faded in and out as the craft flew a grid between the cranberry swamp and Lake Wilhelm. DeMarco thumbed down the button on his radio. "Still nothing?" he asked.

A trooper in the helicopter studied his infrared screen. "I've got your group beside the swamp," he said. "I've got the rest of the troopers making their way to where you are. Between them and you, nothing."

"Take it north of the swamp," DeMarco said.

A few minutes later, he received another report. "I've got one hotspot fleeing easterly," the trooper informed him. "But it jumped over Black Run at about thirty miles an hour. So I doubt it's our man."

DeMarco gazed out across the cranberry bog. *Fifteen acres of freezing water,* he thought. *Fifteen acres of vines whipping at your face and arms and tangling around your legs.*

Where are you going, Thomas? he wondered. *What's that misfiring brain of yours telling you to do now?*

"So how do you think he got out of here?" one of the troopers asked. "You think he caught a ride with somebody?"

Nobody answered.

DeMarco pursed his lips, squinted, and stared out across the swamp. When he inhaled, he could smell a vague scent of something fruity, a subtle tang mixed with the darkness of the bog and the ache of inevitable winter. *Cranberries?* As far as he could tell, there wasn't a cranberry in sight.

He glanced again at his map, then reached for his radio, called the station, and told the dispatcher where to send the vehicles for pickup. Afterward, he walked down the short slope to the edge of the swamp and squatted on his haunches. He scooped up a handful of water and looked at it. Up close and in small amounts, the water lost its darkness, looked as clean and amber as good whiskey. He held it to his nose, inhaled its fragrance. He could smell the winter in it, could smell the dying fruit. He cupped his hand to his mouth, sucked in a sip of water. It was so cold that it burned his throat, so cold that it made him dizzy. He tilted his head back, squeezed shut his eyes, put one hand against the ground to steady himself from falling over.

He did not know what to do with the ache running through him. He wished he could lower his head into the water and let its darkness blind him and let its chill numb his brain. Then he could crawl into a shallow depression in the ground and pull pine boughs atop him, and he would never come out, never think another thought.

He knew that the four troopers up on the road were watching him, maybe whispering to one another. The dogs were probably watching him too. "Let them fucking watch," he muttered to the water. "Let them fucking wonder."

SEVEN

The first thing DeMarco did after returning to the barracks was to wash his hands. He washed his hands frequently, eight, ten times a day. He kept a package of antiseptic baby wipes in his car, another one in his desk. But this time, he went to the lavatory in the barracks because he wanted to splash water on his face too, thought the shock of cold water might knock the cobwebs from his brain. He soaped his hands thoroughly, scraped a thumbnail beneath each fingernail, rinsed off the soap, and splashed four handfuls of cold water in his face.

His hands were clean, but the water on his face didn't work. Fragments of thoughts floated through his brain like charred paper on water, thoughts that would not coalesce.

Instead of returning to his office, he walked to an office down the hall, tapped twice on the glass, and opened the door. Trooper Jayme Matson looked up from behind her desk. She was thirty-six years old, twelve years younger than DeMarco, a tall, thin woman whom some of the troopers secretly referred to as "Ichabod." But DeMarco knew her resemblance to the Sleepy Hollow ectomorph had more to do with the uniform than with her own physiology. He knew that in a sleeveless summer dress and two-inch heels, with her strawberry-blond hair hanging loose to her jawline and not knotted into a bun, she could look as elegant as a gazelle. He also knew the reason for the melancholy smile with which she now, and always, regarded him.

"You still working on that master's in psychology?" he asked as he stepped inside her office.

"Nine more credits," she said. "Why do you ask?"

He pulled a chair up close to her desk and sat down. "Here's a guy who's got the world by the tail. Perfect family, great job . . ."

She was already nodding. "Fame, reputation, respect, the whole package."

"By all appearances without a care in the world."

"And yet he snaps."

"Does he?" DeMarco said.

"It happens, Ry. It does happen. There's

never any way of knowing for sure what's going on inside another person's head."

The way she smiled at him when she said this, the dolefulness of her look, made him avert his gaze for a few moments. He considered his hands.

"Okay, so let's say he does," DeMarco said. "He snaps. In a moment of, what, blind rage? He wipes out his family, one after another?"

"I don't know," she said. "There's the nature of the wounds to consider."

"Right. Very methodical. Deliberate. All except little Davy's."

She waited while he thought it out.

"Okay," DeMarco finally said. "The snap theory. What could make it happen?"

"Just about anything — finances, workload, an argument with his wife."

"The money was rolling in hand over fist."

"That can be its own kind of stress."

DeMarco scowled, thinking it over.

"So maybe he thought he sold out," Matson said. "He's a serious writer, correct? You ever read him?"

DeMarco only cocked his head and looked at her. She had been in his house, had perused his bookshelves. In fact, when she had rolled over in his bed that time, had turned her back to him, it had been Huston's latest novel that she'd picked up off the nightstand. Huston's latest novel she had flung across the room.

As for the sell-out theory, DeMarco couldn't buy it. He had watched the *Good Morning America* spot, then later, the interview with Charlie Rose. In both cases, Huston had been relaxed, confident, almost serene in his responses. "How is all this sitting with you?" Charlie Rose had asked. "Your sudden celebrity status and everything that comes with it?" Huston had said nothing for several seconds, had sat there looking down. Then a slow smile came to his lips. He had looked up at Rose and said, "This last book is the best I've ever written. I'm at the top of my game at last. I feel validated."

And DeMarco, sitting alone in his darkened living room with a glass of warm Jack in hand, had believed every word of it. He had even raised his glass to the television screen. "Good for you, brother," he had said aloud.

So no, fuck the sell-out theory. To Trooper Matson he said, "You know his father committed suicide."

"That was how long ago?"

DeMarco thought it through, thought back to where he had been when he heard the news. Laraine had been pregnant then. He had come home at nearly midnight, a steamy night in August, a bar brawl between Reds and Pirates fans, and found her crying in bed. "That poor man," she had told him.

"It's what he wanted though," DeMarco had answered. He had undressed quickly and climbed in beside her, needing, on that hot night, the warmth of her skin against his, the soothing contact of his hand on the swell of her belly. "I can understand that."

"I mean his son," she had told him. "His only child. Imagine how he must feel right now."

"About four years ago," DeMarco told Matson. "So that could be a factor?"

"His entire past is a factor, Ryan. Question is, what made him take it out on his family?"

"Okay," DeMarco said. "So something set him off. And then what?"

"And then . . . ?"

"I mean after the fog clears. After he realizes what he's done. What happens then? Where is he psychologically?"

"Well," she said, "if he's not, in fact, a sociopath — and they can be very hard to spot, by the way."

DeMarco said, "Let's assume he's exactly what he appears. He's a good, decent man.

59

So when the fog clears . . . ?"

She thought for a moment. "He'll be horrified. Even beyond that. In all likelihood, he would take his own life."

"But he didn't. He walked outside. And he kept walking, all the way up to Lake Wilhelm. Just over three miles from his house."

"Then he detached. Disassociated."

"He just blanked it out?"

"Not exactly," she said. "But for all intents and purposes, yes. He suppresses the knowledge of what happened because it's just too horrific to face."

"So he goes walking out into the woods. And maybe he's still walking. Doesn't know who he is or where he's going?"

"Everybody is different. I mean, there are certain patterns to human behavior, sure, but I'm no expert on this . . ."

"You're the best I have at the moment."

"Maybe he's amnesic," she said. "Maybe he's not. Maybe it all seems unreal to him. Like a bad dream he can't quite remember."

"That's sort of what I was afraid of," DeMarco said.

"Because it makes his movements impossible to predict."

DeMarco nodded.

She waited for him to continue, but he remained motionless, eyes lowered, one thumb moving back and forth across the other hand's knuckles.

Softly she said, "You think he didn't do it."

He looked up at her and smiled. He saw her again with her hair down the night they had gone to dinner. Penne with portobello sauce for her, pasta puttanesca for him. He had ended up eating half of her dinner while she drank too much wine, drank too much on purpose, she later admitted, so that she would have the courage to say what she had said.

Now, looking at her and remembering, he felt his left eye begin to water. He blinked, rubbed his eye, moved his gaze just slightly to the left, over her shoulder, to a blank spot on the wall. "You advised me once that if I truly want to understand somebody's actions, I have to get outside myself and inside that person's head, try to see the world the way they do."

"I advised you a lot of things. Most of which you totally ignored."

"I'm just trying to understand Huston from all possible angles."

Her voice grew even softer. "I wish you would look at me when we talk, Ryan."

He moved his gaze back to her face. "I need to talk about Thomas Huston now."

She lifted her chin slightly higher, inhaled, and lost the melancholy smile. "So if he didn't do it himself but . . . what? Saw it happen? Discovered it after it happened?"

"Either way. Is he going to blank it out or not?"

"Would you?"

DeMarco put both hands on the armrests, got ready to push himself up. "That's a big fucking help, Jayme. You sure you need only nine more credits?"

She leaned back in her chair. "You look tired, Ryan."

He stood. "I've been spending too much time in the pool at the country club. I like to sit underwater and look at women's legs."

"You still like them long and thin?"

"Jayme," he said.

She said, "I could make that penne with mushroom sauce you like."

"Rain check," he told her, and pulled open the door and stepped out.

He was three steps down the hall when he thought he heard her mutter, "Fuck you and your rain checks." Or maybe it was only inside his head.

EIGHT

In his office, DeMarco checked in with the borough police who were monitoring the Huston home on Mayfield Road. "What's it like down there?" he asked.

"I've never seen anything like it," the officer told him. "TV news trucks all up and down the road. It's crazy. Half a dozen people with microphones standing in the front yard of an empty house."

"What are the chances you can get them out of there? Off Mayfield entirely?"

"They'll raise hell and start calling lawyers."

"Close the street," DeMarco said. "Except for local traffic. Tell the newsies their presence is interfering with an ongoing investigation. Tell them we'll hold a press conference soon."

"Where do you want me to put them?"

"It's your town, Officer. You decide."

"That empty lot where the farmers market

63

sets up on Saturdays, it's only two blocks away."

"And no farmers market now?"

"Maybe three, four stands altogether. Apples, late season produce."

"So crowd the news trucks together in the back corner, keep the main entrance free for the produce stands."

"That should work. When's the press conference scheduled?"

"I'll let you know. Thanks for your assistance. I appreciate it."

He went down the hall then, to Bowen's office. The station commander was using a hand mirror to look at the underside of his chin.

DeMarco said, "Pimple cream not working?"

Bowen laid the mirror atop his desk. "Something you want?"

"Did you schedule a press conference yet?"

"As soon as I get your report. How's noon tomorrow for you?"

"Count me out of any press conferences."

"You're leading the investigation. At your insistence, I might add. How about you follow protocol and let your team do the legwork?"

"We're dealing with a celebrity here, and

not just a local one. I know this man. I know more about the way he thinks than you know about the way you think."

"Which is yet another reason why you should handle the press conference."

DeMarco shook his head. "I'm way too pretty for the camera. You're not."

"Listen —"

DeMarco turned and headed back out the door. "You'll have my report within the hour."

At his own desk again, DeMarco stared at the sleeping computer monitor. He envied the monitor's ability to shut itself down from time to time, to turn off the images, extinguish the lights. *You look tired,* Jayme had said.

"I am tired," he told the monitor. He stared a while longer, then pulled himself out of it.

"All right. If I have to stay awake, so do you." He jerked the mouse across its pad. The monitor flickered to life.

In the Google search box, he typed the phrase *Thomas Huston parents,* then read through the long list of hits. Most of the articles were reviews of Huston's books. But two were profiles of Huston and his latest novel, *The Desperate Summer,* a book released three and a half years after his parents' deaths.

The first profile referred to *The Desperate Summer* as "the author's first work following the tragic loss of both parents, one by murder, the other by suicide two weeks later." The other profile, from *Poets & Writers,* recounted how a wild-eyed junkie had walked into the Hustons' hardware store, demanded money, was refused, pulled out a Sig Sauer 9mm and shot Cynthia Huston once in the throat and twice in her chest. He then shot David Huston an inch and a half above his heart. Then emptied the magazine, with no effect, into the black Hayman MagnaVault against the wall behind the counter.

The interview section of the profile probed even more deeply.

P&W: I think it's fair to say that *The Desperate Summer* is your darkest story to date. So is it fair to assume that the novel was colored by the circumstances of your parents' deaths?

TH: I had come up with the basic story line well prior to that. But I did most of the writing in the nine or ten months after. And yes, the story line changed, as they always do.

P&W: Changed because that's the nature

of stories? Or because of your parents' deaths?

TH: Both, I'm sure.

P&W: I'm thinking particularly of the protagonist. Joshua Kennedy has some very dark moments.

TH: He does indeed.

P&W: Do those moments reflect the author's own state of mind at the time?

TH: Well, every character is, in some way, the author. Some aspect of the author. So, in that case . . . Listen, to suddenly be orphaned, even at thirty-five years old . . . I mean, when are the sudden and violent deaths of people you love not a shock? So yes, of course it affected the writing. Of course some of my own thoughts at that time found their way into the novel.

P&W: Now that you have some distance from those events, have you found some peace, some acceptance of what happened?

TH: Distance? You've never lost anyone you loved, have you? There's no such thing as distance.

At that point in the profile, the interviewer shifted gears, moved on to a consideration of the author's work in progress, a novel tentatively titled *D.* Still, DeMarco found Huston's brief responses revealing. It was clear that Thomas Huston, like his character, suffered some very dark moments. But dark enough to cause him to slaughter his own family?

DeMarco knew *The Desperate Summer* well; it was his favorite of the author's three books. The fictional Joshua Kennedy, in anguish over his daughter's rape and his son's arrest for dealing drugs, vents his frustration with the judicial system and with life in general by resorting to petty crimes — first graffiti, then shoplifting, then vandalism of municipal property. He finds his son's stash of ecstasy, but instead of destroying it, he samples the drug and spends the next three days in a motel room with a twenty-four-year-old girl, one of his son's friends. Did that necessarily imply that Thomas Huston himself had ever resorted to crime, drug use, and infidelity as a release from his pain? Of course not. But DeMarco found it interesting that the author would conceive of those activities as emollients for his character's anger and grief.

The sting of his parents' deaths was still raw in Huston after three and a half years. Maybe it was still raw last Saturday night. Maybe it had been festering in him all this time, and some trivial thing — a sarcastic comment, a telephone call — had sent the poisons coursing through Huston's bloodstream, igniting in him a fury that literary palliatives could no longer suppress.

DeMarco made a mental note to pull Huston's phone records from that night. If he could get a handle on Huston's frame of mind, maybe he could make an intelligent guess as to where to look for the writer.

In the meantime, he returned to surfing the Internet. Forty minutes later, he came across a promising article Huston had written for *The Writer* magazine, "Becoming Your Fiction." It cost DeMarco thirty dollars to subscribe online and access the article.

In the article, Huston advised aspiring writers on the importance of honing their observational skills, of listening for nuances of speech patterns, finding the gestures and body language that reveal the nature of hidden thoughts, those small but telling physical details that reveal underlying character traits. "Get into the habit of watching people and *listening,*" Huston had written. "This is your research. Anywhere you can conduct it — at the mall, at a sidewalk café, on a bus or a train or a busy city street — this is your classroom.

"Next, you must learn to translate this observational skill from real people to your characters. You have to come to know your character inside and out, know her history, her childhood, all the traumas and triumphs that made her who she is at the moment your story begins. Only then can you *become* that character as she makes those choices that will propel the story forward. You, the author, sitting there in your comfortable chair, typing away, must simultaneously be the character who is reacting to her lover's betrayal, her promotion, or to that bus speeding toward her down the highway. Because only by becoming that character can you know with any authenticity how she will react to those situations. And only then will she be a credible, believable character. Only then will she be real."

DeMarco leaned back in his chair, stared at the blinking curser. He put himself in Huston's place, saw himself coming to each of the bedroom doorways, tried to envision Huston's horrific moment of recognition. Wife dead, throat slit. Son dead, throat slit. Daughter dead, throat slit. Baby dead, stabbed through the heart.

The rage, the grief, it would have gone off in his head like a mushroom cloud, De-Marco thought. The cloud would have blossomed and swelled and filled every crevice and crenellation in his brain. It would have seeped into every cell, numbed and choked and suffocated them.

It was not difficult for DeMarco to imagine. He could see himself inside Huston's house. He staggered from one room to the next. He had to see, make sure, prove wrong what he already knew. The recognition that they were gone, all gone, would be too much to bear.

How *could* he bear it? DeMarco wondered. One child alone was too much to bear. You never get over something like that, can never shut out the images. The glass will always be shattering, spraying across your face. Laraine will always be screaming, always pounding her fists against your chest. He was slipping back into his own memory then, and he knew it, but he didn't care. Sometimes he even wanted to feel sliced apart again by the pain of it, needed to go sliding down that dark, rain-slick street . . .

He felt a shadow in the doorway then and looked up. Trooper Morgan was watching him. "Aerial report is negative," Morgan said.

"Yeah," said DeMarco, his throat dry and hoarse. He could feel the stream of dampness on his left cheek, could taste salt in the corner of his mouth.

"Park commissioner wants to know if they can open up the trails again."

DeMarco took a slow breath, swallowed hard. "Please remind the park commissioner that in all probability, there is still an armed suspect in those woods. So he can open the fucking trails when I am damn good and sure no more throats are going to be slit open."

Morgan nodded but otherwise did not move.

"That's it," DeMarco told him. "Thanks."

Morgan stood motionless ten seconds longer, then finally turned away.

DeMarco dragged a hand across his face, then wiped his hand dry on a pant leg.

NINE

To keep the nausea from driving him to his knees again, to keep his brain from feeling swollen too big for his skull, his heart so huge with a fiery ache that it would crush the air from his lungs, Thomas Huston struggled to focus his attention on the surroundings. *These woods are ugly, dark, and deep,* he thought. He was cold and his clothes still damp and sticking to his skin. He repeatedly ran a hand across his face, but he could not brush away the feeling of cobwebs.

These woods are ugly, dark, and deep. But I have promises to keep.

What were those promises? To whom had he made them? He could not remember. All he knew was that he could not stand there forever. He might be spotted. Would that be a bad thing? Would that be the best thing? He could not be sure. Nothing was certain. Nothing was clear.

A kind of narrow trail snaked away in front of him, a deer run. He began to see himself as a character in a story that had come to an impasse. The plot faced a fork in the road. The story could continue, or it could come to an end.

I took the road less traveled by . . .

He started walking. He would let the trajectory of the deer run choose the trajectory of the story. His legs pushed through the mist of dawn and began to warm. Movement was not so hard after all. Once started, it would be harder to stop. He felt his joints loosen, felt the muscles gather their old strength. Just two years ago, the legs had carried him to a respectable finish in the Pittsburgh Marathon, three hours and forty-nine minutes, and since then, his legs had logged at least twenty miles per week. They were strong, reliable legs. And now they belonged to a character in a story, a man seeking answers in movement, escape from memory, a man on a narrow, twisting trail.

When this character came to the edge of a wide swampy area, then noticed to his left the road of hard-packed clay and gravel, he crossed to that road, turned north, walked more briskly now, eager until Huston told him, *Wait.* The character stopped. *You can't go home,* Huston told him. *You have to get off the road.* The character pivoted and, moving more hesitantly, uncertain, returned to the edge of the cranberry bog. He stood there and stared at the water and waited for the writer to decide what he should do.

He knows the police are somewhere back there in the woods, Huston thought. *He knows they probably have dogs. He knows they might even bring in a search helicopter once the mist rises and it's safe to fly. So what would he do now?*

With a little effort, Huston was able to achieve the split point of view that allowed him to do his best work. Usually, he was aware first of himself at his desk, blue ink moving across a yellow legal pad, but also aware of himself as the character in the story unrolling in his imagination. This time, the perspectives were reversed. He was the character first, cold and tired and hungry, and then, removed to the background, the writer watching and directing the action.

The character from Huston's story stood by the edge of the swamp and waited. Huston had given him no name and was unwilling to consider the reason for the man's flight. He had filed the man's back-story in a black pigeonhole in his mind. Huston's only concern at the moment was to focus on this troubling plot point before

75

him. What should the character do now?

He's got to get into the water.

The character looked down at his shoes. They were leather Skechers, moccasin style, with rawhide laces. They would offer no protection against the icy water.

A month from now, I would be wearing my Clarks. The Clarks were ankle-high with an inch of protective black rubber around the lower sides, the leather waterproofed against the inevitable sludge that would slicken the campus's walkways until early March. *I should be wearing my Clarks.*

But then Huston pulled himself back and stepped away from the character, because he did not want to be the character beside the swamp, he wanted to be the writer writing the character. *The Skechers are good,* Huston told himself, *because they put him in more peril. And peril is good for a story. The more peril, the better.*

He should go into the water but not too deep.

Gingerly, the character stepped into the water, first his left foot, then his right. The water circled his shins like icy socks. The bottom of the swamp was soft and spongy, a layer of matted grass.

He should work his way around the bog, Huston thought, and the character started moving toward the south. Huston did not know how big the swamp was because he had not written it. The swamp had existed prior to the story and had appeared of its own volition. Huston had no choice as a writer but to take this unforeseen story element and employ it as best he could, with no knowledge of its ramifications. He reminded himself of what Doctorow had said, that writing a story is like driving at night through a fog. The thing to do is to just keep moving.

Just keep moving, Huston told his character. *Even if you can't see very far ahead. Take it one page at a time. Let the story grow organically.*

Huston was pleased to see that the charcoal water swallowed up every sign of his character's passage. With each step, his character had to lift his foot completely out of the water so as not to be caught and tangled in a lasso of wild vines, but at least the water quickly erased his footprints, and the clouds of muddy water were quickly diffused and absorbed back into the swamp. It was not long before the character's feet began to burn with cold, but he had no choice but to keep going. He could not risk setting foot on solid ground just yet. Huston told him to just keep moving as quickly as he could, and the character did so. He was not an absurdist character but a Huston character. He did as he was told, to the best of his ability.

At the southern end of the cranberry bog, Huston's character came to a stream flowing south. The character stopped and waited while Huston regarded the stream. It was not Huston's desire to have his character moving continually southward, but he knew that the stream presented a good opportunity to keep his trail undetectable, and even though the character's feet were now throbbing and burning, Huston could not yet allow him the relief of dry ground.

Huston told his character to follow the stream and quicken his pace. The going was easier now, the water in the stream only a few inches deep, and there was enough exposed bedrock in the stream that the character could find solid footing without having to slow down. And the water seemed a few degrees warmer now. Maybe the character's feet would not be damaged after all, would not be black with frostbite when he sat down to take his shoes off. Maybe they would, but maybe they wouldn't. Huston would just have to wait and see how the story evolved and where the stream might take his character.

It's a strange kind of story to be writing,

Huston thought. He watched his character almost running now down the shallow stream, he heard the slap and splash of water. But he felt the sun on his character's face now too, and he told himself what he always had to tell himself from time to time, every time he felt overwhelmed by a writing project, every time he felt himself about to surrender to frustration. *Trust the process, Huston. Trust the story.*

TEN

DeMarco could not remember ever having used the word *pall* in conversation except in the word *pallbearer,* but now, though he did not utter the word aloud, he felt its meaning as he walked from a campus parking lot to Campbell Hall some sixty or seventy yards away. He felt the pall that had descended over Shenango College as tangibly as he would feel a sudden drop in air pressure. The atmosphere felt sodden and heavy. The students crossing between buildings moved like prisoners trudging from their cells to the gas chamber. Even their laughter, which was in low abundance, rang sour and false.

He had been on the campus several times before, twice for blues concerts but usually to haul in a student on suspicion of selling drugs, for sexual assault, for abandoning his vehicle in a ditch somewhere outside the borough. On those occasions, no matter the season, the ambiance had seemed swollen with promise, almost festive, and buoyant with innocence. Now it felt like the air inside a punctured balloon.

The college administration preferred that any external law enforcement personnel visiting the campus be accompanied by someone from campus security. Normally, DeMarco would have honored that request. But today he did not feel like having an undertrained snot nose watching his every move, maybe making small talk all the while, trying to ingratiate himself, wheedling for an invitation to apply to the state police. Today, DeMarco was in no mood for camaraderie.

Yesterday, he had hiked through Maurice K. Goddard State Park until his legs ached. He had drunk too much burned coffee from too many foam cups, had suffered too many pairs of young eyes following him all day long as if he were the keeper of all secrets and might dribble one forth at any moment, might utter a few precious words of knowledge. Today, he felt depleted of anything valuable, as empty as a pocket turned inside out.

In Campbell Hall, he made his way to the English Department's offices on the second floor. The hallway was empty but for one female student, pale and blond and waifish, sitting on the floor outside a closed door, a notebook open in her lap. DeMarco glanced at the door on his way past; below the nameplate of Dr. Robert Denton, a strip of paper had been taped, and on the paper, typed in bold black script, was part of a poem:

Let seed be grass, and grass turn into hay:
I'm martyr to a motion not my own;
What's freedom for? To know eternity.
                              Theodore Roethke

He recognized Denton's name, the resident poet. The poets, it seemed, always had pretty, young things waiting outside their doors. DeMarco wondered, *And why is that?*

The answer was a simple one: *Because poets and pretty, young things still believe in romance. They still believe that truth heals and beauty sutures. They still believe that love forestalls, deters, and turns away the tragedy that is life.*

DeMarco thought again of his wife, Laraine. She had been a pretty, young thing once upon a time. She too had believed in romance for a while. Until she cradled her broken-necked baby in her arms.

Yellow police tape had been stretched

across the doorway of room 214. DeMarco reached beneath the tape and tried the door, though he knew it would be locked. He then returned past the poet-adoring student to the department office by the stairwell. The secretary was a light-skinned black woman in her late twenties. Her posture was disciplined and straight, her chin held high as she sat at the computer, fingers long and slender and beautifully manicured as they rattled an elegant tattoo over the keyboard.

He approached her desk. "I'll need the key for Professor Huston's office, please."

His voice startled her, but she jerked only a little, kept the look of surprise from her face as she turned to him. "They've already searched there," she said. "In fact, they took the computer and a few other things."

"Yes, we did," he said and smiled. He pulled a leather case from his pocket, showed her his badge and ID card. "That doesn't mean we're finished in there."

She nodded, pulled open a drawer, found the key, and handed it to him.

"I usually go to lunch at twelve thirty," she told him.

He glanced at his wristwatch: 12:21. "And what time do you usually return?"

"A quarter after?" she said.

"Take the full hour. I can wait."

Huston's office felt cold to him, empty of all vitality. DeMarco stood with his back to the closed door, allowed his eyes to scan the crowded bookshelves again, the gray metal filing cabinet, which he knew was now empty, its contents still being cataloged at the station's evidence room. Only a telephone and blotter sat atop the desk. On a small table behind the desk chair was a short stack of students' papers, already graded and waiting to be returned. De-Marco had glanced through those papers two days earlier: twelve short stories from Huston's Craft of Fiction workshop. Beside these papers was a framed five by seven of Huston with his children, little Davy riding high on Huston's shoulders as he stood at the small lakefront dock in his backyard on a summer afternoon, the toddler's fingers buried in his father's thick mop of sandy-brown hair. Thomas Jr. was leaning perilously over the edge of the dock, using a paddle to reach for a red canoe that was about to drift out into the lake. Alyssa stood beside her brother, waiting breathlessly, it seemed, hands held against her chest as if in prayer.

Huston's wife did not appear in the photo. A separate headshot of her in a heavy silver frame sat just to the left of the family photo.

And what does that mean? DeMarco asked himself. *Does it mean anything at all?*

He crossed the room and sat in Huston's leather chair and swiveled around to face the photos. "It could mean a couple of things," he told Claire Huston's softly smiling face. "You took the picture at the dock. That's why you're not in that photo. So you get a photo of your own. But was the placement of your picture here just a gesture on his part, something for public consumption? Or do you get a picture of your own because you hold a special place in his heart?"

He sat and waited then, waited for a whisper, a hunch.

"Talk to me, Claire," he said.

He sat in silence. When the door to the office squeaked open, he swiveled around, expecting to see the department secretary. Instead, he faced a hulking, middle-aged man of weak posture, a surprised individual with a long, sagging face. "Sorry," the man said and quickly closed the door again.

What the fuck? thought DeMarco. He stood so abruptly that the chair flew out from under him and slammed into the small table, knocking both photographs onto their faces. By the time he righted the photos, his radio was crackling.

"The divers found the murder weapon,"

Morgan told him.

DeMarco winced, felt something snag in his chest. "I'll be there in fifteen minutes."

He hurried into the hallway. The corridor was empty now; even the waifish student was gone. DeMarco glanced at his watch again; it was now 12:32. He pulled the door to Huston's office shut, locked it, refastened the police tape, and raced down the steps and outside. The department secretary was climbing into a white Celica. She spotted DeMarco hurrying toward her; she shut the car door and lowered the window.

DeMarco handed her the key. "I locked up. I have to get back to the station."

"Oh," she said. "Okay."

"But there was a man," DeMarco said. "Maybe six-one, six-two. At least two hundred pounds. Sort of reminded me of Thomas Wolfe?"

She wrinkled her brow. "The Thomas Wolfe of *Look Homeward, Angel*?"

"That's the one. So who would that man have been?"

"I'm afraid I don't know what Thomas Wolfe looked like."

DeMarco smiled, tried to slow himself down. His heart always raced when he was excited or in a hurry, and when his heart raced, he sometimes spoke too quickly.

"Actually, I don't either. But the way I always envision him is the way this man looked. Big and kind of slovenly? With a sort of paranoid look in his eyes?"

She nodded. "That would be Professor Conescu."

"Conescu," DeMarco repeated. "And why would he be crossing police tape to go inside Dr. Huston's office?"

"He did that?"

"Apparently he didn't know I was inside." She glanced back at the building, then lowered her voice. "That's just the way he is. Kind of snoopy. Always wants to know everybody else's business."

DeMarco smiled again and backed away from the car. "Enjoy your lunch," he told her.

She started the engine and drove away. Now DeMarco turned to face Campbell Hall. He looked to the second floor just in time to see a shadow duck away from a window.

ELEVEN

Thomas Huston's feet were blue but they were not black. Sitting as high as he could on the inside of the concrete drain pipe, buttocks four inches above the thin stream of water gurgling through the pipe, a foot braced against the other side, he had removed his soggy shoes and socks and now rubbed one bare foot and then the other until they no longer felt like packages of refrigerated meat in his hands. He rubbed away the agonizing needle prick and then kept massaging until he could flex his toes without fearing they might break off.

He had scuttled into the culvert just minutes earlier, awkwardly straddling the little stream until he was fifteen or so feet inside the pipe at more or less the center of the asphalt road overhead. According to his wristwatch, it was now 11:40 in the morning, though the hour or even the date bore little meaning to him. Something had happened to his concept of time. Time had been shattered and broken, some of the pieces melted together, others wholly lost. Ten minutes might carry the pain of a month, two days nothing more than a sliver of glass in the corner of his eye.

Maybe he had been inside that drainpipe forever. Maybe he was a character in a play by Beckett and what he thought of as his memory was merely seepage from his creator's brain.

He pulled the collar of the dirty jacket tight around his neck, then tucked both hands into the side pockets. And only then saw that he was wearing a jacket and knew it wasn't his. He had no idea where it had come from or when he had put it on. It felt too loose across his chest and shoulders, was the jacket of a bigger man. An old, quilted jacket, dark green, stained with dark blotches that smelled of motor oil, with long tears in both sleeves through which the dirty white batting showed. Small patches of dried clay marked the front, the sleeves, every surface he could see. He sniffed a patch of dirt; it reminded him of the cave. But the memory of the cave was itself uncertain, dreamlike, and unreal. When had he been in a cave? And why?

What was not dreamlike was the heavy,

deep ache in his chest, the feeling of *grief* that made his head feel swollen, made every breath feel like a bruise. He wanted desperately to weep, he wanted that comfort. But he was not sure why.

Now and then, a vehicle rumbled down the asphalt road, and when it passed atop him, Huston reflexively hunched his shoulders and lowered his head. Afterward, he smiled to himself because he recognized the uselessness of that posture. Part of him was helpless to resist the urge to take a defensive posture, and part of him could not help being amused by it.

He sat with both legs stretched over the stream now, bare feet braced against the other side, knees bent just enough to keep them from locking up with stiffness. He kept his wet shoes and socks cradled in his lap. The smell of wet leather and sodden, sweaty cotton was somehow comforting — the end of a morning run, just another part of his daily routine. He would rest for a few minutes and then head for the shower, get dressed for his eleven o'clock class. *What day is this?* he wondered. *If it's Monday, I teach Contemporary Lit. If it's Tuesday, the Craft of Fiction.*

But he could not hold the truth at bay for long. It came back with the speed and suddenness of a bullet, it roared through the pipe and slammed into him, left him sitting there shivering and sobbing, convulsing with grief. "My babies," he moaned. "My sweet, darling babies . . ." But the pain was too much and it took him under; it made him sink into sleep, doubled over with his arms hooked around his knees.

After a while, his arms slipped apart and he awoke with a start, gasping for breath. The air was dim now, gray and damp, and the first image to flash through his brain was of the knife going into Davy's chest. He shrieked with pain then, had no power to contain it. His cry bounced off the concrete, split in half, and shot down both sides of the pipe, echoed and echoed and pounded like a hammer at his brain.

For a while, he could only sob and gasp for breath. Eventually, the part of him that stood apart, detached, said that he was useless like this. He could accomplish nothing as long as the pain controlled him. He would have to get back to thinking of himself as a character in one of his stories and not as Thomas Huston, not as the man whose family had been butchered, the man whose life no longer existed, a mere body shot full of poison now, a corpse deprived of death. He knew this and was even able to marvel at this apparent division in his psyche, this dissociative split that allowed him to experience his pain while also regarding it from a distance.

He was both a fiction and the truth. The stronger of the two was truth, however, and the truth sickened him and hollowed him out. He felt hollowed out by hunger too and knew he would have to eat soon, even though the thought of food was nauseating. Water, on the other hand, was not a problem. The area was as wet as Alaskan taiga, soaked by hundreds of small ponds and swamps and streams. Before leaving the last stream, Huston had cupped its waters to his mouth. He remembered doing that. The water was so cold that it burned his throat and made him dizzy. Even so, he had gulped one mouthful after another, had filled his stomach with it. But he would have to find food of some kind soon. And now that his body temperature had been compromised, he would have to find a better place to gather his strength and make his plans.

He thought about trying to work his way to Oniontown and the O'Patchens, but Oniontown was at least twenty miles away, and Ed O'Patchen would be likely to shoot him on sight. Huston still had his wallet, his debit and credit cards and probably a little cash, but all of that belonged to another life, a life eradicated, an eviscerated life.

He could not go on living, he knew that much. But he had one thing to do before he could stop. He thought of the men and women he worked with and the students he taught, and he did not believe he could trust any of them to help him. They claimed to love and admire him, but that was yesterday or the day before, that was part of an expired dream.

Was there no one he could trust?

There was Nathan, yes, but no, Huston would not involve him in this. Let him have his own life. He had struggles of his own.

So there was only Annabel. Only Annabel who would understand. Only Annabel who would know. She might not want to help him, but maybe she would. She owed him that much. He had helped her when she'd needed it, and not lightly but with sadness in both their hearts, and he believed she would help him too. It was all sad business now. No business but the saddest. He had to try Annabel.

He did not know how to contact her except at work, and she did not work except on weekends, on Thursday, Friday, and Saturday nights. How many days until Thursday?

Some things remained quite clear to him. Other things he saw as if viewed in the pieces of a shattered mirror. This jacket, for example, seemed to have no beginning. Where had it come from?

What day is it? he wondered again. He went back in his mind to late Saturday night, worked hard to find his way back to it and harder still to stop short of the house. He did not want to go back inside the house in his memory. He was outside of it now, a man wandering the streets with a knife in his hand. A heavy, ugly knife, something to cut through the darkness and then the fog, something to give him weight. He remembered the way the knife had sliced through the water, how it fell straight down, stabbed through the water with hardly a splash, disappeared into the murk.

No, wait, he told himself. *That was the next day, wasn't it? Didn't I have the knife when I found the cave? Yes. Yes! Sunday night I found the cave. How did I get there? I don't know. I walked, I guess. I walked all day. Then I found the cave and I broke off some branches and I crawled inside. I had the knife. What about the jacket? I don't know, but I had the knife. I wanted to use it on myself, I remember that. I wanted to open up my wrists and fill the cave with blood. And I almost did* it, didn't I? Or did I dream that? No, I almost did it. I put the blade against my wrist. I wanted to do it. God how I wanted to do it.

Then the next morning . . . Monday. It was Monday; today is Monday. I went back to the road. I was going to flag down a car, get a ride back home. I wanted to go home. I wanted everything back. But nobody would have picked me up if they saw that knife. So I dropped it in the water. I watched it going down. I hated it but I hated to let it go. Why was it so hard to let that damned thing go?

That was Monday, wasn't it? Or was that Sunday?

Then what did you do? he asked himself. Then you remembered. How could you go home? There was nothing there, nobody there, everything gone. So you started walking again. You walked to the bog. You walked down the stream. You came to the road and the drainage ditch, and you couldn't go any farther so you climbed into the culvert. And then you did what?

You found the jacket. You were wearing it. You found it when you saw that you were wearing it.

Then you slept all night.

No, he remembered, first my feet were blue. I held them, and they felt like packages of frozen meat. So I rubbed them awhile, and *then I didn't care anymore and I fell asleep. I woke up and it was dark. It was dark everywhere, and I was shivering. I thought I was underwater, and I tried to swim to the top but I banged my head on the pipe, and I went to sleep again. I passed out; some more time passed.*

And now it's daylight again. Another morning. So this must be Tuesday.

Huston looked down at his stockinged feet. He put a hand over each foot. The socks were no longer wet, his feet no longer icy to the touch. Somewhere, he had lost most of a day. That day was in the drainage ditch somewhere, had maybe leaked away from him in the trickle of water beneath his feet. *Where did it go?* he wondered, and he watched the water awhile — he watched himself trickling away with it.

Then he brought himself back.

This is Tuesday, he told himself. Craft of Fiction. But there would be no class today. He wasn't there. No class unless Denton took over his classes. Who else could they ask? *Not Conescu, for Chrissakes. A janitor would be better than Conescu.*

Never mind, the other part of him said. *Find Annabel. You have to talk to Annabel.*

But Annabel is only for Thursdays. I know where to find her on a Thursday. And today is

96

only Tuesday.

Then you have to wait, he told himself. *You have to stay alive and wait.*

Two more ugly, impossible days. He doubled over again; he hugged his knees. He wept and trembled and muttered aloud, "Two more fuck fuck fucking fucking days."

TWELVE

Under the fluorescent light bar in the middle of the evidence room, DeMarco examined the knife in its clear plastic bag. The tapered blade was eight inches long, the full tang triple-riveted in a handle made of a shiny, black composite material. He said, "It's an attractive piece of craftsmanship."

Morgan told him, "It's called a chef's knife."

"And it's the one?"

"Lab says it matches the wounds on all four victims."

DeMarco squinted at the inscription on the blade, but he could not make it out. "Fucking fluorescent lights," he said.

"Wüsthof. Made in Solingen, Germany."

"And we're sure it's Huston's?"

"There's one empty slot in the knife block. This one fits."

"All the others are Wüsthofs?"

"All twenty-five."

"Twenty-six in the set? Somebody has a serious knife fetish."

"It's a professional quality set. Retails for around a thousand."

"You can't be serious."

"We found the receipt in a drawer with all the warranty stuff. Charged to Claire's Visa last December 12. So apparently the set belonged to her."

"Unless she bought it for him as a Christmas gift."

Morgan pointed to the scalloped edge. "These indentations are supposed to keep food from sticking. The style is called *Santoku.*"

"And I suppose you know what that means."

"The three virtues. Slicing, dicing, and mincing."

"Christ," DeMarco said.

"There were descriptions with the warranty papers."

"Anything in the descriptions about why he did it?"

DeMarco turned the knife back and forth in the light. In the two indentations closest to the bolster were tiny rust-like stains. The rest of the blade was clean. DeMarco said, "I'm betting this isn't rust here."

"It's the baby's."

"Nobody else's?"

"None that can be identified."

"I'm surprised there's any left at all. It was in the water how long?"

"Approximately thirty-eight hours."

"Long enough to wash any prints off the handle."

"Unfortunately."

"So we can't place it in the hands of any particular individual."

"But we do know it's the murder weapon."

"Yippee," DeMarco said. He handed the bag back to Trooper Morgan. "Anything else?"

"Lab reports on the bed linens. I left a copy on your desk."

"Summarize them for me."

"The blood smear on the cover in the master bedroom is Claire's blood only."

"So he slit her throat, then wiped the blade clean."

"Not completely clean. The smear on the boy's cover is mostly his blood but with a bit of Claire's mixed in."

"And on the girl's?"

"He took a little more time here. Actually wrapped a corner of the sheet around the blade to clean it instead of just wiping the blade across the sheet. And the blood this time is mostly the girl's, trace amounts of the boy's."

"None of Claire's or the baby's?"

"A trace amount that might be Claire's. The lab can't say conclusively."

"None of the baby's?"

"None."

"But only the baby's is on the blade currently?"

"Correct."

"So . . . first he killed Claire. Then the boy. Then the girl. He slit each of their throats, wiped the blade clean each time afterward, did an especially good job after the girl. Maybe even washed the blade clean. Can that be right?"

"It's how it looks."

"Why would he clean the blade so thoroughly before stabbing the baby? It doesn't make any sense."

"The rest does?"

"Also, the baby was *stabbed*."

"Yes, sir. Twice."

"Why?"

"Apparently to make sure he hit the heart."

"Why didn't he slit its throat too? Why did he change his method of killing for the baby?"

"I guess only he knows that."

"I guess you're right. You got anything else?"

"The vaginal swabs on the girl came back negative."

"Thank God for that."

"But the DNA profile of the sperm sample matches the DNA from the kids."

"So it was definitely her husband's. Was the lab able to determine the age of the sperm?"

"It was from that night."

"No sign of forcible rape?"

"None."

"So he made love to his wife that very night."

Trooper Morgan said nothing.

"He makes love to his wife. Then he gets dressed again and methodically murders his family one by one."

"Unless he murdered them first and then got dressed."

"I guess we won't know that until we find him, see if there's any blood on him."

"How could there not be?"

"You ever see a murder scene as clean as that house was? Not a single bloody foot-print. Not a blood splatter anywhere except in the beds. Nine drops of blood leading from the baby's crib to the hallway. That's it. Nine fucking drops."

He was angry and the fluorescent light hurt his eyes. "So you know what we've got here?" he asked.

Morgan spoke softly. "No, sir, I don't."

"We have a lot of fucking questions and not a single fucking answer."

THIRTEEN

It is important to understand things. This was what Thomas Huston kept telling himself. *You need to figure things out.*

He was walking through the woods now, picking his way between the hardwoods and birches, moving in what he hoped was a northeasterly line. He guessed the time at midafternoon; the light had softened and was slanting in behind him through the mostly leafless branches. There was a peculiar sensation of tunnel vision, of a blurry, black periphery wherever he looked, and when he tried to see into the distance, his gaze seemed too weak to travel more than forty yards or so. His head felt heavy, full of dark clouds, and though he ached in his neck and shoulders, knees and feet, the aches seemed somehow apart from him, as if he were experiencing another man's pain.

You are a writer and a teacher, he reminded himself. *A writer first and then a teacher. As a writer, it is your job to make order out of disorder. To find the meaning in metaphor. And as a teacher, it is your job to explain that meaning to your students. And now you are the student. You are the writer and the teacher and the student.*

Find the meaning and explain it, he told himself. *That is your job now.*

Annabel could help. His writer's instincts told him that Annabel would understand more of this than he did. Annabel lived in the kind of world where these things happened. He did not live like this. His life was blessed.

First things first, he thought, and paused for a moment, and looked around. *Today is Tuesday. Thursday, you can see Annabel. So first things first: Find something to eat. Then find a place to stay. A warm place and dry.*

Maybe somebody would help him, take him in. Give him a place to wait until Thursday. Who could he go to for help?

One by one, he considered his neighbors, his friends, his colleagues. Their faces seemed distant to him, people he had known a long time ago. Memories of memories. Only Annabel seemed clear and real, approachable. He had helped her and she would help him. *But Annabel is Thursday,* he told himself. *Today is Tuesday.*

Maybe you should go to the police. They will feed you and give you a place to stay. Yes, but they will want answers in exchange, and I have none. They will say where is the knife and I will say I drowned it. They will ask why did you drown it. I will say it was either that or cut myself to pieces with it.

And they will keep me from my job. My job is to find the meaning. Find the meaning and explain it.

Why can't the police find the meaning?

Because they don't know where to look.

You can tell them where to look.

No, I want to find the meaning myself. This is what I do. I will find the meaning and explain it, and then I will find my family again.

Do you really believe that is possible, Thomas?

I have to believe it. I have no choice but to believe it.

You stopped believing when you were fourteen, remember? Who was Cain's wife? you asked. If God is the only God, why is he a jealous God? Who was God talking to when he said Let us create man in our own image? If God is love, why is there so much hate? You had so many questions that Mrs. Lehner got red in the face and called you impossible. If you are going to keep interrupting me, Thomas Huston, you can just stop coming to

Sunday school altogether, how would you like that?

I liked it fine, he said. That was when I really started looking for the meaning. And I saw one good Christian after another sniffing at another man's wife, another woman's husband. I saw a deacon accused of pedophilia, then disappear and leave his wife and children behind. I heard my father's friends laughing about payoffs to building inspectors, bribes to the zoning commission. I saw who was selling drugs and who was buying them. I saw who was keeping a woman on the side and who was being kept. I saw who cheated on their taxes and who liked to steal lipstick from Woolworth's and who was collecting social security checks for dead spouses.

If God is love, you asked, why are we supposed to fear him?

Turn to page 193 in your hymnal, Reverend Barrett said. "How Great Thou Art."

So if you remember all that, he told himself, what makes you think now that you can ever find your family again? If there is no God, there is no heaven. If there is no heaven, your family is gone.

And with that realization, the pain in his stomach exploded like a gasoline fire, it dropped him to his knees, to the leaf-matted earth. The fire was black and it devoured the sunlight; it sucked all the oxygen from the woods. It laid him down flat with his face to the wet leaves where there was nothing but the chill and the damp stink of rot.

FOURTEEN

DeMarco was still in his office at six that evening, still trying to piece together the disparate shards of Thomas Huston's life. He thought of all the times he had seen the Hustons together at public events — the summer carnival, the Pumpkin Parade, a spaghetti dinner fund-raiser for a local girl with leukemia. In every case, they had appeared the epitome of a happy family, smiles on all their faces, Claire and Thomas holding hands, the kids laughing, little Davy all eyes and sloppy grin. They could have been poster models for the traditional family unit.

He knew how easy it is to mask the darker emotions from most people, to hide sorrow, anger, a glowering hostility in the shadows of the heart. Most people have no desire to peer into those shadows. Who needs the extra weight of other people's burdens? But some people, the unlucky few, are wired to see the shadows first. DeMarco considered it a kind of handicap, like color blindness or extreme myopia. And on those occasions when he had seen Thomas Huston in public, DeMarco had sensed that the man's happiness was genuine, the joy he took from his family. But there had been shadows too. They lurked in the corners of Huston's eyes. They pulled at the corner of his mouth when he smiled.

And Huston noticed the same in me, De-Marco told himself. *That sadness in your eyes,* he'd written.

Because Huston had his demons too. He had been very good at keeping them caged, of channeling them into his fictions, at least until this past weekend. Then, for some reason, the beasts had escaped. But where had they taken him after the slaughter? And where would they lead him next?

A knock on the doorframe interrupted his thoughts. DeMarco looked up from the lined white pad on which he had been scribbling notes. Trooper Carmichael stood in the doorway, a plastic jewel case in hand.

"The Outlook Express files," Carmichael said. He strode forward and laid the case atop DeMarco's notepad. A small man with a tight mop of curly, black hair, Carmichael had a wide-eyed, nervous look that always reminded DeMarco of a Chihuahua his mother had had when he was a boy. The dog's name was Tippy, a frenetic, little creature full of useless energy. It had had a passion for digging holes in the yard, then running from one to the next like a frenzied treasure hunter, shoving its muzzle in deep. Carmichael was like that with computers. He was happiest with his nose close to a keyboard, his fingers scrabbling to claw treasure from computer code.

"I'm still working on the deleted files and a few password-protected documents. Should have those for you by tomorrow afternoon."

DeMarco eyed the jewel case with the shiny disk inside. "Anything interesting?"

"I don't read them, Sergeant. I just pull 'em."

"Thanks," DeMarco said. "Now take a break, okay? I don't want you working through the night again."

Carmichael grinned. "I've got plans for tonight."

"They involve a woman, I hope."

The trooper blushed. "My buddy and I are writing a program that sends spiders out through the entire Internet."

"Spiders?"

"Little pieces of program. They scour the Internet and grab whatever type of information they're programmed to grab. In our case, they're looking for juvenile offenders, anybody between the ages of six and eighteen who's ever been picked up for anything from fighting at school to committing an actual crime. Within whatever radius we want to establish. Plus any kid who's blogged or sent email with any kind of inflammatory language in it, whether it's directed at an individual or a group or whatever."

"Sounds ambitious," DeMarco said. "And its purpose?"

"To compile a database. Of every juvenile in the county predisposed to become an adult offender."

"Predisposed?" DeMarco said.

"Anything happens in a particular city or town, the program will tell us precisely who to pick up based on the nature of the crime. Think of the guesswork it will eliminate!"

"No more detective work."

"Not only that but, and here's the exciting part, we'll be able to see them coming."

"Now you're scaring me."

"Remember that movie with Tom Cruise? Where they can see a crime coming before it happens? We're almost there. We can almost really do that. Our program will build a profile of intent based on past history. It's not only informative but deductive. Removes all possibility of human error."

"Christ," DeMarco said.

"I know! Homeland Security has their own version already. Problem is, they don't like to share. I don't really care though, because we're having so much fun just putting this thing together."

Sometimes DeMarco felt that the world had come to a standstill. At other times, and this was one of them, he felt that the world was spinning so fast he was in danger of being flung into the void.

He laid a hand on the jewel case. "Well, in the meantime . . ."

Carmichael winked. "I'll have the rest of it by tomorrow noon."

"Good," DeMarco said. "Unfortunately, I just thought of something else. You have time to monitor social media for any chatter about the case? Not just the usual kind of talk about it, but anything implying, you know, insider knowledge. Any one individual taking an inordinate amount of interest in what's transpiring. You got time for that?"

"If you need it, I'll find the time."

"I appreciate it. Thank you."

Carmichael's brisk exit seemed to suck the air from the room. DeMarco sagged in his chair, rubbed both hands over his face, and felt the world spinning like a centrifuge.

He got up, still feeling wobbly, and headed to the restroom to wash his hands.

FIFTEEN

For dinner that evening, DeMarco opened a can of white albacore tuna and dumped it onto a plate. He sliced tomatoes, onions, and mozzarella for a quick caprese salad, sprinkled it with dried basil, drizzled Italian dressing over everything. He carried this and half a water glass full of Jack Daniels to the dining room, where his computer sat on the table amidst an ever-growing accumulation of file folders and miscellaneous papers.

On the CD Carmichael had made, there were sixty-seven emails to or from eight different sources, most from the inbox, none more than six weeks old. Apparently, Huston was not an email pack rat and kept his files cleaned out. Carmichael had organized the messages into separate folders labeled with the names of the correspondents.

The first folder contained messages between Huston and his literary agent. The agent's tone brimmed with optimism about the buzz *The Desperate Summer* had generated. He reported that inquiries about film rights were coming in daily, that he was negotiating audio rights and, through his subagents, foreign language rights in nine countries. A large print edition was scheduled for release in February, the mass market paperback the following May. In one of the emails, he predicted a half-million dollar advance for Huston's next novel. "So for Chrissakes, Tom, get fifty pages or so to me along with an outline," he wrote. "We've got to strike while the iron's hot, man, and the fire is fucking blazing right now. Plus, I recently met a woman who's working in *Spamalot,* drop-dead sexy brunette with legs that go all the way to the most exquisite ass I've ever drooled over. Promised I'd take her to Ibiza if she'll sleep with me, so I need that fucking commission!"

Huston's replies showed a more literary concern. "I plan to take my time with this one, Harry. For one thing, the plot is a lot more convoluted. Plus the research isn't easy. I have to watch my step. Maybe that brunette would settle for Roosevelt Island instead of Ibiza? Tell her there will be fewer terrorists."

In another email, he complained about his reputation. "My problem is I succeeded too well with my goal of bridging the gap between serious and commercial fiction. I made the plots too strong. The books have sold too many copies. So now according to the *Washington Post* I'm a 'veteran mystery writer.' And not one of my books is a true mystery."

In another: "Did you notice that every fucking review so far has started off by announcing that I got a 200k advance for *Summer*? Is that how everybody judges a book these days, Harry?"

DeMarco sipped his whiskey. "So he does have a few bugs up his ass," he said. "Not a happy camper at all."

But Huston wore a different face in the emails to his students. Most were filled with encouragement and practical advice: "Don't even worry about publication for now. You're a strong writer, Nicole, and will get even stronger. So concentrate on that. Publication will come when you're ready for it."

"It's all in the execution, Ben. Learn when to dramatize and when to summarize. You do too much of the latter and not enough of the former."

All told, there were emails to or from nineteen different students. Huston signed all of his emails *TH.* In all of his remarks there was a kind but insistent honesty that DeMarco had to admire. "Not a man for blowing smoke up your ass," DeMarco said.

Most students had received only one or two emails from Huston, but a student named Nathan Briessen had rated at least one each week for the past five weeks. All were responses to messages sent by Briessen with questions about structure, first- or third-person voice, amount of backstory to include. What struck DeMarco as interesting, though, was that three of Huston's responses, though each started out with practical advice and encouragement, ended with some small variation on the same statement and question: *Research this week. Care to join me?* Even more intriguing was the most recent message, eight days old: *I need to talk to Annabel again. Want to come along?*

"Annabel?" DeMarco said. "Who the fuck is Annabel?"

He wrote *Nathan Briessen* on the tablet beside the keyboard, and beneath that name he wrote *Annabel?*

Two files contained correspondence between Huston and the dean of humanities, Huston, and the provost. Congratulations from the administrators, invitations to lunch, effusive glad-handing and backslapping, polite thank-yous from Huston. The only interesting message from the inbox had come from the dean, who wrote, *Just wanted you to know that I've received a cc of Professor Conescu's diatribe. Be assured that my response to it will be the usual one. Still, we must tread lightly here. Litigation can be messy, whether justified or not.*

"Hmmm," said DeMarco, tilting up his glass, which was empty. He considered refilling it but was too eager to open the file labeled *Conescu.* The first message was a two-page, single-spaced, and sometimes barely comprehensible denunciation of Huston. Its salutation was ominous. *Sieg Heil, mein Chairman!* The letter then went on to blame Huston and some other individual — "you and your sycophant henchman both" — for the department's recent decision to deny Conescu's application for tenure. Conescu promised a lawsuit charging "ethnic discrimination." The letter was punctuated with pejoratives, most of them in all caps or bold type: villainous, despicable, contemptible, sadistic. He called Huston a "yuppie neo-Nazi," a panderer, a harlot, an asswipe. He wished him "a cancerous life full of pustules and misery."

DeMarco wrote *Conescu* on the tablet.

Seriously pissed.

Huston's response to the message was more measured:

I understand your anger, Valya, but I am only one of nine colleagues who voted against tenure. And I assure you that I have nothing against you personally and not a single negative feeling toward Romanians in general. You know my concerns; I've made them very clear in the department meetings. As the chair of the tenure committee, it is my responsibility to do so, and I take that responsibility seriously. But, for the record, here they are again: I consider it improper that you charge your students $60 each for a textbook you wrote and paid to have published. Had the book been brought out by a reputable trade publisher, it would have been better edited. As you will recall, I made a photocopy of the first two pages for you and marked 19 spelling, grammatical, and typographical errors in those pages alone. And this is a composition text for beginning writers. How can we justify its use as such? It is one thing to self-publish for your own pleasure but another thing to force your students to purchase a book that is otherwise unmarketable and, unfortunately, riddled with the kind of errors we hope to teach these students to avoid. I consider it an abuse of our academic freedom that the administration has allowed this practice to continue for the past three years. That is why I cast my vote against awarding you tenure.

DeMarco reached for his tablet. He put an exclamation point after Conescu's name. The remaining file also contained three messages, two from Huston's colleague, the poet Robert Denton, and the other from Huston to Denton. In the first, Denton stated that he too had been cc'd a copy of Conescu's angry letter, and added:

I want to see that slimy, slinking bastard's balls cut off and nailed to the wall. But chickenshit you know who is quaking in his Guccis over the possibility of a lawsuit.

Huston, in his response, cautioned restraint.

The vote was 9–3 against him. Is he going to sue all of us? It's all bluff, you know that. He blows off steam in these letters, then he sits in the department meetings and never makes a peep.

Denton's follow-up message was dated the Friday before the murders.

Why don't you write something for the *Chronicle of Higher Ed,* maybe even the *NY Times*? Talk about how all these academics who couldn't write a fucking greeting card are turning to self-publishing and then patting each other on the back for getting "published." About how the poor fucking kids who have to use those books don't know any better. Talk about what a damn fraud the whole business of self-publishing is in academia. You've got the rep, man. You could pull it off. You're the wine master. I'm just a lowly grape picker.

The folder contained no response from Huston. Had he responded in person or not at all? On the tablet DeMarco wrote *Robert Denton.*

It was nearly eleven p.m. when DeMarco finished reading the emails. His back ached and his eyes stung, but he now had a list of four individuals he could consider persons of interest. Huston was still the primary suspect, but it was now clear that his life had not been as idyllic as it had seemed. DeMarco took no pleasure in that discovery.

SIXTEEN

I have my wallet, Thomas Huston told himself. *I have my debit and credit cards. I have ninety-three dollars in cash. I have my wedding band. My wristwatch . . . Where is my wristwatch?*

It was not on either wrist nor in any of his pockets. A Concord Saratoga chronograph, silver-and-black face set in a brushed stainless steel case, black rubber band, a birthday gift from Claire and the kids. All of his nice things were gifts from Claire and the kids. But where was it now? He was wearing it yesterday, wasn't he? And the day before?

He remembered climbing into bed with Claire on Saturday night. Removed his clothing, looked at the watch, decided to leave it on because he planned to do a little work that night, didn't want to let himself get carried away and remain at his desk all night, and there was no clock in his office, just the computer. But he preferred to consult his watch every now and then; he saw not just the time but his family's love in it, carried that love on his wrist.

So he had been wearing the watch when he and Claire made love, then he held her until she fell asleep, then he slipped out of bed and quietly dressed again. He was worried that the garbage had not been taken out, and he had some thoughts in his head that he wanted to get down before they slipped away from him, but they were still rough edged and awkward so he let them tumble over and over, repeating and colliding and polishing themselves while, after taking care of the garbage, he took a slow, short stroll through the night, stood and breathed in the air, then returned to his office and wrote in his journal for a while.

What was the last thing you wrote? he asked himself, and tried to remember. *You wrote, "He knew what he had to do," didn't you? That scene, those opening lines? And then you wrote about Claire, right?*

The sentences had been forming ever since he had lain in bed and watched Claire undressing, had kept working in his head all through the lovemaking. *She is a dark-haired woman, green eyed and dusky with secrets. Her mouth is sensuous but sad, limbs long and elegant, every movement languid. Even her smile is slow with sorrow.*

And now a flush of panic, a writer's terror. *You got that down, didn't you?* Yes, he was sure he had. He had written that and more, a long descriptive passage that he planned to break up later, a brushstroke here and there. And then he would —

No, he told himself, *stop it. Keep your mind here and now. The watch is gone, it doesn't matter where or when or how. Everything is gone. The past is history, pages torn from a book. Be here now. Right here.*

You've got some money and your useless credit and debit cards. You can buy food. Where are you going to buy some food?

From within the line of trees that began just ten yards off North Street, he surveyed the possibilities. Across the street and to his right, maybe thirty paces away, the Country Fair, an all-night gas station and convenience store. Beside it sat Basic Kneads, a sandwich shop that specialized in home-made breads and croissants. But the sandwich shop was dark, as was the Giant Eagle a block and a half east. *So it's at least nine o'clock,* he told himself. *Probably an hour later, maybe two judging from the lightness of traffic.*

He turned his attention to the convenience store again. Two cars at the pumps. One man pumping gas, the other car empty. Passengers in the store. He waited and watched. Soon the first car drove off. Several minutes later, a teenaged boy and girl came out of the store laughing, each carrying a large plastic cup, sipping from straws. She climbed in behind the wheel, the boy on the other side. Engine noise, headlights, little blue car moving away and down the street, happy lives continuing.

As far as he could remember, he had never been inside this store, always bought his gas at the BP close to home, did his shopping at the big Americo's on the edge of town, went there nearly every Saturday morning, he and Claire, on their weekly shopping date, each with a cart or a basket, communicating across the store with their cell phones. How he loved that hour together wandering through the banked displays of fruit and vegetables with the misters erupting every now and then like little fountains while the music of André Previn, John Tesh, or Yanni wafted overhead. The olive bar, the bins of bagels and croissants, the racks of hard-crusted baguettes and artisan breads, the cases of Stilton and Shropshire Blue, the Asiago and fontina, the bûcheron and pecorino. The deli and meat cases, the thirty kinds of seafood on their beds of sparkling ice. And Claire, beautiful Claire, her voice on the cell phone: "These Dungeness crabs are huge!"

He loved the sensuality of it, the anticipation, the sensory assaults from all directions. And when *gone* came into his head now, *all gone,* it struck like a hammer blow so vicious and sudden that he fell sideways against a tree and sobbed and whispered "Claire" again and again, his cheek scraping, abrading against the bark . . .

Time passed . . .

He breathed . . .

He could not will his heart to stop.

The convenience store across the road. Cold lights, cold asphalt. He watched the vehicles come and go.

Christ, how he ached for the snuggery of his office, the familiar building. There were vending machines in the basement, a coin changer. This was Tuesday. He could live on crackers and candy bars until Thursday, couldn't he?

But no, the keys to Campbell Hall were on his key chain and his key chain was hanging from the peg by the kitchen door. *And the police,* he told himself. *They'll be watching the building, won't they? And everybody will know, the whole town must know by now.*

This is Tuesday, he told himself. *It hap-pened Saturday night.*

Every time Saturday night came back to him — and it was never far away now, always crouching in the nearby shadows — every time it came back to him, it was worse than a hammer blow, it was alive and fero-cious, sprang out like a lion, ripped him to pieces.

For a long time, he stood against the tree and could not move, tried to will his heart to cease. But it would not work, it never worked. So he had to keep going for a while yet. He had to live a while longer.

Get some food, he told himself. *Do what you have to do.*

He watched the convenience store. A pickup truck at the pumps now.

He wished the numbness would come back, that strange sense of watching himself from a distance. But it had abandoned him for some reason, the two selves coalescing. He knew now that he was not a fictional character clinging to a fictional tree, waiting for his creator to tell him what to do. It was Thomas Huston standing there on the edge of the woods, Thomas Huston dirty and hungry and cold. He had only to look at his hands to confirm it. They were filthy and scratched now, but they were Thomas

Huston's hands, the hands of a writer and professor, callus free, hands made for typing, for wielding a pen or a stick of chalk. Hardly a semester passed that some coed did not say something complimentary about his hands. In response to his question "What did you like most about this course?" on the end-of-semester evaluation form, one of them had written, "Your hands. Your voice. Your butt in tight blue jeans."

Those hands in front of him now, yes, they were his, but he detested them, wished he could cut them off, wished he had cut them off a week ago. Had they ever really held a pen or had Saturday night erased all that? Had they ever stroked the hair of a sweetly scented woman? Ever traced a circle of desire on her breast, felt the soft rise of her stomach, the slow curve of her thigh? Had this hand ever lay in her velvet cleft of heat, ever felt the undulations of her muscles ripple and tighten around his fingers?

He wanted Claire's body against him again, wanted her breasts crushed against his chest, wanted his dick in her mouth, wanted to taste her pussy and to feel her body rocking against him wave after wave. He wanted all of it and he would never have any of it ever again. Only a man like Thomas Huston deserved those things. Who he was now, he did not know. And the whimpering noises rising from his throat now, these were not his sounds. He had never heard such sounds before.

Christ, why did you ever leave her bed? he wondered. *You and your fucking writing. You and your fucking words.*

Again he could not breathe. There was no air. *Breathe,* he told himself. *Inhale. Exhale.* Nothing came naturally anymore. Nothing happened of its own accord.

He sagged against the tree, clung to it, pushed hard against the horrible images while he chanted to the bark, *She is a dark-haired woman, green eyed and dusky with secrets. Her mouth is sensuous but sad, limbs long and elegant, every movement languid . . .*

SEVENTEEN

Now begins the hard time, DeMarco thought. He had washed and dried his dinner plate, washed and dried his hands, and refilled his glass with four more inches of whiskey. He stood by the kitchen sink now and looked out the window at the small back lawn enshrouded in darkness. When he was a younger man, he used to sit on the porch step on summer evenings, a cold beer or glass of iced tea in hand, and talk to Laraine while she worked in the flower beds bordering the porch. She had especially loved daffodils and lilies and gladioli, tall, stately flowers that required a lot of attention. His own preferences ran to mums and marigolds, black-eyed Susans and sunflowers — showy blasts of exuberant color. But even more than those, he had loved watching Laraine's elegant hands as they worked the topsoil and peat moss and excised weeds. Back then, he had thought her care

131

merely evidence of a meticulous nature and never guessed the fragility of spirit at its foundation.

But that was all a long time ago, and flowers no longer grew around the house.

It was for her that he had started the brick path from the back porch to the small barn-like garage across the alley. For her he had started converting the second floor of the garage. It was going to be her sewing room, exercise room, reading room, whatever she wanted it to be. "You can use it too," she had told him. "I don't want you to think of it as just mine."

But he had. It was all for her. Now the unfinished path. Now the unfinished room.

DeMarco stared into the darkness and wished he had the energy to return to work. He wished he had the stamina to work twenty hours a day, to push himself to an exhaustion that would reward him with four hours of dreamless sleep. Unfortunately, his body tired and his attention always began to wander before he was ready for sleep. If he dragged himself to bed now, he would end up having to silence his thoughts with an all-night radio talk show. His favorite was a program devoted to the supernatural, to considerations of shadow people, spirits and demons, poltergeists and ghosts. Stories of a happy or purposeful afterlife held his attention, kept him listening for shreds of credibility. Other times he dozed off, only to have the demons and poltergeists ride their radio waves into his brain.

He knew he had at least three hours to kill before he could crawl into bed with any realistic expectation of sleep. He could drink himself into a stupor, but he would pay for it all the next day, and right now he wanted to keep his wits about him, wanted to keep the puzzle of Thomas Huston's life laid out in distinct pieces to be fitted together eventually, not all jumbled together in a sloppy pile blurred by hangover.

He knew how he was going to kill those three hours but was reluctant to admit it to himself. Only once or twice a month would he give in to the impulse to drive to Erie. The activity always stung him with self-loathing for several days afterward, as if he were a boy who had been caught masturbating to pornography. He knew he would do it again tonight but remained standing at the window for another fifteen minutes. Finally he admitted his weakness, as he always did, and told himself, "Just fucking go, why don't you?"

The drive from his home to the I-79 on-ramp was less than twenty miles, just enough time for him to settle into the whiskey-smoothed rhythm of the road. Headed north on the interstate, he listened to a blues station out of Cleveland and occasionally lifted his glass from the cup holder for another sip. The whiskey was warm on his tongue and throat. It carried the old reconciliation into his core, the old surrender to the way of things, and he paid small attention to the familiar landmarks briefly revealed by his headlights, let the muscles in his shoulders and neck release their angry tension, let his grip on the steering wheel give up its vehemence. Sometimes he felt as if the car were doing the driving, making this decision for him. In the morning he would know better, but for now, he indulged himself in the illusion.

The little Cape Cod was dark except for a soft light in the first-floor eastern window. *The stove light,* he told himself. It was the only light Laraine left burning when she went out for the evening. It would provide just enough illumination to guide her and a companion to the staircase and upstairs into darkness.

He drove past Molly Brannigan's on State, but Laraine's white Maxima was not visible anywhere. A car that looked like hers was parked outside the Firehouse on Old French

Road, but the number on the license plate was wrong. He continued winding his way through town, following the worn path to Laraine's favorite nightspots. The car responded as if on autopilot. He set his brain on low idle, tried not to envision anything unpleasant, tried not to imagine the inevitable.

On East Eighteenth Street, just a block from the little theater he and Laraine used to frequent during the first five years of their marriage, the only good years among the past eighteen, he parked facing west, as far from the nearest streetlamp as possible yet within sight of the white Maxima across the street in the Holiday Inn's elevated lot. She could have parked less conspicuously, he told himself, could have hidden her vehicle from view, but she never did. He acknowledged this fact but chose not to ponder it. Pondering was best reserved for the daylight hours. Too much cerebration at night could lead to harder drugs.

He watched her car and tried not to think about her in the hotel bar, waiting for some man to buy her a drink. Or maybe no longer waiting. Either thought was not a healthy one. So he thought instead about the little studio theater nearby. He wondered if it was still operational. He and Laraine had attended a lot of plays there, had spent many pleasant hours in that small, dark room. *Coyote Ugly* had been the first one. He smiled when he remembered how shocked Laraine had been when, in the second act, the lead actress walked onstage completely naked.

How quickly things change, he thought.

Then asked himself, *But what else did you see? We saw* True West *there.* American Buffalo. Glengarry Glen Ross. The Skin of Our Teeth. Greater Tuna. Children of a Lesser God.

It was Laraine who had introduced him to live theater. Introduced him to poetry and literature too, the magic of words. Now he could quote Rilke or Marquez at the drop of a hat, but now the height of Laraine's current cultural life consisted of pornographic reruns playing on an endless loop inside her own brain, dulling images of the same scene over and over again. He knew what movie she watched in her head because he often watched it too.

The scene always opened with a long shot of a red pickup truck racing toward them down a dark, rain-slick street, a two-thousand-pound torpedo with one of its headlights out. Laraine had spotted it before he did. He had been staring straight ahead, driving too slowly through the intersection, thinking not about the light turning from yellow to red but about the examination he would take the next day, his possible promotion. "Move!" Laraine had screamed. But he had looked to his right first, saw her hands on the dashboard as she stared out her side window, saw the single headlight bearing down on them, and only then mashed down on the accelerator.

He regained consciousness to the sound of people hammering on his windshield. The Taurus he was driving that night had been rammed across the sidewalk and tight against a clothing store. He remembered turning his head to the left and looking through his shattered window at a mannequin in a bikini looking down at him. It had been a red bikini, fire truck red. The mannequin had had red hair and her nails were painted red and her fiberglass skin was a very pale red too. In fact there had been red everywhere he looked that night. The wetness dripping from the side of his face and from his left eye was red. The drunken driver of the red pickup truck crushed against the Taurus was now lying facedown on the hood of his truck, halfway out his own windshield, and his head was drenched in red. Vehicles were converging on the scene from two different directions, and their flashing lights were red too; their sirens were red, and Laraine's screams as she struggled against her seat belt were as red as her limp right arm, the side of her yellow summer dress splotched bikini red, siren red, as she wrestled with the seat belt and tried to turn to the rear seat, tried to climb into the back, reaching with her one good arm for Ryan in his car seat behind De-Marco. Until Laraine touched the boy, there was not a drop of red on him anywhere, yet he continued to sleep peacefully, his head canted too far to the side, his wisps of corn silk hair still as yellow as pale sunlight, still as alive as summer except for the wash of color DeMarco saw everywhere he looked each time he blinked another red tear from his eye.

Or maybe that's only my pornographic movie, DeMarco told himself now. *Maybe Laraine doesn't even see it anymore. Maybe she's managed to shut it all off.*

But he doubted it. Otherwise, she would not have been coming out of the Holiday Inn at nearly midnight in the middle of the week, would not be standing beside her car while a man DeMarco had never seen before rubbed a hand over her breasts, up under her blouse, let his other hand fall between her legs. It always intrigued De-Marco to see the aplomb with which Laraine absorbed these pawings and gropings. Her hands rested lightly atop the man's shoulders. She stood as still and stately as a gladiola while his hands moved over her.

Five minutes later, Laraine's car pulled out of the parking lot and was followed by a dark green Hyundai. She would drive home in no hurry now — she always did. De-Marco, on the other hand, sped down familiar side streets so as to reach the Cape Cod before she did. He parked half a block away.

He waited until she had unlocked the front door, until she and her friend for the night were inside. Then he drove forward and parked at the curb in front of the house. He climbed out and walked to the front door and rang the bell.

Laraine opened the door and stood there looking at him. There was no surprise on her face, no anger.

"Do you even know this one?" he asked.

She said nothing. She blinked once but otherwise did not move.

"You've got to stop doing this," he told her. "You don't know who these guys are, what they might do. Sooner or later, you're going to get yourself hurt."

And now she smiled, as if there were an inherent humor to the notion of being hurt.

"I'll be in my car," he finally said. "In case you need me."

Her look was void of any emotion he recognized.

She closed the door and turned the lock, and he returned to his vehicle. He laid the seat back until he was comfortable, then he watched the dark house for a while, and then he didn't. He listened to the radio for twenty minutes or so, listened to Ry Cooder's agonized guitar weeping all the way from Texas, listened to Norah Jones, Dinah Washington, Clapton and Raitt and John Lee Hooker. Then he turned the radio off because he did not need a soundtrack for what he was feeling.

He spent the next half hour or so reciting snatches of prose and poetry to himself, phrases first heard aloud when Laraine had read to him in bed. She had loved what she called the music of words, and when she read to him, he heard the music too. Later, when she stopped reading to him and the house was too empty, he would read the same books alone and always hear them in Laraine's voice, but with a sadness then in both her voice and in his heart because he did not know if she would ever speak to him again.

"My mother is a fish," Faulkner had written. "Roosters wear out if you look at them so much," Marquez had said. He remembered the entire first paragraph from Hemingway's "In Another Country." But he could not recall the lines from Rilke's "The First Elegy" that followed *Oh, and the night, the night, when the wind full of cosmic space invades our frightened faces . . .*

After a while, Laraine's new friend came sauntering out of the house. At the door he turned to kiss her, but she said good-bye with a smile, stepped back, and closed the door. He stood there perplexed for a few seconds, wondering what he had done wrong. DeMarco sipped the last of his watery whiskey and thought, *They are always perplexed.*

Finally, the man turned and crossed to his Hyundai, climbed in, and drove away.

A few minutes later, the light blinked on in the upstairs bathroom. *She'll be taking a shower now,* DeMarco told himself. Then she would towel dry her hair, brush her teeth, run the blow-dryer for a while. The important thing was that she was safely alone inside her home now and the doors were locked. DeMarco started the engine and turned the radio on again. He was grateful for the company on the drive back home.

EIGHTEEN

Inhale, Thomas Huston told himself. *Exhale. Do it again. Do it again.*

Nothing came easily anymore. Nothing came naturally.

You need to keep your thoughts straight, man. Get some food. You need to eat.

It was surely midnight now, maybe later. No car had stopped at the convenience store in quite a while.

Go now, he told himself.

He came out of the trees and crossed the street and tried his best to look like a man out for a stroll. He kept his head down, knew there would be security cameras. He looked up only long enough to glance through the window before entering, saw the boy behind the counter. Tall, thin, scraggly, reddish beard. *Not one I know,* he thought. *Not one of mine.*

So he pulled open the door, walked inside, and headed straight down the center aisle as if he knew where he was going. What he knew was that the restrooms would be in a rear corner, and there they were, to his right, between the fountain drinks and the milk cooler.

At the sink, Huston avoided the mirror until the soapy water he had rubbed over his face had been rinsed off. Then he raised his head, allowed himself to look. His face was more familiar than he expected. Maybe he was still Thomas Huston after all. A three-day beard, bits of hair sticking up here and there. But he knew that face. The eyes were tired, face drawn, but that was not the face of a beast, was it?

Next he scrubbed his hands clean, picked the dirt from beneath his fingernails. Then he scrubbed himself again with a damp paper towel, as far down the neck as he could reach without getting his shirt wet. He dried himself, finger combed his hair, rinsed his mouth out, scrubbed a finger over his teeth, and rinsed again.

Out in the store, he shopped carefully, tried to think ahead. Protein, nutrients. *Be smart so you don't have to do this again.* A loaf of bread, a jar of peanut butter. A can of cashews, four small bags of beef jerky. When he opened the cooler to reach for a gallon of orange juice, the tin of cashews

144

clattered to the floor. He sank to his knees, gathered it in, and cradled everything against his chest.

"Here you go," the cashier said, startling him. The boy had come up behind him and stood there smiling now, holding out a small plastic basket.

"Yeah, thanks," Huston said. He dropped the items into the basket, took the basket from the boy's hand. "Car food," he told him.

"Where you headed?"

"Toronto," said Huston. "Started out from Texas two days ago." He stood facing the cooler, kept his head turned to the side as if he were searching for another item.

"That's what? Fifteen hundred miles at least. You drive straight through?"

"We stopped at a rest area a couple times for a little sleep, but yeah, mostly straight through."

The boy nodded and stood there waiting, apparently eager for conversation.

Huston turned his back to the boy, faced the shelves stocked with chips and crackers, little boxes of overpriced cookies. "My wife drove Jamie over to Mickey D's for a Happy Meal. Which makes me the designated shopper."

"You finding everything you need?"

"I was hoping for something healthy, you know? Kind of hard to find in a convenience store."

"At the end of the aisle there's some apples and bananas."

"No kidding?" said Huston, turning away.

The bananas were three for a dollar, the Fuji apples seventy-five cents each. Huston chose three of each, then crossed to the counter. "How much for one of these pizzas?"

"The whole thing? Nine ninety-five. Two dollars extra for pepperoni."

"Skip the pepperoni," Huston said. He set the basket on the counter. "Tell you what. If you want to start ringing me up, I'll grab one or two more things real quick."

"Will do," the boy said.

Huston felt strange again, a character in a story. A character pretending to be a corpse pretending to be normal when in fact the world had ended, the bomb had gone off, all was devastation. What else did this corpse need to keep the show going a while longer? A toothbrush and a tube of toothpaste. A pair of mirrored sunglasses. A black ball cap with a yellow *P* embroidered on it. He placed these on the counter with the other items, watched the digital display adding up the prices. He could feel his reflection looming in the convex mirror suspended from the ceiling, could feel the probing eye of the security camera.

The cashier said, "Sixty-eight fifty-six."

Huston withdrew three twenties and a ten from his wallet, then dropped the change back inside. *Twenty-four dollars and a few coins left,* he told himself. *The sum assets of your life.* He picked up both plastic shopping bags and the jug of orange juice with his left hand, the pizza box with his right.

"You going to drive through to Toronto tonight?" the boy asked.

"That's the plan." He started for the door.

"Well . . . have a good one."

"You too."

Already the night felt several degrees cooler. *Where to now?* he wondered. He tore the tag off the ball cap, bent a curve into the bill, placed the hat on his head. The McDonald's was several blocks to his left so he headed in that direction just in case the cashier was watching. After a block, he turned back toward the woods. *Think!* he told himself. *You know where you are. Think of a place to go for the night.*

Twenty yards into the woods, he could wait no longer. He sat behind a tall pin oak, pulled the pizza box onto his lap. He ate quickly, two slices in little more than a minute, a long swallow of orange juice, with little recognition of the flavors. Then he forced himself to slow down. Unfortunately, that allowed the memories to start again — Tommy at his last birthday party, stuffing his face at Pizza Hut, letting long streamers of cheese dangle from his mouth . . .

Huston squeezed shut his eyes, drove the happy images away. Gone, gone, all was gone.

" 'Whose woods these are,' " Huston mumbled aloud and focused his thoughts, tried to fill his mind's eye with the words themselves. " 'I think I know. His house is in the village though . . .' "

NINETEEN

DeMarco awoke to the gray emptiness of dawn. The house was empty and the world was empty and all he had to fill it with was another day's work. This day and the next day and the next day and the next. For a while, he did not care about any of it, did not want to face another parade of slow hours, but as always, after staring at the dull light in the window for a couple minutes, he told himself to get his sorry ass out of bed. "Do somebody some good today," he said.

A few minutes later, coffee was dripping into the decanter. Then he was in the shower and the water was steaming the glass. Then he dried himself and wiped the fog off the mirror, and just like that, the routine took hold as always, the mechanics of living, step one, step two, step three, and the wind-up man was moving again.

On his desk at the barracks, he found

another CD from Trooper Carmichael. The trooper had managed to unlock all of Huston's password-protected and deleted files. DeMarco inserted the disk and opened the file marked *Deleted.* The file contained drafts of several letters of recommendation for former students, each letter distinguished by a kind but insistent honesty.

I have no doubts that when Matthew manages to impose a discipline on his capacious imagination, he will produce some truly outstanding work . . .

I have encountered no student writer with a more impressive technical mastery of the craft. Certainly someday Andrea will have acquired the life experience necessary to give depth to her work. Until then, her keen editorial eye will make her an asset in any graduate writing program . . .

A file marked *Home* included drafts of homework assignments written by Alyssa and Thomas Jr. and critiqued by their father. These too displayed Huston's delicacy and tact. He managed, for example, to remonstrate his daughter for her reliance on clichés and words such as *cute* and *sweet* while praising her sense of pacing and narrative structure. He underlined numerous misspelled words on his son's paper and wrote in the text: *Spell-check, Tommy! You're being lazy.* But he also wrote *I love this description! A beautiful phrase.* And *Very clever!*

Huston's *Misc Notes* file revealed another aspect of his character, and these random thoughts intrigued DeMarco:

for essay about fathers and sons: Sometimes I think that the lucky boys, the lucky men, are the ones who grew up despising their fathers.

story about obit writer: It's all in the obituary, trust me. Easy to read between the lines once you get the hang of it. Easy to tell if he was a brotherly man, a joiner, a glad-hander and friend to all, or maybe a loner, curmudgeonly and mean, a small-spirited recluse not even his family is going to miss.

short story, possible title "Dry Wood": A couple goes into the wilderness for a weekend in an attempt to get their passion (fire) back. But their planning is bad; it's late in the season; an icy rain catches them off guard. As they search for dry wood to build a fire, they blame each other more and more for their predicament, bring up old wounds, until the fire of rage causes the woman to attack her husband . . .

essay: Close to death, closer to life.

essay: I don't mind a little poetry now and then but I have no time for poets.

No time for poets? DeMarco wondered. *Referring to Denton?* He made a mental note to probe the poet a bit, poke around for soft spots and old bruises. Then he returned to the *Misc Notes* file, read through three more pages of brief glimpses into the writer's mind. Something about the rhythm of Huston's prose seemed to match DeMarco's rhythm. He found himself thinking that he and Huston were tuned to the same frequency.

"Difference is," DeMarco said aloud, "you've got talent and I've got sleep deprivation."

The file labeled *Office Emails* contained more messages between Huston and Denton. All but one series were concerned with departmental matters. Carmichael had listed these in chronological order beginning with one from Denton. The emails made DeMarco lean forward in his chair.

Turns out C's "writer-in-residence" position cost him $300/week! Available to anybody! No duties, no application process. There are as many as 20 "artists-in-residence" at any given time. It's little more than a hotel that caters to wannabes. B

Bob — Keeps digging his own grave, doesn't he? However, he never claimed it as a sinecure or award, did he? Do you still have a copy of the faculty newsletter? Tom

". . . spent the month of July as writer-in-residence at the James Bryce Carwell Institute in Palo Alto . . ." The writer-in-residence! Subtle but misrepresentative nonetheless. The devious bastard. B

Bob — Okay, another nail in the coffin. Share it with the committee next week and let's see how they take it. Tom

Will be more effective coming from you, don't you think? My credentials are legit too but admittedly obscure. Better to have the condemnation come from the king rather than from a mere princeling, eh? B

DeMarco leaned back in his chair. *C for Conescu,* he told himself. He read the emails again. It seemed clear that professors Denton and Huston were intent on exposing Conescu as a fraud, a poseur. The emails also suggested that Denton was leading the attack but attempting to position Huston as point man.

"Very interesting," DeMarco said.

He went online then to access the English Department's telephone number, punched it in, and spoke with the secretary. When he asked if Denton was expected in that day, she pulled his schedule. "Monday, Wednesday, Friday, he teaches from two to two fifty, then from three to three fifty. Office hours on Monday and Friday but none today."

"How about his home address? You have that?"

There was a pause, then a timid response. "I know you're the police but . . . I'm not sure I'm allowed to give that out."

"No problem," DeMarco told her. "Wouldn't want to get you in dutch."

Next, he telephoned the county courthouse, asked Cheryl in the Recorder of Deeds office to search the database for Robert Denton. Two minutes later, he wrote the address on his notepad: 619 Locust Drive, Greenwood Valley.

Greenwood Valley was an eighties subdivision of sprawling ranch and mock-Tudor homes. DeMarco calculated that Denton would need ten minutes to get from his home to campus, maybe more if he ran any errands on the way or stopped for a cappuccino. In any case, he probably wouldn't leave the house before one in the afternoon. It was now only 10:47.

"Plenty of time for me to ruin his day," DeMarco said.

TWENTY

Robert Denton's house in Greenwood Valley was a vinyl and brick split-level on a quarter-acre lot of grass that probably hadn't seen a mower blade since mid-August. The mulch beds were overrun with creepers gone wild, the flower beds full of leaves. DeMarco arrived in an unmarked silver Impala from the motor pool, parked half a block from the poet's house, then approached by foot.

The curtains were all drawn in the front of Denton's house. At the first-floor entryway, DeMarco pressed the doorbell three times. With the two-note chirp echoing throughout the house, he crossed briskly to the corner, then hurried along the side of the house until he could see the rear entrance. A door thudded inside. Footsteps scurried. A rush of muted voices. A minute or two later, the back door opened and the waifish girl DeMarco had seen in Campbell

Hall outside the poet's office exited the house at a canter. She crossed the rear yard and hurried through a narrow opening in the privet hedge.

DeMarco returned to the front door and again thumbed down the doorbell.

Finally the door swung open. A barefoot and rumpled-looking Denton, wearing a blue-and-green-striped bathrobe and holding a mug of coffee in one hand, a thick literature anthology in the other, blinked at him.

"Morning," DeMarco said and smiled through the screen door. "I'm Sergeant Ryan DeMarco with the state police. And you are Robert Denton?"

"That's right," Denton said. He stood very still. DeMarco thought that except for the poet's deer-in-headlights look, except for the bare feet, bare legs, and bathrobe, he might be posing for a yearbook photo.

"I was wondering if you would have a few minutes to talk with me about your colleague, Professor Huston?"

Denton remained motionless for two more blinks. Then suddenly he became animated. "Oh sure, absolutely. Come on upstairs." He turned from the door and spoke quickly as he mounted the stairs. "Just let me jump into some clothes real quick. I've been working on today's lesson plans. I'll meet you in the living room, top of the stairs."

DeMarco pulled the door shut behind him. He said, "I haven't gotten around yet to taking my screens down either."

At the top of the stairs, Denton paused long enough to look back down. "Screens?" he said. Then, "Ah, the storm doors. Right. I hadn't even noticed."

"Those lost BTUs add up fast."

"One of these weekends," the poet said. "Come on up. I'll just be a second."

The stairs opened directly onto the living room, a room that would have been full of sunlight had the horizontal blinds across the wide picture window been open. De-Marco stood at the top of the stairs and let his eyes adjust. A brown leather sofa. A bookcase full of books. Indentations in the beige carpet where another piece of furniture had long stood against the side wall, where now, in the corner, was nothing but an acoustic guitar on a metal stand. *A piano?* DeMarco thought. The mantel over the fireplace was empty, the grate full of old ashes. All around the room were other indentations in the carpet, bare nails stuck in the walls. *Entertainment hutch,* DeMarco thought. *Recliner. Coffee table. Matching end tables. Pictures there and there and there.*

The only sign of inhabitance was last Sunday's newspaper spread out on the floor in front of the sofa.

Wearing beltless blue jeans and a loose, blue-striped white Oxford shirt, cuffs unbuttoned, tail hanging out, Denton returned from his bedroom. "Please, sit down, Officer. Can I get you a cup of coffee?"

DeMarco smiled. "Looks like you've been cleaned out here."

"Ex-wife," said Denton. "Estranged wife actually. But at least she left me a place to sit, right?" He motioned toward the sofa. "Please, have a seat. I'll grab a chair for myself."

He retrieved a low barstool from beside the kitchen counter, positioned it just inside the living room, sat with his bare feet on the top rung. Then he noticed how awkwardly DeMarco was sitting, his feet spread wide to avoid the newspaper.

Denton hopped down off the barstool. "Christ, I'm sorry," he said and scooped up the newspapers, tossed them into an empty corner. "I live like a fucking bachelor, you know? Can't seem to bring myself to get this place organized."

"You and your wife trying to work things out?" DeMarco asked.

"Who the fuck knows? I mean, she wants

us to date, you know? So we date. But all she ever wants to do is to haul out all the old baggage. Sorta makes me wonder why we even try."

DeMarco nodded, said nothing.

Denton grinned. "I do miss the piano though. And she doesn't even play! She just took it to piss me off."

DeMarco smiled and said nothing. He already knew that Denton was uncomfortable with silences.

"Anyway, about Tom," Denton said. "I mean what a fucking shock. The whole university is reeling over it. You guys have any idea where he is? Why he'd do such a thing?"

DeMarco said, "I stopped by your office the other day but you weren't in yet. I talked to a student who was there waiting for you. Thin. Pretty. Strawberry-blond hair?"

"Heather Ramsey," Denton said. He waited but couldn't tolerate the pause for long. "Good student. Very bright." He shuffled his bare feet on the barstool's rung. "So uh . . . I guess you wanted to ask me some things about Tom?"

"I'm just hoping to figure him out," DeMarco said. "Get a feeling for who he is."

"He's my fucking hero," said Denton. "I mean not now, not after what he did, but . . . He was my sanctuary, I'll tell you that. I don't know how I'm going to survive without him around anymore."

"Your sanctuary."

"Yeah, it's like . . . I guess you have to know what academia is really like. Inside the ivy tower, you know? It's filled with pettiness like you wouldn't believe. Fucking careerists who care more about office space than ideas. Anal, dysthymic . . . completely dysfunctional outside of the classroom, you know?"

"Except for Thomas Huston."

"We are the only published writers in the department, did you know that? In an English department of seventeen people. Two creative writers. It's fucking pathetic."

"There's a Professor . . . Conescu?" De-Marco said.

"He's a dickhead."

"How so?"

"In every way so. He is the epitome of academic paranoia. Thinks the whole department is out to get him just because he's Romanian. Because he has an accent. Because his gypsy grandfather was hanged at Buchenwald. Or so he claims anyway."

"And are you?"

"Am I . . . ?"

"You and Professor Huston. Were you out

to get him?"

"We were out to get rid of him, yes. But only because he's fucking incompetent. He's a blight on the entire department."

"And that's why he was denied tenure?"

"He never should have been hired in the first place. He should be in a padded room somewhere."

DeMarco smiled. He reached into his jacket pocket and pulled out a small notepad, looked at what was written there, put it away again. "So it was you and Dr. Huston who led the vote against him."

"He's not a doctor."

"Excuse me?"

"Tom. He doesn't have a PhD."

"But you do."

"MFA, UC San Diego. PhD, University of Denver."

DeMarco nodded.

"I mean, that has never mattered to me. The guy's written two bestsellers."

"I thought it was four books," DeMarco said.

"Right, four, same as me. But only two of them, the last two, had significant sales. The first one barely sold at all. It's my favorite though. For some reason I've always liked it the best."

"You've written four books too?"

162

"It's poetry, of course. Small presses. Not for the masses."

DeMarco nodded. He remembered what Huston had written. *It's easy to read between the lines once you get the hang of it.*

"So this Conescu," DeMarco said. "Would he be capable, in your opinion? Of what happened to the Huston family?"

"Are you saying Tom didn't do it?"

"I'm asking which of the two would be more capable."

"Jesus fucking Christ," the poet said. "More capable? There's no question. Not in my mind anyway. I mean Tom isn't perfect . . . He has his shortcomings, sure, just like everybody else. But something like that? Wiping out the whole family? I just can't fathom it."

"What shortcomings?"

"Department wise mostly. He just wasn't terribly concerned about the business of the department. If it wasn't his family, his students, or his own writing, he had to be nudged, you know?"

DeMarco thought, *His own writing?*

"So you think Conescu might have been involved somehow?"

DeMarco smiled. "We don't know."

"But you think it's a possibility?"

"At this point, everything is a possibility."

DeMarco put his hands on his knees. "I should let you get back to your lesson plans." He stood. "Thanks for taking the time to speak with me."

"Anytime, honestly. I'm more than happy to help."

DeMarco paused before descending the stairs. "By the way, just for the record, where were you last Saturday night?"

"You're kidding, right?"

"Standard procedure."

"Well, let me think. I guess I was here."

"You guess?"

"I mean I was. I was here all night."

"Anybody else?"

"Here? Just me and my muse."

"She have a name?"

"I call her the Bitch. But it was just the two of us all Saturday night. I was in the bedroom at my computer until, I don't know, well after midnight. Revising a manuscript for a chapbook contest."

"So if I have my resident computer geek dig into your computer and pull out all the time signatures on your hard drive, he'll be able to confirm that?"

A muscle twitched in Denton's jaw. "They can do that? I mean, the computer keeps track like that?"

"To the minute," DeMarco said. He had

no idea if it was true or not. He hoped it was. He smiled at the poet.

"No problem," Denton finally answered. "Absolutely."

DeMarco nodded, then headed down the stairs.

Denton remained at the top. "Could you tell me though? Do you guys have any idea where Tom has disappeared to?"

DeMarco did not look back. "Have a good day, Professor."

TWENTY-ONE

DeMarco stood in the center of the communal living room of apartment 312 North Hall. The girl who had answered the door, then went to 312C to alert Heather Ramsey of his presence, now stood with her back to him at the kitchen sink as she washed the same juice glass over and over again. When Heather came into the living room, the girl at the sink shut off the faucet and meticulously dried every millimeter of the glass.

"I just have a few questions is all," DeMarco said to Heather Ramsey.

"I need to be in class in twelve minutes. It's an eight-minute walk from here."

"Professor Denton's class?"

She nodded. "So I really don't have any time right now . . ."

"I'll walk with you," DeMarco said. He let her cross ahead of him and go out the door, then he turned back to the kitchen. The other girl had already moved away from the sink. *On her way to the front window,* De-Marco thought. The sound of his voice brought her up short.

He said, "Could you tell me how frequently Miss Ramsey doesn't return to her apartment at night?"

The girl was small and reed thin, her eyes huge. "Uh . . ." she said.

"Is it every night or just now and then?"

"I don't really . . . keep track, you know?"

"Could you tell me what the university policy is concerning professors sleeping with their students?"

Her eyes widened even farther. "I guess I don't . . . really know anything . . . about that?"

"Thanks very much," DeMarco said.

Outside, he cut across the grass to catch up with Heather Ramsey. She took long, adamant strides and walked as if leaning into a wind. Her hands were empty, fingers opening and closing as she walked. As he came up beside her, she offered a tight smile and said, "I saw you in Campbell Hall, right? You went into Professor Huston's office?"

DeMarco said, "And I saw you sneaking out of Professor Denton's house this morning, right?"

She cut him a quick look, then jerked her

gaze forward again. Her gait stiffened. "I don't know what you're talking about."

"That's not what your roommate said."

She shook her head and blew out an angry breath. "I hate this place."

"Are you the reason his wife left him? Or was it the girl before you?"

Her pale face reddened.

"Has he told you that he's still sleeping with his wife?"

When she looked at him this time, there were tears in her eyes.

He said, "You need to talk to me, Heather."

Her pace slowed. She cast a glance about at the other students hurrying to their classes. None was more interested in getting to class than in trying to ascertain with a glance why she was being escorted by a state trooper. In a voice barely louder than a whisper, she asked, "What does any of this have to do with Professor Huston?"

"That's what I need to figure out. And that's why you need to talk to me."

"I'm going to be late for class."

"You don't use books in this class?" he asked. "You're not even carrying a pencil, Heather."

Her pace slowed even more. Finally she came to a halt. "Everybody's watching."

"Just smile," he told her. "See? Big smile for everybody to see."

She tried one out but to DeMarco it looked more like a grimace. "Good," he told her. "So what's that place over there? With the picnic tables under the awning?"

"Student union," she said. "The patio."

"Can we get a cup of coffee there?"

She blew out another breath. "Whatever."

Loud music blared from inside the union, an indecipherable clash of bass thumps and slurred hip-hop lyrics. DeMarco emerged onto the patio carrying two paper cups of coffee, set the hazelnut latte in front of her, kept the black dark roast Columbian for himself as he took a seat beside her at the scarred picnic table. She sat with her legs beneath the tabletop and faced the Union's smoked-glass wall. He straddled the bench and faced her.

"That music in there gives me a headache," he said.

She nodded.

He sipped his coffee.

She said, "How do you know he's still sleeping with his wife?"

"He told me they were dating."

"Really?" she asked. Then, "But just dating, right?"

He looked out across the campus. The lawns and sidewalks were mostly empty now, students in their classes, in their dorms, maybe two or three in the library. He said, "After I saw you this morning, before I came here, I made some inquiries about your poetry professor. This last one was his third marriage, did you know that? He's got four kids to the first two wives."

"He told me all that."

"Did he tell you he's still sleeping with the last one?"

"You're just saying that. You don't know."

"I do know that the dean has spoken to him twice, unofficially, because of complaints from the parents of previous students. Officially the university can't do anything because the girls, like you, were all at least eighteen. He's been at the university now for, what, nine years? My guess is he averages one or two coeds a year."

Her tears left small black circles on the weathered tabletop. "He says I'm special."

DeMarco laid his hand atop hers. "You are," he told her. "But not to him."

TWENTY-TWO

Thomas Huston awoke shivering. An hour or so after midnight, he had curled into a tight ball in a small room on the second floor of the university president's new mansion. The ten-thousand-square-foot building had been under construction since March and the ribbon-cutting ceremony was not scheduled until May of next year. All four stories had been framed in, but there were no windows installed anywhere, no wiring or plumbing except beneath the concrete of the basement and garage floors.

Just inside the basement entrance at the rear of the mansion, workers had stored some of their materials: boxes of floor tiles, rolls of electrical wire, a cardboard box full of electrical wall boxes and plugs, a stack of two-by-fours, and, taking up at least a third of the spacious room, a dozen or more rolls of Tyvek insulation. Slung over the stack of two-by-fours was a dirty chambray shirt, stiff with dried perspiration. Huston pulled the work shirt over his short-sleeved knit shirt, buttoned it to the neck, rolled down the sleeves, and buttoned them too. The shirt, like the dirty quilted jacket he pulled over the top of it, was an extra large, but he did not mind how it looked on him, and the odor it gave off was no more offensive than his own.

Then Huston crept upstairs to look around, wincing at every creak of the subflooring. Illumination from the sodium vapor streetlights flooded in through the open windows at the front of the house, so he kept to the rear, tried always to keep a wall between himself and the front windows, and ducked quickly past open doorways.

On the second floor, he found a small interior room with only one opening, a door that faced the center of a much larger room. *A walk-in closet,* he told himself. *Off the master bedroom.* He huddled up in a corner of this room, pulled his bags of groceries close, and tried to sleep. But all he could think about were the evenings he and Claire had spent in unfinished buildings like this one.

During his last two summers in college, he had worked on a construction crew but had lived with his parents. Claire O'Patchen lived with hers in a village six miles away. The young couple had tired quickly of making love twisted and cramped in the backseat of Huston's battered Volvo parked along the side of a dirt lane, of pulling apart with every flash of headlights. Then one night, in search of a more secluded place to park, he drove past the construction site where he and the crew were building a two-story colonial.

In mid-June, he and Claire made love on a sleeping bag in the cement-block basement. The first night went so well, despite the hard surface, that he took to carrying a sleeping bag and backpack in his car, of filling the backpack with a bottle of wine and an assortment of midnight snacks. By late August, he and Claire were spending most of their nights together beneath an open window on the second floor. Back at college in the fall, he quickly familiarized himself with every building in town under construction, places much more private than the frat house, much less expensive than a motel. Places where their only real concern was how far through the night Claire's cries and moans might carry.

Now he faced the corner of the closet and smelled the fresh wood, the scent of open air. He pulled his knees to his chest, squeezed himself into a ball, but he could not squeeze out the ache, the heavy, hollow anguish.

The chambray shirt and quilted jacket seemed to have no effect against the chill night air. He convulsed with sobs and he shivered with cold. After a half hour of lying huddled against the wall, his body stiff with the tension of violent shivering, he climbed to his feet and made his way back to the basement. He carried a roll of the Tyvek up to the second floor, unrolled it and buried himself beneath the foil liner. He pulled the bags of groceries close and held them tucked against his stomach, something to wrap himself around.

Somewhere before dawn, he awoke enshrouded in gray. He awoke thinking he still held the knife in his hand, and he recoiled from it and flung the knife away, rolled away from it and felt the strangely soft obstacle at his back, batted and kicked at the Tyvek and sent the bags of food scattering, kicked and flailed to get clear of the insulation until he had rolled hard against the opposite wall. There he lay blinking, breathing hard. His eyes felt scratched and sore, his throat scraped raw, body chilled to the bone.

Gradually, the previous night came back to him, bits and pieces coalescing. He was in the president's new mansion. It was morning, maybe six, six thirty. Construction workers would be showing up soon. Traffic on the streets. Too many eyes.

Quickly, he gathered up and bagged the food and made his way down to the basement. He peeked out the rear entrance. The world outside was deep in gray. But he knew these fogs, had moved through them most of his life. In an hour, the world would be clear again. He had to get back to the woods. Plan his next move. *Today is Wednesday,* he told himself. *Tomorrow night I can see Annabel.*

He pulled the ball cap down low on his forehead. Checked the pocket of the chambray shirt to make sure the mirrored sunglasses were still there. Patted his wallet. Then he picked up the grocery bags and stepped outside, moved stiffly but quickly down the gentle slope of the long backyard. Before long, he broke into a trot, a shadow through the fog. *I need to start making my way to Annabel,* he told himself. *There's a long way to go yet. Miles to go. Miles and miles before I sleep.*

TWENTY-THREE

For the second time in the past four minutes, DeMarco knocked on the door of Professor Conescu's office in Campbell Hall. The first time, three minutes earlier, there had been no reply, so DeMarco went to the English Department office and asked the secretary when might be the best time to catch the professor in.

"Any time between eight and six," she said. "Maybe even later, for all I know. I leave at six and he's always still here."

"What days?"

"Any day. I'm here five days a week and he's always here. He teaches Monday, Wednesday, and Friday at ten, eleven, two, and three, but the rest of the time he's in his office. All day on Tuesdays and Thursdays."

DeMarco looked at his wristwatch: 1:17.

"I knocked but he didn't answer."

"Oh, he's in there," the secretary said.

"Trust me. He's always in there."

So this time DeMarco knocked and knocked again. Every fifteen seconds he knocked three quick raps against the door, each series louder than the last. And finally a growling voice from behind the door demanded, "Who?"

"Sergeant Ryan DeMarco of the Pennsylvania State Police."

Silence for another ten seconds. Then, just as DeMarco was about to rap on the door again, the dead bolt clicked. He waited for the door to be pulled open, but the metal knob did not turn. He reached for it, gave it a twist, and threw the door open.

Conescu had organized his office so that the only part visible from the doorway was a narrow corridor leading to the window six feet away. To the left of the door stood a wall of metal bookcases. The books were crammed in vertically and horizontally, books on top of books. To the right, two metal filing cabinets, each five feet tall and with more books piled atop them, blocked the view into the office.

DeMarco stepped forward to the edge of the cabinets, turned to his right in the narrow opening between the front of the cabinets and the forced-air heating unit beneath the window, and there, crammed into the corner with his desk facing the wall, sat Conescu, big and slouching and messy haired. He sat with his head cocked toward a filing cabinet, his gaze locked onto the gray metal. The knuckles of both hands rested against the edge of his computer keyboard. On the screen was a text document crammed with words from margin to margin.

"I apologize for the interruption," DeMarco said. "I just need a few minutes of your time."

Conescu sat motionless for a few seconds, then opened his hands, laid his fingers atop the keyboard. He typed furiously for a couple of lines, said, "Too busy right now. Come back at three o'clock maybe," and hammered at the keys again.

"You teach at three o'clock," DeMarco said. He came the rest of the way into the room and took up a position to Conescu's left, sat on the edge of the metal desk, his body only inches from the professor. Conescu stiffened, which made DeMarco smile. "So now will work better."

Conescu stopped typing. Then he scrolled down the page until only white space was visible on the screen. He leaned back in his chair, turned his head toward DeMarco, lifted his eyes, and glowered. Every movement was distinct and separate, almost detached from the one that preceded it.

Paranoid schizophrenic, DeMarco told himself. *Classic.*

He said, "How would you characterize your relationship with Professor Huston?"

Conescu considered his response. Finally he said, "I don't like Nazis. Nazis don't like me."

"And why do you call him a Nazi?"

"What is Nazi? Full of hate. Prejudice. The desire to stifle, persecute, destroy those who threaten them."

"Did you threaten him?"

Conescu stared at him through slitted eyes. Then he faced his monitor. "Professional disagreements."

"He was one of the committee members who voted against tenure for you. You've threatened him personally and the university in general with lawsuits."

"My reputation is at stake."

"And what is your reputation?"

Conescu's shoulders stiffened and rose. His neck all but disappeared. DeMarco could hear him breathing through his nose, the slow inhalations, quick bursts of expelled air.

Finally DeMarco said, "From what I've been able to determine, Professor, all the threats were coming from you. I have copies of the emails and the letters. So I have only one other question for you. Where were you Saturday night between ten or so and dawn the next day?"

"Where is any decent person at that time? Asleep in bed."

"You're not married, are you?"

"I have no time for those things."

"Those things? You mean a wife?"

"Romance! Love affairs! I live a life of the mind."

"So there's no way to actually confirm that you were where you say you were?"

This time, Conescu blew a mouthful of air out through his teeth. "Check the tapes," he growled.

"And what tapes would those be?"

"Security cameras on every floor of my building. I arrive home at seven. Stay in till four the next day. Order dinner between eight, eight thirty. Check the tapes if you want to know."

"You had food delivered?"

"Steak stromboli and mozzarella sticks."

"Name of the restaurant?"

Conescu glared up at him. "You think I'm a liar?"

"Just asking for the name of the restaurant is all."

"Pizza fucking Joe."

"Pizza Joe's on Twelfth?"

"You want to smell the empty box in my garbage can?"

DeMarco smiled. "I'll let you know if that will be necessary."

Out on the street three minutes later, on his way to the parking lot, DeMarco was hit by a sudden cold shiver. "Higher education," he said out loud. "Jesus fucking Christ."

TWENTY-FOUR

By ten that morning the woods were no longer misty. From time to time, Huston emerged from the woods to check his position against an unobstructed view of the sun, but whenever possible, he remained hidden on his northward march. He had followed Sandy Creek out of Lake Wilhelm to its headwaters, a narrow stream that burbled up out of the ground. By his calculations, he had hiked ten to twelve miles since dawn. If his calculations were correct, Annabel's place of employment was fewer than three hours away.

You should start heading west now, he told himself. *No, stop for a while. Eat something. Don't wear yourself down to nothing.*

He knew that he was already nothing, that nothing remained of him save his ignorance and rage. He hoped to alleviate the ignorance by talking with Annabel, then shortly thereafter to expiate the rage. It sounded easy, but he knew it would not be. Annabel might not know anything. Even if she did, would she be likely to tell? In that case, what would he do?

He sat on the ground and ate one of his apples and a few pieces of beef jerky. He still had half the orange juice left and knew he should ration it out to last as long as possible, but the plastic jug pulled heavily on his arm when he walked. *You can always find something to drink,* he told himself. *Every little town along the way has at least one soft drink machine outside of a community center or a playground. Drink the orange juice. Keep your strength up.*

He wondered if he should contact Nathan Briessen. All morning long, Huston had been running names through his head, assaying each individual's potential for assistance. The only name that did not get crossed off the list of candidates was Nate's. *Nate knows about Annabel,* Huston told himself again. *He could drive me there. Drive me away again. Bring me clothes that don't stink, shoes that aren't soaked through. Maybe get me a weapon.*

But what right do I have to involve him in this?

Not since a boy had Huston felt so utterly alone. Yes, in his interviews, he had frequently spoken of the solitude of the writer's life, but his solitude had never been more than temporary, the manufactured solitude of a few hours each morning. There had always been Claire to fill the empty spaces. To shine her brightness in all his dark corners. Ever since February of his junior year in college. The Sweetheart Dance. Their first kiss. With that kiss, she had swept away his loneliness, poured light into his soul.

Now he was a twelve-year-old boy again. The one who left the house every afternoon to escape his parents' screaming. Their arguments that never ended. Every day after school he had hiked the woods alone and slept in fields and wished his parents would get a divorce if they hated each other so much. But they had stayed together despite the shouting matches. Three or four nights a week, the mattress on its metal frame thudded in their bedroom. The closest Huston ever came to understanding their relationship was the time he had complained to his father. "Why can't she ever talk in a normal tone of voice?" he had asked. "Why does she have to sound so angry all the time? Pretty soon you start screaming too. That's all I ever hear around here." His father, who at the time had been changing the oil in the Pontiac, crawled out from under the car, wiped his hands on a blue rag, and shrugged. "Your mother's a passionate woman. I have to take the good with the bad."

There was a lot more of the good when Tommy Jr. came along. Something mellowed then in Huston's mother and father. Tommy was his grandmother's jewel, and then Alyssa, her grandfather's princess. Then one day Huston's parents were gone.

But always there had been Claire. His light giver. The keeper of his soul.

Now that too was gone. Now he had only Annabel to rely upon. Only Annabel, his ignorance, and his rage.

He tossed the ravaged apple core aside. Climbed stiffly to his feet. Bent over and hefted the grocery bags. *A few more miles,* he told himself. *You don't deserve to rest.*

■ ■ ■ ■

DECEPTION

■ ■ ■ ■

TWENTY-FIVE

DeMarco had one other stop to make on campus. The registrar was a brittle-haired blond with a round face, bright green eyes, and an easy smile. But somewhere underneath the tight, flowered dress and eye-catching cleavage beat a schoolmarm's heart.

"All I'm asking," DeMarco said, trying not to sound as exasperated as his five minutes with her had made him, "is for his class and home address."

"And as I've told you," she answered, "we consider that personal information. It can only be supplied with the student's permission. Or with a warrant."

"Then please call him and ask his permission."

She smiled. "I'm afraid you will have to do that yourself."

"Then tell me his telephone number."

"I'm sorry but I can't do that."

"You understand that this is a police matter?"

She grinned so hard that her nose wrinkled. "I noticed that right away," she said.

"So the university has no desire to cooperate with the police?"

"We always cooperate with the police."

"By refusing to provide information?"

"I'm sorry, but it's against our policy."

"You're giving me a headache," DeMarco said.

She gave him another nose-crinkling grin.

"Will you tell me this much?" he asked. "Does he have any classes today?"

She thought about the request for a few moments, turned it over in her mind, flipped it inside and out, and finally typed *Nathan Briessen* into the search engine box.

"He does not," she answered.

"How about tomorrow?"

"I'm sorry," she said. "It's against university policy to provide that information."

"You know I can get a warrant easily enough."

"I'm sure you can get lots of things if you really want to."

The thought popped into his head that maybe she was flirting with him. Was it possible? He considered again the overdone hairdo, the overly tight dress, the overabundant cleavage. But he dismissed the possibility. He knew this kind of woman. She laid out all the necessary bait but only so as to lure the victim close enough that she could slap him silly.

DeMarco chose to stay out of reach. From his jacket pocket he took the small notebook on which he had written Heather Ramsey's address and telephone number. He punched the numbers into his cell phone. She answered in the middle of the fourth ring. Her voice was small and glutinous with tears.

"It's Sergeant DeMarco again," he told her. "I'm trying to locate Nathan Briessen. Do you know him, by any chance?"

"The grad assistant?" she said.

The registrar's nose uncrinkled. Her grin turned out to be not permanent after all.

"Would you happen to know where he lives?"

"Somewhere downtown," Heather Ramsey told him. "Over a bakery, I think. I don't know the exact address."

"How about you?" DeMarco asked. "You doing okay?"

"To be honest with you, I don't know how I'm doing."

"You call me, okay? If you need anything. If you just want to talk."

"Thank you," she said.

DeMarco pocketed his cell phone and smiled at the registrar.

"Thank you for your time," he told her.

"Who was that?" she demanded.

"Have a lovely day."

TWENTY-SIX

DeMarco knew of only two bakeries in town. The first, Basic Kneads, was housed in a small one-story cottage. The other, Schneider's Bakery, occupied the first floor of a large three-story brick building on Main Street. An open doorway to the side of the bakery gave way to a landing and a locked door. Outside the locked door were four call buttons. Stuck beneath the button for apartment 3B was a black label with white printing that read *Briessen.*

DeMarco held the button down for five seconds.

A male voice came through the speaker. "Yes?"

"Sergeant Ryan DeMarco of the Pennsylvania State Police, Mr. Briessen. I'd like to speak with you for a few minutes please."

The reply sounded heavy with resignation. "Come on up."

The student stood waiting in his open

doorway at the top of the third-floor landing. He said, "It's pronounced Bryson, by
the way. Not Breeson."

"Sorry," DeMarco said.

"Happens all the time. Come on in."

The young man was older than DeMarco
had expected, maybe thirty, give or take a
couple of years. He was taller than De-
Marco, six-one or so, a black man of medium build, clean-shaven, fit, his hair
cropped close to the scalp. He wore loose,
faded jeans, white cotton socks, and a faded
blue T-shirt with the word *SeaWolves*
emblazoned in orange across the chest.

"Don't see many of those," DeMarco said
with a nod toward the shirt. "You a fan?"

Briessen closed the door behind DeMarco
and followed him into the living room.
"Second baseman for three seasons. Never
got called up, so I sold insurance for a while.
Now I'm back in school. Have a seat. Can I
get you something to drink?"

DeMarco sat in a canvas sling chair
wedged into a corner beside the front
window. Briessen pulled the leather swivel
chair away from his desk, turned it to face
DeMarco, sat down, and said, "I was sort of
wondering when you guys would get around
to me."

DeMarco smiled. He liked this young

man. "The wheels of justice turn slowly."

"Not that slowly, I guess. It's only been four days. Seems more like four months though."

DeMarco nodded. "You from Erie originally?"

"Chicago. When the Tigers signed me, they sent me to Erie."

"What brought you here?"

"Thomas Huston."

"You knew him before you came here?"

"Only by his work. I came here to study with him."

"How long have you been here?"

"This is my third semester, my last for coursework."

"And you had a class with him this semester?"

"Independent study. Plus he's my thesis director and advisor. I also took classes with him each of my first two semesters."

"So you've gotten to know him fairly well."

"That's what makes this all so unbelievable. I just can't seem to . . . get my head around it."

"You never thought he was capable of something like that?"

"It's inconceivable. His family was everything to him. Everything."

"So if not him . . . who else might have

done it?"

"Christ, I can't even . . . I mean . . ."

DeMarco waited. The young man was fighting back tears. He lived here in an apartment with two chairs, a hundred books on plastic bookshelves, a kitchenette, and a bedroom. The heat and the aromas from the bakery made the air thick and too sweet. A constant drone of traffic noise came through and sometimes rattled the windows. By the look of his graceful hands and long fingers, he was a privileged boy from Lincoln Park or Streeterville, but he had failed as a baseball player and had gotten bored with selling insurance. He lived alone and dreamed of being a writer, and now his hero was finished, whisked away from him by unfathomable tragedy.

DeMarco said, "What about Conescu?"

Briessen looked up at him. "He's a first-class weasel but . . . a murderer? Honestly, I don't think he's got the balls for it."

"How about Denton?"

"Dr. Denton?"

"I sensed a lot of professional jealousy there."

"Well, yeah, but . . . who wouldn't be jealous of Tom? He was . . . perfection."

And now DeMarco understood. Softly he

said, "Did he know how you felt about him?"

A tiny movement flitted at the corner of Briessen's eye, a twitch, a wince. Then he shrugged. "It was never expressed, never talked about. But I'm sure he knew."

DeMarco waited for the rest of it.

"The thing about Tom is, right from the start, he treated me like an equal. I mean I might never publish a single word. But he respected my . . . intent, you know? He respected the dream. More than anything else, that's what made him so special to me."

DeMarco allowed half a minute to pass in silence. "You have any idea where he might be, Nathan?"

"I wish like hell I did. Imagine what he must be going through right now."

"I've been doing my best to imagine just that. Where would he go? What would he do?"

"I think he's looking for the killer."

"You do."

"Wouldn't you, if you were him? I know I would. Hell, I'd be helping him right now if I could."

"Do you think he knows who did it?"

"I've thought about this a lot. And I can't imagine that he does know. I mean . . . have you found any other bodies yet?"

"So you *do* believe he's capable of violence."

"Under the right circumstances? Aren't we all? I mean, could Tom ever hurt his family? Never. *Never.* Could he waste somebody who did hurt his family? Could you?"

DeMarco chewed on his lower lip, looked at his hands. He still sometimes fantasized about torturing the man who had run the red light and plowed his pickup truck into the side of DeMarco's car. The man had spent seven months in prison for vehicular manslaughter, but seven years would not have satisfied DeMarco. Not even seven times seven years. Not seven score and ten.

DeMarco felt the stiffness in his jaw, felt his molars grinding. He brought himself back to the apartment, away from the impossible. "So you've had no contact with him whatsoever."

"Not a word. I keep hoping though."

DeMarco nodded. "As for your whereabouts last Saturday night?"

The young man sat motionless for a while. Finally he said, "A club in Erie. The Zone."

"And after closing?"

Briessen blew out a slow breath. "Alex Ferris. He's a student here. Just tread lightly, okay? His parents are . . . unaware.

Un . . . enlightened."

Christ, DeMarco told himself. *So much fucking tragedy in this world. So much fucking pain.*

"Who's Annabel?" he asked.

"Annabel . . . ?"

"From Professor Huston's email to you. He said he was going to visit Annabel and invited you to go along."

"Ah," Briessen said. "A woman he was using as his model for Annabel. From the novel he's working on. Was working on."

"She's a character in his new novel?"

"Right. The Lolita character."

"You're losing me here. Annabel is a character based on the Lolita character?"

"His new novel, the one he was calling *D.* It's a contemporary take on Nabokov's novel *Lolita.* Tom was calling his character Annabel. The woman he invited me to meet was, I think, the physical model for that character, who, yes, is modeled after Nabokov's character Lolita."

"And you met this woman? Professor Huston's Annabel?"

"I wanted to. In fact I had planned to until late that afternoon."

"And?"

"A friend of mine called from the road. He was headed north, thought he might swing by if I had the time."

"Which you did."

"I mean, I wanted to go with Tom. I hated to turn him down. But at the same time I didn't want to go with Tom."

"I'm not sure I understand."

"Strip clubs, you know? They're just not my thing."

"He was meeting Annabel at a strip club?"

"His Lolita character, his Annabel, works at a strip club. In his novel. So that's where he was doing his research."

"You're going to have to bear with me here because I've never read *Lolita*. But what you're saying is that Annabel is the name he gave to a character he was modeling after a character named Lolita in the novel *Lolita*?"

Briessen smiled. "No. Lolita is a nickname for a character in Nabokov's novel *Lolita*. She's a young girl, what Nabokov called a *nymphet*. Not a child but not yet a woman. And the narrator of that novel, Humbert Humbert, is a literature scholar who has an unhealthy obsession with nymphets. He traces that obsession back to his very first intimate encounter, when he was still a boy, with a twelve-year-old girl named Annabel, who died of typhus. Tom took that same name as the name of his Lolita character.

He also intended for his Annabel to have some association with Poe's Annabel Lee, from the poem of the same name, just as Nabokov's Annabel did."

"Whew," DeMarco said. "I think I'm getting dizzy."

"All of Tom's novels, as I'm sure you know, have borrowed characters and situations from other novels. Tom intended his novel to be like Nabokov's in its use of wordplay and lots of literary allusions, and to be a comment on contemporary American society. The plot would be different, of course, just as all of Tom's plots were wholly his own creation, but in theme, you might say, his *D* was going to echo *Lolita* in that both would be about desire and the moral implications of how we respond to our desires."

"This is very helpful information," DeMarco told him. "Though I can't help but wonder how you came to be so well informed."

"I told you, Tom was my advisor. I went to his office nearly every day. I picked his brain every chance I could. He's a very, very generous man with his time and advice. And I like to think that he saw some potential in me as a writer and that's why he was so supportive."

"So if I want to find this Annabel character . . . You say she was only twelve years old?"

"In Nabokov's novel. But not in Poe's poem. And not in Tom's novel either. But she would be somebody still young enough to have a kind of wounded innocence to her."

"A wounded innocence."

"Someone who has been hurt but is still . . . vulnerable, I guess. Trusting. Not yet jaded. Not yet cynical."

"Someone like you," DeMarco said.

Nathan Briessen flinched. "Funny you should say that. Tom said that once."

Strange irony, DeMarco thought. Huston was writing a novel about an older man who falls in love with a girl, and here was a young man who was in love with the older man.

"Desire," DeMarco said. "That's what the title stood for? *D* for *desire*?"

"The book was to be divided into four parts: Desire, Deception, Despair, and Discernment."

"Discernment? It was going to have a happy ending?"

"That I don't know. In all likelihood, Tom didn't either. What I do know is that discernment doesn't always lead to happiness.

Sometimes just the opposite."

"Well," DeMarco said. Then, a moment later, "Do you know which club it is? Where Annabel works?"

"I know that Tom had been visiting various clubs for a couple of months now, trying to find the one girl who seemed to have the qualities he was looking for. The one who wasn't faking it, you know? He said that some of them were very good at faking it."

"Faking interest in him?"

"Faking innocence."

"Is that possible? For a woman to work as a stripper and still be an innocent?"

"Apparently Tom thought so."

"And you?"

Briessen shrugged. "I guess it's fair to say that my own view of life isn't quite so . . . conciliatory. Not that I don't wish I could share Tom's view. And you, Sergeant?"

"Excuse me?"

"How do you view the world?"

DeMarco smiled. "Did Professor Huston happen to mention the name of the club where Annabel works?"

"He mentioned others, ones he had crossed off the list. But this new one? I don't think so. I know he'd visited it three, maybe four times already before he invited me to go along. I think he just wanted me to look at the girl too, you know? See if I thought she was the real thing."

"Very strange place to go searching for innocence."

"I made the same comment. And you know what he said?"

"I'd like to."

"He said that's what makes it worth writing about. The apparent dichotomy. The internal conflict."

"The human heart in conflict with itself."

Briessen cocked his head and smiled. "You've read Faulkner."

"Once upon a time," DeMarco said. "As for the name of this strip club . . ."

"It wasn't anything local, I know that much."

"He couldn't risk being seen by someone he knows."

"Right. I mean his wife knew, but even so."

"She knew he was going to strip clubs?"

"It was research. She understood. They trusted each other completely."

"And this you know because . . . ?"

"He told me."

DeMarco smiled and nodded. *We believe what we want to believe.* He said, "So it wasn't a local club. Can you give me anything more than that?"

"I think he said something about going north. The first time he went to this club, I mean. Must have been three, four weeks ago."

"North to Erie?"

"No . . . no, he asked me about a golf course that was nearby. Twin Oaks something. Twin Oaks Country Club, that was it. He asked if I knew how to get to Twin Oaks Country Club because the strip club was off the same road, just a couple of miles away."

"Twin Oaks straddles the Pennsylvania-Ohio border. Just north of Pierpont."

"There you go. That's where the club is. Somewhere not far from there."

DeMarco smiled. "You've been a great deal of help today."

"I only wish I knew more."

"This novel he was writing. The one he called *D*. I haven't found it anywhere. Not on his computers, not in any of his papers."

"You wouldn't find it on his computers. Bits and pieces maybe. Random notes, things that occurred to him at the time. But he always wrote his first drafts in longhand."

"You're sure about this?"

"Positive. He encouraged all of his students to do the same. He said that writing in longhand is less mechanical, more organic and sensual. That it encourages a freer flow of thought."

"And how much of the novel do you think he had written?"

"It couldn't have been much because he was still doing his research. He wouldn't start the actual writing until he knew his subject inside and out."

"And he had only recently found his Annabel."

"Right. So I'm sure there's a journal of some kind because I saw him writing in it in his office. But I wouldn't be surprised if most of the book still exists only inside his head."

DeMarco sat motionless for a while. Then he pushed himself to his feet. "So what does this do to your thesis project? Will you ask Denton to take over as your advisor?"

Briessen shook his head. "I'm trying to be like Tom. I'm still holding out hope that everything will work out."

DeMarco's smile felt forced and crudely drawn. But he held it until he was down on the street.

TWENTY-SEVEN

From behind a thicket of thorny bushes on the edge of a field, Huston studied the collection of small, white buildings two hundred yards to the northeast. One, two, three . . . seven wooden buildings in all if he did not count the dugouts at the two ball fields. Each of the buildings was painted white, each with a red metal roof. He knew he had seen them before but he could not remember when. Two equipment sheds, both centered between the Little League field and what was probably the girls' softball field, one building maybe thirty feet long, twice as long as the other. Two restrooms, actually one building with two entrances back to back. Then a small building behind the batting cage, and beside it a building of identical size — a pump house and a shed for the power boxes and meters? And the largest building, the long narrow one between the two ball fields, recessed equidistant some twenty yards behind the backstops and boarded up tightly, the concession stand. Both ball fields had lights and electronic scoreboards. Both had expensive fencing and an array of stadium bleachers. The entire complex seemed more suitable for a small college than for a tiny village twenty miles from nowhere.

Then he remembered. The Little League All-Star playoffs two summers ago. "This is Bradley," he said aloud. "The name of the town is Bradley." The town itself was tiny, no more than four hundred residents. But the birthplace of a woman who was now a famous actress. Bradley Community Park had been her gift to the town.

"We call it Blow Job Community Park," a woman had told Claire that breathless July day. Tommy was at second base, playing defense, still early in the game. On offense, he would go three for three that day, a double and two singles. Two stolen bases, three RBIs. The All-Stars' coaching staff comprised the head coaches from four different teams, so Huston was in the stands that day, was trying to watch the game but couldn't help listening in as the woman explained to Claire the origins of the park. She looked to be in her late thirties, maybe a few years younger than Claire, and spoke with a deep-throated coarseness that he knew his wife found offensive but would never comment on, not even to him.

"I went to school with her," the woman said. "Trust me, I know. She screwed and blew her way through high school. Rumor was she had two abortions her senior year. Day after graduation, she hopped on a plane out of here. Next day she started sucking and fucking her way through Hollywood. They say she gives the best blow jobs in Beverly Hills. Personally I wouldn't know, but my ex says he can believe it. So anyway, she came back here, must've been five, six years ago, told the town council she'd build the kids a park if we'd rename Main Street after her. So why not, what'd we care? Street's hardly fifty yards long end to end anyway. She probably thinks she bought herself some kind of big eraser, you know? I laugh about it every time I come here."

Huston had wanted to concentrate on the game, but she was a great character, the way she sat there in the bleachers in her tight jeans with her knees spread wide, her blue flip-flops perched on the bench in front of her. He had meant to make some notes about her when he got home, the pretty but hard-edged face, the mass of black hair that gleamed in the sun like a crow's feathers, the smoky, lusty growl in her voice. But Tommy's team had lost the game by one run, was knocked out of the playoffs, so the family took him to Chuck E. Cheese in Erie to cheer him up, made a long night of it, and by the time they returned home, the woman had fled from Huston's memory. But here she was back now. All of it was back.

It hit Huston like a blow to the chest — the day, the sunshine, the grin on Tommy's face every time he had stood safely on base and looked into the stands. The pain pierced his chest like a spear, mushroomed into a toxic cloud of pain, filled him from top to toe. He dropped to his knees behind the thorny bush, fell forward onto his hands. "It can't be gone," he said aloud. "I can smell the hot dogs. I can hear the game." His arms quivered, his body shook. The thorns jabbed at his skull.

TWENTY-EIGHT

Both Huston's house and his office had been searched thoroughly. *So where,* De-Marco asked himself, *could the manuscript of* D *be hiding? And why would Huston hide it?* If DeMarco could answer the second question, maybe he could hazard an intelligent guess to answer the first.

He sat in his car along the street outside Nathan Briessen's apartment. He had his window down, needed a feeling of openness, a sense of forward movement. The traffic noise did not bother him, but the odors of sweet rolls and doughnuts and bread coming from the bakery made his stomach growl. *I need to walk,* he told himself.

Four minutes later, with a cup of coffee in one hand and half of a pumpernickel roll in the other, he walked north on Mulravy Street. The street slanted uphill toward the college, through a residential neighborhood of older two-story houses, shingled and vinyl-sided working-class homes. Dogs chained in side yards barked at him. Old women peeked out from behind faded curtains. All of this registered on DeMarco along with the soft, yeasty warmth of the fresh roll and the rich bitterness of strong black coffee, but he kept it as background to the thoughts that scrolled through his mind.

He hides the manuscript to protect it, he told himself. *Because it's an original copy, valuable, one of a kind. In which case he isn't really hiding it but securing it somewhere. In a fireproof box?* No such container was found in his office. The small safe from the house had already been opened. Passports, social security cards, birth certificates, a copy of the deed, and titles to the vehicles. A few pieces of Claire's best jewelry, including a gaudy diamond ring that had probably belonged to her grandmother. A copy of her parents' will, a copy of the Hustons' will. An old gold watch that had probably belonged to Huston's father. No manuscript.

Okay then, he hides it because . . . because he's superstitious? He thinks it's good luck to put the manuscript away in exactly the same place every day? A place only he knows about?

Or he hides it because he doesn't want it read? Doesn't want his wife to know about his visits to the strip clubs? Doesn't want anyone from the university to know — especially anyone who might take delight in tarnishing Huston's image?

Whatever the reason, the manuscript, if one existed, could be anywhere. But the forensics team had already turned over every rug, vacuumed every carpet, luminoled and black-lighted every surface. The desk in Huston's offices had practically been torn apart, every closet emptied, every cubbyhole probed. No manuscript.

The early forensics report had identified black nylon fibers of three different kinds in every bedroom and Huston's study, consistent with nylon socks, a nylon warm-up suit, and nylon batting gloves. No such fibers were found underneath Huston's chair at his home, however, where he himself might have left them, which indicates that they came from somebody else, somebody who had stood near his desk and chair and in fact walked all around it. But who? The boy? Claire? Somebody else? Forensics was currently attempting to match the fibers to clothing taken from the house. Similar black fibers had also been found just inside the back door. Unfortunately, probably dozens of people passed through that house every week. The kids' classmates. Neighbors. Newspaper reporters. Impossible to identify and track all of them down.

Okay, forget the fibers for now, DeMarco told himself. *Let's say that Huston hides the manuscript because he's afraid that it might be damaged by two active children and their friends. Occam's razor — the simplest answer is the best answer. The manuscript is the sole record of his current project, everything he's been thinking about for the past few months. So he hides it for safekeeping. But in this case, he just needs to secure it out of their reach. A filing cabinet will do. A desk drawer. The top of an armoire. A bookshelf. All places already searched. No manuscript.*

DeMarco went back to the university and spent another fifteen minutes inside Huston's office at the college. Poked around in every crevice large enough to hold a tablet or sheaf of papers. Nothing.

He used his cell phone to call Nathan Briessen. "I'm hitting a wall here, Nathan, and I think you're the only one who can help me get through it."

"Whatever I can do, just ask."

"This manuscript you told me about. The work in progress. I can't for the life of me figure out where it could be. Where did

Professor Huston do his writing? At home, at the college, in his car, at the local coffee shop maybe?"

"Home and university office to be sure. The other places? I doubt it. He likes solitude when he works. Maybe a little music but nothing else."

"He told you this?"

"It's something every student asks him sooner or later. Every interviewer. *How* does a writer work?"

"So the manuscript could be in either place? Either the home office or the university office. He carried it back and forth with him?"

"That's right, yes."

"Well . . . it's not here in his office. And our previous searches didn't uncover it at his house. It's apparently not anywhere it might logically be."

"I really don't know where else to tell you to look. I'm sorry."

"Could he have left it in his car, by any chance? The night he went to the strip club, for example? It's not in the car now. I know that already, but I'm just wondering if he might have left it in the car at some point and left the car unlocked . . ."

"I highly doubt it. First of all, I don't think he would have taken it with him to a place like that. And secondly, I last talked to him on Friday. If he had somehow lost his work, he would have been . . . beside himself. Absolutely devastated."

"You're sure a manuscript exists?"

Briessen said, "I'm sure the novel in progress exists."

DeMarco cocked his head, thought for a second. "I say manuscript, you say novel in progress. Is there a difference?"

"I guess it all depends on how you're conceiving of a manuscript."

"Well, you said he does his first draft in longhand. So I'm thinking a tablet of some kind? A legal pad? A notebook?"

"He used a bound journal. A lot easier to carry around."

"Like a diary, you mean?"

"Bigger," said Briessen. "Maybe nine by twelve. It would look just like a hardcover book. Like a smallish coffee table book, you know? It has a dark maroon cloth binding."

"Like a book without a jacket," DeMarco said. "I don't recall seeing anything like that. And he's written four books so far."

"You wouldn't find any of the older journals. Once he's put the second draft on his hard drive, he stores that journal in a safe-deposit box at the bank."

"Could the novel in progress be there too?"

"It's probably right under your nose. And I just now realized why."

"I do wish you would share that information with me."

"You get to be famous," Briessen said, "and people start stealing little pieces of you. I once stole a shot glass out of the Hemingway house in Key West."

"If the journal's been stolen, how could it be right under my nose?"

"That's not what I meant. Tom was wary of the possibility that somebody might try to steal it. Now that he'd become a kind of celebrity. I mean if you're nineteen or twenty years old and all you want is to be a writer, and one day you happen to be in a famous writer's house or office and you see his journal lying there on his desk or sticking out of his briefcase —"

"And students came to his house?"

"Frequently. Three or four times a semester he'd have gumbo night for a small group of students. He makes a mean pot of gumbo."

"Always the same students? During any particular semester?"

"There was some overlap, but he tried to include everybody at least once. Everybody from his advanced fiction workshop."

DeMarco made a mental note to get the class roster from the department secretary. "So if one of those students happens to see his idol's journal, he just might grab it if the opportunity presents itself?"

"That's how I got my favorite shot glass."

"So then, to prevent that possibility, the thing to do would be to conceal the journal somehow. So that it doesn't look like a journal."

"Right. It looks just like a big book, so you put a book jacket on it."

DeMarco stepped up close to the metal bookshelf. With his free hand, he pulled the first book of appropriate size off the top shelf, laid it open on the desk, and unfolded the jacket. "I don't suppose you would know what the jacket looks like."

"Civilization," Briessen said.

"Excuse me?"

"Last time I saw it, he was using the book jacket from Kenneth Clark's *Civilization.* Tom figured that most people would be intimidated or bored by such a book. Especially students. Therefore, not tempted to steal it."

Quickly DeMarco ran a hand across the titles. "Not on the top shelf. Not on the second . . . not the third . . . and not the bottom. Might he have changed the jacket?"

"Might have but I doubt it. I mean, why bother if it was doing what he wanted it to do?"

"So if it's not here, it must be at the house."

"I'd bet money on it."

After satisfying himself that none of the books in the office was the journal in disguise, DeMarco drove to Huston's house. From his trunk, he took a pair of gloves and booties and put these on just inside the foyer. Then he went to Huston's spacious den.

And there it was, square in the middle of the second shelf from the top in the wall-length mahogany bookshelf. "Son of a gun," DeMarco said. His hands shook as he used a pen to lay the book open, then to lift away the jacket. A journal with a plain cloth cover the color of burgundy wine. From the looks of it, not many pages held Huston's tight but neat handwriting. Maybe twenty in all. "Not much," DeMarco said aloud. But maybe it would be enough.

He replaced the cover, then wrapped the book in a dish towel from the kitchen drawer. At the barracks, he logged both items in at the evidence room, then immediately logged out the journal, minus the jacket. Before returning to his office, he washed his hands with plenty of hot water, but they were still shaking when he pulled on a pair of thin white gloves.

TWENTY-NINE

Huston decided on the smaller of the two equipment sheds. The larger one, the one with the wide barnlike door, probably held a mower or two, maybe even a lawn tractor, the drag-along for raking and smoothing the fields, bags of lime and quick-dry for the infield, grass seed, shovels, probably a pitching machine plus miscellaneous tools. The floor would be wheel dirtied and probably crowded. The other shed would have the bats and balls and helmets, catcher's equipment, and extra bases. These, he guessed, considering the orderliness of the complex, would all hang out of the way on the inside walls. There would probably be plenty of room on the floor for him to stretch out. Maybe rain ponchos to wrap around himself for warmth. The catcher's chest protector to use as a pillow.

The parking lot was empty except for a few pieces of windblown litter. From forty yards away, it looked to Huston as if the place had been battened down for the winter. If he could get inside the shed without being seen, he could hole up there with his remaining groceries. Then make his way to Annabel. He tried to remember the probable distance. Tried to see the topless club on a map in his mind's eye, the squiggling two-laner heading north-northwest, snaking toward the Ohio border. "Slouching towards Bethlehem."

Why did you think of that? he wondered. *Yeats and his mystical anarchy. His spiritus mundi, his hell-raising Sphinx. "The blood-dimmed tide is loosed, and everywhere the ceremony of innocence is drowned . . ."*

For just a moment, he imagined himself at the front of the classroom again, reciting to his students, trying to tap into Yeats's mad vision. How he loved those moments when he lost himself in words. Stirred himself and others with the music and the power.

Focus! he told himself now. He squeezed his eyes shut, then with one quick jerk, shook his head like a drunk trying to stay awake. *Thomas Huston is dead,* he told himself. *The teacher is dead. The writer is dead. Words and music and stories are all dead now. Now only power remains. The power of the dead.*

He stared hard at the equipment shed. "It will be locked." Yes, but all the buildings will be locked. Nothing will be easy now, nor should it be. Everything will hurt. Everything does.

He needed a tool. Metal. Strong enough to force a padlock or to splinter the wood around a dead bolt. He was too far away to be able to see how the door was secured, so he would just have to assume the worst. He needed a pry bar of some kind. Couldn't bang or pound or hammer, not even at night. The sounds would echo like a jungle drum.

To his left lay the town of Bradley, a quarter mile south. He had skirted it by hiking through the trees. Could he risk going back now to assess the possibilities? "You have to," he told himself. "You have no choice." He would stay off the main drag. Keep to the backstreets. Maybe somebody's garage door would be standing open. Somebody's garden shed. *People are trusting out here,* he thought. *People don't know.*

He stood up. Brushed the leaf litter off his knees. Left his groceries nestled in the thorns.

"You don't look that bad," he reassured himself, though he did not believe it.

"What choice do you have?"

"Okay. Try to look normal."

THIRTY

To DeMarco's eyes, the first several pages of Huston's journal appeared to contain nothing but random, spontaneous notes. Ideas for scenes, characters' names, a tentative plotline, passages quoted from Nabokov's novel.

"When I try to analyze my own cravings, motives, actions and so forth, I surrender to a sort of retrospective imagination which feeds the analytic faculty with boundless alternatives and which causes each visualized route to fork and re-fork without end in the maddeningly complex prospect of my past. I am convinced, however, that in a certain magic and fateful way Lolita began with Annabel." (Lolita)

main character named Howard (means noble watchman) Humphreys? Harold? Houston? (means hill town; might be fun to pique readers' curiosity)

main character needs a nemesis to parallel Nabokov's Quilty. Denton as physical model: smooth, charming, designer clothes, lots of styled hair. He should be younger than main character, more attractive to women/girls. Somewhat predatory. Doesn't love women the way main character does. Loves their attention, their idolatry. Narcissistic.

contemporize Lolita, but how? College freshman — too easy?

nemesis gets jealous when the narrator gets more attention than he does from the sexy new student. But why does she prefer narrator? She's intellectual? Disdains her beauty?

Maybe as story progresses, Lolita character gets more and more aggressive in trying to ruin her beauty. Hacks off her hair. Starts cutting herself. This makes narrator only want her more. Aches to heal her. So that his empathy overrides his common sense?

Nabokov's narrator on "nymphets": "Good looks are not any criterion; and vulgarity, or at least what a given community terms so, does not necessarily impair certain mysterious characteristics, the fey grace, the elusive, shifty, soul-shattering insidious charm. I was consumed by a hell furnace of localized lust for every passing nymphet whom as a law-abiding poltroon I never dared approach. Humbert Humbert tried hard to be good. Really and truly, he did."

These entries were followed by more of the same, plus occasional allusions to some of the strip clubs Huston had visited.

McKeesport place: Smoky, noisy, big bouncer. All in all a bit frightening. Men at horseshoe-shaped bar mostly older, middle-aged or more, mostly blue collar but a couple in suits. Watered-down draft beer is free with $20 cover charge. Most of the girls look stoned. Only one of them looked me in the eye. Afterward came to my chair, sat on my lap, made me squirm. She looked fourteen but surely must have been older. Are there age limits for strippers in this state? In the booth later, she told me her real name is Joyce. Pretty but not up close. Christ she was hungry for something, not just my money. I kept think-

ing about Alyssa. Went home so fucking
sad.

His visits to clubs in Titusville, Wheeling,
Beaver Falls, Ambridge, New Castle, and
one along Exit 7 of Interstate 80 left him
similarly depressed, not only for the way the
dancers must have felt, how they viewed
themselves, but also for the way he felt when
they thrust their shaved pussies at his face.

Is it even going to be possible to make the
Lolita character sympathetic?
  How can men enjoy this kind of thing? I
feel like scum.

DeMarco found the entries interesting,
but not until the ninth page did he come to
one that he thought might be useful. *Opening scene!* he read. The entry was dated only
four weeks earlier.

If you get up early enough, or better yet
fail to close your eyes at all the night
before, a morning in gray can lay all the
night's detritus before you, all the night's
litter emptied now of its noise and bluff and
whiskey-ed bravado, leaving nothing but
the sticky, squeezed-out wrapper of a self
licked clean of its truculence. In that last
misted hour before sunrise, all of your

shrieking spirits will have lapsed into a muted misery, their throbbing hearts squeezed into something akin to reconciliation but not quite, a weary truce perhaps, not yet surrender.

It was in this frame of mind that I first encountered Annabel. After a long night with my heart pressed against the dented metal edge of the bar at the old Claireborn Hotel, recently renamed the Erie Downtowner but still as shabby as ever, still dark with old, scarred tables and chairs with stained cushions, the carpet still stained and threadbare, the air, though now "smoke free" still stale with the ghosts of cigars and sixty years of filterless griefs, yet "fragrant with gin" as Twain might have said — after such another long night, I had staggered to the sidewalk and then down State to the docks, there to fill my lungs with lake oxygen seasoned with the diesel fumes of barges and freighters, spiced with whatever gases of hospital waste the ships had dredged up. There I stood against the rail and let the night lap against me. From time to time I heard footsteps in the dark but never once looked up. I smiled at the water I could hear but not see, smiled at the thought of black unconsciousness, and only hoped it would come quickly if it came, no mere mugger's threats and demands, no bargaining for my life, which I was not inclined to do. Unfortunately I was not interfered with. In time, I made my way back up State to Perry Square and there claimed a bench as my own chair of forgetfulness. But the power of the chair had apparently leaked away, or been diluted by dog piss, or rattled away by all the blows of all the blow jobs and anal fucks and fingerings and baby puke and ice cream drips and farts and soiled diapers of all its days and nights because I could forget nothing, not a single blow of my own.

Another hour passed. And then . . . and then the sound of pain at a gallop. I did not recognize it as such at the time and can hear it so only now in retrospect, but that is surely what it was, more pain than I had ever known, more wrenching of a soul I thought already wrenched apart. It came in the guise of a young girl jogging, only a slim figure of gray at first, a girl made of mist who emerged from the mist, then bare legs and bare arms as she trotted down the path toward my bench, a slender loop of wire hanging from each ear, swinging as she ran. I heard the music as she approached and wondered how her ears could tolerate such noise, the thump of heavy drums and screaming chant. Stride by stride, she closed the distance, oblivious to me. I was a charcoal lump on an otherwise empty park bench. She had no doubt passed this bench a hundred times before at this hour, always empty then, so, therefore, she must have assumed without even thinking about it, empty now. She was nearly upon me when I registered on her consciousness. She gasped, stopped short, and jerked to the side, stumbled off the edge of the path, twisted an ankle, and fell, and too aghast to speak, only huddled there and stared.

I raised both hands. "I'm not moving," I said.

She fumbled at a little bag attached around her waist. "I have pepper spray!"

"You won't need it. I swear. I'm not moving an inch." I must have bitten my lip, for I tasted blood and whiskey in my mouth. It both chilled and intoxicated me.

"Jesus," DeMarco said. "Is this supposed to be funny?"

Below the entry, Huston had written *Strive for Nabokovian prose? Maybe similar but contemporary, less self-conscious, more like Bukowski?*

DeMarco pulled a tablet close and on the first page wrote *Who is Bukowski?*

Huston's next entry was dated one day later:

There is to her eyes a nakedness that denudes me. Her nakedness is an innocence more than primal. I imagine she could lay with me, let me do all manner of dark things, every base act I have ever conceived, yet her eyes would shine with purity. They are greener than polished jade and brighter than jade in full sun. In them I see myself more than bare: transparent. With every stain and cancer streak of sordid self etched out like oil spilled on snow.

DeMarco flipped to a clean page in his tablet, and at the top of it in large letters, he wrote *Annabel.* Below the name he wrote *appears innocent* and, below that, *green eyes.*

The next two entries were undated. They were separated by several lines and were the only writing on that page:

I have fallen in love with a dying girl. Anyway, she says she is dying, though she looks as healthy and sensuous as a Triple Crown winner.

When she sleeps, I want to ravish her. I want to devour her, swallow her down as a boa constrictor would a fawn. Then I would lick her taste off my lips and lie in the sun with her inside me, and I would sleep until her every cell has been absorbed into mine.

A troubling thought kept apace with De-Marco's reading: *Who is this character? Is this Huston imagining how a sick, deranged man thinks?*

Then came an even more troubling thought: *What if this isn't Huston's character speaking? What if this is Huston himself?*

"Jesus fucking Christ," DeMarco said.

A minute later, he reached for his calendar. The opening scene entry had been written on a Sunday, the next on Monday, the others undated. DeMarco asked himself why every entry wasn't dated. Was Huston in a rush sometimes? Or were all entries from one day given just the one date? Did it even matter?

Nathan Briessen had said that Huston thought he had finally discovered his Annabel at a strip club, maybe six weeks before his disappearance. But what if he had met her prior to that? Something about the woman had resonated with him, stuck to his consciousness. Maybe he was smitten, maybe not. Next day, he was still thinking about her. Maybe Thursday night he went to her club for the first time. Would she have told him, when they first met, that she was a topless dancer? She must have. Maybe he had told her about the book he was writing. Maybe she had recognized him — maybe *she* was the smitten one! In any case, Huston had made the last entry, the one about eating her alive, on an undesignated date.

On his notepad DeMarco wrote:

Did he become obsessed with Annabel and end up killing her?

Did Annabel help to kill his family?

Possible others with motivation? A crazed fan? A crazed associate of the junkie who'd killed Huston's mother? Maybe Annabel has a boyfriend who found out she was doing Huston. Or maybe the motive was professional jealousy. Denton? Conescu? Somebody else?

He stared at those questions for a while, tried to think each one through. But why would Huston kill Annabel? When? No missing strippers reported. No extra bodies. He drew a line through the first question, looked at the others. An accomplice would explain the two methods of killing — stabbing for the baby, slit throats for everybody else. Then he told himself, *Hold on, wait. You're confusing the writer with the character. This is fiction, it's just a story. This isn't Huston at all.*

He was about to cross out the questions when he stopped, lifted his pen off the paper, looked at the questions once more, then let them stand.

Had the writer become the character? Had the murder and suicide of Huston's parents loosed something in him, spawned a rage he struggled with but, eventually, failed to contain? DeMarco understood repressed rage. He understood how a single event could shred a privileged life, leave it tattered and flapping in the black gales of night.

But DeMarco was having a hard time keeping things straight now. Was the Annabel of these passages real? What about the strip club Annabel? Or were both a fabrication? Where did Huston end and the author

235

of those dark passages begin? Huston's writing had never before been so sanguinary, so grim. Where was the hopeful story Nathan had said Huston was writing? Or was it far too early for the end?

This was a whole different writer at work than the one DeMarco thought he knew. How much of the voice was artifice and how much a reflection of the man?

DeMarco leaned back in his chair. He looked at his white-gloved hands. *How much of you is artifice?* he asked himself.

"We are all made up," he answered aloud. "We are only real at night."

THIRTY-ONE

Huston retraced his steps through the woods, back toward Bradley, deep enough behind the trees that his chances of being spotted were small, but close enough to the cluster of buildings that he could scan for a good place to emerge. A place where, if spotted from a distance, he would provoke no suspicion, a day hiker out for a stroll, just another yuppie pantheist who didn't have sense enough to wear sturdy shoes.

You have to anticipate the reader's questions, then address those questions, he always told his students. Questions about motivation. Intent. Nothing in fiction can be aimless. Anticipate and address.

From the woods, he could see the backs of a vinyl-sided two-story and a small clapboard cottage, and between them a garage with a gravel driveway that ran out to the highway. Huston angled toward the garage, and then, maybe twenty feet inside the woods on the far side of the garage, he came upon a ring of stones, charred logs inside the ring. An old kitchen chair, half-rotted seat on a rusty metal frame. Cigarette butts that had been tossed toward the fire ring but fell short.

Somebody's quiet place, he told himself. He studied the two houses. The cottage looked dark, the windows curtained. The backyard was empty but for a bare wooden picnic table and two benches. The grass was thick and heavy with dead leaves blown in from the woods. *Summer home. Maybe a hunting camp.*

An elaborate swing set sat behind the two-story. The aluminum crossbar was bowed, the red paint dull. He guessed that the child or children who had played on those swings, who had slid down that now-canted slide, were too big for it now. Teenagers maybe. In any case, that house too was still and dark. *Parents at work,* he told himself, *kids at school.* And that glint of sunlight on glass, the garage's side entrance, wooden door with a window chest high.

The door might be locked or it might not.

You're not going to find a better place than this.

He knew how to do it. A couple of his characters had done it; he had written them, had watched them. He had already thought it through. Stride purposefully to the garage's side door, quick test of the knob, if it's unlocked you're inside. If it's locked, no hesitation, crisp elbow jab to the corner of the glass, reach inside even as the glass is still skidding over the concrete floor, find the lock, turn it, open the door, and step inside. The sound of breaking glass might catch somebody's attention a house or two away, and they would stop what they were doing, listen, wonder where the sound had come from. But by then, he would be inside, searching for a tool. Getting away unseen would be more problematic than getting in.

You know all this, he told himself. *Just do it.*

He pulled the sunglasses from his pocket, fitted them on. Pulled the bill of the cap low over his eyes. Gathered his energy and made himself ready.

But the swing set undid him. It sucked his energy dry.

The children come home from school. They run to the backyard. They climb onto the swings. They talk about their days; they laugh. Alyssa puts her feet to the ground, pushes the swing back as far as she can, lifts her feet, and glides forward. Tommy swings more gently, holds little Davy securely on his lap.

The sound of breaking glass, all movement stops, feet flat on the ground. Alyssa says, *Who's that man over there?* And Tommy tells her, *Run inside and get Dad.*

He staggered back to the fire ring, clutched the top of the old kitchen chair to keep himself from falling. Stared into the ashes. Felt the pulse of bruising sobs building in his chest again, wanting out, banging inside him, choking off his air until he could resist them no longer. He went down on his knees then, toppled the chair, and fell onto it. And sobbed, wanting to die, *Please let me die.* His fists squeezing ashes. *Please, God, let me die.*

THIRTY-TWO

DeMarco made three wrong turns before finding the place. "You go about ten miles, maybe a little less, north on 58," he had been instructed by one of the troopers. "After you pass the country club on your right, it's only another mile or so. There'll be the Vita-Style beauty shop on your left — fancy name for a beauty shop in a converted garage, isn't it? Then a couple of houses. Then start watching for a dirt road on the same side. It's about a mile and a half down that road. It's called Whispers."

But there was no sign along the highway, no billboard advising him where to turn, and in the moonless dark of early night, intersections with unmarked, unpaved roads were not easy to distinguish until he was upon or past them. His first dirt road led him to a Baptist church in a yellow, steel building. The parking lot was empty and the building empty. A lighted sign in the small strip of lawn advised: *In the dark? Fol-low the Son.*

The second wrong turn dead-ended at a farmhouse, from whose driveway DeMarco could see into the dining room. The room was well lighted and clearly illuminated four individuals seated around the table. Nearest the window sat a man who appeared to be in his seventies, then, clockwise around the table, another man maybe thirty years younger, then a middle-aged woman with short, brown hair, and finally a boy wearing a red baseball cap. When the headlights from DeMarco's car swept across the dining room window, all four individuals looked his way. "Sorry," he said aloud and quickly swung the car to the left so that he could back up. But none of the faces watching him showed any surprise or concern, and he knew he was not the first driver to take this lane by mistake. It probably happened several times every weekend night, half-drunken men in search of nude women, their attention, their touch, the illusion of desire.

The family watched DeMarco's car for five seconds or so, then the white-haired man turned his gaze back toward the table and raised his hand, and DeMarco saw that they were playing cards at the table. He smiled to himself but also felt a twinge of jealousy. He was the end of a generation himself and unless a miracle of God or chance intervened, he would never play cards or any other game with one of his grandchildren.

He put the car into reverse, then pulled away quickly. Out of nowhere, four dogs suddenly appeared at his bumper, yapping mongrels of varying breeds and sizes but all uniformly loud, all apparently hungry for the taste of metal or rubber. When he reached the highway, the dogs turned as if by signal and trotted home again. In the end, he was as inconsequential to the dogs as he had been to the family in the farm-house, a fleeting distraction.

The third dirt road, narrow and potholed, rounded a sharp turn after a mile and seven-tenths, and there, behind a row of tulip poplars denuded by the winds of autumn, was a two-acre parking lot of packed dirt in front of a long, low wooden building. The boards were weathered and unpainted except for a white door on which someone had brushed *Whispers* in sloppy, red letters. The tin roof nearly blended into the black-ness of the sky, and the whole building looked as if it had once been an equipment shed of some kind, or maybe an old sawmill.

Maybe the white-haired man in the dining room had once owned this land and farmed it, had built his house from timber harvested off his property. Now the family grew a few acres of soybeans and lived off government subsidies while the owner of Whispers harvested a steady crop of dollars from the fertile soil of fantasy.

From inside the building came the muted screech of guitars, the kind of screaming rock music that always set DeMarco's teeth on edge. He preferred the more soothing tones of Norah Jones, Rickie Lee Jones, Corinne Bailey Rae, and even, when the mood seized him and the back of his throat had been warmed and numbed by ample Jack, Billie Holiday and Dinah Washington, the amazing Etta James. But he had not come here for the music.

The white door opened onto a small anteroom emblazoned by floodlights. The sudden brightness and blast of music hit DeMarco like a punch and made his bad eye water. He stood there blinking, staring at the yellow wall in front of him. From his left came a man's voice, sounding like rocks falling through a pipe. "Fifteen dollars, please."

The man was seated on a low chair behind dirty glass, a thin, smallish man with a thin smile on a pale, thin mouth. Somewhere between fifty and sixty-five, half mummified by alcohol and smoke. A stray-dog kind of look in his eyes, wizened and tough, alert and wary.

DeMarco pushed a twenty through the opening in the glass. He was handed five ones in return. "I need your left hand, sir," the man said and showed him the rubber stamp he held.

DeMarco stuck his hand through the opening, then pulled it back and squinted at the blotch of black ink. "What is this, a squirrel?"

"Your guess is as good as mine," the man said. Then, "Enjoy."

When DeMarco faced the yellow wall again, he could make out a yellow knob and the seam of a door. The door rattled with the boom of music from the other side. He steeled himself for the punch of even louder music, then pulled the door open.

Again, he squinted and blinked. This room was as dark as the one at his back was bright. He kept his hand on the yellow door, held it open by a few inches until he had surveyed the room and allowed his eyes to readjust.

On the wall directly opposite him, across a plank floor maybe thirty feet wide, a dim red Exit sign hung above a closed door. To its left was a Coke machine and beside it a large trash barrel, then another doorway, this one open, with a sign above it that read Restroom. Most of the illumination in the room came from the two signs and the vending machine and from the light in two doorways on the wall to his left, one open doorway at each end of the wall. Both doors led, he surmised, to the stage area where the young girls danced.

Two of the five tables were occupied, one by three dancers in skimpy costumes, the other by a small, bald, and bespectacled man who sat staring at his can of Diet Coke while a dark-haired woman in leopard panties and a matching halter top rubbed his leg.

This woman and the three others all turned to regard DeMarco when he stepped inside. Everybody smiled at him. They sized him up as if they could see straight through to his bank account, could see how high his twenties were stacked. He had dressed for the evening in khaki slacks and brown loafers and a white poplin jacket over a black knit shirt — his idea of casual. He hoped that, tonight at least, he looked like a businessman of some kind, maybe a sales rep. The dancers kept smiling at him, and he interpreted this as a good sign. His face, he knew, might give him away. People sometimes told him he looked like Tommy Lee Jones, but he considered this an insult to a good actor.

Then one of the dancers stood and came toward him, and for a moment, he felt again like a sixteen-year-old at his first high school dance, like he wanted to bolt for the door before he could make a fool of himself. His stomach fluttered.

In her high heels she was maybe five foot eight. She had long red hair that looked chestnut brown in the dimness, and a nose like Julia Roberts's, one that widened with her smile. But he doubted that her face garnered much attention from the customers. Her only clothing was a short, white coat held together by one button and trimmed in rabbit fur at the neck and hips. A quick glance informed him that there was no other fur in the vicinity. He felt his body warm, felt the heat and movement of blood.

She took hold of his arm and leaned close so as to be heard above the music, spoke into his ear so that her hair fell across his arm, so that her scent washed over him. His stomach quivered at her touch.

"You look like a virgin," she said.

He said nothing in reply, only raised his

eyebrows a little when he looked at her.

"Your first time here," she said.

"It is," he told her.

"Don't worry. Virgins are my specialty."

She led him to a table. After he sat, she put her hands on his knees and swung his legs around, away from the table, then sat sidesaddle atop them. Now her coat fell open below the waist and he could clearly see the smooth paleness of skin from her knees to her belly button. "So what's your name, sweetie?" she asked.

"Thomas," he told her, the first name to come to mind.

"We get a lot of Thomases in here," she teased.

He smiled. Her hair smelled like Obsession, the scent his wife used to prefer. "And what's your name?" he asked.

"I'm Ariel. Like in *The Little Mermaid*. You know, the Disney movie?" She put her mouth against his ear now and made a sound that both startled and disarmed him, drained him of all awareness for a moment. It was a low purring sound made by simultaneously moaning and rolling her tongue, and the warmth of her breath in his ear dizzied him.

Now she slid a hand along the inside of his thigh. Things were happening to him over which he had no control. His bodily response to her touch frightened and enlivened him.

She asked, "So what brings you here tonight? Looking for some fun? Or some good fun? Or some really good fun?"

The current song blasting from the speakers came to an end with her question, leaving him to sit there with the silence and dimness and an agitated crotch. Before he could formulate his reply, another song erupted, this one a hard-driving country song. "If it don't come easy," sang Tanya Tucker, "you better let it go . . ."

"I came to watch you dance," he said.

"We don't start dancing for another hour, sweetie. What are we going to do in the meantime?"

"I guess I don't know," he said. "How about I buy you a drink and we discuss the possibilities?"

Ariel lifted a hand in the air and waggled her fingers. DeMarco followed her gaze to a woman behind a short bar near the stage entrance. The woman soon approached his table. She set a split of champagne and a fluted glass in front of Ariel. "And you, sir?"

He thought he had seen something in her eyes when she looked at him, a shadow of disapproval. She appeared to be in her late thirties, with a long-legged body and ample breasts slowly succumbing to gravity, a face still fighting entropy.

"Double Jack," he told her. "Straight up."

The bartender turned and walked away.

Ariel laid a hand on his cheek and turned his face toward hers again. "We could do a couple private dances," she told him. "That would pass some time."

"I'm afraid I'm not a very good dancer."

She giggled softly. "It's twenty dollars a song for a room dance," she said. "But for fifty dollars you can have a twenty-minute couch dance." She spoke with her mouth against his ear again. "And there's a curtain across the door in the couch room."

He nodded.

"Sound good?"

"Sounds very good." He poured some champagne into her glass. She lifted the glass and took a sip. Then she placed her lips against his and forced a trickle of mouth-warmed champagne over his tongue. He tasted its wetness and the sweetness of her lips, and when the dizziness passed, he thought, *That's a good way to get hepatitis.*

The bartender returned then and set his glass in front of him. "Thank you," he said. She smiled tightly. As she walked away, she gave Ariel's shoulder a quick tap.

Ariel's eyes widened at the touch. She cut a glance at DeMarco's face, then quickly looked away. "I'll be right back," she told him. She reached for her glass and the small bottle of champagne, slid off DeMarco's lap, and walked away briskly. The fur trim on her white coat tried to cover her backside but fell short. He watched her go and knew that she would not be coming back. He wished he had stroked that fur when he'd had the chance.

DeMarco sipped his drink for a while. Finally he stood, glass in hand, and crossed to the bar. He smiled at the bartender, whose eyes held a dull sheen of resignation. "We know each other?" he asked.

"Don't believe I've had the pleasure," she said.

"You made me for a cop. I saw you tap her shoulder."

"I guess you look the type," she said.

"My guess is we've met before."

She shrugged. "In a previous lifetime maybe."

"When I was working vice, no doubt."

"No doubt," she said.

He sipped his drink. She brought out a bottle from behind the bar and poured another inch into his glass.

"I'm not here to make trouble," he told her.

"Neither am I."

"I'm just looking for some answers."

She stared at him hard for a few seconds. Then looked away. Then looked at him again. "If it's about that professor, there's not much I can tell you."

"Good guess," he told her.

She shrugged. "He's the only one of our customers been in the papers lately."

"And?"

"He was a customer. That's the grand total of what I know about him."

"Except that he's a professor."

She shrugged. "Some of the customers don't know enough to lie about who they are."

"What else didn't he lie about?"

"To me? I never even spoke to the man except to take his drink order."

DeMarco nodded and sipped his whiskey. He was feeling more comfortable now, playing a more familiar role. Ariel's scent and warmth and touch had unnerved him for a few minutes, took him to a place of uncertainty he had not visited in a very long time. It had reminded him of how easily a man could succumb to such an invitation, how quickly he could find himself lost in that

252

beguiling place.

But, he asked himself, a man like Thomas Huston? Huston had been married to a beautiful woman and, by all accounts, blissfully so. On the other hand, thirteen years of married life can make a man restless. Curious. Wistful for the unknown, the only imagined. Maybe even fearful of the slow slide into old age and all the loss it portends.

And what was it Bill Clinton had said when asked, *Why would a man in your position, Mr. President, a man who has achieved everything he could ever want, ever stray?*

Because I can, Slick Willie had said. He had done his best to look remorseful, repentant, self-chastising, but had been unable to banish a sly and arrogant smile from his lips.

Had Thomas Huston succumbed to a similar weakness?

"If you never spoke to him," DeMarco asked, "how did you find out he's a professor?"

"Girl talk," she said. "Besides, just because I work in a place like this doesn't mean I'm totally illiterate. I read the paper every once in a while."

"That's what puzzles me," DeMarco said. "Why a man so well-known would jeopardize his public image by —"

"Fraternizing with us lowlifes?"

DeMarco considered her face. It was beginning to look familiar.

"Let me save you the trouble," she said. "You took me in a couple times maybe ten, twelve years ago. Me and a couple of friends."

"For keeping a disorderly house."

"So they said. Personally, I consider myself a meticulous housekeeper."

"Meticulous," he repeated and smiled.

"Dust bunnies run at the mention of my name."

"On Fourth Street," he said. "Just up from the marina."

She nodded. "There's a gift shop there now. Some guy gives glass-blowing demonstrations in the basement."

The way she said "glass-blowing" made him smile again.

"Guess who taught him his technique," she said.

He grinned and shook his head. Another sip of whiskey. Then it came back to him. "Bonnie," he said.

"Good for you. You remember the names of all your busts?"

"Just the ones who proposition me with sex."

Again, she shrugged. "Use what the good

Lord gave you, that's what my mama always told me."

"I imagine that's a popular opinion around here."

"More like gospel. The eleventh commandment."

"You remember the other ten?"

She rattled them off without cracking a smile. "No spitting, no swearing, no touching the dancers, no fighting, no smoking, no cell phones, no cameras, no minors, no food near the stage, no drinks that weren't purchased at the bar."

"I bet you can name the seven dwarves too."

"We have them booked for New Year's Eve. You should come. They put on quite a show."

DeMarco chuckled, then felt guilty when he realized how much he was enjoying himself. "Maybe we'd better get back to the subject."

"Let's refill that glass first."

He considered it. He wasn't officially on duty. In fact, if he were home right now, he would have a glass in hand and his eyelids would be drooping. "A small one," he told her.

She poured his glass half-full.

"You call that a small one?"

"I don't call any of them small. Just hurts a guy's feelings."

"Stop it," he said.

"I would if I thought you really wanted me to."

He turned his back to the bar so she would not see his unmanageable grin. From that position, he could peer into the stage area. Around a low stage built of plywood, its floor boxed in by low plywood walls, were several inexpensive chairs with black seat pads. Eight customers were already seated around the stage in anticipation of the first dancer. A mirrored ball hung above the stage and flickered shards of light throughout the room.

The rear and one sidewall of this room each had three openings cut into them. Two of the open doorways on the rear wall led to tiny rooms with nothing inside but another chair; in one of these rooms, a naked girl was straddling a fully-clothed man who sat with his head back, eyes closed, arms dangling limp at his sides while the girl writhed atop him, sluggishly bumping and grinding to Usher's "Nice and Slow." The third tiny room appeared empty, but DeMarco thought he could make out another door deeper inside. *The dressing room,* he told himself.

Each of the three doorways on the far wall had a dark, heavy curtain hanging over it. *Couch dances,* he thought. *Fifty dollars for twenty minutes.*

He turned back to Bonnie. "So what was Thomas Huston's preference? I'm guessing the couch dances."

"Couch dance. Singular. One per night."

"That was it? Twenty minutes and then he'd leave?"

"He'd watch the dancers for a while first, have a couple of drinks. Then the couch dance. Then good night."

"Always with the same girl? In the room, I mean?"

Bonnie looked away for a moment. She gazed at the mirrored ball. When she returned her gaze to DeMarco, she smiled. "It's not my job to notice things, you know? Just the opposite."

"It's not your job, but you notice them all the same. You're too clever not to."

"All I know is that he doesn't come here anymore, and because of that, I've lost a regular source of not much income."

DeMarco nodded. "You own this place, Bonnie?"

"More or less."

"So tell me about the girls who work here."

"What's there to tell? If you're pretty, if you're friendly, you can make a lot of money. All cash."

"How much is a lot?"

"On a busy night? Five, six hundred. Sometimes more."

"Is this a busy night?"

"Around eleven o'clock it will be. That's when the really pretty girls come on."

"The ones here now aren't pretty?"

"You've looked at them all. You tell me."

"I think Ariel's a beautiful young woman."

"She could work second shift if she wanted to."

"So why doesn't she if it would mean more money?"

"She likes to tuck her little boy in at night." Then, after seeing the look of surprise that crossed DeMarco's face, "What, you think none of these girls have maternal instincts?"

"You know them better than I do. You tell me."

"We've got our crack and heroin whores, sure. You've probably spotted a couple of them already. We've also got our girls trying to put themselves through college. Then we've got our single mothers trying to feed their babies. And then we've got the usual assortment of head cases."

"Tell me about the head cases."

"How long you been a cop? You know them better than I do."

It was true; he remembered them all. He remembered the sadists, the masochists, the ball bashers, the cutters, the little lost girls, the thrill junkies, the sin lovers, the nymphos, the fetishists. He knew why women fucked when they didn't fuck for pleasure or money. They fucked because they wanted to be loved or they wanted control or they wanted to hurt themselves or somebody else. They fucked for annihilation, temporary as it might be.

"Did Professor Huston have a favorite?"

"I just pour the drinks."

"I know, it's your job not to notice. But I'm asking you, Bonnie, okay? I'm just asking if you happened to notice a pattern of any kind."

"Most nights after nine, ten o'clock, I'm so busy pouring drinks that the only thing I pay attention to is the money coming in. Speaking of which, you owe me thirty dollars. Plus tip."

"Thirty dollars? I didn't order that triple you poured me."

"I didn't charge you for it. It's twenty for the champagne, five each for your single Jacks. The rest was on me."

Scowling, he laid two twenties on the counter. "A night at Whispers doesn't come cheap, does it?"

"You want cheap, there's places for that. You probably know them all already."

He let the comment pass. Then, "So he comes in every Thursday night . . ."

"For the past month or so. Maybe a little more."

"At about what, ten o'clock?"

"Sometimes a little earlier. And he's always gone by eleven."

"He watches a few dancers. He has himself a couch dance . . ."

"Pays his bar tab and calls it a night."

"Uneventful."

"An ideal customer."

"Now then, as to those couch dances . . ."

"I'll get Ariel for you."

"Not for me. I'm talking about Huston's."

"You sure? I could swear I saw something special between you two."

"Knock it off now."

"I think I saw love in bloom."

"Bonnie, please."

"She could use a nice daddy for that little boy of hers."

"I'm not interested in being anybody's daddy. Sugar or otherwise."

"She played the French horn in high

school. She tell you that?"

"Tell me this: What actually transpires inside those rooms?"

"You see those curtains?"

"I do."

"Can you see what's behind them?"

"No."

"Neither can I."

"Does the eleventh commandment apply behind those curtains?"

"I don't go there myself, except to vacuum. So I don't really know."

"So who would?"

"You, for fifty dollars."

"Plus tip."

"You're a fast learner, DeMarco."

"Not as fast as you." With that he drained his glass and set it softly atop the bar. "I need to know who Huston's regular girl was. She would be young —"

"Nobody here under twenty-one."

"— or at least she looks very young. Green eyes. Long legs. Maybe even a limp but very subtle, something most people wouldn't even notice."

"No limpers here," Bonnie said. "Green eyes and long legs we've got by the bushel. Stay awhile and see for yourself."

"She keeps herself in shape. Jogs in the park probably."

"I don't fraternize with joggers," she said.

"Could you please be serious for a minute?"

"Look," she said. "Give me something specific and maybe I can help you."

"Young, pretty, long legs, and green eyes. That's not specific enough for you?"

"That's about as specific as a telephone psychic."

"Then how about this? Names and addresses of all the girls who work here."

"Not even if I knew them."

"You don't know their names?"

"I don't take résumés here, okay? Everybody's an independent contractor. They give me a name, and that's what I call them. They come and they go. I don't get personal with them."

"None of them ever need a little mothering?"

She winced, a momentary thing. "I'm not the mothering type."

He watched her face for another reaction, but none came.

"I need your help here, Bonnie. Otherwise, I might have to come back again. Maybe interview all the patrons as they come through the door. Maybe just park a patrol car out front."

She stared at him again. He stared back.

Finally she said, "Two names. That's the best I can do. No phone numbers, because I don't have any."

"Real names or working names?"

"As far as I know, they're real."

"I appreciate your cooperation."

She reached for a pen and small pad on the cash register, wrote on the top sheet, tore it off, folded it, and handed it to De-Marco. She said, "I can't tell you what a pleasure it's been to see you again. Let's do it again another ten or twelve years from now."

He stood, slid the paper into his shirt pocket without looking at it, gave her a smile, and turned away.

"I'll tell Ariel you said good night."

"Don't," he answered without looking back.

"I know love when I see it," she said.

THIRTY-THREE

Like some character out of a Flannery O'Connor story, Huston thought. This was what he had come to. Hiding in a shed. A misfit. Hunted. Hated. Huddled like a criminal in the dirty darkness.

He had lain beside the fire ring for a while, falling through his darkness. Eventually he realized he was not going to get his wish and he would never hit the bottom of that darkness. He had no choice but to live awhile longer. When he stood and reached down to set the kitchen chair aright again, he saw that he had the tool he needed right there in his hands. If he could work one of the metal legs loose from the rusty screws that held it to the seat pad, he could flatten one end and use it for a pry bar. Thirty minutes later, he was safely inside the equipment shed at Bradley Community Park.

The shed had no windows, but he had

wedged the door open with the handle of a baseball bat. Through the inch-wide gap along the doorframe, the night's darkness seeped into the shed and lightened what would have been pitch-blackness. He could make out the three long shelves holding boxes of dirty baseballs and softballs, bases, batting helmets, and two sets of catcher's equipment. Beneath the shelves were two fifty-gallon plastic drums, one holding baseball bats, the other, softball bats. His two grocery bags and the nearly empty jug of orange juice sat an arm's length away.

In his wallet were two tens and four ones. Two credit cards with a combined credit limit of fifty-four thousand dollars. Two ATM cards giving him access to another thirty-eight thousand. He owned a beautiful home filled with the mementos of a hard-won comfort, but the home was no longer habitable, it was a cursed place now. It cried out to him for fire and obliteration.

He knew that O'Connor would have rendered this scene with a gentle humor. The narrative would unwind slowly, building to a moment of grace for the desperate man. Huston had been an admirer of O'Connor's stories and the sometimes-wild incongruity of their characters' lives. The incongruity of his own situation would have made him smile as O'Connor's stories had, if only he were not so acutely aware of its permanency. He knew that his life would never get better than this. He could never climb higher than this, his lowest point.

He knew he should eat something, but just the thought of food made his stomach roil with nausea. It seemed a very long time ago that he had eaten the pizza. He had only one thing left to do, and then, if all went well, he could return to his beautiful house and gather his family around him one last time and send all their spirits wafting into the clouds on the rising thermals. He knew too that he would have to sit there among the flames and watch the spirits rise, but he was prepared for that as well.

Another incongruity, Tom. He heard those words in Claire's voice. He let her speak for him. Her voice could be trusted, but his own could not.

You're going to send our spirits to heaven, she said, *when you don't even believe in heaven? How does that work?* He could feel her fingers playing with the hair at the nape of his neck, could feel her sweet breath on his face.

Yes, he told her. *I want you all in heaven.*

And what about you? Have you started to believe in hell now too?

266

Only this one, he said.

And is this where you will always be?

He stared at the crack of gray light along the door, but he could discern no answer there. No answer in the scent of dry dust on the floor. No answer in the grocery bags or in his wallet or in the nausea that never left him.

I love you, baby, was all he could think to say. *Please forgive me. Please try to forgive me someday. Please, baby. Please.*

THIRTY-FOUR

DeMarco felt too restless to go home. His last cup of coffee had been at least eight hours earlier, yet he felt as if his nerves were spiked with caffeine, as if his skin did not quite fit and he wanted to wiggle out of it. If he drove straight home, he would get there before ten thirty. And then what? Turn on the television, unscrew the Jack, sip, and stare until sleep overtook him.

So leave the television off and think about Huston, he told himself. *Try to figure the guy out. Get inside his head. Walk around inside his brain awhile.*

But he was too restless to maintain the necessary focus. Ariel's scent had gotten under his skin, seeped into his pores. And Bonnie's wisecracks, her quick, easy sarcasm . . . God, how he missed the company of a woman. He missed the touch and scent and warmth of a woman. A woman's kindness and playfulness. A woman's soulful gaze.

He could go back and sit with Ariel awhile longer, tell her that police officers are men too. Not that she would need to be told. He had detected, or believed he did, a sweetness beneath the playacting. Something real. If she had green eyes instead of brown, he might have wondered if she was Huston's Annabel.

Instead of making the turn onto 417 that would have led him home again — the place he knew he should have gone, the only place he truly belonged, where no harm could be done to anyone but himself — he continued straight for another quarter mile, then followed the signs to the interstate, and twenty minutes later parked his car across the street from Laraine's Cape Cod. He hated himself for the weakness that kept returning him here, two nights in a row now; hated his inability to shake off the naive belief in change.

He silenced the engine and slipped a CD into the player. Norah Jones sang to him about darkness and shady corners, sang, "Hot like to burn my lips. I know I can't win."

A light from Laraine's living room shone pale blue through the curtains. He told himself, *She's probably reading, maybe listening to music.* She was a teacher of English at an Erie prep school, taught literature and creative writing. She used to read to him in bed. *Now she reads to herself,* he thought. *Reads to herself and picks up strangers in bars.*

Sooner or later, she would lift her head and glance out the window. She seemed to always know, always intuit when he was out there. He told himself he didn't want it to happen tonight. He told himself he would listen to Norah sing four songs — only four — and then he would start the engine and drive home again. He told himself that was what he wanted to happen.

In the middle of the third song, the porch light snapped on. He drew in his breath, winced as the old ache deepened, felt the disturbance in his chest that was like a stone dropped into a very deep well. So, she had looked out and seen his car. And now the front door would be unlocked. Next she would turn out the living room light . . . There, the window went dark. *She's going upstairs now,* he thought. *She's waiting there at the top but I won't go in this time. This time I'm not going in.*

Norah sang, "Truth spoke in whispers will

tear you apart . . ."

When he eased the front door open and stepped inside, she was standing in profile at the top of the stairs, facing the bedroom, her hand on the banister post. She was a shadow in a darkened house, and he felt heavy with the darkness that had brought them both to this place, always brought them here, kept them always in this darkness. She went into the bedroom then without looking down at him. He leaned against the door. *Go home,* he told himself.

But he knew he would not. He would not have come into the house if he intended to go home. He pried off his shoes and locked the door. First he went into the kitchen, washed his hands with dish soap. Then he went up the stairs.

In the darkened bedroom, with the curtains drawn, as always, and with even the radio turned to face the wall so that its dim blue glow cast no light upon the bed, he eased himself down beside her, smelled her scent in the darkness, felt the hollowness engulf him. "How are you?" he asked. His voice was a whisper and whiskey hoarse.

She said nothing. After a minute or two, she rolled onto her side and faced him. He could not see her body yet, but he felt its heat and knew that she was naked, and he wanted to fall against her, wanted to pull her close and drive this ache from them forever. But all he did was to raise a finger to her face, trace the softness beneath her jaw.

She moved her hand against him, slid her hand between his legs, cupped her hand around him through his khakis. He told her, "We don't have to do this."

She said nothing. She always said nothing.

He told himself he wished they could throw away the script for once, but he also knew he had come here counting on the script to be followed. With her hand moving against him and her scent filling the darkness, he suddenly wanted only that the script be played out as written. She would not kiss him but he could touch her, so he laid one hand between her breasts and slipped his other between her legs. He was always surprised by how wet she was when he touched her, always wondered what it was about these infrequent nights that excited her. Was it the thought of how much he needed her? The thought of the grief he would feel afterward when he drove home alone?

She touched him without words until touching was not enough for him. Then he rolled away and stood and removed all of his clothing. When he eased onto the bed again, she rolled onto her side and presented her back to him, and when he entered her and gripped her waist, she sucked in a quick breath but otherwise remained silent.

Because of her passivity he always tried to go slowly. Now and then a nearly inaudible moan would escape from her, but she would give him nothing more, would never lay her hand atop his or say a word to him. He concentrated on being gentle and slow and hoped he would feel the muscle on the inside of her right leg begin to quiver, hoped that her back would arch toward him and that she would let herself go the way she used to before the accident, back when she would cry out so loudly that they had to close the windows in the summer, and after Ryan was born had to press her mouth to the pillow so as not to wake him.

But of course it did not happen that way anymore. As per the script she had written a long time ago, all that happened now was that her breath quickened and her stomach muscles went rigid and she held herself hard against the mattress. Then he came too, and he tried to be as quiet and controlled as her, but he felt himself falling and falling and disappearing into blackness.

Half a minute later, he opened his eyes and felt her stillness beside him. He ran a hand up her stomach and felt her arms crossed at the wrist atop her breasts, both hands clenched.

Finally he pulled away and lay there looking at her. When he touched her spine between the shoulders, she jerked and went stiff.

He knew he should not talk, but he hoped it might be different this time. He hoped that maybe she was ready now and that this woman who loved words and who taught the beauty of words to eleventh-grade boys might permit him a few words to attack the circles of sadness rippling through him.

"Laraine," he said.

She pulled away and swung her legs over the side of the bed.

"Laraine, wait."

She went into the bathroom and locked the door and turned the hot water on so that it gushed and splashed and steamed into the tub.

When he drove home that night, he played a Paul Winter CD filled with songs that had no lyrics, no voices, no heartfelt, useless words.

THIRTY-FIVE

Morning brought the kind of clarity that only a chill November morning can. At a few minutes after eight, DeMarco stood sipping coffee on his front porch, using the bite of the air to wash the heaviness from his eyes. The grass in his yard shone neon green in the new sun and sparkled with frozen dew. Shadows from the slender poplars around the perimeter striped the grass. Everything looked clean and new to him in the morning and he hoped the illusion would last. He was determined not to beat himself up anymore over his weaknesses; he needed to stop sapping his energy and concentration with regret. A woman and her three children had been slaughtered and the primary subject was still at large, a man DeMarco knew and had liked. It was DeMarco's responsibility to bring the suspect in, not to determine his guilt or innocence. He did not want to let another day pass without making some progress on the case.

With enough caffeine and sunshine, maybe he could have a productive day.

When he first entered his office that morning at the barracks along Route 208, he stood for a while at the window behind his desk. Across the road, the digital sign outside Citizen's Bank registered a temperature of thirty-seven degrees. Behind and on both sides of the bank, a cornfield of stubbled stalks continued in shades of khaki and sage to the distant woods. Those woods, he knew, continued northward all the way to Lake Wilhelm, broken only by a few villages and asphalt roads and the ceaselessly rumbling four lanes of interstate highway.

"You're out there somewhere," he said. "You're cold and you're hungry, and as far as I know, you're completely out of your mind. But you're out there. And I'm coming to get you. I'll find you, my friend."

He turned then and sat at his desk and pulled from his shirt pocket the slip of paper Bonnie had given him the night before. He had already passed the first name, Tracy Butler, on to Trooper Carmichael. The other name, Danni Reynolds, would keep him busy for the next two hours.

He ran the name through a couple of

databases on known criminals. No priors, no hits. He checked the Department of Motor Vehicles, both Pennsylvania and Ohio. No vehicle registered in the name of Danni Reynolds. He did a background check through the court records. He called the Registrar of Deeds at three county courthouses for a listing of any property held in the name of Danni Reynolds. He keyed in the name on Google, Classmates.com, Facebook, EmailFinder.com, People Finder, Zabasearch, ThePublicRecords.com. He tried four different zip codes on Whitepages.com. No address available for a Danni Reynolds. No Danni Reynolds. No Danielle Reynolds. No Danna, Danique, or Danica Reynolds.

As a last resort, he ran the name through the cell phone registry. No hits on either Danni or Danielle or any of the other variations, but there were seventeen listings for D. Reynolds. Only four — two D. Reynolds, a D. J. Reynolds, and a D. L. Reynolds — were within fifty miles of Whispers.

He used the office landline and blocked the number. The first call was answered by a deep male voice. DeMarco said, "Is this D. J. Reynolds?"

"Who's this?"

"I'm a friend of Danni's, Mr. Reynolds.

Would you happen to know where I could reach her?"

"Hell, I don't even know who Danni is, pal."

The number for D. L. Reynolds connected to the voice mail for a landscaping business. The call to the first D. Reynolds was answered by the recorded greeting of what sounded like a teenage girl. "Hi, guys! I can't take your call right now. Leave me a message!"

DeMarco circled that number on his notepad and dialed the last. This call was answered by another female voice but older, tired. "Hello?"

"Hi, Ms. Reynolds. My name is Bob Leland. I'm with the County Census Bureau and we're doing an update of our records in anticipation of the next census. Could you just confirm for me that I am speaking with Danielle or Danni Reynolds?"

"Sorry. My name is Darlene."

"Well, that's a good name too. Yep, there you are, three names below Danielle. And you are residing at the same address as provided during the last census?"

"Unfortunately I am," she said.

"Okay, thank you very much, that's all I needed to know. Unless . . . any chance you would know the address for a Danni or

Danielle Reynolds? I'm having a heck of a time tracking her down."

"Sorry. Nobody I know."

"Well, thank you anyway. Have a beautiful day."

Next DeMarco did a reverse lookup of the number he had circled. Thirty seconds later, he had what he needed. D. Reynolds, 14 East Pearl Street, Apartment 2C, Albion, Pennsylvania. She lived fewer than fifteen miles from the strip club. "You're my girl," he said aloud.

It was 10:09 a.m. If he left now, he could be in Albion around eleven. "A good time," he told himself. A stripper who worked until two or three in the morning would probably still be in bed, but not so soundly asleep that a phone call wouldn't rouse her. She would be groggy, not thinking straight, might blurt out a few words he could use.

He stuffed the notepad into his jacket pocket, then walked down the hall to Carmichael's desk. "You get me anything?"

The trooper handed him another small slip of paper. "Cell phone number, that's it. No address yet."

DeMarco looked at the listing, then took out his cell phone, blocked his number, and made the call. Tracy Butler answered on the third ring. Her voice was throaty and slow,

279

still groggy with last night's Xanax. "Hello?"

"Annabel?" DeMarco said.

"Who, baby?"

"I'm looking for my Annabel. Are you her?"

"Not last time I looked. But it's a pretty name, isn't it?"

DeMarco pressed End, crumpled up the slip of paper, and tossed it onto Carmichael's desk.

"Sorry," Carmichael said.

DeMarco patted his jacket pocket. "No worries. I have her in here."

Before leaving the building, he stepped inside his station commander's office. "I'm headed north to check out a person of interest. She might know something about Thomas Huston's current whereabouts."

"How does she know him?" Bowen asked. "University stuff?"

"Whispers stuff."

"Say again?"

"It's a strip club just east of Pierpont, Ohio."

"You telling me the man had a secret life?"

"Research for his novel."

"That's a handy excuse, isn't it? Covers just about everything a guy could get into."

"I'll be back in a couple of hours."

"You taking a cruiser?"

"Not this time. Low profile."

"Well, that piece of shit of yours is certainly low profile. Think it will get you there and back?"

"I'll buy a Lincoln when I get your job." He turned toward the hall.

"Hey!" Bowen said.

DeMarco looked into the room again.

"You taking 62 west to the Interstate?"

"I am not bringing back any fucking spinach rolls," DeMarco told him.

"They make them one day a week. What's the harm?"

"Do I look like a delivery boy to you?"

"You drive a delivery boy's car."

"Fuck you and die," DeMarco said.

"If you go past the place. That's all I'm saying."

"If I go past," DeMarco said. He turned away and started down the hall.

"And this time don't forget the dipping sauce!"

Thirty-Six

With fewer than two thousand residents, Albion has three distinguishing characteristics. The B&LE occasionally rattles through the south end of town, loaded with coal and other freight on its way to the Lake Erie loading docks in Conneaut, Ohio. A medium-security state correctional facility opened for business just outside of Albion in 1993 and now housed a few hundred more adult male offenders than the town had residents. But the thing most locals remember Albion for happened on the last day of May 1985, the day forty-one tornados ripped across Canada, Ohio, and Pennsylvania. The F4 twister that swept the quiet streets clean of all cars, trucks, and Amish buggies hit Albion at 5:05 in the afternoon, two minutes after the warning was issued from the Erie National Weather Service. It obliterated a hundred or so homes.

DeMarco had heard all the stories. A man

had been watching from his porch as the writhing black mass approached, only to have his leg sheared off by flying debris. House trailers were lifted off their foundations, spun through the air, smashed into the ground. A car was sucked two hundred feet into the funnel, heaved over the top of a silo, and slammed into a field, a young woman and her dog inside. Bodies were found as far as two miles from where they had been yanked into the air.

The neighboring towns of Wheatland and Atlantic had also been laid flat. Dozens of lives lost, thousands forever damaged.

DeMarco thought about that twister, thought about the sudden, random violence of life as he drove into Albion an hour before noon on a sunny autumn day. He remembered what Samuel Butler had said, that life is a long process of getting tired. He and Laraine had laughed when she read that line to him out of *Bartlett's Quotations*. But DeMarco knew now that Butler had had it wrong. *Life is a long process of being destroyed,* he thought. *And not, in fact, a very long process at that.*

Danni Reynolds's apartment was on East Pearl Street, a street that had been wiped clean by the tornado and rebuilt in a hurry. The building was of post-and-board construction, two stories high, with slapdash balconies, railings and stairways that looked as if they could not withstand a heavy breeze. Where the yellow vinyl siding was buckled or missing in places, wisps of pink insulation stuck out like dirty cotton candy. Most of the windows were covered with towels, sheets, or heavy curtains to keep out the drafts.

DeMarco parked across the street and studied the building. Four apartments on the first floor, four on top. Apartments A and B in the front, C and D in the rear. Danni lived in the rear.

He drove around back to a paved parking area. No access from there to the next street behind the building unless she climbed a chain-link fence. She had two ways to get to ground level. Down the rear stairway to the parking area. Down the side stairway to East Pearl Street. He guessed that she owned a car, one of the five compacts in the parking area, none newer than four years old, none without a few scrapes or indentations. *Chances are,* he told himself, *if she runs, it will be to her car.* And if she ran, it would tell him a lot. Everything he needed to know.

DeMarco drove back toward East Pearl but parked his car at the end of the driveway, blocking its entrance. Then he climbed out and crossed to the side stairs. On the second floor balcony, he walked just past the door of apartment D, close enough to Danni's apartment that, if she were inside, he would hear her phone ringing. Then he pulled the cell phone from his pocket and dialed her number. Four rings, then her voice mail answered. "Hi guys! I can't take —"

No faint ringing sound had emanated from her apartment, no muted musical ringtone. Maybe she kept the phone on vibrate. Maybe she shut it off when she slept. Maybe she wasn't home.

He waited ten seconds and hit redial. Then again. Then one more time.

"Hello?" she finally said. Groggy, she sounded even more like a little girl, a child.

He tried to soften the gruffness of his voice, gave her little more than a whisper. "Annabel?" he said.

He was answered with silence. He waited.

"Thomas? Is that you?"

"No, Danni," he told her. "This is Sergeant Ryan DeMarco of the Pennsylvania State Police. And I need to speak with you."

Immediately, his phone went silent. *Call Ended,* the screen message said.

THIRTY-SEVEN

He stuffed the phone back into his pocket, moved two steps closer to Danni's door, and waited. She was either sitting there on her bed, feeling the panic mount, unsure of what to do next, or she was stuffing clothes into a bag. Maybe she was whispering urgently to Thomas Huston. Maybe she was calling him, asking what she should do.

DeMarco thought he heard movement inside. No heavy footsteps, no mad rushing about, but soft, quick steps, the clink of what might have been keys. He was aware then of a quickening of his pulse, that familiar excitement of the chase. But as soon as he recognized the heat of the adrenaline rush coming, he suppressed it, smothered the flame. This wasn't some gooned-up punk he would have to throw against a wall and cuff; this was a frightened young woman, a girl he had yanked up out of her sleep with just the mention of a name. And the plaintiveness in her voice when she had said, *Thomas? Is that you?* — the memory of that voice brought a sudden heaviness to his chest, an ache that extinguished all traces of excitement.

The door opened quickly, startling him. She stepped out onto the balcony, saw him, and gasped audibly.

He smiled.

She looked away. Turned back to the door, pulled the door shut, nervously fitted her key in the lock. "I'm sorry. I have to get to work. I can't talk right now."

"Whispers doesn't open for a while yet, Danni. A long while."

She took a breath. Still facing the door she turned her head slightly, lifted her eyes to him. "I mean class. I have to get to class."

She was dressed in yellow basketball shorts, a gray hoodie, low-cut Nike running shoes, no socks. She had probably rolled out of bed after his phone call, pulled on the shoes and hoodie, yanked her long brown hair into a ponytail. DeMarco imagined her jogging toward him through the mist as he sat alone on a park bench.

Softly he told her, "I'm not here to arrest you, Danni. Not if you're honest with me."

"I don't . . ." She glanced down at the dirty blacktop of the parking lot. Green eyes wet with tears. "I don't know anything."

"Is Thomas Huston inside your apartment, Danni?"

"No! No, why? He's never been in my apartment."

"Then why don't you and I just go inside and sit down and have a conversation, okay? That's all it will be."

Now she began to tremble. Tears streaked both cheeks. Her voice quivered when she spoke. "I haven't done anything wrong."

"I know you haven't." He moved closer now, stood next to her, spoke very softly. "I know you wouldn't. I just need to talk to you, that's all. Five minutes and I'm gone."

She sniffed back her tears, blinked twice. Then faced the door and again raised her key to the lock.

DeMarco watched as she fumbled to open the door. She looked barely into her twenties, five and a half feet tall, maybe a hundred fifteen pounds. A tiny thing, really. A child. His chest began to ache again, a heaviness of breath. His left eye watered.

"I'm going to move my car out of the driveway," he told her. "I'll be right back." And he turned away quickly, quickly brushed the wet sting from the corner of his eye.

■ ■ ■

Underfurnished living room, tiny kitchen, a bathroom the size of a closet, a bedroom behind a curtained doorway. Furnishings were minimal, a futon for a sofa, two collapsible chairs, one green, one yellow, $12.95 each at Walmart. He guessed that she slept on a secondhand mattress on the floor in the bedroom, no dresser or chest of drawers, that she kept her clothes neatly folded in cardboard boxes lined against the wall. But everything was neat, no dust, no dirty dishes in the sink. The air smelled vaguely of strawberries. An unlit candle on the kitchen counter.

She sat on the futon, feet drawn up beneath her. He stood by the window, over which she had hung a vinyl blind and a sheer, cream-colored lace curtain.

"When was the last time you saw or heard from Thomas Huston?" he asked.

She chewed on her lower lip. Then said, "I guess it was a week ago this Thursday. Last Thursday night."

"And where did this occur?"

"At Whispers."

"Did you spend time with him there?"

"A little."

"A private couch dance?"

"That's what he paid for but . . ."

"But what?"

"That's not what we did. We never did that."

"Then what did you do?"

"Just talked."

"In the room where the couch dances are held. You talked."

"That's all we ever did, I swear."

"Okay. And what did you talk about?"

"He was writing a book about a dancer. So he would ask me stuff."

"What kind of stuff, Danni?"

"Stuff a writer would want to know, I guess. Like how did it feel when I was up on the stage or in the champagne room with a guy. What I thought about when they were watching me. What I thought about when I went home."

DeMarco nodded. "That's only three questions though. And he visited Whispers five, six times, am I right?"

"After the first time it really wasn't like an interview, you know? I mean . . . we just talked. He was a nice guy, he was very sweet."

"Are you telling me that there was no physical involvement between the two of you in the champagne room?"

"There wasn't. I swear. I sat beside him on the love seat. We just talked. That's all we ever did."

"And you never saw him outside of Whispers?"

"Just that first time."

"Tell me about that first time, Danni."

"I was jogging one morning. I like to jog early when there's nobody else around."

"And this was in Erie?"

"No, it was here."

"I didn't see a park here in town."

"There's the Borough Park, but that's not where I was. It was on the bike path. It runs alongside the railroad tracks and across the extension canal. All the way into Shadytown."

"And Shadytown is where?"

"About three miles south of here."

"And where along this bike path did you meet Thomas Huston?"

"Shadytown is just a tiny, little village. I don't think it even has a post office. But just off Route 18, there's this little place beside the canal. I don't even know if it has a name. It's just a couple of picnic tables and barbecue grills, but the bike path runs through it for another hundred yards or so. Then it just ends."

"So you run in one direction, then you

turn around and run back."

She nodded, chewed on her lip, sat with her hands shoved underneath her thighs.

"And Thomas was where along this path?"

"In the park. At the first picnic table."

"And you came jogging along and . . ."

"Most of the way, there's either the railroad tracks or the canal on the one side of the path. On the right side going to Shadytown, on the left coming back."

"And on the other side there's what? Route 18?"

"Yeah, but you can't see it from the path. There's always trees or heavy brush on that side. Except for the traffic noise, you'd never even know it's there."

"And you feel safe running there in the early morning?"

"I carry pepper spray and a whistle."

DeMarco smiled. *Christ,* he thought.

She said, "So anyway, just as the bike path enters the little picnic area, that side opens up into a big clearing with the tables and stuff. The first table is like right beside where the brush ends. In fact, when you're on the path, you can't even see the table until you're right beside it, and it's like maybe three feet from the edge of the path."

"And that's where Thomas was sitting."

"It was so startling, you know. I've *never*

seen anybody there in the morning. Then suddenly there's this guy."

"So what happened?"

"He scared me. 'Cause he was like . . . He told me he had heard my footsteps coming. He could hear me breathing, you know? So he was sitting there sort of leaning forward, trying to see around the edge of the brush. But it's sort of misty, the way it always is in the morning, especially if it's rained the night before. And I'm on top of him before either one of us knows it. I almost ran into his head."

She was smiling now, staring at the floor. DeMarco waited.

She said, "He jerked out of the way just in time, and I guess maybe I screamed a little bit, more of a loud gasp, you know? Anyway, I tripped over my own feet and almost ended up in the canal."

"Then what?"

"He got up to help me. But by then I had my pepper spray out." Her smile widened. "He was so funny. He put both hands in the air and sat back down and said, 'I'm not moving. I'm staying right here. Just tell me if you're okay.' "

"And were you?"

"Except that I'd twisted my ankle."

"So how did you get back home?"

"We just stayed like that for maybe fifteen minutes, him on the picnic table, me with my pepper spray out. He told me his name, where he taught, the names of his kids and his wife . . . He even tossed me his wallet so I could look at the pictures and his ID. So finally . . . I said okay. I let him drive me back home."

"And that was it?"

She shook her head. "I knew who he was by then. I knew he was a famous writer. I told him about reading his second novel in lit class."

"State university?" DeMarco asked.

She nodded. "I'm a senior. Elementary Education major."

"And so . . ."

"There was just something . . . so easy about him, you know? I mean he actually seemed interested in me, this famous, big-shot writer. It was flattering. So when I asked him what he was working on now, and he told me . . ."

"You told him about Whispers."

"On the way back to my place, he stopped at a convenience store and got us each a cappuccino. Then we just sat in his car outside my apartment for a while and talked. And yeah, I told him about Whispers."

"And you became his Annabel."

"He never actually said that. I mean, he did spend more time with me there than with the other girls, but he never said I was the one he was writing about. Anyway it was fiction, wasn't it?"

"You're the only girl he paid for private dances with?"

"As far as I know."

"So maybe that part wasn't just for talking?"

She looked up at him. "He told me I reminded him of his wife when she was my age. Except that her hair is darker than mine."

"That doesn't answer my question though, does it?"

"He never touched me. Not like that. He never once even tried."

DeMarco considered asking what would have happened if Huston had tried to touch her. Then he decided that the answer was irrelevant.

"And after that first meeting in the park, he came to Whispers every Thursday night. You spent twenty minutes with him in the champagne room, and you had a conversation."

"That's it," she said. "That's all of it." A few moments passed before she added,

"Except that it wasn't every Thursday night after that. He missed one."

"Do you remember which one?"

She gave it some thought. "It would have been the time before the last time he was there."

"Did you ask him about it?"

"He said he had to go out of town on business."

DeMarco tried to think of something else he might ask. "Anything else you can tell me about your relationship with him?"

She thought for a few moments. "I gave him my phone number."

"You did? When was that?"

"The last time he came to Whispers. I mean, it didn't make any sense to me that he had to pay a cover charge and all just to talk to me. So I told him that. And I gave him my number. He promised to thank me in his new book. He said he'd like me to meet his wife sometime."

With the final sentence, tears pooled in her eyes. DeMarco said, "Did he give you his number?"

She nodded. "He said that if I ever needed anything, just to let him know."

"And did he ever call you? Or you call him?"

"Neither," she said.

DeMarco watched her for a few moments. She was sitting with her head down, picking tears from the corners of her eyes.

And he asked himself, *Was it just his kindness? Is that why she's crying? And was his kindness real?*

He had no answers. Finally he said, "So why did you run from me, Danni?"

"I don't know. You're a policeman. Thomas's family has all been killed and he's missing. I spent time with him at the club . . . I was scared, I guess."

He studied her for a moment. "So you're a senior this year?"

"I do my student teaching in the spring. Then I'm done. Graduate, get a job, maybe have a normal life for a change."

"You have a boyfriend?"

"There's a guy I'm seeing."

"Does he know you dance?"

"He lives in Pittsburgh. I only see him when I go down there."

"How about your parents? Do they know?"

She did not move. Only her shoulders quivered. He saw one small dark spot appear on the edge of the sofa cushion, then another.

He crossed toward her, laid a hand on the top of her head. He said, "I might have to call you again, Danni, if I think of anything else to ask. Be safe when you run, okay? I know that mornings are nice but . . . be safe."

THIRTY-EIGHT

Back at the barracks, he dropped the white paper bag, long and slender, on Commander Bowen's desk. "You want half of this?" Bowen asked.

"I want six dollars and forty-nine cents."

Bowen reached for his wallet. "Learn anything useful?"

"At the moment I'd say no. But I have to process it to be sure. Something feels off."

"You locate the contact?" He laid a five and two ones on the far edge of the table.

DeMarco picked up the bills, folded them, and slipped them into his pocket. "I found her, but there were no revelations. She's just a kid. Decent kid at that."

Bowen unwrapped the spinach roll, a long tube of baked pizza dough stuffed with spinach, mushrooms, and gooey mozzarella. "You sure you don't want some of this?"

"Nah, I'm not hungry. I already licked it a few times on the way back."

299

Bowen grinned, lifted the spinach roll to his mouth, and bit off the end. "She wasn't getting it on with the suspect?"

"Says no. I'm inclined to believe her."

"And why is that?"

"Can we have this conversation when there's not cheese and spinach hanging out of your mouth?"

"I want you to know that I still have my concerns."

"Hemorrhoid cream, liberally applied. Works every time."

"All I'm saying is you knew the guy. Maybe it colors your judgment, maybe it doesn't."

"Maybe you wouldn't get hemorrhoids if you didn't sit around on your flat ass all day."

Bowen waved him away. "Go. I'd rather be alone with this beauty anyway. I'm in heaven here."

In his own office, DeMarco sat at his desk and stared at the screen saver on his monitor, a black background with what were supposed to be stars rushing forward as if he were speeding through deep space. To De-Marco it looked more like a snowstorm at night, the Arctic Express blasting toward him off Lake Erie.

He asked himself why he felt so tense.

Ever since leaving Albion, his nerves had felt raw and abraded. Something sat leering at him from the edge of his consciousness, something he could not quite identify — something he should know, almost knew, but couldn't quite put his finger on.

He reached for a legal pad, turned to a clean sheet, laid the tablet horizontal. Across the top he wrote three names, evenly spaced: *Danni. Bonnie. Huston.*

Under Danni's name he wrote *a.k.a. Annabel.* And under that, *I believe her.*

Under Bonnie's name he wrote *don't trust her.*

And under Huston's name *why Shadytown at dawn? missed one Thursday at Whispers why? told Danni out of town on business. Bonnie failed to mention the missing night.*

But Bonnie hadn't failed to mention Danni. She could have given him the names of any two dancers. Instead, one of them just happened to be Huston's connection. Why had Bonnie done that? She could have protected Danni, provided another's name. Was it a gift? Or was it a diversion?

He stared at the paper. There was more to the situation than what he had written, he knew there was. But what was he missing? His brain wasn't working right, wasn't seeing the connections. He got out his cell phone, called Danni's number. This time he didn't bother to block his own.

"Two questions," he said after her hello. "Who's the bouncer at the club?"

"You mean Tex?" she said.

"Kind of scrawny, mouthful of crooked teeth. Collects the money at the entrance."

"That's Moby," she said.

"So who's Tex?"

"He's kind of big? Not tall but beefy, you know? Shaved head, looks like a butcher?"

"There wasn't anybody like that around when I was there."

"You might not have seen him, I guess. He spends most of his time upstairs, watching everything through the one-way glass."

"You know his last name? Where he lives maybe?"

"No, but Bonnie would. I'm pretty sure there's something going on between them."

"Why do you say that?"

"Just a feeling, I guess. The way they stand when they're talking to each other, you know? The way he looks at her."

DeMarco wrote *Tex* on his tablet. Then *Moby.* "And Moby?" he said. "What can you tell me about him?"

"Just that he's a sweetheart. Oh, and that he's Bonnie's brother."

"So what makes him such a sweetheart?"

"He just is. I mean it used to worry some of the girls, him being so scrawny and sweet and all."

"Why would that worry them?"

"Until Tex came, I mean. Everybody feels safer now with him upstairs this past couple of months. Moby couldn't hurt a fly, but Tex . . ."

"Tex is new?"

"I don't know the exact date when he started, but it wasn't more than two, at most three, months ago."

"Okay, good. Thank you for this. One last thing."

"Am I going to get in trouble with Bonnie for talking to you?"

"Are you going to tell her you've been talking to me?"

"No way."

"No way will I either, Danni."

"You promise?"

"You have my word."

"Because I need this job. Just a little while longer. Just until I start my student teaching. Then I'm going to have to quit anyway. I mean I can just imagine what could happen. Parent-teacher conference in the afternoon . . ."

"Champagne room conference with the father that night."

"There you go."

"So listen," he said. "Final question. The night Huston didn't show up as usual."

"Two Thursdays ago."

"Right. Did all of the other regular girls work that night?"

"Geez, I don't know. They sort of come and go, you know?"

"Try to remember, okay? Was there anybody missing the same night as Thomas? Anybody who is usually there when he is?"

Silence for fifteen seconds. Then, "I'm pretty sure that was the night Bonnie missed too."

DeMarco felt something slam into place. A piece of the puzzle. "Bonnie didn't show up that night?"

"I'm pretty sure it was that night, yeah."

"Any chance you'd know why she wasn't there?"

"According to Wendy, her grandmother was really sick and she had to take care of her. Bonnie's grandmother."

"And Wendy is . . . ?"

"One of the dancers. She's like forty or something. Three kids. I guess Bonnie had asked her to watch the bar that night. And it's not like Wendy brings in the big tips anyway. She said later she'd tend the bar every night if Bonnie would let her."

"And that same night. Was Tex at the club?"

"Yes, he was."

"And Moby?"

"Yep. Moby's always there."

"So the only two regulars who weren't there were Thomas Huston and Bonnie."

"As far as I can remember, yes."

DeMarco pursed his lips, nodded, and filed that information away. "The next Thursday," he said, "the last time you saw Thomas. When he told you he'd missed a night because of business out of town. Did he get any more specific than that?"

"I remember I teased him a little. I asked if it was monkey business. I thought it was kind of strange that he didn't laugh at that, you know? I mean he was always a very upbeat kind of guy."

"But not that night?"

"Usually he came with a question or two he wanted to ask me. Like, did the girls talk about sex much? Did they like men? Did they hate men? Did their boyfriends and husbands know what they were doing? Trying to understand our psychology, you know? All of our messed up psychologies." She delivered the last line with a tone that smacked of self-contempt. DeMarco knew the sound well.

He said, "Yours doesn't seem so messed up to me, Danni."

"Sometimes I wonder."

"I've known a lot worse."

"I guess you would, being in the business you're in."

He thought, *Right. The business of being human.* "So that last Thursday night," he said. "Thomas wasn't as upbeat as usual? How would you describe his mood that night?"

"I don't really know," she said. "Kind of subdued? Pensive?"

"Like he had something else on his mind?"

"Exactly."

"But you don't know what?"

"I wish I did."

"You sort of liked him, didn't you?"

The question obviously took her by surprise. DeMarco waited out the silence.

"The truth is," she finally said, "I did look forward to seeing him. He made me feel . . . I'm not sure if you can understand this or not."

"Try me."

"Most times I leave that place and I'll come home and sit in the tub for an hour. Then I climb out and I still don't feel clean. I mean, it's not like I'm proud of what I do, you know? But where else can a girl make a thousand a week dancing? And that's all I ever do. Unlike some of the girls there."

"But with Thomas, you felt different."

"I guess I felt like everything was going to be okay. Like I really would get my degree, get a job, end up with money in the bank instead of being in debt the rest of my life. And that someday I'd be able to forget all about this past year or so."

He envied her optimism, her capacity for hope. He had hope too, but of a whole different nature than hers. She hoped for a happy life. He hoped for a good night's sleep and an occasional dulling of the pain. "I appreciate you talking to me like this," he told her. "I'll try not to disturb you again."

"Actually I don't mind it at all now that I'm not scared anymore. You're sort of like Thomas in that way."

He said nothing.

"I just can't believe he's responsible for what happened."

"You know," DeMarco began, but left the rest of it, *neither can I,* unsaid. "You call me if you think of anything important. Anything at all."

"I will," she said.

He held the phone to his ear a few seconds

longer, listening and waiting. Then he lowered it and hit End.

■ ■ ■ ■

DESPAIR

■ ■ ■ ■

THIRTY-NINE

"This is Sergeant DeMarco, Nathan. Do you have a minute to talk?"

"Did he . . . ? Have you found him?"

DeMarco stared at the legal tablet on his desk. Only seconds before telephoning the student, he had added Nathan's name to the others. "Not yet," he said.

"Christ, I've had this awful feeling lately."

"What kind of feeling?"

"Just that something's happened to him. Something bad."

"I hope you're wrong," DeMarco said. "Meantime, I wonder if you could help me out with something."

"Sure, anything."

"What I'm trying to figure out are Thomas's routines, patterns of movement, things like that."

"I'll tell you whatever I know."

"For example, the way a writer works. The way he comes up with things, I mean.

Thomas was working on a novel, and a novel is fiction. So he was making the story up, am I right?"

"Well, that's the nature of fiction, yes."

"But he can use things that actually happened too."

"Sure. Real experiences are often the foundation for stories."

"So he might take, for example, an actual meeting he had with somebody. The first time he met Annabel, let's say. But for the novel he'll change where that meeting took place."

"Sure. I mean look at Hemingway. Most of his work was in some way autobiographical. A fiction writer takes what's real but changes it around, makes it more dramatic, more intense and interesting."

"But there's no way of knowing which parts actually happened and which are made up."

"Not unless the writer tells you."

"Okay. That's what I thought. A couple more things. As far as you know, was it Thomas Huston's habit to be up at dawn, maybe take a drive somewhere, find a quiet place to sit and think? I mean he had a big, beautiful house, an office there and one at the university."

"Sure, but . . . Can you hold on for a

second? Let me just pull something up here on my computer."

"Take your time." While he waited, he looked over the names on the yellow legal pad. Danni, Bonnie, Huston, Moby, Tex, Nathan, Conescu, Denton. He drew circles around the first and sixth names, the only individuals he believed he could trust.

"Here it is," Nathan said. "Let me read this to you, okay? Thomas sent me this note, must have been like the second week of the semester. I actually fell asleep in workshop one night, but he was very understanding about it. He just teased me a little and then we moved on with class. Afterward, I apologized and told him I'd been having trouble sleeping, story ideas rushing through my head all night, things like that. He didn't say much at the time, but next morning I found this note in my campus mailbox. I scanned it onto my hard drive. Can I read it to you?"

"Please do," DeMarco said.

"Okay, this is what he wrote. 'Dear Nathan, For the first few years, you might look upon your insomnia as a romantic affliction common to your profession, a creative badge of honor. Maybe you even enjoy it in a perverse sort of way, because after all, it is the ideas that are keeping you awake, all

313

those potential stories and poems and novels, more validation that you have been chosen and gifted. But trust me, after you have lain awake a thousand or so nights, exhausted and longing for sleep, foggy and dulled throughout the day, the glamour of insomnia wears thin. The sooner you learn to discipline your hammering mind with meditation and progressive muscle relaxation, the more productive you will be. It would be quicker to take a sleeping pill or half a bottle of vodka, but then you would be ruined for work the next morning. You might even try soothing music or reading the work of some of your duller classmates. The thing you must never do is to reach for a pen or you will be awake and scribbling until dawn, then have to struggle all week long with a maddening kind of narcolepsy. Establish and maintain a discipline, Nathan. There are a lot of writers with talent but not a lot of talented writers with discipline. Good luck, keep writing, but get some sleep. Thomas.' "

"Sounds like he knew what he was talking about."

"That's just it. Later that day I thanked him for the note, and he admitted that he had never been able to put the advice into practice. He said he's been a polyphasic sleeper most of his adult life. But a reluctant one."

"Polyphasic. Sleeping in phases?"

"Right. What he told me is that he and Claire would go to bed around ten or so every night, watch a little TV, do what married couples do, I'm sure. Sometimes he would fall asleep after an hour or so, and sometimes he wouldn't. He never slept for more than two or three hours. So whenever he could in the afternoon or after dinner, he'd catch another hour or so."

"And when he was awake in the middle of the night. What would he do then?"

"Write. Read. Do research. If he was feeling especially restless, he might even take a walk or a drive."

"So for him to end up thirty miles north of here at dawn some morning, sitting in a little park somewhere . . ."

"Not at all unusual. He told me that often he would use those times to scout out locations, like in a movie, you know? Except in his case for a novel. He liked to be able to visualize a scene in his head before he wrote it. It was a way of creating a strong sense of authenticity."

"This is very interesting, Nathan. Thank you."

"You know about his family history, right?

About what happened to his parents?"

"I do."

"So you can imagine how hard it must be for him to sleep."

"Yes, I can."

"Listen, you don't think . . . I mean I don't even want to consider this but . . ."

DeMarco waited.

"What happened to his parents. You don't think it might have finally tripped something in his brain, do you? Caused him to just . . . Jesus, I hate myself for even thinking such a thing."

"He was a troubled man. He hid it very well, probably channeled most of the grief into his writing. Even so."

"But he was so fucking kind. To take the time to write me that note. To show such concern for me."

The young man was weeping now — DeMarco could hear it in the quality of his voice, the hoarse deepening of sorrow.

"We're almost done here, Nathan, and then I'll let you go. Two weeks ago. You wouldn't happen to know how Thomas Huston spent that particular Thursday evening, would you?"

"Thursday two weeks ago," Nathan said. "He didn't go to the club that night? The one with Annabel?"

"He didn't. That's why I'm asking."

"Wait a minute. Was that the night he gave a reading at Cincy State? I think it was."

"He was in Cincinnati that night?"

"Right, he did a reading Thursday night, then met with some classes there the next morning before coming back to campus here."

"And you accompanied him there?"

"I would have gladly. Most of the class would have. I mean, we had done it before, even took a university shuttle bus once to Case Western. But he didn't tell us about the one in Cincy that Thursday until afterward, at the next workshop."

"Do you find that unusual? That he didn't tell his students about it beforehand?"

"Honestly . . . yes. In fact I was a little bit hurt by it. A lot of us were."

"And this reading he did. It would have been through the English Department at CSU?"

"Through the MFA program in the English Department, right. Did something . . . Is there something about that particular night that interests you?"

"Just trying to account for his movements prior to last Saturday night."

"He did give a reading, didn't he?"

"I'm sure he did. Thank you, Nathan, for

indulging my curiosity about the writing process."

"He wouldn't have lied to us about the reading, would he? Is that why he didn't tell us about it until afterward?"

DeMarco paused to gather his thoughts. "As far as you know," he finally said, "did Thomas appear to take a special interest in any particular female student?"

"He took special interest in all of his students."

"You know what I'm asking, Nathan."

"I never saw any evidence of it. Not once."

"He never confided in you about his interest in anyone?"

"No."

"Okay. Then tell me this. Do any of his female students have a serious illness? Maybe a terminal illness?"

"What? No. Why would you ask that?"

"How about a slight limp? Can you think of any female student who walks with a slight limp?"

"I don't . . . No. No, none of that. He wasn't having an affair. Why are you asking me these things?"

"Take care, son," DeMarco said, and he ended the call.

DeMarco was working on a feeling now, the

kind of thing people call a gut instinct, though with DeMarco the feeling was lodged a good eight inches above the gut, just below his sternum, something with the heaviness of metal, warm, and irregularly shaped, as if he had swallowed a chunk of lead steak and it was lodged there, making both swallowing and breathing difficult.

Perhaps the heaviness sat like a lump of lead in DeMarco's chest because he was a hundred percent certain that a telephone call would reveal that Huston had not given a reading in Cincinnati on the Thursday night in question. He was certain that Huston had been with Bonnie that night. Shacked up somewhere? If so, he wouldn't have wanted the motel charge showing up on his credit card statement. So before De-Marco looked up the telephone number for the English Department at Cincinnati State University, he made a short visit to Trooper Carmichael's desk.

"Do me a favor and pull all of Huston's bank records for the past three months. What I'm looking for are any withdrawals made on Wednesdays or Thursdays during that time. From all checking accounts, joint or otherwise. Probably from an ATM. Let me know when you have something."

In his own office again, DeMarco opened

Cincy State's website, clicked his way to the English Department, MFA program, director Alice Bramson. She wasn't in her office so he left a voice message asking her to return his call ASAP. Then he tapped the side of his thumb against his desk, thought about walking down the hall for another cup of coffee, knew he didn't need it, didn't want it pooling atop the lump of lead steak working its way up into his throat. "I hate fucking waiting," he said aloud. It didn't relieve any pressure. "I hate fucking waiting!" he shouted. That felt better, but it didn't accomplish anything except to bring Trooper Carmichael to his threshold.

"You just gave me this a minute ago. I'm working as fast as I can."

Softly, DeMarco told him, "I wasn't speaking to you. Thank you very much. Please close my fucking door."

FORTY

By midafternoon, DeMarco knew three things.

Fact one: According to Dr. Alice Bramson, Thomas Huston had not given a reading at Cincinnati State University since the publication of his second novel. She would have loved it if he had appeared there more regularly; she adored his work; she still had fond memories of his previous visit. Nor had he given a reading anywhere in Cincinnati that night, guaranteed; otherwise, she would have been in attendance, her copy of his latest novel in hand, awaiting his signature.

Fact two: On each of the nine Thursdays previous to the death of his family, Thomas Huston had made withdrawals from an ATM approximately twelve miles from his home. All were made not from his and Claire's joint checking or savings accounts but from his personal checking account. All of those withdrawals but one had been for eighty dollars, all made within twenty minutes of 7:30 in the evening. The other withdrawal, made two Thursdays before his family's deaths, occurred at 6:42 in the morning and was in the sum of three hundred dollars, the maximum withdrawal allowed per day. On the day previous to that withdrawal, at 4:16 on Wednesday afternoon, he had made a similar withdrawal of three hundred dollars.

From this information, DeMarco was able to surmise two things: that the withdrawals of eighty dollars each week were used to cover his admission to whatever strip club he had visited that night, his drinks, plus his champagne room visits. The combined six-hundred-dollar withdrawals were not.

The third fact DeMarco was able to glean from his information was this: Bonnie had lied.

DeMarco stared at the notes on his legal pad. He said, "Where would she and Huston spend six hundred dollars on a Thursday? Or maybe on Friday. Or both." He already knew, thanks to an earlier call to the English Department secretary, that Huston had taken a personal day on the Thursday in question but had shown up for his afternoon office hours on Friday afternoon, then had rushed home in time to catch Tommy's sixth-grade basketball game.

By all appearances, the writer's life had veered from its routine only from approximately 6:30 a.m. Thursday until noon or so on Friday. A thirty-hour anomaly.

DeMarco asked himself who besides Bonnie could account for this change. Not Danni. Not Nathan. Possibly Bonnie's brother, Moby, but DeMarco knew that if he contacted Moby, Bonnie would soon be alerted to it. What about Tex? Tex who? No last name, no last known residence, nothing but his association with Bonnie.

DeMarco needed another coffee after all. But he had filled his mug only halfway when a thought occurred to him. With coffeepot in hand, he walked briskly to Bowen's office. He said, "I'm going to need Carmichael and Morgan for a little overtime tonight."

"Of what nature?" Bowen asked.

"Tits and asses."

"You want to see theirs?"

"Keep your fantasies to yourself," DeMarco said. Then, "Plainclothes. I need them to watch Whispers from the inside while I watch it from the outside."

"You have reason to believe Huston is going to show up there?"

"No. But the woman who owns the place. There's something not right about her relationship with Huston. I think it went deeper than she claims. Plus there's another character there who might be of some interest."

"You sure this isn't just an excuse to look at naked girls again?"

"That's what I subscribe to Showtime for. Just authorize the fucking overtime and expense money, okay?"

"Expense money for what? Let me guess. The three of you are going to have to buy a few lap dances, right?"

"It costs fifteen dollars to get inside. If they don't sit around the stage, they won't have to tip the dancers. Besides, I want them sitting at a table, where they can keep an eye on the entire place. But they'll have to look legitimate, for Chrissakes. A couple beers each, maybe a drink or two for the girls. It's a hundred dollars max. Quit your bitching and take it out of petty cash."

"That's three troopers with what, four hours OT each?"

"Or pull our guys back and let the sheriff's department and game commission handle it."

Bowen blew out a noisy breath. "Any thoughts on what might be going through his head right now?"

"Huston's? Pain. Grief. Anger. Murderous rage."

"You have a theory, don't you?"

"I always have a theory."

"You going to share it with me?"

"E equals mc squared."

Bowen sat motionless, staring hard at De-Marco's face.

"What? It's revolutionary. People are finally going to realize what a genius I am."

Nodding his chin toward the coffeepot in DeMarco's hand, Bowen said, "You drinking straight from the pot now?"

"I brought it for you, asshole. You want a refill or not?"

Bowen pushed his empty cup across the desk. "I'm getting a little annoyed with your insubordination, Ry. From now on, it's Sergeant Asshole."

DeMarco filled the cup. "In the spirit of love, peace, and harmony, sir, I will do my best."

DeMarco returned to his office and set his coffee mug on the edge of the desk. Instead of refilling it, he had emptied it out and rinsed it clean in the lavatory. No more caffeine. His stomach was sour enough already, his mouth foul. He wished he had some chewing gum or breath mints, a candy bar, something to create the illusion of sweetness and cleanliness. But he had nothing. There was a vending machine in the lounge, but that was half a building away. Too far to walk for an illusion that would dissipate after a few minutes.

He turned to his right and looked at the whiteboard on which he had copied the names and notes from his legal pad. What usually happened when he was deep into an investigation was that one or two of his scrawls would appear to stand out from the rest, appear darker or slightly raised off the surface of the board, and he would know then that those names or clues were pivotal and held the keys to a resolution. But not this time. The longer he stared, the less distinct the writing became, the less legible, until all of it swam before his eyes in a blur.

"Go home and take a nap," he told himself. He turned to the window behind his desk. It was still a beautiful day outside, blue skied and sunny. Warm enough that he could sit on his back patio with a jacket and gloves and a ski cap on, stretch out on the chaise lounge, lose consciousness for a while. Maybe he would try Huston's prescription of meditation and progressive relaxation. Except that he didn't know how to meditate. Did it involve prayer of some kind? Prayer had never worked for him. Television sometimes worked, but only at two or three in the morning with the volume low and the flickering images muted behind a glass of Jack and melting ice. Not a good prescription for an afternoon nap.

His eye was drawn then to the rose of Sharon bush outside his window. That bush had put him to sleep once. He still remembered how restful the nap had been, one dusky afternoon last spring. He had spotted a movement of some kind in the center of the bush, had pulled his chair close to the window for a better look. At first, he had had difficulty making sense of the object in the shadows; it fit no preconception. Gradually, the object separated into two objects, and he saw that the lower one was a bird lying on its back. The other object, a second bird, was standing over it and lightly pecking at the first bird's neck. His first thought was cannibalism, one bird eating another. But as he watched he realized that he was witnessing a courtship, two cardinals engaged in foreplay. The female, on her back, would turn her head this way or that, allowing the male to nuzzle his bright beak against her.

DeMarco remembered the sense of lightness he had felt while watching the birds, a quiet kind of happiness. He had leaned back in his chair and watched them just over the windowsill, and at some point, he had closed his eyes and fallen asleep. When he'd awakened a half hour was gone, but he'd felt as if he had slept for ten hours. Afterward the day had been clean and new again. On his way home that afternoon, he had stopped at a local travel agency and picked up brochures about Puerto Rico, Hawaii, the Bahamas. He had made up his mind to take a vacation in the summer, leave everything behind in drab Pennsylvania, all the crimes and bloodstains and adumbrations. He had held onto that plan well into July. Now it was November and he could not remember where he had put the brochures.

FORTY-ONE

The night was cool and smelled of woodsmoke, the kind of late autumnal night that, in other circumstances, might have found Thomas and Claire Huston lying on their backs on a blanket in the backyard, holding hands and watching the stars with Alyssa snuggled against her father, Tommy with his head on his mother's shoulder. The adults would take turns pointing out constellations, maybe telling the story of Orion and Artemis, recounting how the Seven Sisters had committed suicide and were then turned into stars by Zeus. Tommy would probably turn the talk to aliens, while Alyssa remained contemplative and silent, alert for a shooting star. A foot or so behind Thomas's head, a speaker from the baby monitor would be humming softly, a barely audible murmur of comforting white noise.

But tonight, there were no comforting sounds for Thomas Huston. Music from inside Whispers came to him disjointed and jarring, bass thumps and screeching guitars. The temperature was in the midfifties, but he could not stop shivering. Before leaving the equipment shed in Bradley that afternoon, he had anticipated the night's chill and had searched the shed for something extra to wear, something less filthy than the torn quilted jacket. He had found a navy-blue hooded sweatshirt that had been rolled into a ball and stuffed onto the top shelf behind some batting helmets. The sweatshirt was a good fit, had probably belonged to one of the coaches, who had pulled it off on a warm day, threw it aside, and forgot about it. It was stiff with dust but loosened up after a vigorous shaking. He wore it now with the hood pulled low over his ball cap, the drawstring snug beneath his chin, his hands drawn up into the sleeves. It had kept him warm enough while hiking, but now, every minute or so, as he huddled in the trees behind the gravel lot, a spasm of shivers would seize him, spreading out from his solar plexus and down his spine.

At other moments he felt feverish. His eyes burned and his stomach fluttered with nausea from time to time. He had been too nervous all day to eat anything, had drunk only a can of Diet Pepsi purchased from a vending machine outside of a gas station just thirty minutes earlier.

Now he lowered himself onto his knees in the darkness of the tree line. The low trees and bushes grew to the very edge of the gravel lot, which left him a mere twenty yards from the building, from Annabel. The only illumination at the rear of the building came from the bare yellow bulb above a door with neon-yellow lettering that said *Employees Only. All Others Use Front Entrance.*

On a couple of occasions in the past, he had waited in his Accord for Annabel to come out that door and join him in his car so they could talk. If he had his cell phone, he could call and she would come immediately — he knew she would — and surely she would have the answers he needed. She would help him now just as he had helped her. But all he could do was kneel and wait. Eventually she would step outside for a break from the noise and strobing light, the smells of beer and desperation. Only three weeks ago, though it seemed months past to Huston, she had done just that. "I'm going to take a breather in a few minutes," she had said. "How about if we continue this conversation out in your car?"

Tonight, there had been only seven cars in the lot when he'd arrived, but four more had pulled up in the last thirty minutes, one with two males, one a single male, and two cars each occupied by a dancer. He wished he could have called out to one of the girls, asked her to tell Annabel he needed to talk to her, but he could not take that chance. After his first visit, the word had quickly spread that he was a mere spectator, that except for his single private dance each night, he was there only to observe, and that if he wanted anything else, he would smile and nod his head and a girl would come to his table. So now it would not be safe for him to speak to anyone but Annabel. He would have to wait.

He thought that maybe Annabel would let him go home with her when Whispers closed, let him have a shower and shave, feel like a human again, at least on the surface. She would have information for him, answers, an explanation. Maybe a weapon of some kind. She seemed like the type of woman who would keep a gun at home.

He shivered and waited. From time to time he looked up at the stars.

It happened sooner than he expected. He thought he might have to wait until midnight for her breather, but suddenly the door opened and she was there, standing in the yellow light, peering out into the darkness. At first he could not believe it had happened so soon, and he stared for a moment as if she were an apparition. Then he pressed a hand to the tree trunk and pulled himself to his feet. He had not thought about how to best approach her at this moment, how to make her aware of his presence without frightening her. He blew air through his teeth, just wanted to catch her attention. "Sssss!"

But it wasn't loud enough. She remained in the doorway, kept scanning the parking lot. He took a step forward, felt a thorny branch against his neck, put out a hand to push it away.

Then a car door opened, the dome light dark. "Over here," the man inside said, and blinked a flashlight on and off. He was sitting in a light-brown Bonneville, one of the seven cars that had already been in the lot when Huston arrived.

Annabel strode toward the man's open door. Huston thought she appeared angry, walking with an adamant stride, leaning forward. But before she reached the car, the man pulled his door shut, then the passenger door popped open. Annabel altered her path, crossed in front of the car, bent down beside the open door. Huston heard her say, "All right, so what's this about?"

The man's response was muted and indecipherable. Annabel straightened, looked back toward Whispers, stood motionless for a few seconds. "This is bullshit," she said. Then she faced the car again, climbed inside, and shut the door.

Huston retreated a bit deeper into the trees. He watched the car but could see only the silhouettes of their heads and shoulders. She did not move close to the driver, nor he to her. Over the next fifteen minutes, bits of their conversation were loud enough to reach Huston but only as dull intonations, mere sounds. He had no idea what was transpiring inside that car. More importantly, no idea about what to do when Annabel emerged from the car. If he revealed himself so as to catch her attention, the man in the car would see him too, would see a hooded figure calling out from the edge of the woods. But if he did not, Annabel would return to Whispers, in which case he would probably have to wait until the club closed for her to come back outside.

In the end, he decided that the best course of action was to wait. At two a.m. the customers would all leave, then the employees. So he should wait. He would sit and tremble and wait.

Annabel remained in the man's car for approximately twenty minutes. Then suddenly the rear door of Whispers sprang open. The rectangle of yellow light was filled by the figure of a large man, his shoulders nearly as wide as the doorframe, arms thick with muscle. In his right hand, he held a baseball bat against his leg.

Now the driver's door on the car in the lot popped open. His dome light did not come on. Huston looked back and forth from the two men, one standing and enveloped in light, the other seated in darkness. The man in the car said, "You need to go back inside, pardner."

The man in the doorway started forward. The baseball bat swung back and forth beside his leg.

The man in the car slid out and stood up, turned on a powerful flashlight, and aimed it directly into the other man's eyes. "This is state police business," the man said. "And I am telling you to go back inside. Now."

The man with the baseball bat stood motionless. Five seconds passed. Finally he took a step and a half backward, then turned, retreated inside, pulled shut the door. The other man slid inside the car again and softly closed his door.

Thomas Huston could not breathe. He could hear the sound of breathing coming from his mouth, one quick gasp after another, but he could get no air into his lungs. There was only blackness now, no oxygen, everything extinguished by the face of the man with the baseball bat, the voice of the man in the car. He had recognized both of them. And now, everything else except that knowledge was suffocated, stabbed out. Huston stumbled backward, back through the trees, falling against one and then another until he finally wheeled around, gasping for air, sucking in the blackness, plunging blindly through the branches. He could not breathe, could not think, could do nothing but plunge deeper and deeper into the woods while his chest ached as if stabbed again and again and again by the knife of recognition.

FORTY-TWO

With his car radio turned low, DeMarco could occasionally hear a particularly loud blast of rock music from inside Whispers, and it never failed to set his teeth on edge. More often, he felt the noise as a thrum of vibration on his skin, a recurring itch. He had the radio tuned to Erie's NPR station in hopes that the soft-voiced host and the strains of Coltrane and Monk would lessen the unquiet he felt, the jitteriness that resulted from having to sit too long with empty hands and a sober mind. He had been watching the parking lot for nearly eighty minutes now, only a few minutes longer than Morgan and Carmichael had been inside, dressed like golfers fresh from nineteen holes. During that time, each trooper had made a visit to the men's room to make a cell phone call to DeMarco. Bonnie remained at her station behind the bar, they reported, and displayed no signs of

nervousness, no particular interest in anybody there. None of the customers bore any
resemblance to Thomas Huston.

DeMarco could not have explained, had
he been asked to do so, why he expected
Huston to show up there tonight. Yet he felt
certain of it. Somehow, this place or Huston's relationship with Bonnie was integral
to the slaughter at the Huston home. De-
Marco knew it, Huston knew it, Bonnie
knew it. And Huston was a creature of
routine, a man who, like many, employed
routine as a palliative, a damp blanket laid
over the fires within. He had spent several
Thursday nights in a row in the same place
Bonnie had, even the one Thursday night
neither had shown up at Whispers — this,
DeMarco knew in his gut. Then Claire,
Tommy, Alyssa, and Ryan had been murdered, and Huston had been spotted wandering through the dawn in a daze. Now it
was Thursday night again. Where else would
Huston go, distraught as he surely was,
consumed by either guilt or rage?

DeMarco checked his wristwatch again:
10:07. "Where the fuck are you?" he said.

Finally he had to admit to himself that he
had been wrong. Huston was not coming.
DeMarco sent a text message to both troopers: *Send her out.* With luck, one of them

would feel the vibration through the booming rattle of Def Leppard.

A quarter of an hour later, the door at the rear of the building swung open. A woman stood there in the yellow light, peering out, slowly scanning the row of vehicles. DeMarco could not see her face because she was backlit, but she was wearing loose slacks and a short-sleeved, collared shirt — not a dancer's outfit. DeMarco opened his car door, leaned out, and said, "Over here," blinked his flashlight once, then pulled his door shut.

Now Bonnie came toward him without hesitation, long, angry strides. Whispers's door banged closed behind her, and in the sudden darkness, he lost her for half a minute, then found her again as she neared the front of his car. He leaned across the seat and popped open the passenger door.

She put both hands on the roof, bent down to look in at him. "All right, so what's this about?"

"We're having a conversation," he told her. "Get in."

She blinked twice, and now he saw the anger in her eyes for what it was, a mask for something else. When she spoke, there was no heat in her voice, only the chill of fear. "I have a business to run, you know."

"Not if you don't get in," he said.

She drew back then, straightened up, looked toward Whispers. "This is bullshit," she said. DeMarco said nothing. He was feeling better now, less jittery.

She climbed in and slammed the door and sat there glaring at him. He shut off the radio. Then he turned to her and smiled.

"This is harassment," she said.

His smile did not waver. "Where were you two Thursday nights ago?" he asked.

He felt the flinch more than saw it, knew that even with the dome light on, he would not have seen it on her face but he had felt the negative energy of it, sudden and brief and then gone. "Where do you think I was?" she said. "Same place I always am. I was here. Working. Tending to my business."

"If you're going to start this conversation with a lie, Bonnie, we can have this conversation somewhere else. Someplace where the seats aren't as comfortable."

"Someplace I can have my lawyer present," she said.

"That's fine with me. I can hold you for questioning for seventy-two hours. You and me and your lawyer can have several conversations in seventy-two hours."

She stared out the windshield.

DeMarco said, "I know you were with

Thomas Huston that night. The Thursday night he missed coming here."

"Yeah, right, I went to a literary reading. Probably my favorite thing to do."

"Last time we talked you had no idea where Huston was that night."

She was sitting hunched forward now, silent and still. Half a minute passed. She said, "I swear to God I didn't do anything."

"I know you didn't. Why would you? You liked Thomas Huston; he liked you. You spent a lot of time together talking, didn't you?"

"Who told you that?"

"So where did the two of you go on that Thursday?" he asked. "I know you were together. I know you spent the night together and it wasn't at a literary event in Cincinnati. So you can either tell me where you were, or within twenty-four hours, I'll find out for myself and be back here to arrest you and shut you down."

"This is illegal, what you're doing."

"I'm questioning a witness, Bonnie. There's nothing illegal about that. So far I have no reason to arrest you. But if I know that you're withholding evidence, I do. And I will. So the choice is yours."

He allowed her a few seconds to mull things over, then added, "Bear in mind that this is a homicide investigation. Not a trivial matter. Four people are dead. Three of them children."

With every minute in the car, she had leaned slightly more forward in the seat, and now sat with her forehead nearly touching the dashboard, fists pressed tight to her stomach. He waited for her to sort out her options. A full minute passed. The thump of music from Whispers no longer bothered him. He was feeling calmer now.

"He took me to get an abortion," she said.

Now it was DeMarco's turn to flinch. "Thomas Huston did?"

"That's who we're talking about, isn't it?"

"Took you where?"

"Cleveland. I had it done Thursday afternoon. We spent the night at the Super 8 out by the interstate. Then came home in the morning."

"You know I can check all this out," he told her.

"Do it," she said. "It was the Cleveland Women's Center on Water Street. I gave my name as Bonnie Jean Burns. He came up with the name. Apparently it's from some old poem by somebody."

"Why Huston?" DeMarco asked. "Why was he the one to take you there?"

Now she turned her head his way, looked

at him through the darkness. "Why do you think?"

"You're telling me that it was his baby?"

She sounded exhausted when she answered. "That's what I'm telling you."

"He was cheating on his wife with you?"

"Do you find that so hard to believe? Or you just don't want to believe it?"

He had no answer, none he wanted to give. "Did the two of you ever talk about being together? Permanently, I mean."

"Christ no," she said.

"You never talked about what might happen if maybe his wife and family weren't in the picture?"

"It was a fucking fling, DeMarco, okay? He knew it and so did I. I sucked his dick three times and fucked him twice. You want to know what positions we used? Is that relevant to your investigation too?"

"Neither one of you was smart enough to use protection?"

"I wear a diaphragm. Apparently they aren't foolproof."

DeMarco leaned back in his seat and stared at the steering wheel. The exhaustion he heard in Bonnie's voice seemed to have spread to him now. The calmness was gone, replaced suddenly by a heaviness in his body, a dull numbness of the limbs. For the first time in a long time, he felt that if he closed his eyes, he would almost certainly fall asleep.

The light that flared abruptly from Whispers startled him. In the rectangle of yellow light, a large man stood, broad, bald, heavily muscled. In his right hand he held a baseball bat. He shoved the door open the whole way so that the spring hinge locked, then he came forward a few steps, paused, and squinted at the vehicles. Within seconds, he spotted the silhouettes in DeMarco's car and strode toward them.

DeMarco threw open his car door. "You need to go back inside, pardner."

But instead of halting, the bouncer increased his pace. Now DeMarco climbed out, turned on his flashlight, and aimed it at the man's eyes. "This is state police business. And I am telling you to go back inside. Now."

The big man stood in place for a moment. Then he took a step and a half backward, then turned and retreated into the building and pulled the door shut behind him. DeMarco slid back behind the steering wheel and eased his door shut.

"Tell me about Tex," he said.

"His name is Tex," she answered.

"Anything else?"

"He's the bouncer."

"Last name?"

"I think he said it was Doyle."

"You think?"

"What did I already say about names in this place? And now I suppose you want to arrest me for giving a guy a job without clearing him through Homeland Security."

"Why is he so interested in you being out here?"

"Because that's what I pay him for: to watch over the girls and me."

"He's new?"

"Yeah, a couple of months or so."

"Who was your bouncer before he came along?"

"My brother, Moby. You've seen him. So you know why I needed a new one."

"Where's Tex from?"

"Probably Texas, you think?"

"From what I hear, the two of you have a thing for each other."

"Right," she said. "I don't even know his last name for sure, don't know a damn thing about him, but I'm fucking him anyway. Hell, I guess I'm fucking everybody in the place. I'll fuck you if you want me to. I run a club where girls shake their tits and pussies at men, so obviously I'm a fucking whore myself, right? I'm a fucking nymphomaniac, right? So whip out your dick for me, DeMarco, and let's have at it."

DeMarco allowed a few moments to pass. Then he asked, "Which of these vehicles is his?"

"How would I know?"

"You don't know what car he drives?"

"I'm inside when he gets here. I'm inside when he leaves. For all I know he gets dropped off by a flying saucer."

"So you're going to force me to run down every license plate in this parking lot. Just to find out who your bouncer is."

"I'm not forcing you to do anything. Besides, what difference does it make who he is? He's got nothing to do with any of this."

"Maybe I just don't like guys who come at me with a baseball bat."

"That's your problem, not mine."

He leaned his head back against the headrest and closed his eyes. The thump of music was grating on his nerves again. He felt the vibration in his eyeballs.

"So are you going to whip it out or not?" she said. "What's the matter? Afraid to show me what you've got?"

He did not open his eyes. They sat in silence for another minute. Finally he asked her, "How can you work in such a sad business as this?"

"Haven't you noticed?" she said. "It's a sad fucking world."

Another minute passed. DeMarco sat up, buckled his seat belt, put a hand on the ignition key. "I'll let you know if I have any other questions."

"I can hardly wait," she said.

The slamming of the door jarred his bones. He started the car and the headlights flared on. He watched as she crossed the gravel lot. Her stride on the return trip had none of its previous adamancy. Now her gait was halting and weary. She had thrown her shoulders back and lifted her chin in an attempt to show that he had had no effect on her, but the trudge in her gait betrayed her. At times she almost appeared to falter and list to one side. He leaned forward to watch her more closely, but then she was at Whispers's door. She yanked it open, stepped into the yellow light, and then was gone.

"Son of a bitch," he muttered. He turned in his seat, reached for his briefcase, laid it open on the passenger seat. He turned on the dome light, then found Huston's journal among the papers and paged through it until he located the passage he wanted.

There is some quality of furtiveness about her, some pale aura of shame. She looks like a dancer trying to hide a limp, but there is nothing wrong with her legs; her legs are fine. Better than fine. No, her limp is elsewhere, somewhere in her mind or in her heart, in the shuffle and drag of her soul.

And there was another passage too, something about the mouth. It didn't take him long to find it.

She is a dark-haired woman, green eyed and dusky with secrets. Her mouth is sensuous but sad, limbs long and elegant, every movement languid. Even her smile is slow with sorrow.

The passages, he realized, applied more to Bonnie than to Danni. In fact, they fit Bonnie perfectly. He looked up at Whispers, the closed door, the dim, naked bulb. "She's Annabel," he said. He did not yet know what it meant, but he was nonetheless certain. "They're both Annabel."

FORTY-THREE

On the drive home, DeMarco thought three times about calling Nathan Briessen. After the third time, he placed the call.

"I hope you don't mind my calling again. But I guess you've become my go-to guy for all things literary."

"I don't mind at all," Nathan said, although to DeMarco's ears his voice sounded sleepy. "Not that I'm any kind of authority."

"Well, you're in training to be a writer. So you know how writers work. How Thomas works. I've read lots of novels, sure, but that doesn't give me any insight into what goes on in a writer's mind."

"I think you're giving me too much credit, but I'll help if I can. What do you want to know?"

"Is it reasonable that Thomas could have based his Annabel character on two women? One young and the other one older?"

Nathan took a long time before answer-

349

ing. DeMarco did not hurry him.

"A composite character," the young man finally said. "I mean . . . I don't see why not. Maybe he used one as the younger version of Annabel and one as the older. Or maybe he took qualities from each of them to build the character. The one thing he always preached to us was the need for complex characters. It's the contradictions in a personality that make for conflict, he said. And that's what a story is all about. Do you know the Faulkner quote from his Nobel speech? He said that the only thing worth writing about is the human heart in conflict with itself."

"The heart in conflict with itself," De-Marco said.

"Right. So . . ." Then Nathan went silent.

"Is there something else?" DeMarco asked.

"Sorry, I was thinking about something he said about building characters. That we — as writers, I mean — have to really take our time getting to know them. To not just jump into a novel until we have a full sense of who our main characters are as people. That we have to let them build bit by bit."

"I'm not sure what that means, Nathan."

"In terms of his Annabel. He was still building her. Figuring out exactly who she was as a character. And probably using various people, not just one or two. The way this one looks, the way that one talks, bits of history from somebody else."

"You're saying that his Annabel wasn't based wholly on one real person."

"It's unlikely that she was. After all, he was starting with Nabokov's and Poe's Annabels. And building his own from there."

DeMarco suppressed a sigh that would have emerged as a groan. "Okay," he said. "Thanks. I appreciate this. I apologize for disturbing you."

"Not a problem," Nathan said.

Afterward, in the reclining chair that, most nights, served as his bed, DeMarco tried to ignore the recognition that something had fallen in him, some inarticulable thing that left him feeling heavier than he was before, as if his center of gravity had dropped to his knees. Not only had Huston's Annabel become more amorphous than ever, but the notion that Huston had cheated on his wife was even more troubling. DeMarco had wanted Huston to be better than that, someone he could admire. But now the equation was changed. It was a kind of Occam's razor for law enforcement that adultery explained nearly everything. Infidelity. Lust. Stupidity and weakness.

It did and it did not. To be attracted to the kind of life Bonnie represented, to be drawn to that hedonism and self-indulgence when one's own life is otherwise so structured and controlled, this much DeMarco could understand. But to lay a knife across the throat of a woman you apparently adored, to take the life of your own son and daughter and baby boy, this was incomprehensible. Mere lust, sexual attraction, the desires of the flesh — how could any of it account for such madness?

In the darkness and silence of his living room, with a cool glass of melting ice and whiskey in his hand, DeMarco wondered if he was trying to apply reason to a situation where reason did not exist. To a casual observer, Huston's life would have appeared blessed. But this was the illusion Huston had created and maintained. A man patient and generous with his students, a picture-perfect wife and family, shirts and chinos always neatly pressed, fame and financial success; a man respected, envied; a man with a life each of his students longed for. Was it all a construction meant to conceal in himself the same dark urges that drove Huston's characters? His life had seemed a sunlit lagoon, but what currents made the blue water shimmer? A lifetime of struggle and ambition. Parents taken away by violence. Professional jealousies. The stresses of fame, the loss of anonymity. The pressure to live up to the hype, to always be better, brighter, more successful, more worthy of praise.

Was it as simple as that? The facade, as thin and brittle as all facades are, had shattered? Huston had snapped?

DeMarco sipped his drink and wondered how it must feel to let everything go. Was Huston now deliriously happy in his insanity? Completely weightless and free? No shame, no remorse, no obligations, no sin?

DeMarco could not imagine such a state of being. Not in this world or any other.

FORTY-FOUR

At first light, after three hours of restless sleep, he returned to Huston's journal. He told himself that he was looking for the madness that would explain everything and solve the equation. He read each entry aloud, hoping to hear some vague insinuation he had missed on previous readings.

DeMarco now understood that much of a novelist's life can show up in his fiction, thinly disguised as somebody else's life. Portions of the journal were total fiction, but others were not. Discerning the difference would be the hard part.

If Annabel was a composite character, part Danni and part Bonnie, probably even part Claire, maybe Huston's nameless narrator was a composite too. More than likely, some of that composite was Huston. Were that character's desires actually Huston's desires brought to the surface?

It wasn't long before certain entries

seemed to leap out at DeMarco as they had not during earlier readings. He had wanted it to happen while studying the names on the whiteboard, but it had failed him then. Now it happened in Huston's journal. Not once, but three times.

Earlier, DeMarco had read the entries while assuming they were statements made by Huston's protagonist. But if viewed as expressions more accurately ascribed to the author . . . The hairs on DeMarco's arms bristled as he read them again:

I am reminded of Nabokov's contention that there are always two plots at work in a story. The first is the plot of the story, but above it, hovering ominously like a fat, black-bellied cloud, is the writer's consciousness, which is the real plot of everything he writes. If a book is filled with love, it is because the writer longs for love. If the book drips violence, it is because the writer burns to levy justice, to decimate his enemies. The writer composes such books as a means of survival. Otherwise, his psyche would unravel. And the unraveling, depending upon its form, can be either pitiful or disastrous.

The next entry was even more chilling:

But doesn't every guilty man hide his deeds behind his words and hide his thoughts behind his smile? Or behind other deeds? Doesn't the pedophile hide behind the Little League team he coaches or the school bus he drives or the Masses he conducts? And doesn't the wife beater hide behind the sidewalks he cleans for the old lady next door, and behind his punctuality and efficiency at work? The pornographer, the rapist, the serial killer — the predatory stockbroker, the ambulance chaser, the Medicare-bilking physician — the congressman, the senator, the president — don't they all cloak their evil behind silk ties and thousand-dollar suits?

Why would you expect any less from me?

The last troubling entry had been made some time on the Saturday immediately following Bonnie's abortion in Cleveland. Suddenly the two short paragraphs assumed new meaning:

I keep wondering how long it will be before I can become reconciled to what I have done. What right did I have to do such a thing? Though it is true that I was merely an assistant, a facilitator, does this absolve me of all guilt? What we did goes against the grain of all I believe. Then why did I do it? Because she asked. She had no one else to help her.

I see both of us now in a wholly different light. Her complete absence of regret, her relief that the thing is done, is abhorrent to me. But maybe this feeling is the result of a simple case of transference. It is not Annabel I should hold in contempt but myself. I feel certain that the other man would agree.

"The other man?" DeMarco said aloud. A shiver rattled his spine. He read the passage again, slowly. And again.

"The other man? What other man?"

And then it dawned on him. "Jesus H. Christ," he said. "She lied again."

FORTY-FIVE

At 7:59 that morning, DeMarco strode up to Trooper Morgan as he stirred powdered creamer into his coffee in the break room. DeMarco shoved a sheet of folded paper between two buttons on the trooper's shirt. "Run these through the DMV ASAP. Get me copies of all the photo IDs."

"Okay if I take a sip of coffee first?"

DeMarco was already on his way out the door. "No," he said.

In his office, DeMarco went online, typed in the website he needed, found the phone number and office hours. The female who answered with a question on the third ring sounded sleepy and young, as if her first cup of chai tea had not kicked in yet. "Cleveland Women's Center?" she said. "How can I help you?"

"This is Sergeant Ryan DeMarco of the Pennsylvania State Police," he told her. "I'm investigating a multiple homicide here in

Mercer County, and I have reason to believe that a recent patient of yours is involved."

"My gosh," she said.

"Here's what I need. Do you have a pen to write this down?"

"Oh," she said. He heard a desk drawer being pulled open, a hand rummaging inside, the rustle of paper. Then, "Okay, ready."

"Her name is Bonnie Marie Harris, but she probably registered under a false name, possibly Bonnie Jean Burns. Possibly with the first name of Annabel. She's five foot nine, forty-one years old, weighs approximately 145, brown hair, green eyes. She would have been very early in her pregnancy, no more than six weeks probably, and she would have paid for the procedure with cash. What I need to know is if it's your practice there to ascertain the blood type of the fetus, and if you did, what that blood type is. And I need that information ASAP. This is a matter of some urgency."

"Uhh," she said, "Sergeant? I'm not sure I can give you that information. We have a confidentiality policy and we're not supposed —"

"Let me speak to your supervisor," he said.

"Uhh, there's just me and the nurse and

the doctor right now."

"Nurse or doctor, either one. Now. Thank you."

"Okay, uhh . . . may I put you on hold?"

"No you may —" he managed to get out before the Muzak began, an orchestral version of the Lennon–McCartney song "Here, There and Everywhere." "Fuck," he said. "No respect for authority."

As he listened to the Muzak, he was reminded of his favorite cover of the song, the one by Claudine Longet, former French wife of the balladeer Andy Williams. Then she had been arrested for the murder of her lover, the Olympic skier Spider Sabich. Longet had beguiled the jury and the judge, and spent thirty days' worth of weekends in a plush cell for negligent homicide, a misdemeanor. As far as DeMarco could recall, her singing career had ended with the bullet that went into Sabich's belly. DeMarco had been just a boy at the time, but he could still picture the singer's waifish and fragile beauty, could still hear her whispery voice. She had been one of his first infatuations. Even then, apparently, he had been attracted to murderers.

"Sergeant Ryan?" a deep male voice said.

"Yes. Who am I speaking with?"

"This is Dr. Atwater. I'm the physician on

duty today. Jolynn has passed on your request to me, and I'm sorry to say that our policy prohibits the release of personal information."

"I understand that, Doctor. And I'm sure you realize that if necessary I can obtain a court order and —"

"Sergeant? If I could finish, please."

"Go ahead."

"If I were able to provide such information, and if a patient fitting your description did avail herself of our services on the day specified, it would most likely be the case that our services were limited to an ultrasound and the administration of the prescription drug RU-486 to induce termination of the pregnancy. In which case, the patient would have undergone a miscarriage some time during the next twenty-four hours or so."

"Are you telling me that this was the case with Bonnie?"

"I am telling you that if a patient came here only six weeks into her pregnancy, RU-486 would have been administered. I'm afraid that's all I can tell you."

DeMarco said, "Okay. Thank you, Doctor."

"I'm sorry I can't be more precise."

"I understand. Would you be able to tell

me anything about the man who accompanied her?"

"Not even if I knew anything."

"Okay, well . . . thank you for your cooperation."

DeMarco had hoped that the clinic performed routine tests on all aborted fetuses, and that, in this case, the blood type could be matched to Huston's. Given the commonality of blood types, Huston would not be entirely ruled out or definitively identified as the father, but it was a hunch De-Marco had had to play. Now he was left with only the unsubstantiated certainty that Huston's phrase *the other man* had no relevance to the novel in progress. It applied only to Huston's own certainty that he had not fathered another baby. And there were only two ways to account for that certainty. Either Huston had never had sex with Bonnie, or he was no longer capable of producing children.

"The in-laws," DeMarco said. He grabbed Huston's file off the corner of his desk, slapped it down on the blotter, and started flipping pages until he found the home phone number for the O'Patchens. De-Marco hoped that Rosemary would answer, and she did.

"Would you happen to know," he asked

after his greeting, "if your son-in-law ever had a vasectomy?"

Rosemary's voice remained as flat as the first time he'd heard it. "How is that important now?" she said.

DeMarco cautioned himself to slow down, to take his time with her. She had been delivered a blow from which she would never recover. If for no other reason than that, she deserved whatever patience he could muster. He said, "In your heart of hearts, Rosemary, you don't really believe that Thomas could ever have hurt his family, do you?"

"Ed says I have to accept it. That I need to see things as they are. But I just can't get my head around such an idea. I can't."

"Well, I'm working on a theory that might prove you right."

"You are? What . . . I mean can you tell me what it is?"

"Not just now I can't. I'm sorry. But I will when I can, I promise you that. In the meantime, about the vasectomy . . . ."

She said, "Right from the start they both wanted a boy and a girl. And it worked out exactly the way they'd planned. First Thomas Jr. and then Alyssa."

"But ten years later, along came another one."

"Ever since Alyssa, he'd intended to have a vasectomy. But Claire was on the pill, so . . ."

"It just never happened?"

"They changed their minds. After Alyssa started school, I think it was."

"They changed their minds about . . . ?"

"Only wanting two."

"Ah. And so . . ."

"I think they waited until the seventh month. Seventh or eighth, I'm not sure which. Until they knew that the baby was healthy and everything would be okay. That's when he had it done."

"Are you telling me that Thomas did have a vasectomy?"

"They had a barbecue that night. As stiff and sore as he was afterward, he insisted on making steaks for us. Ed teased him unmercifully."

Her voice was quivering now, growing weak and hoarse.

"Thank you," he told her. "That's exactly what I wanted to hear."

"It is?"

"Yes, it is. And I'm sorry I had to call. I know how painful this is for you."

"Do you?" she said. "How can you really?"

He said, "I lost my own boy when he was just a baby. His name was Ryan too. Ryan

DeMarco Jr."

"Oh my God," she said. "Oh my God."

"So I have a sense, you know, of what you're going through now."

"It's all so terrible," she said. "How did it happen?"

"A car accident."

"Oh no."

"He was in his safety seat and everything. All buckled in. But even so."

"Oh my good Lord, Ryan. And your wife? Was she hurt?"

"Not visibly. But she left me not long afterward."

"It's all just too much," she said, sobbing now. He could feel her shoulders shaking, could feel the heavy, black ache in her chest. His left eye started to water. He put a finger to the moisture and dragged it away.

"I'm sorry," he told her. "I didn't mean to add to your troubles. I just wanted you to know that . . . I do understand how you're feeling right now. I really do."

"It never leaves you, does it?" she said. "Ed keeps telling me it will get better, but I know it won't. We can expect to feel like this for the rest of our lives, can't we, Ryan?"

What should I tell her? he wondered. He searched his mind for the right words, but his mind was a blank, empty of everything

365

except the heart-emptying truth. "I suspect we can," he said.

"Okay," DeMarco asked himself, "what do you know?"

He stood in front of the whiteboard in his office, black marker in hand. Under Bonnie's name he wrote *abortion.* Under Thomas Huston, *vasectomy.* "So Thomas took her to Cleveland for the abortion," DeMarco said. "He probably even paid for the abortion, but it wasn't his baby. He knew it wasn't his baby. So why the fuck would he do it?"

He wrote *The other man?* and underlined it twice.

DeMarco was still staring at the whiteboard when Trooper Morgan appeared in his doorway. "You better have what I need," DeMarco told him and snatched the packet of printouts from the trooper's hand. On each page was a photocopy of a driver's license, owners of the vehicles parked at Whispers the previous night. One was registered to Bonnie, four to dancers, and four more to men who bore no resemblance to Tex, the bouncer.

"That's it?" DeMarco said. "This is all of them?"

"All but your car and mine."

"And these four guys?"

"No priors for any of them. I checked with Carmichael and he confirmed that these were the four customers inside with us that night."

DeMarco shoved the papers against Morgan's chest. "I told you to get what I need. This isn't what I fucking need."

The trooper remained calm. "What do you want me to do?"

"Go away and let me think."

Morgan turned toward the door. Then DeMarco said, "Wait a minute. Get a car and meet me out front."

"Squad car?"

"Fuck no."

Alone again in his office, DeMarco studied the board. "So no car for Moby. No car for Tex. Moby, I know . . ." he said, then stepped within a foot of the board, stared so hard at the other name that the letters blurred, "but who the fuck are you? And who gave you a ride to Whispers?"

FORTY-SIX

Bonnie Marie Harris's home was a small brick ranch in a seventies subdivision in the town of Linesville, twelve miles east of Whispers. DeMarco, dressed in the wrinkled chinos and OSU sweatshirt he kept in his office, scanned the windows.

Morgan had parked the undercover car on the opposite side of the street. "Looks like nobody's home," he said.

"Unless she's sleeping." DeMarco reached for his cell phone. "Where's that number?"

Morgan handed him the notepad.

"You're sure this is the landline?" De-Marco asked.

"I'm sure."

DeMarco punched in the digits. The number rang four times, then went to Bonnie's voice mail.

"Just what I thought," Morgan said.

"Tell you what," DeMarco said and popped open the passenger door. "Stop thinking. Just sit here and keep your eyes open."

DeMarco crossed briskly to the front door and rang the bell. The sound echoed throughout the house. He cupped his hands to his eyes and peered inside through one of the glass panels alongside the door. The foyer was small and empty and dark. No lights on anywhere in the house as far as he could determine. He tried the door. Locked. A bronze Schlage lock, matching the Schlage dead bolt three inches above it.

Without looking over his shoulder to see how many busybodies might be peeking out from behind their curtains, he strode across the front of the house as if he knew where he was going. He knew enough to know that the back door would be in the back. Ten seconds later, he found it more or less where he'd expected it to be. It opened onto a small wooden deck, empty but for a single inexpensive patio chair — no patio grill, no garden hose, no wind chimes or hummingbird feeder. The outer aluminum door was unlocked; the wooden door with three diamond inserts of glass at eye level was not. He peered into the kitchen. An Amana refrigerator, gas stove, the corner of a small breakfast table. By all appearances, uncluttered and clean. He raised a fist to the door and rapped five times.

The house remained silent. He lowered his gaze. No dead bolt. He considered his options. The rear decks of two other houses had views of this back door, but was anybody watching? The entire neighborhood was quiet, the kind of bedroom community that had once been fashionable but was now home to high school teachers and small-business owners and factory workers, middle-aged, middle-class, and struggling first-time homeowners. He hoped that everybody was too busy making a living to pay any attention to the man leaning close to Bonnie's back door, the man using his body to conceal the credit card he was sliding along the doorjamb.

A minute later, he was inside with the door closed behind him. He stood motionless in the corner beside the door and listened for the sounds of movement. The refrigerator hummed. The wall clock ticked.

Walking heel to toe, he crossed the kitchen to stand on the threshold of a long, narrow living room. He stepped just inside, grateful for the ugly shag carpeting, a pale, lifeless green. The living room opened onto a short hallway, and he kept his eye on that dark corridor as he crossed toward it. He told himself that if Bonnie was in the house, she would be in a bedroom. He could only hope that no one else was in there with her.

There were three bedrooms in all: one completely empty, another with nothing but a bare futon on the floor, the other fully furnished with a suite of heavy pieces — mission style, a fumed oak dresser and chest of drawers, two nightstands, and an unmade bed. A dozen clothes hangers lay scattered on the floor, the closet door standing open.

He turned on the bedroom light. Indentations in both pillows. The closet half-empty, another tangle of hangers on the floor. The room smelled of cigarette smoke. Was Bonnie a smoker? Huston, he felt certain, was not. And if that was not the indentation of Huston's head on the second pillow, whose was it? He shut off the light and returned to the living room.

On the coffee table in front of the sofa were two empty beer bottles. Bud Light. To the left of the farthest bottle, a saucer with three cigarette butts in it. "Possibilities," DeMarco said. "Bonnie smokes, Huston doesn't. Or some other man doesn't. Or some other man does and Bonnie doesn't." He could detect no lipstick on the filters.

After he returned to the car, DeMarco telephoned his station commander. "I'm going to need a search warrant ASAP," he said, "and as soon as you get it, send a team from the nearest barracks over here to collect the prints. Somebody was with her when she bugged out. They left a couple beer bottles and a plateful of cigarette butts behind in the living room."

"And just how do you know this?" Bowen asked.

"I peeked in the fucking window. How do you think I know?"

"So the curtains are open?"

DeMarco looked toward the plate-glass window with its tightly drawn curtains. "Could I see inside if they weren't? And while you're at it, get a search warrant for Whispers too."

"And how do I justify all this?"

"She spent the night with Huston two Thursdays ago. Plus she lied to me about it. Plus she's smart enough to know that it wouldn't take long for me to figure out that she lied. So now Huston is nowhere to be found, his family is dead, and she bugged out of here probably a few hours ago with most of her clothes."

"How do you know she didn't just take them to the dry cleaner?"

"How would you like having to pick up your own fucking spinach rolls from now on?"

When the call ended, Trooper Morgan asked, "Where to now?"

DeMarco patted his breast pocket. "I think I dropped my pen when I was out back."

"There are two or three in the glove compartment. Help yourself."

"This was a special pen. Give me a minute."

DeMarco climbed out and walked quickly to the back door. Inside again a few moments later, he made his way to the front window. With a hand on the drawcord, he pulled the curtain aside just enough to peek out. Morgan was examining his teeth in the rearview mirror. DeMarco drew the curtains open by a couple of inches, then hurried back outside and to the car.

"You find it?" Morgan asked.

"Nah, it's gone. Let's go."

"I can help you look for it."

"Forget it," DeMarco said and pulled his seat belt tight.

"But if it's special to you . . ."

"It's a fucking pen," DeMarco told him.

Morgan started the car. "Do you realize you've been swearing a lot lately? A lot more than you usually do."

"I'm sorry," DeMarco told him. "Really. I am just overcome with fucking regret."

FORTY-SEVEN

The haze around the moon seemed to suggest a softening at day's end, but DeMarco felt only the approaching chill of night. The time was not yet six p.m., but the sun was low and weak on the western horizon, the gibbous moon rising pale and clouded on the other side of the sky.

DeMarco sat on the top of three steps off his back porch, feet on the pad of interconnecting bricks he had started to lay nearly a decade earlier. He had removed the sod, excavated, and leveled the path from his porch to the side door of the garage some sixty feet away, but had laid only the first three sections of the pathway before everything was interrupted. The bricks were arranged in a herringbone pattern and ended nine feet from the porch step. He had started the pathway so Laraine would be able to walk from the garage to the house without having to step through the puddles that accumulated in the backyard after heavy rains. Now when it rained, the last fifty feet of the trench filled with muddy water, temporarily submerging the weeds that sprouted from the packed earth. Now he parked on the street and only occasionally unlocked the garage to drag out the mower. Old, split bags of grass seed and mulch and potting soil still sat in the dark corners, the clay pots Laraine had used to start her herb garden every spring, filmy plastic bags filled with dried-up gladiola and tulip bulbs.

DeMarco was weary of the unfinished path and overgrown yard, of the nubilous moon and the lowering sun. He tried to remember the energy and exuberance for life he had felt during those long ago days when he had started the brick path and the room above the garage. But it was like trying to remember a decade-old dream. The nostalgia was there, the sense of loss, but little else remained.

He dipped the edge of a whole-wheat bolillo roll into a plastic pint container filled with kalamata and other olives, sun-dried tomatoes and roasted garlic gloves, but the pleasant slipperiness of the garlicky oil registered on his tongue only distantly, it too like little more than a memory of something once savored. The cold beer in its brown, beaded bottle satisfied only in the slight burn as it went down his throat.

He had been waiting all day for the results from the search of Bonnie's house. He knew that pubic hair from two individuals had been recovered from the bedsheet, and that a few tiny splatters of somebody's blood had been recovered from the lavatory faucet. But it would be several days before the DNA tests were finished. Even then, they would tell him nothing until he had other DNA samples for comparison. In particular, he wanted to know whose fingerprints were on the second beer bottle on Bonnie's coffee table. They would belong, he knew, to whatever man was with Bonnie now. He did not want to believe that Huston was that man, could not conceive of a single valid reason why Huston would make such a choice, but he also knew enough of human behavior to know that logic seldom applied when an ample supply of testosterone was stirred into the mix.

Unfortunately, Trooper Carmichael had not yet been able to run the prints through the national fingerprinting database. Computers were down somewhere. Meanwhile, another forensics team was searching Whispers. DeMarco had nothing to do but sit and wait. Bowen had ordered him to go home and get some rest — "And get something to eat, for Chrissakes" — a couple hours of enforced downtime.

DeMarco sucked on a kalamata olive, then spit the pit into the grass. *Maybe an olive tree will grow,* he thought. *The tree of life. Maybe he would plant an apple tree beside it. The tree of knowledge.* "My own fucking Garden of Eden," he said.

The muted jangle of his cell phone startled him. He yanked the phone from his hip pocket and put it to his ear without looking at the caller ID. "It's about fucking time," he said.

"Excuse me?" the male voice said. "Is this Sergeant DeMarco?"

"I'm sorry. I was expecting another call. Is this Nathan?"

"Yes, sir, it is. I, uh . . . I just got home a couple of minutes ago and I found this disturbing message on my answering machine. I thought you should know about it."

"Disturbing how?"

"It's from Thomas."

DeMarco sat up very straight. "And?"

"It came in at 4:19 p.m. I've been away from my apartment all day and —"

"What did he say, Nathan?"

"Hold on a minute. I'll play it for you."

A button clicked. Nathan's recorded greeting. A beep. Then the voice of Thomas Huston, hoarse and slow, chilling in the flatness of its delivery:

"It was many and many a year ago,
In a kingdom by the sea,
That a maiden there lived whom you may
    know
By the name of Annabel Lee;
And this maiden she lived with no other
    thought
Than to love and be loved by me.

"I was a child and she was a child,
In this kingdom by the sea:
But we loved with a love that was more
    than love —
I and my Annabel Lee —
With a love that the winged seraphs of
    Heaven
Coveted her and me.

"And this was the reason that, long ago,
In this kingdom by the sea,
A wind blew out of a cloud, chilling
My beautiful Annabel Lee;
So that her highborn kinsmen came
And bore her away from me,
To shut her up in a sepulchre

In this kingdom by the sea.

"The angels, not half so happy in Heaven,
Went envying her and me —
Yes! — that was the reason (as all men
    know,
In this kingdom by the sea)
That the wind came out of the cloud by
    night,
Chilling and killing my Annabel Lee.

"But our love it was stronger by far than the
    love
Of those who were older than we —
Of many far wiser than we —
And neither the angels in Heaven above,
Nor the demons down under the sea,
Can ever dissever my soul from the soul
Of the beautiful Annabel Lee:

"For the moon never beams, without
    bringing me dreams
Of the beautiful Annabel Lee;
And the stars never rise, but I feel the
    bright eyes
Of the beautiful Annabel Lee;
And so, with the night-tide, I'll lie down by
    the side
Of my darling — my darling — my life and
    my bride,

In her sepulchre there by the sea —
In her tomb by the sounding sea."

This recitation was followed by several seconds of silence, then the beep that ended the recording. Then Nathan said, "Did you hear it okay?"

"He was reciting a poem, right?"

"Poe's 'Annabel Lee.' It's the last poem Poe ever composed."

"I got the Annabel Lee part," DeMarco said, "but why would he do that? Why would Thomas call you just to recite a poem?"

"I'm trying to figure that out myself. I think there's a message in it."

DeMarco pushed himself to his feet. He stared at the hazy moon. "Go on," he said.

"We can assume, I think, that Annabel Lee refers to his wife, Claire."

"I thought you said that the dancer from the club was part of his Annabel?"

"Well, yes, for the novel he was writing. But if you listen to the other lines of description, Claire is a better fit here. I mean they married young and she died too young. So that seems obvious. And they both grew up in the area, not by a sea but by Lake Erie, which, from certain rocky points, can look as vast as a sea. So that makes the first stanza fairly straightforward and autobiographical from Thomas's point of view."

"Okay, I'll buy that. Keep going."

"Of course, all of the poem can't be autobiographical because Tom didn't write it. But there are some lines that especially apply. The lines about the angels killing her because she was so beautiful — I don't know if he meant those to apply or not. I mean Claire is gone, obviously, and I'm sure he's grieving her. Maybe it's no more than that, that he's using the poem to express his own grief. But here's the part that's giving me chills, it's four lines from the bottom. On the tape, Tom's voice slows down and he's sobbing. I mean, he sounds like he's choking on his grief . . . And he says, 'And so, with the night-tide, I'll lie down by the side of my darling — my darling — my life and my bride . . .'"

"And that means something to you, Nathan?"

"It's not the way Poe wrote it. Not exactly the same words."

"How is it different?"

"Poe wrote, 'And so, *all* the night-tide, I lie down by the side of my darling,' and so forth."

"And Thomas's version again?"

" 'And so, *with* the night-tide, *I'll lie down* by the side of my darling.' "

For a few moments DeMarco considered the implications. "What are the chances that he just got it wrong? That he remembered it wrong?"

Nathan said, "Not a chance. I've heard him recite it in class. He knows dozens of Poe's poems by heart. 'The Raven,' 'Lenore,' 'The Lake,' 'To Annie' . . . dozens of them. Sometimes I think he fucking *channels* Poe."

DeMarco said nothing. Slowly, his head turned from east to west, his gaze scanning the empty sky. On the far horizon the fallen sun had left a wide, irregular band of color, a graduated blending of rose, scarlet, and deep plum muted behind a haze of cloud. It reminded him of blood soaking through a bandage.

"Sergeant?" Nathan said. "Do you think it means what I think it means?"

DeMarco told him, "I'm afraid it might."

The young man began to sob. "He called to tell me he's going to kill himself. Tonight. That's why he called me, isn't it?"

"There were no other messages?" De-Marco asked. "Did I hear everything?"

"Just the poem, nothing else. Not even good-bye. Christ, can't you guys do something to trace it? Plug into my phone records or something and find out where the call came from?"

"We'll try, of course, but . . . I'm just not sure what good it will do. He's not carrying his cell phone — we found that at the house — so he's probably long gone from wherever he made the call."

The sobbing became more desperate. "So it's too late to stop him, isn't it? Because I wasn't here. If I had been here a couple of hours ago —"

"Listen, he reached out. That's important. Maybe he'll do it again. So you just sit by your phone, okay? Can you do that for me?"

"Of course I will."

"Okay, I'm going to get to work on this. But you call me the instant you hear a word from him. The instant. You understand?"

"I will. I swear to God I will."

FORTY-EIGHT

DeMarco hurried back inside his house, left his beer and olives on the back porch, grabbed his car keys, and headed for the front door. He had his car in sight when the officer on duty at the barracks answered his call. He gave the officer Nathan Briessen's phone number and the time of Huston's call. "The second you get the address, get back to me with it."

A minute later, he started the engine and sat in the idling vehicle, anxiously tapping his thumb against the steering wheel. He needed movement, but which way to go? He had no idea where Huston might be. He had last been seen near Lake Wilhelm, so DeMarco eased away from the curb and headed for Interstate 79. He wanted to flatten the accelerator to the floor but kept the speedometer needle at forty. He did not want to go too far in the wrong direction and have to reverse himself.

Just over fourteen minutes later, his cell phone jangled. "The call was placed from a public phone at the Qwik Stop convenience store in Conneaut, Ohio."

"Ohio? Shit." Then, "Wait a minute. Conneaut is straight up seven, due north of Pierpont, am I right? I'm coming up on seven now."

"Yes, sir."

"He *did* go to Whispers."

"Sir?"

"I need a street address."

"The store is along Route 198 on the west end of town. Corner of Franklin Avenue."

DeMarco swung his car onto the entrance ramp. Conneaut was a full hour away. The speedometer reached seventy and kept climbing. "Okay, alert the Conneaut Police Department to send a car to the store. Huston's probably long gone by now, but he might still be hanging around somewhere. And no fucking sirens or he'll head for the woods again. And get the Ohio boys from the nearest barracks in the vicinity too. Have them checking out any abandoned buildings, warehouses, anyplace he might have holed up for the night. And I'm going to be flying low, so inform any of our guys who might be on traffic control on the

interstate. I'm driving a light-brown Bonneville."

"Ten-four, Sergeant."

"Anything yet from the search of the strip
club?"

"I'll check on that and get back to you,
sir."

DeMarco hung up the radio, grabbed his
dash light off the passenger seat, stuck it on
the dashboard, and turned it on. The strobing light pulsed through the gloaming,
punching softly into the gathering dark.

A local black-and-white was parked along
the side of the convenience store lot, parking lights on, a young officer behind the
wheel, a paper cup of coffee on the dash.
DeMarco spotted the car while he waited
for the light to change so he could turn into
the lot. He had turned off his dash light
upon entering town and stowed it on the
floor, but here was a townie in plain view,
as conspicuous as a one-ton, glowing wart.
DeMarco knew that if Huston had been
lingering anywhere near the store, he was
long gone by now.

DeMarco backed his vehicle into a space
facing the street, climbed out, and crossed
to the police car. The young officer behind
the wheel rolled down his window, and De-

Marco showed him his ID.

"The clerk never saw your man," the officer said. "Phone is there on the outside of the building. Probably the only pay phone left in town."

"Huston didn't go inside to get change for the phone?"

"Clerk says no. Says he never saw the guy."

"So Huston was either carrying a few dollars in change or he bought a phone card somewhere."

The officer nodded and reached for his coffee. "Every gas station and grocery store sells them. We could ask around, I suppose."

"Doesn't matter where he bought it," De-Marco told him. "He's not there now. Not here either."

"What would bring him up this way anyway?"

DeMarco gazed out past the gas pumps. The lights threw a cold white illumination onto the concrete. A teenage girl was pumping gas into her Toyota, laughing loudly into a cell phone.

"I was surprised to even see a pay phone here," the officer said. "They're like relics."

DeMarco watched the girl awhile longer. She was very pretty — long brown hair, long legs, and a thin, well-defined profile. He wondered if she was the kind of girl his son would have been attracted to. Ryan would still be just a boy, more or less the same age as Huston's oldest son, but old enough to be sneaking glances at every girl who passed by, old enough to be wondering what it would be like to hold her and touch her, what it would be like to be wanted and loved.

When the girl climbed into her car, De-Marco took a step away from the officer's. "You pulling second shift tonight?" he asked.

"Overtime," the young man said. "Just waiting for you actually. We've only got a three-man force here."

"Well, thanks for hanging around." He glanced at the officer's left hand. "I guess I kept you from your dinner, right?"

The officer shrugged. "Wouldn't be the first time I had to eat cold meatloaf."

"Give your wife my apologies."

"No problem. Comes with the territory."

DeMarco leaned down to look at him. "Nah, really, tell her I'm sorry. Tell her you're sorry too. Tell her how much you missed her. How much you love her meat-loaf."

"Okay," the officer said and smiled crookedly.

"It's important," DeMarco told him.

"Don't wait till you're my age to learn that."

But he recognized that look in the young man's eyes, the smile that was almost a smirk. *Okay, pops,* the look said. *Whatever you say.*

The look lingered with him even after the officer was gone, as DeMarco sat in his own vehicle again, watching past the gas pumps as car after car moved through the intersection, the light changing ceaselessly from red to green to yellow to red. He knew he was accomplishing nothing by remaining there, that Huston could be miles away by now. He was out by the lake somewhere, somewhere along those miles of ragged coast. Maybe already with his Claire. With his family again, if that kind of thing were possible. DeMarco had no idea what was possible and what wasn't. He was only sure that in this lifetime, at least, he never would know.

The Ohio troopers knew the area, and they were out there patrolling it, cruising the back roads, looking for a campfire in the woods. Huston would need a fire tonight to keep him warm. If, indeed, he had any intention of lasting through the night, which DeMarco doubted. The troopers had DeMarco's phone number and were supposed to call him if they spotted anything. A light in an abandoned building. A solitary pedestrian. A body in the water.

DeMarco kept his window rolled down despite the chill. He liked the vague scent of water in the air, the damp scent of night. He thought it might be nice to live up there, so close to the water. It might be nice to have a boat that he could motor out a mile or so and shut off the engine and listen to nothing but the water, feel nothing but the movement and the low lap of waves.

He laid his head back against the headrest and turned his face to the open window and closed his eyes. Christ, he was tired. Now that he admitted it, he could feel the heaviness in every limb. His neck and shoulders ached, his spine felt stiff. The air smelled of concrete and water.

When the phone rang in the distance, he thought he was at home and tried to push himself up out of his chair. He rammed his chest into the steering wheel and that brought him awake. Now he thought the ringing was coming from the public phone mounted on the corner of the building, so he threw open the door and stood and only then felt the vibration in his pocket. But by the time he had his cell phone out, the call had gone to his voice mail. The number looked familiar, but he could not remember whose it was. He immediately tried to call it, but it went straight to voice mail without ringing, and when he heard the greeting of "Hi, guys, this is Danni," he hung up and waited for the beep that would tell him that Danni had completed her message to him and hung up. He did not bother then to listen to her message but called her back. She answered on the first ring.

"He just called me!" she said. "Just three minutes ago, he called me."

"Thomas Huston called you?"

"Yes. Didn't you listen to my message?"

"No, I didn't want to wait. What did he say?"

"The first thing he did was to ask if I like poetry. Then he recited a poem for me."

" 'Annabel Lee' again," he said.

"What?"

"The name of the poem he recited. 'Annabel Lee.' "

"No, he said it was called 'The Lake.' And that's what it was about. The loneliness of the lake."

"Danni, listen. Was it about anything else, anything having to do with death?"

"I think so," she said. "There was something about a grave in it."

"Do you have a computer?"

"Yes."

"Can you go to it now? While I have you on the line?"

"Sure, it's right here."

"Okay, go online and see if you can find a copy of 'The Lake' somewhere."

"I don't even know who wrote it," she said.

"Try Poe. Edgar Allan Poe."

"Okay, give me a minute."

DeMarco walked from one side of the parking lot to the other. He returned to his car, stood there a moment, then started walking again.

"Okay, I have it," she said.

"Read it to me."

She did so.

"That last part," he said. "Starting with the word *death*. Read that part again for me."

This time she read more slowly. " 'Death was in that poison'd wave,/And in its gulf a fitting grave/For him who thence could solace bring/To his lone imagining/Whose solitary soul could make/An Eden of that dim lake.' "

When she finished, he told her, "Thank you, Danni. Now tell me anything else he said."

"What does it mean?" she asked.

"It means he hasn't killed himself yet, not

as of four minutes ago anyway. So I need you to please just think hard and answer my questions now, okay? Did he say anything else or did he just recite the poem?"

"Yes, he said, uh . . . he said something about seeing the whole way across the lake. About being able to see the lights in Canada."

"He said he could see them from where he was?"

"No, he said he'd be looking at them in a few minutes. He said there were no stars out tonight because of the clouds but he was near a place where he could . . . how did he put it . . . 'ascend to the heavens' I think. That was it. He said he could ascend to the heavens and from there look down on the lights in Canada as if they were stars. So that he would have to come down to them to get to heaven. It just made no sense to me, and the way he sounded, his voice was so low and tired or something. It's hard to explain."

"You did fine," he told her. "You did wonderfully. I have to hang up now, but if he calls back, you try to find out exactly where he is, okay? And then you call me immediately."

"I will," she said.

He hit the End button, then brought up

his call log for the telephone company's number. Then he realized that it would take several minutes to get the necessary information from them, so instead, he pocketed the phone and hurried into the convenience store. In addition to the middle-aged female clerk behind the counter, there was a thirty-something male standing at the dairy cooler, half a gallon of chocolate milk dangling from his hand while he studied the display of Ben and Jerry's pints, and a teenage couple loading up on chips and Slim Jims.

"Could I have your attention please?" he said loudly and held his ID above his head. "My name is Sergeant Ryan DeMarco of the Pennsylvania State Police and I need your assistance. I am looking for a place, probably within a couple of miles of here, where it would be possible to see across Lake Erie to the lights of Canada. Can anybody think of *any*place like that?"

The man at the dairy cooler said, "That's like forty miles across."

The clerk said, "You can see lights from that far, I think."

The man with the milk came toward the front. "No, because of the curvature of the earth. It would be like trying to look over the horizon."

DeMarco said, "A high place. Somewhere

a person would have to climb. A hill, a tower, something like that."

The clerk said, "There's a cell phone tower just a mile or so up the road toward North Springfield."

"The lighthouse," the teenage girl called out.

"What lighthouse, miss?"

The man said, "Would that be high enough?"

"Miss?" DeMarco said again. "What light-house?"

To her boyfriend she said, "You tell him."

"Just out at the point," the boy said.

"Tell me exactly where."

The man said, "I don't think it's high enough. Besides, it's all fenced off. I don't think you can even get to it anymore."

DeMarco crossed to the teenage couple. He looked directly at the boy. "This is extremely important," he said.

The boy said, "It's high enough. And you can get to it. You just can't take your car up to it because the road is blocked off. And you have to climb over a chain-link fence."

DeMarco said, "Tell me how to get there."

"Just take 531 east until it swings south. There's a dirt road there that veers off to the left, straight toward Perry Point. But you can only drive about twenty yards, then there's these three metal poles you can't get past. The old lighthouse is another couple hundred yards up that road. Behind an eight-foot fence."

"And you're sure you can see the lights from there?"

The boy said nothing for a moment. Then, "I, uh . . . that's what I heard anyway. I mean there's No Trespassing signs all over the place so . . ."

DeMarco looked at the girl. She smiled and said, "We're sure."

FORTY-NINE

His headlights blinked out behind him when DeMarco was thirty feet or so beyond the three metal security posts. He stood in the middle of the lane in sudden darkness. Low trees and sumac and a heavy tangled wall of fox grape vines on both sides of the lane blended with the now-black sky. He felt enclosed in a long, narrow closet, and because all directions were now uniformly black, he felt a dizziness swoop into him, and he lurched a step to his left before catching himself, standing still with his legs spread wide. He knew that it was only an illusion that he was falling — he had both feet on the ground; the earth was still flat beneath him. He could hear his engine ticking as it released its heat, as hot oil flowed back into the oil pan, as hot metal cooled and contracted.

He felt an urgency, yet knew that it would do neither him nor Huston any good if he went rushing headlong into the bushes. The lane was still there. It had not disappeared from existence just because his headlights went out. His eyes would adjust. *A step at a time,* he told himself.

He was carrying his flashlight but decided not to use it here. It would have cast a powerful beam, enough to illuminate the path for two hundred feet ahead. But if Huston was indeed up ahead somewhere, and DeMarco felt certain he was, he would see the light coming toward him, jerking back and forth, and some vague premonition told DeMarco that the only productive approach would be a cautious one, that he needed to move in on Huston as carefully, as reverently, as one might approach a wounded animal that had crawled into the brush to die.

He thought for a moment about taking out his cell phone and using its dull blue glow to illuminate his path, but he did not want to chance even that. His eyes would adjust. He was moving north toward the lake, and in all likelihood, Huston was facing north, if indeed he was not already facedown on the boulder-strewn shore. But an anomalous blue light bobbing up the lane might still catch Huston's attention, might force a tragic decision that had not yet been implemented. Most suicides, De-Marco knew, were anything but sudden. Most victims sat a long time with the gun in their lap, the razor pressed between finger and thumb. It took a long time to summon the courage or despair sufficient for the next step.

DeMarco drew hope from the fact that Huston had reached out twice. Unfortunately, the first call had been answered by a machine. Nathan would have had the pre-science and empathy necessary to intuit Huston's motives and might have swayed the man's resolve somehow, might have pulled him in. Danni, however, was very young — too young to know the depth of Huston's sorrow. Too far away, in a sense, to extend a hand into the chasm of Huston's grief.

DeMarco wondered why Huston had chosen Danni and Nathan to contact. A stripper and a student. Did the man have no friends, no trusted confidante? At first, DeMarco thought this very strange. Then he asked himself, *Do you?*

DeMarco knew that his only choice was to proceed cautiously under the assumption that the implication of Poe's poetry had not yet been fulfilled. His own arm was long enough to reach into any chasm. No chasm was deeper than the one gouged out by the loss of a child.

Ten minutes later, having stepped off the lane several times before pulling himself back toward its center, and having felt his trajectory making a slow turn toward the north, he now saw the blackness shift ahead of him, saw it open up into a lighter shade of blackness. His eyes were adjusting now, cones and rods taking in more light. Ahead, at a distance impossible to calculate, maybe forty feet and maybe forty miles, was a charcoal wall. Vague silhouettes darkened it here and there, but the only one that interested DeMarco was the one that rose like an obelisk, like a lighthouse without a light, an obsolete beacon of hope.

He could smell and hear the lake now. The scent of wet earth, so too like the scent of sex. A soft rumble. Water lapping against rounded stones. Soft darkness washing against a harder darkness, sighs against groans, tears against grief.

He did not see the security fence as much as he sensed it, so black had the night become. No moon or stars, an absolute occlusion of sky. Something told him to put out his hand as he walked, and soon he felt the coldness of wire emanating toward him, so unlike the chill of a living night. He slowed his approach but kept moving and, a few seconds later, touched the fence, the mesh of thick wire against a palm.

The boy had said that the fence had to be climbed. He had not said whether the top was laced with spikes or barbed wire or some other deterrent. DeMarco gazed upward but saw only more darkness.

The fence rattled softly when DeMarco pushed himself against it and pulled himself off the ground. He held himself there, letting the noise dissolve away, until his fingers ached. The boy had said "an eight-foot fence." DeMarco was two inches short of six feet tall and had pulled himself a foot and half off the ground. So the top of the fence should be only a few inches above his head. Spikes or a coil of razor wire would be a foot higher.

He slid his left hand up the wire. A rounded bar looped with chain-link wire. Emptiness above. And DeMarco thought, *Thank God for small favors.*

Every inch of his ascent produced another creak or rattle from the fence, another wince from DeMarco. He wondered if Huston could hear the sounds.

From his perspective at the top of the fence, with the rounded bar painfully hard against his crotch, the lighthouse seemed to stand out in sharper relief now, a silent shell. DeMarco balanced himself, felt the quickness of his heart, the ache in his shoulders. Then he slid his leg over the top rail as quietly as he could, achingly eased his body perpendicular to the ground, and hung there by his fingertips. The ground, he knew, could be no more than five inches below his feet. Unless the fence was erected along a cliff face. But that would mean that the lighthouse sat perched in midair.

He held on a few seconds longer, told himself to stop being so foolish, then uncurled his fingers and let himself drop. Logic promised that the ground was there but it still came as a surprise to him. He felt the jolt in his knees and hips. Stood with his face to the fence for a few moments to catch his breath. Then turned and walked as surely and quickly as he could toward the lighthouse.

The door at the bottom of the tower stood open. Maybe Huston had opened it, maybe it had been knocked open long ago. DeMarco took one step inside. The air smelled of closure, dampness, and mold. Now he pulled his cell phone from his pocket and flipped it open. Shone the blue light around the small, circular room. Graffiti scrawled on the naked stuccoed walls. A littering of trash, beer cans and bottles, wine bottles, cigarette butts, and food wrappers. An old woolen blanket, green and filthy and twisted into a stiff tangle. And in the far corner, a metal staircase corkscrewing toward the top.

DeMarco turned the ringer and vibrator off on his cell phone. Then pocketed the phone. Laid his left hand on the rusty rail of the staircase and began a slow ascent. Without the cell phone, he was in total blackness again. He tested each stair with his foot before settling his weight atop it. Kept waiting for the missing stair that would send him tumbling to the ground.

■ ■ ■ ■

DISCERNMENT

■ ■ ■ ■

FIFTY

DeMarco felt the stairwell walls tightening around him but gradually detected a freshening of the air. All the lenses and mirrors would have been removed long ago when the lighthouse was decommissioned, and by now, vandals would have stripped the upper platform bare and smashed out all the windows. He could feel the coolness on his face now, the damp tickle of moist breeze.

His hand slid onto a downward curve in the stair rail and there was nothing beyond it. He leaned forward and felt in the darkness with his right hand, touched the rough planking of the upper platform. He was three steps from the top. He asked himself which way was north. Turning his head slowly, he felt for the touch of breeze on his face. Found it, rose another step higher.

The lake splashed against the rocks below. Far out in the lower darkness, a long broken string of dim lights glowed, a scattering of dull pearls. And between the center and the left end of that broken necklace, a shadow. A man standing with his back to DeMarco. A man leaning hard against the rail. De-Marco could hear the man's breath, ragged and quick inhalations. The man's shadow was as black as grief.

DeMarco searched his mind for the right words. A phrase that might pin the shadow to the rail instead of sending it leaping forward. For a few moments, he could think of nothing. His mind was a swirl of black-ness. Then it came to him, and he said it without hesitation and tried to blend the whisper of his voice to the lake's.

" 'It was many and many a year ago, in a kingdom by the sea . . .' "

An abrupt turn from the shadow. A dam-ming back of breath. Both men stood mo-tionless. Huston's voice when he finally spoke was a barely audible rasp, a serrated breath drifting out toward the water. " 'That a maiden there lived whom you may know . . . by the name of Annabel Lee.' "

DeMarco said, "I'm sorry, Thomas. I can't remember any more of it. I wish I could."

Huston spoke without moving. "Ryan De-Marco," he said.

"I've been trying all week to find you, my friend."

Huston said nothing. DeMarco could not see his face, but he felt the man's brokenness, the pain that comes from knowing that what is broken can never be made whole. DeMarco smelled dread in the air blowing in across the lake. He smelled grief and sorrow and despair. He felt the chill of the darkness and he felt the loneliness of the rocks on the battered shore below. And suddenly he was very tired again. He did not want to have to do anything else tonight. He eased himself down on the edge of the landing and leaned back against the wall. "I am so fucking tired," he said.

It was a while before Huston spoke again. His voice was muted and reached DeMarco as if from another room, a whispering through thin walls. "I came up here to jump," he said.

DeMarco told him, "I know you did."

"Claire and the kids and I came here once. Long, long time ago. Before Davy was born. Tommy was only six, I think. I had to hold Alyssa the whole time, she wouldn't let me put her down."

"You must have a lot of fine memories. I envy you that."

What DeMarco wanted was to stand and

join Huston at the rail. He wanted to see the lights across the lake. He wanted to see through the long miles of darkness. He said, "How did you get here, Thomas? You're a long way from home."

Huston did not answer, and after a while, DeMarco told himself, *You're going to have to get up now. You're going to have to try to go to him before he climbs over that rail.* But before he could make himself move, Huston spoke, and DeMarco decided to stay where he was for a while longer.

Huston said, " 'I was a child and she was a child, in this kingdom by the sea. But we loved with a love that was more than love . . .' "

DeMarco supplied the finish. "Just you and your Annabel Lee."

A few seconds later, Huston said, "Writers."

"What about them, Thomas?"

"We're all such romantics."

"I'm not sure I know what you mean by that."

"We love our misery. Until it gets to be too much to bear."

DeMarco sat very still and thought about that for a while. He was sitting with his head against the rounded wall and he had to fight the urge to close his eyes. His eyes were heavy with exhaustion and the left eye was watering profusely in the chilly air. The line of moisture down his cheek was cold on his skin, but the scar at the corner of his eye stung and throbbed with his pulse. He thought it remarkable all the things he could feel when he sat motionless in the darkness without a drink in his hand, all the things he could smell and taste and hear and remember. He did not understand what he was feeling for Huston at that moment — it seemed a peculiar emotion to feel for another man. He wondered how long he might have to sit motionless in darkness before he could understand such a thing.

After a while, he thought about Nathan and Danni sitting by their phones, waiting for Thomas to call again. He thought about the calls he was expecting. As quietly as he could, he eased the cell phone from his pocket. He held it below the top step so that its light would not startle Huston. Then he depressed the button and saw that he had two voice messages. He tapped the Select button and raised the phone to his ear.

The first message was from a sergeant from the Erie barracks. His men's search of Whispers had turned up nothing that might help DeMarco track down Bonnie. The upper floor was an unfinished attic space, bare but for an overflowing ashtray, a cardboard box full of empty beer bottles and fast food wrappers, and a faux leather swivel chair set between two one-way mirrors, one looking down into the barroom, the other into the stage room. "It's a pretty standard security setup," the sergeant said. "Places like this are usually run on the cheap. Anyway, we took in all the bottles and other items. Get back to me when you can and let me know if you want any of it sent to the lab or not."

The second voice message was from Trooper Morgan. He said the reports had come back on the beer bottles from Bonnie's apartment. The second set of prints had matched those of an individual in the NCIC database, a man named Inman, a name DeMarco recognized. Trooper Morgan wanted to know if a BOLO alert should be issued for the man as "a person of interest." DeMarco typed a quick text to Trooper Morgan. *BOLO immediately.*

DeMarco quietly laid the phone facedown on the step. He let out a long slow breath.

"Thomas," he said, and was a little surprised by the plaintiveness in his voice, "can you tell me what happened that night?"

FIFTY-ONE

After the dinner of Cornish game hens, after Thomas and Claire had cleaned up the dining room and kitchen and set the dishwasher to humming, after the Monopoly board had been reset for four players, everyone but little Ryan took a turn rolling the dice for the honor of picking that night's movie. Alyssa won with a pair of sixes and chose *Once in a Lifetime.* As per family rules, Thomas Jr. exercised his one-time veto option and forced Alyssa to pick again. Her next choice, *The Princess Bride,* went unopposed. Swordplay and fighting for Thomas Jr., romance for Alyssa, a mix of goofy and sophisticated humor for the adults. The Monopoly game progressed in halting fashion, interrupted frequently with comments such as "Hold on a minute. I want to watch this scene."

Throughout the evening, the baby moved from one lap to another, played alone for a while with his Barnyard See'n Say, and finally fell asleep snuggled against Thomas Jr. A part of Thomas Huston Sr. watched and absorbed every move and word and laugh from his family, felt keenly every moment of their typical Saturday night together because he knew how transitory it was. All too soon, he knew, Thomas Jr. would be spending his Saturday nights elsewhere, first just hanging out with a small group of friends, then with that one special girl. Alyssa would not be far behind. Then there would be just three of them to share a quiet evening, and in the blink of an eye, only two.

In bed that night, just after midnight, with Claire nestled against him with her head on his chest, her hair still damp and scented by a mango-infused shampoo, Thomas spoke of the ache of wistfulness he felt, and she comforted him as she always did. She said, "Things change but we'll always be a family, baby." She said, "Someday we'll have a house full of grandkids." She said, "Baby, make love to me again. I can never get enough of you."

Later, he listened to her hair dryer in the bathroom, then she came back to him and quickly fell asleep in his arms. He waited another half hour or so before slipping out of bed. He had some lines he wanted to get down before the night spirited them away, a few words for his protagonist, some lines of description for his Annabel, lines that had appeared out of the ether while watching Claire undress. Plus, he was concerned about the garbage. He had forgotten to check to see if Tommy had carried the garbage outside after dinner as asked. Sometimes the boy got distracted during his chores and left them unfinished, and now Thomas could not rest with wondering if the plastic bag full of chicken bones and skin had been left somewhere between the kitchen and the garbage cans outside the garage. If so, the bag would leak and Thomas would find it in the morning, probably torn open with its contents dragged all over his and his neighbor's yards.

He slid out of bed and, well aware that his restlessness went deeper than the chicken bones, deep enough to keep him awake awhile longer, deep enough to require a slow walk through the neighborhood, he gathered his clothes off the floor, where he had left them in a pile, then dressed in the hallway, took his shoes out of the downstairs closet, and slipped them on, and quietly made his way into the kitchen. No bag of chicken bones there. The battery-operated clock on the wall, the one Claire had purchased online with *Bienvenue au café Huston* written in red script across the face, ticked off the seconds. The dishwasher was silent now. Thomas opened the door and laid it open so the dishes would be dry by morning.

Then he crossed to the door that opened into the garage, unlocked it, reached around the jamb, and switched on the garage light. The bag of chicken bones was sitting on the roof of the car. Tommy liked to climb into Claire's silver Altima and pretend he was driving. He would work a make-believe gearshift through its five gears, braking and downshifting, mashing down the accelerator on straightaways. He had probably completed several laps around Daytona's brickyard before bringing himself and the car back to the garage. Through it all, four Cornish game hen carcasses had ridden on the roof.

Thomas Huston smiled to himself as he retrieved the plastic bag, opened the side door of the garage, and went out into the darkness. A pair of twenty-gallon plastic garbage containers stood against the garage wall. He opened the nearest one, placed the bag inside, then snapped the lid on tightly, so a marauding raccoon could not pry it off. Then he came back to the front corner of the garage and stood looking at the sky. The night was clear, cool but not cold, still in the high forties though many of the leaves on the four maples in the front yard were already down. He smelled winter coming, and the nameless ache began in him again, that strange longing he often felt when alone, especially at night, that desire for something he could not articulate or identify. Sometimes it came over him so forcefully that he felt like weeping, and occasionally did. Sometimes it helped to walk.

He went out to the sidewalk and turned to the right. He would go only as far as the end of the street, three blocks to the intersection with Redfern, then turn back again. He had left the garage door standing open, the garage light on, and if he stayed away too long, the garage would fill with moths.

He had been thinking about Poe a lot lately. Two years before that, it had been Steinbeck. And before that, Faulkner. A trinity of troubled men. He felt a kinship with all of them, felt he understood their misery. Lately he had been thinking about Poe's "imp of perversity," that compulsion toward contrariness that always had Poe shooting off his mouth when he should have bitten his tongue, his inability to keep from criticizing his colleagues. Huston, by comparison, was a master of restraint. His anger simmered well beneath the surface, visible only to himself. He had learned that trick from his father, whom most people had considered the most congenial of men, always smiling, always nodding in agreement. Not until Thomas's mother and father were gone did it occur to Thomas that there was more to his father than had met the eye.

At the intersection with Redfern, Thomas Huston paused for a while. There was no traffic in the development at that hour. The houses were dark. No dogs barked, no alley cats prowled the shadows. All quiet on the suburban front.

By the time he returned to his garage, he had finished crafting several sentences for the novel. The first two would introduce the scene in which his protagonist first succumbed to his desire. *He knew what he had to do. His heart knew what was necessary and right, but he could not make his body move away from her, could not summon the strength to resist what he would have to live with forever and which would give him no peace.* The other sentences were about Annabel by way of Claire, about his protagonist's desire by way of Huston's own.

In the garage he closed and locked the door and crossed toward the kitchen. He thought he detected a faint odor of cigarette smoke. Maybe a neighbor had stepped outside for a midnight smoke. Surely Tommy hadn't sneaked a quick one earlier in the evening? Huston paused for an instant and sniffed the air. Was it really cigarette smoke he smelled? Maybe the odor had come from the bag of chicken bones. Maybe he was just imagining things.

He locked the inside garage door behind himself and crossed toward his study. *He knew what he had to do,* he thought, and repeated the sentences again, working on the cadence, the pauses, getting them just right. Sometimes a comma made all the difference.

He sat at his desk and laid his journal open and wrote down the sentences. A few more sentences followed. He worked on each one in his head until it sounded just right, then he wrote it down. *She is a dark-haired woman, green eyed and dusky with secrets.* Maybe twenty minutes passed, not long, certainly no more than thirty. A creak of footsteps upstairs. Tommy taking a leak probably. Maybe sneaking in some time on his laptop. Huston read over what he had written, was pleased with the sound of it.

Then he closed up the journal and returned it to the bookshelf.

Suddenly the scent of cigarette smoke intruded again, this time he was sure of it. He had never smoked, always abhorred the stupidity of the habit, its selfishness and self-destructiveness, and his sensitivity to its stink had always been keen. But he felt no anger, only sadness, because now he would have to go upstairs and catch Tommy in the act and read him the riot act. The boy would be embarrassed. Maybe he would cry. And Thomas Huston's only desire was to fill his house with happiness. Disciplining his children was a duty he accepted but never enjoyed.

Just outside Huston's office, a man he had never before seen was waiting in the unlit foyer at the bottom of the stairs. The man stepped into the doorway before Huston reached it, a big man, not as tall as Huston but broad shouldered, thick necked. His head was shaved and gleaming with perspiration. The scent of cigarette smoke clung to his tight black T-shirt and jeans.

Huston gave a small start of surprise at the sight of him, an involuntary chuff of air, a barely audible "unh." It was as if all the rest of the house went dark around him but the man remained clearly illuminated in the light from the office. In that first instant Huston took in everything about the man, the broad, round face and gray eyes that seemed too small for his head, the black nylon batting gloves, the black enameled pistol in his right hand, the chef's knife in his left. *That's my chef's knife,* Huston thought, and was suddenly disoriented by his recognition of the knife, the dreamlike incongruities of *stranger, knife, gun, my home.* For several moments, all he could understand, all that registered on him, was the soreness of every breath, the sudden heavy hurt in his gut. It was not fear that paralyzed him but this sudden interjection of the inexplicable, and in the dark congestion of his mind, he could think only of his mother and father.

"Back up," the man told him.

Huston only stood there. He tried to swallow but could not. The smell of stale smoke was nauseating.

The man raised the pistol. Huston stepped back.

"Keep going. Back further."

Three halting steps. The movement broke something loose in Huston's chest and he sucked in three desperate breaths. The man was fully inside the room now, and now the room felt tight to Huston, a carpeted cage.

"Who are you?" he said.

"I'm the man whose baby you killed."

"What? What are you talking about?"

"Don't fuck with me, man. You know what I'm talking about. You took her to Cleveland and you killed my fucking baby."

In a distant part of his brain, Huston thought *Bonnie,* he thought *the abortion pill,* he thought of the long night in the motel room while she waited for the cramping and the flow of blood to begin. He thought of the silence as they drove back to Pennsylvania Friday morning. Yet even those thoughts would not cohere to explain that pistol, that knife, this man whose presence choked like a hand around his throat.

From that point on, the night warped into a gelatinous blur for Huston. He was not sure how long it lasted. Maybe an hour, maybe more. The knife pressed into his hand. The horrific choice. *Your baby for mine. Either that or your whole fucking family. Every last fucking one of you.*

He remembered leaning over little Davy's crib. The soft sibilance of breath. The sweet, powdery smell. Then the tears and the terrible ache that mushroomed through his every cell. *Now,* the man whispered from the doorway. *Or else I start shooting.*

The baby looked to Huston like a small,

pale fish underwater. Asleep at the bottom of an ocean of tears. The first push of the blade was too tentative and off the mark. The second was an act of mercy. It carried all the terrible weight of a father's inestimable love.

FIFTY-TWO

Huston was bent double now and sobbing convulsively, hands to his face, his back bucking hard against the lighthouse rail. De-Marco climbed to his feet an inch at a time, closed the distance between them. He laid a hand on Huston's back, felt the searing heat between his shoulder blades, felt the chill of lake air on his face. He stood like that without moving, staring into the long darkness. The broken necklace of lights in the distance blurred. They seemed to float and wobble, yanked back and forth in a current of grief.

Then DeMarco too bent forward, his forehead against the other man's back.

After a while, Huston eased himself to his knees. Then fell sideways onto a hip and elbow. Then, after several minutes, he pushed himself into a sitting position, knees raised, arms crossed atop his knees, chin on his chest. DeMarco turned his back to the lake. He wanted to sit too but remained standing, knew he had to begin.

"How long before you found the rest of them?" he asked.

"I don't know."

"But after a while. When you realized he wasn't there anymore. Wasn't standing behind you outside Davy's room."

"He wasn't anywhere," Huston said.

"So you went into the other bedrooms then."

Huston said nothing. His head moved twice, nodded against his arms.

"And you have no idea who this man was?"

"Bonnie. That's all I know."

DeMarco wondered how much he should tell him now. Should he get him down and into the car first? Or would the information help to accomplish that?

Huston said, "I went to see her last night. To ask her. But he was there. He came outside and I saw him."

"You were there?" DeMarco said.

"That's when I knew she wouldn't help. I saw you there too."

"Why didn't you call me? Right from the beginning, you should have called me."

"You're my friend. And a policeman.

You'd be torn apart over what to do. What I wanted to do."

DeMarco was silent for a few moments. Then said, "The man's name is Carl Inman. Calls himself Tex now. He was the bouncer at Whispers but kept himself out of sight most times. He was released from prison three months ago, has a long list of offenses, most of them involving violence. He did a four-year stretch this last time. I remember him from a dozen or so years back when I first met Bonnie. He's changed a lot since I saw him back then. My guess is he's been on a steady diet of steroids."

Huston was looking up at him now. "Do you know where he is?"

"Not at the moment. But we will. We'll find him."

Huston shook his head. "I never thought," he said. "I never would've imagined."

DeMarco said, "We never can."

More minutes passed. DeMarco was beginning to feel chilled now, a bone-deep shiver. "We need to get down from here, Tom. Get you a place to rest. Some decent food."

After a few seconds, Huston leaned onto one hand and gradually pushed himself to his feet. But instead of moving toward the stairs, he slid away from DeMarco, four feet away against the curving rail.

"Thomas," DeMarco said. "C'mon."

Huston shook his head. "You go. Just leave me be."

"To do what?" He took a step toward Huston but stopped when the man backed away and leaned his upper body over the rail. "Thomas, think. Forget Poe. There's no Eden by the lake. And your Annabel isn't here."

"Then leave. Or else I'll have to find out if that's true."

"Does that mean that if I leave you here, you won't try to find out?"

Huston looked down at the rocks.

DeMarco said, "We'll catch him, Thomas. We will."

"Then that's when I'll come back."

DeMarco considered his options. He could lunge for Huston, one long stride and grab, but would it be quick enough to stop him from going over the rail? Probably not. Was it really possible that Huston might take the plunge? *His family has been butchered,* DeMarco thought. *What would you do?*

He could call for backup, surround the lighthouse with men and safety nets. *And they'll get here just in time,* he told himself, *to scrape Huston off the rocks.*

Or he could take the man at his word. He

wasn't a criminal; he wasn't a murderer.

"Okay, I'm going to trust you," DeMarco told him, "on one condition." He reached inside his jacket and took a business card from the pocket. He held it out toward Huston. "My number is on here. You can get to a phone, right? So you check in with me every . . . six or so hours, okay? Agreed?"

"Lay the card down. Don't come any closer."

"It's going to blow away."

"Then put it inside somewhere."

DeMarco lowered his hand. "Will you give me your word? Because I know you're an honest man, Thomas. I know you're a man of honor."

Huston blew out a puff of breath. "I'm not the man I used to be."

"We are who we are," DeMarco answered. "And I believe in you. Deal?"

A few seconds passed. Then, "Leave the card inside."

DeMarco placed the card and three twenties at the top of the stairs. At the last moment, he decided to lay his cell phone atop them.

The instant he got back to his car, he used his police radio to call the telephone company and instruct them to track the movements of his phone at all times. Then he began to question his own judgment. Had he made the right decision? Was he letting his identification with Huston influence him?

Of course he was. It's what a friend would do.

He grabbed the police radio again and notified the Ohio State Highway Patrol that a potential suicide was at the top of the Perry Point lighthouse. "Bring a psychologist and rescue equipment," he said. "No lights or sirens. I'll meet you at the lighthouse."

He climbed out of the car and made his way back to the security fence. Up and over again, as quietly as possible. He crept low to the open lighthouse door. Sneaked to the top of the stairs, wincing with every creak. At the top he found his cell phone, nothing else. He knew that the rocks too would be empty of everything but spindrift. In Eden, who needed money or Sergeant Ryan DeMarco's number?

He called off the trace on his phone, canceled the rescue unit, waded back through the darkness to his car, his flashlight beam swinging like a sickle.

FIFTY-THREE

Before the morning debriefing, DeMarco met with his supervisor in Bowen's office. The BOLOs on Inman, Bonnie, and Huston had already been updated. Huston, if spotted, was to be approached with caution and if possible picked up and held in protective custody. Bonnie was to be considered a possible hostage of Inman, a possible accomplice. Inman was to be apprehended by any means necessary.

Bowen said, "I'm going to be honest with you, Ryan. This part about you just leaving Huston at the rail and going back to your car, I'm more than a little uncomfortable with that."

"That's because you weren't there," DeMarco said. "Another step toward him and he would have jumped. Would you be more comfortable with that?"

"You shouldn't have been there on your own in the first place."

"I was following a lead. Like I said, you can't know because you weren't there."

"So why didn't you just back away from him for a minute, out of sight, and use your cell phone?"

"Did you read the report?"

"It's six pages long. I skimmed."

"Then skim it again. And this time read the fucking thing."

"You going to get testy with me?"

"It's eight o'clock in the fucking morning, I didn't sleep all fucking night, and the fucking report is right there on your fucking desk. Judgment call. Quit busting my fucking balls, why don't ya?"

"You think because you used to be my supervisor you can talk to me like that?"

"Yeah I do. So drink your fucking cappuccino mocha latte grande and leave me the fuck alone for a while. I've got a debriefing to conduct." With that, DeMarco turned and strode out of Bowen's office.

Four seconds later, he stepped onto the threshold again. "By the way, I apologize for swearing."

Bowen licked the foam off his lips. "Apology accepted."

After the debriefing, DeMarco stood at his office window for a while and stared at the abandoned cardinal nest. *So maybe you saved his life,* he told himself. *Think of it that way.*

Yeah and maybe you didn't.

He imagined himself in Huston's place, imagined himself doing the thinking for Huston, feeling Huston's emotions. *You've just now found out the name of the man who forced you to stab your own baby and who slaughtered your family. You found out that the woman you trusted and helped — for no other reason than because your innate compassion told you to help her, despite your own misgivings — later betrayed you to her troglodyte boyfriend. Maybe she was coerced into it, beaten, threatened, who knows. Does that matter? No, what matters now is that you know the man's name. So you don't jump off the lighthouse. Your previously depleted body now swells with purpose. Fuck compassion, you're through with that. You can maybe spare an ounce or two of compassion for Bonnie, for what she might have gone through, but not a drop for Inman. Him, you want to make suffer. Him, you want to punish with extreme prejudice. Your own life is over, you know that. You accept it as an irreconcilable fact. But before it officially ends, you want to see Inman suffer. You need it. Fuck food, fuck sleep, fuck oxygen. Your heart pumps lava now. Your pulse pounds revenge.*

DeMarco felt the heat in his own veins and was uncertain whose thoughts were fanning that fire, Huston's or his own. Not that it mattered. He wanted Inman as much as Huston did. Huston's chances of finding the man were slim to none. No vehicle, no weapon, no knowledge of Inman's whereabouts, no means of locating him. DeMarco's chances, with the nation's finest law enforcement units all backing him up, were better.

FIFTY-FOUR

A long, gray day filled with long, dark thoughts. DeMarco quietly seethed through the first two hours of the morning, waiting for the telephone to ring. When he thought himself capable of conducting an interrogation that did not involve strangulation or similar means of persuasion, he drove north to a small mobile home on the periphery of a sand quarry and hammered on the metal door until Bonnie's brother, Moby, appeared, blinking behind the filmy glass. He was wearing a wife-beater and gray sweatpants cut off at the knees, a two-day beard, and the look of a scrawny rat terrier that had recently been kicked in the balls by a Siamese cat.

DeMarco didn't wait for an invitation to go inside. Moby's empty hands were all the invitation he required. He pushed past the startled man and strode through the compact kitchen/dining/living room. "Where's your sister?" he asked.

Moby rubbed his crust of beard. "I wish to fuck I knew."

"How about Carl Inman? Seen him lately?"

"What the fuck is an Inman?"

"Tex. The bouncer."

"Far as I know Tex's last name is Snyder."

"Uh-huh," DeMarco said. He poked his head into the first bedroom. A tangle of sheets and a green wool blanket on the mattress, the thick scent of farts and old sweat. Dirty clothes on the floor, a soup bowl filled with and surrounded by broken peanut shells and dust, an open bottle of Lake Erie Rhine wine beside the bowl, four inches of wine remaining.

Unless that's his piss jar, DeMarco thought. He was careful not to touch the bottle when he knelt beside the bed to look underneath. Three balled-up socks and what appeared to be the twentieth-year reunion of a large class of dust bunnies.

"There's nobody else here if that's what you're looking for."

The other bedroom was filled wall to wall with cardboard boxes and white garbage bags crammed with empty wine bottles. Moby said, "Those are all going to the recycler when I can get somebody to haul them away for me."

"Good to see you're living green," De-Marco said. He took a quick glance in the bathroom, winced, and turned back toward Moby, who backed into the living room as DeMarco approached.

Moby said, "Aren't you supposed to have a warrant or something before you can look around in a fella's place?"

"I just came for the pleasant conversation," DeMarco answered. "And to admire your talent for interior design." He put two fingers against Moby's shoulder and pushed him down onto the sofa. DeMarco sat across from him on the edge of the orange vinyl banquette bench. He felt the little mobile home shiver on its foundation. He felt the fragility of Moby's life.

When DeMarco leaned forward, Moby leaned back. DeMarco said, "So as far as you know, the guy your sister has been banging for the past, what, seventeen years or so if you count the conjugal visits, is a guy named Snyder?"

Moby looked at him and blinked.

"Don't even try to fucking bullshit me," DeMarco told him. "She's your sister and she's been taking care of you most of your life. I understand that. I also understand that a guy who looks and smells the way

436

you do has a liver that's only going to last a couple more years if he's lucky. A couple more years you'd probably rather not spend in a little concrete room where the only wine you'll get to drink is what comes squirting out of some fat prison guard's dick."

"Prison for what? I didn't do anything."

"How about as an accomplice to murder? Multiple homicides, to be specific."

"Bullshit."

The man's surprise seemed genuine to DeMarco. "Maybe you're not in the loop on those, but you know what? Tough shit. You withhold knowledge of your sister's whereabouts, you're still going to spend your last days sipping golden wine through a hairy straw."

"Look, she told me to call him Snyder if anybody asked. And that's all she told me."

"When was the last time you saw her?"

Moby scratched beneath his chin. "What day is this?"

"It's Saturday, the original Sabbath. I should be sitting in a church pew singing praises to the Almighty, but thanks to you, I'm sitting in this tin shithole instead, and I don't much feel like singing. So I swear to God, I'm going to drag your scrawny ass out to my car in about five seconds if you

437

don't stop scratching and tell me what I want to know."

"She brought me home after we closed up Thursday. Then yesterday morning, her and Fuckhead come by to tell me they had to go somewhere for a couple days."

"They came in Bonnie's car?"

"I was in bed, man. Barely awake. They let themselves in and came to my room and told me."

"A couple of days."

"That's what she said. Said she'd be back in a couple fucking days. At most."

"And what did Fuckhead have to say?"

"Told me to keep my mouth shut or he'd twist my balls off with a pair of pliers."

"And yet here we are, chatting like this."

"Hey, nobody said nothing about there being murders involved. I don't believe in hurting people."

"But you know that Fuckhead believes in it, don't you?"

"I know how he treats my sister."

"And you too, I bet."

"I couldn't care less how he treats me."

"Still, you probably wouldn't mind much if I were to give him a nice room of his own far away from here for the next hundred years or so."

"All I care about is that you fix it so Bonnie can't hear from him or know where he is. When it comes to fucking up your life, I don't have much room to talk, but I'll be damned if I can figure out why a woman ever lets herself be suckered by a piece of shit like him."

"It's a mystery, no question about it."

"That place where I work?" Moby said. "Why do those girls do that to themselves? I mean some of those girls are so fucking sweet."

"They do it for the money, I guess."

"Hell, man. Women could own this whole planet if they wanted to. They lock up their pussies long enough, every red-blooded man alive would be on his knees within a couple months."

"Maybe so. Or maybe human nature is a little more complicated than that."

"There's no complication to it. Men want pussy and they'll do whatever they have to, to get it."

DeMarco thought, *This from a man whose pecker probably hasn't worked for years. On the other hand, maybe that's why he's so smart.*

"I mean, I just don't understand it," Moby said. "Women should be treated special, you know? Yet they let themselves be treated like crap."

"Happens every day, Moby. All over the world."

"Which only makes it an even bigger fucking mystery, don't it?"

FIFTY-FIVE

Monday dawned like a mile-long freight train filled with radioactive sewage. De-Marco trudged through it. All he could do now was to wait for a tip, a sighting of Inman or Bonnie. He felt as heavy and hollow as a gut-shot dog dragging its ass uphill. He wondered where Huston had spent the night, wondered if he was still alive. *You never should have let Huston go,* he told himself. *Should have taken him into protective custody, tricked him, told him a lie, whatever was necessary. You should have recognized Inman that night you saw him at Whispers, should have looked back through the fog of all those years, instantly recognized Inman, instantly fit all the pieces together, instantly shot the beast on sight. You should have never become a cop. A teacher, maybe, like Laraine. Social studies and history, that's what you would be good at. Lesson plans and field trips.*

He busied himself with paperwork and chastised himself and second-guessed the way he had handled things. The mistakes went years into the past. If he had made better choices on a rainy night twelve years ago, little Ryan might still be alive. His house might not be a stinking, sunless cave. His soul might not be a dead leaf, empty shell, dried-up turd, whatever it had become.

"You look like crap," Bowen told him in the afternoon.

"You are crap," DeMarco said from the threshold.

"What is this, like your twelfth trip to the coffeepot?"

"Go back to your Internet porn and mind your own business."

"Get in here," Bowen said.

"I'm busy."

"Get in here now. And close the damn door."

DeMarco stepped over the threshold and pulled the door shut. He stood with his left buttock pressed to the doorknob.

Bowen told him, "You look like a junkie, you know that?"

DeMarco slurped his coffee because he knew Bowen hated the sound.

Bowen opened a desk drawer, rummaged

around inside, brought out an amber prescription bottle, shook two white tablets into his hand, laid them on the far edge of the desk. "Pick those up, get your ass home, swallow those pills, and go to bed. And don't give me any shit about it."

"I don't take medications," DeMarco said.

"Right. Caffeine all day, Jack all night, no food, no sleep. You're destroying yourself. You realize that, don't you?"

DeMarco smiled, then took a longer, louder slurp.

"Here's the deal, Ryan, and it's the only deal you're going to get. You take those pills, go home, and get some sleep. Or else I'm taking you off the case."

"You wouldn't fucking dare."

"You're supposed to be heading this investigation, but look at you; you're a mess. I don't know what it is about Huston, but you're taking this case way too personally. It was probably a mistake for me to let you head the investigation in the first place. But just because we're friends doesn't mean I'm going to keep looking the other way while you rip yourself to pieces over this guy."

DeMarco remained with his back pressed to the door. He tried to still the caffeine jitters streaming through him, watched the ripples in his coffee cup.

Bowen's voice softened. "Or maybe this isn't about Huston at all. Maybe it's about Laraine somehow? Or Ryan Jr. maybe?"

DeMarco gripped his cup with both hands. His mouth felt sticky and sour. He spoke in a whisper. "Don't talk about my family," he said.

Bowen stood and scooped up the white tablets. He crossed to DeMarco. Took the coffee cup from his hands, pressed the tablets into his palm, closed DeMarco's hand around the pills. He stood very close, his fingers still clenched around DeMarco's.

"Go home, Ryan. If there's any news between now and morning, I'll send a trooper to drag your ass out of bed. That's not a suggestion; it's an order. And this time, you're going to fucking listen to me."

For some reason, DeMarco could not bring himself to look Bowen in the eye. For some reason, all he wanted was to go to sleep now. He wanted to sleep a hundred years, no dreams, no night sweats, no thoughts of another day.

He leaned slightly forward, reached behind himself, and gripped the doorknob. With a sliding, turning motion, he faced the door and pulled it open and said as he stepped into the hallway, "Make sure you scrub my mug out when you're done fondling it."

FIFTY-SIX

The long, cool shadows of afternoon. On the edge of his back porch, DeMarco stood for a while and looked at his unfinished brick path. Streaks of soft yellow sunlight slanted in low across his yard. He remembered that Laraine had told him once that photographers and painters call this hour of such clear, soft sunshine the hour of magic light. He wondered what a painter would make of the scene from his back porch. Dandelions and crabgrass had grown up between the bricks and out of the bare soil. The grass in his yard was four inches high and hadn't been mowed for over a month. At the far end of the yard, the windows in the unfinished apartment in the small barn looked back at him like cartoon eyes, black and unblinking.

For just an instant, he thought he saw himself looking back from one of those black windows, but then the image was gone. *Must have been the me that never was,* he thought. *Never was or will be.*

He wanted a drink, but Bowen's white pills were in his pocket and he knew he should not mix them with alcohol. He told himself he should heat up a can of soup. He should eat some soup and maybe a can of fruit cocktail. Eat something sensible, then take the pills and sleep for twelve hours, then wake up refreshed and ready to kick some tail again.

It was a good, simple plan. He was glad he had thought of it. To celebrate, he went inside and took a bottle of Corona out of the refrigerator and drank it down in four gulps. He drank another one while studying the eight cans of food in the cupboard. There was one can each of sliced beets, whole potatoes, mushroom pieces and stems, and five cans of tuna. He drank another beer while standing at the back door and looking out through the screen. *Beer is okay,* he told himself. *Beer is mostly water. Water is supposed to be good for you.*

To keep the first three beers company, he carried a fourth beer into the living room and swallowed the white pills and turned on the TV. With the beer in one hand and the TV remote in the other, he surfed channels for a while before finally settling on a cooking show. He watched a slender, pretty woman demonstrate how to prepare a chicken breast with caramelized onions and mushrooms and a sauce made with white wine, capers, and the juice of one lemon. The pretty woman told him that the sauce could also be used with shrimp and that it was wonderful for poaching salmon.

"That's wonderful to know," he told her. He imagined that if he lifted the hair off the back of her neck, she would smell like moonlight with a hint of lemon. He watched her until his eyes grew heavy, then he closed his eyes and listened to her voice become a murmur, and when she leaned close to whisper to him, he could feel her breath on his cheek and the clean, cool scent of her body filled him with the soft, unhurried heaviness of magic light.

"That's wonderful," he told her, and he let the empty bottle slip from his hand and onto the floor.

Fifty-Seven

The remote slid upward past DeMarco's fingers. He thought about tightening his hand around it, but he was in a gray, soft place and could not summon sufficient interest to hold on. He heard the television click off and the silence that followed, and he wondered about that too but from a long distance away.

After what seemed a long time, the thought registered that somebody other than himself must have lifted the remote from his hand and shut off the television. He tried to force his eyes open, but they were enormously heavy, so he surrendered to the heaviness and went back into the grayness.

After a while the grayness lifted again, and again the thought registered that someone else must be in the living room with him. He hoped it was the pretty woman with capers and the juice of one lemon, but when he looked back at the grayness from just outside the edge of it, he saw that it was separating into rising wisps like fog over water. He did not want it to go, but it was quickly becoming too thin to take him in again, too thin to cover and hold him.

A while later he reasoned that Bowen had sent a trooper to wake him. He did not wonder how the trooper had gotten inside or which trooper it was. After all, he had left his back door open. Maybe he had left his cupboard open too. Maybe the refrigerator as well. None of that mattered. All that mattered was that the white pills were a wonderful thing and the gray nothing had been wonderful too and also the sweet indifference that came with it.

What finally intruded upon the indifference and spoiled it was the scent of cigarette smoke. It began distantly, like a memory that nagged but would not quite materialize. Had the scent been sweeter, as of leaf smoke on an autumn evening, he might have used it to deepen the indifference, a boost to the white pills' sedation. But the stink of cigarette smoke was unmistakable. And as the scent increased in his consciousness, the wonderful indifference gave way to annoyance.

The scent buzzed and pricked at him. De-

Marco wanted to return to the gray nothing, but the scent would not allow it, and before long, he was hearing his own thoughts again, and he knew he had to listen.

His instincts told him to remain still while his stumbling thoughts found their footing, and when they did his pulse began to hammer and his breath grew quick and shallow. The last time he had experienced that scent was in Bonnie's house. But he had never seen Bonnie smoking nor had he smelled the scent on her. And he finally put a name to the scent and the prickling sensation that accompanied it.

He kept his eyes closed and wondered how close Carl Inman was to him, on which side of the recliner. He listened for Inman's breathing and tried to sense the heat from Inman's body and decided that the man was on his left and very close. Probably he was sitting on the sofa and watching DeMarco, had been there long enough for his eyes to adjust to the darkness. Probably he was holding a knife, though maybe also the handgun he had used to threaten Huston. DeMarco wondered what fraction of a second would be needed for him to vault up out of the chair and dive for cover and, with luck, race into the bedroom where his service weapon in its holster hung from the chair.

Not time enough, he told himself. He was still groggy from the white pills. He was still struggling to piece his thoughts together, to fit them into a linearity. Whereas Inman was wide awake and alert.

You don't stand a chance, he thought.

He opened his eyes and slowly turned his head toward the sofa. In the darkness, Inman was little more than a hulking shadow. The only light in the room came from the blue digital readout on the DVD player atop the television and from the dull glow of the streetlamp against the Persian blinds and drawn sheer curtains. He remembered the day he had hung those blinds. Remembered Laraine as his cheerful assistant, her hand on the small of his back as he drilled the pilot holes. *You're so sexy with a power tool in your hand,* she had teased. She was young and beautiful and clear-eyed in his memory. The man drilling the holes was middle-aged and tired beyond his years, and he knew he was soon going to die.

To the silhouette, DeMarco said, "Nothing you do to me is going to change your fate, Carl. There's already an alert out for you and Bonnie. You've got nowhere to go."

"Then I guess this will just have to be for

the fun of it."

Yet Inman did not move. He was seated on the edge of the sofa seat but slouched back with his head and shoulders resting against the top of the cushion. He said, "You're a sound sleeper for a cop."

"You caught me on a good night."

"So you think this is a good one, do you?"

DeMarco turned away from him. The digital readout on the DVD player said 3:27. DeMarco told him, "I've been asleep for almost nine hours. That's more sleep than I've had all week."

Inman's laugh was a single grunt.

"So fuck you," DeMarco said. He let his hand fall toward the wooden lever on the side of the recliner, then felt his pinkie finger graze something cool and smooth. He gripped the empty Corona bottle around the neck and lifted it off the floor. Now he moved his hand to the wooden lever on the recliner. He took in a slow, deep breath and held it.

Then he yanked the lever up. As the footrest banged down, he threw himself sideways over the armrest and landed on his knees with the recliner between him and Inman.

He heard Inman stand, but the man did not rush toward him. Calmly, Inman said,

453

"Seems to me like you're the one with nowhere to go."

So no gun, DeMarco thought, *or he would have shot me already. A knife is more fun. He wants to play awhile.*

DeMarco climbed to his feet and faced him. He held the beer bottle behind his leg. "Anybody ever tell you that you stink?" he asked. "Literally. You smell like a fucking ashtray."

Inman grunted again and strode around the back of the recliner.

DeMarco swung at the hips, brought the bottle up in a wide arc toward the side of Inman's head. But Inman leaned back from the waist and the momentum of DeMarco's swing pulled him off balance and he fell into the recliner again, his back against one armrest, legs one atop the other. Inman moved quickly then, stabbed a hand around DeMarco's throat, yanked him forward off the front of the recliner, hammered his head onto the carpeted floor.

DeMarco raised his arm so as to smash the bottle against Inman's body, but every movement felt glacial, heavy and drugged and slow, and before the bottle could make contact, DeMarco's arm was pushed to the floor and pinned under Inman's knee. De-Marco tried to drive his free hand upward through the heavy air, push his fingers through the heavy darkness and into Inman's eyes, but Inman blocked it with his elbow, then yanked DeMarco up off the floor and smashed his head down again, and for just a moment, the room flared red, then blinked into darkness and sucked DeMarco all the way down to the black basement far below the sweet nothing.

FIFTY-EIGHT

A distant sound of breaking glass. No, not glass, too sustained. More like bells, jingle bells. Christmas? The ice cream man?

Whatever the sound it was getting closer, louder, or else DeMarco was getting closer to it, coming up out of the blackness, the hole that had sucked him down. He tried to move, lift his head, open his eyes, but his brain throbbed with every pulsebeat now, felt too big for his skull, Christ the pain of it. And that jingling sound only made it worse, so fucking loud now. And there was something wrong with his arms, his body — he couldn't even get his mouth to open. *What the fuck is the matter? Why can't I move?*

Second by second, the darkness grew thinner, and DeMarco pushed up through it toward a diffuse glow that he thought might be the sun. He thought he might be underwater and pushing toward the surface, but he realized then that he was breathing through his nose, that the air was warm. The light was not the sun. He was sitting — no, lying on his back. The jingling sound near his head now, metallic. Something cold touched his ear and he jerked away from it. The weight of the darkness was evaporating, and he could open his eyes now, saw nothing but light and smelled the stink of cigarette smoke in his face and realized then that he had been unconscious, and now he knew where he was and he knew that he was fucked.

He was lying beneath the floor lamp in the corner of the room. Inman leaning close, smiling, jingling a key ring against DeMarco's ear. DeMarco leaned away from him. Looked down the length of his body. Wrists bound with duct tape, arms bound tightly to his sides. Ankles bound too. A strip of tape pulling hard and tight across his mouth.

"Good morning, sunshine," Inman said.

DeMarco looked across the room. The blue digital readout said 3:42. *Only a few minutes,* DeMarco thought. *Long enough to be thoroughly screwed.*

"Here's what we're going to do," Inman said. "You following this?"

DeMarco turned his head. Inman on his

457

knees, face too close, stink all through him. Inman dragging on a cigarette. Smoke stinging DeMarco's bad eye, fouling up the house.

"I got your keys here," Inman told him, and jingled the key ring in his face. "Thanks for leaving them on the counter. So I thought maybe you and me could take us a ride in that sorry-ass car you got parked out back. Go up to Niagara Falls maybe? Scoot into Canada for a while? I saw you got a police radio in your car, so we'll have some entertainment along the way. What do you think? You up for a road trip?"

DeMarco's heart and brain hammered in syncopation. Both eyes stung from the smoke, the left eye watered. He was breathing hard, quick rasps of air through his nose. His answer was a furious, inarticulate mumble behind the tape. "I'll fucking kill you, you worthless fucking piece of shit."

"Excellent," Inman said. He stood, held the cigarette in his mouth, leaned down, and seized DeMarco under both arms and yanked him to his feet. They stood face to face. Inman took the cigarette from between his lips, blew out the smoke. With his free hand, he drew a long, heavy-handled knife from the leather sheath strapped to his belt, and he laid the side of the blade against De-

Marco's cheek, the point near the corner of his good eye.

Inman said, "There's a couple places up along the border where I'm pretty sure we can slip through. We do, I just might let you go. We don't . . ." He grinned and took another drag from the cigarette. Then, "We clear on this?"

DeMarco squinted his eyes and said nothing. *You're fucking dead,* he thought.

"So everything's cool," Inman said. "Hold this for me, will you?" He took a last drag from the cigarette then dropped the butt into DeMarco's shirt pocket. Then he stepped behind DeMarco, laid the knife blade against the side of DeMarco's neck. Immediately a pinpoint of heat stabbed DeMarco's left breast, then the heat blossomed and spread, and he smelled his shirt burning.

Inman chuckled while DeMarco squirmed. Finally Inman stretched an arm over DeMarco's shoulder and slammed his palm against the burning cigarette, hard enough to jolt the air from DeMarco's lungs. Inman said, "Don't say I never did nothing for you." He shoved him toward the kitchen.

DeMarco moved with small, stuttering steps, taking as much time as he dared, breathing deeply through his nose. Thanks to the adrenaline and the blow to his chest, all grogginess was gone now and his head was clear. He thought about dropping low, leaning back, and driving his skull up into Inman's chin. He thought about spinning away, hooking his foot against Inman's, and bringing him down. He thought about diving forward while bringing his right heel up into Inman's crotch.

But he was also clearheaded enough to know that none of those moves would work. Inman was keeping himself an arm's length away, only close enough to hold the blade against DeMarco's jugular. Inman was stronger and younger and quicker.

I'll have to take my chances in the car, De-Marco told himself. *Maybe send us both into a ravine somewhere. If I'm going to die, this shitbag is going with me.*

Just inside the kitchen door, Inman grabbed DeMarco by the collar and brought him to a halt. He turned the knife slightly so that the blade bit into the skin. Softly, Inman told him, "Your neighbors are sound asleep. There's not a single light burning on either side of this house. You can't run, you can't call out, there's not a thing you can do to change that. You understand?"

DeMarco gazed through the screen door

into the blackness of his yard. *There should be a lamppost out there. A beautiful brick path lined with solar lights. A child's swing. A place to play catch.*

Inman slid the blade off DeMarco's neck, jabbed the point into his spine. "You understand, pig?" he said.

DeMarco nodded.

"Then move it."

So many thoughts on the way to the barn. A slow tumbling of emotions. He realized that a part of him had always hoped that everything could be set right somehow, Ryan and Laraine and all the dark, sodden nights, a dozen years lived in error. And he realized too what a foolish hope that had been. There could be no erasure of mistakes engraved in time, no cleansing. One careless night, three wasted lives. Done is done. Dead is dead.

His shoes were wet with dew from the high grass, his ankles were wet, his cuffs were heavy. He smelled the dew, and its scent filled him with sadness. The sadness was heavy and wet and cool on his feet. He smelled winter in the night air, the coming of the end. And he knew suddenly that this was where he wanted to die, not in Canada or anywhere in between but here at the end of a path he would never finish building.

He saw that Inman had already opened the barn door and backed the car most of the way inside, and when they reached the front of the car, he saw that the trunk lid was open. *That's where I'm going. Except that I'm not.* He knew that Inman planned to stuff him into the trunk under concealment of the barn, had even removed the bulb from the trunk light. He would keep De-Marco where he could cause no trouble, arrive at the border around dawn. DeMarco was insurance, nothing more. When the insurance was no longer needed, the policy would be canceled. No refunds, no dividends.

The other possibility was that Inman would shove DeMarco into the trunk, slit his throat, close the lid, and leave him there to stink up the garage. The story about driving DeMarco's car to Canada merely a ruse to get DeMarco to the car. After all, Inman must have a car of his own parked nearby.

But if he planned to kill DeMarco immediately, why not do it in the house? In fact, why come after DeMarco at all? What did that accomplish? None of Inman's actions made any sense.

What also made no sense was the peculiar feeling of calm that enveloped DeMarco when he stepped inside the barn. So cool inside, so dark. He hadn't parked his car in here in years, hadn't opened the door except in daylight, to pull out the lawn mower or get one of his tools. He liked the strangeness he felt now, the slow sense of dreaminess, as if he could die in slow motion here and let all the past slip away from him, all mistakes quietly swallowed by the darkness.

Inman shoved him toward the rear of the Stratus. *At the turn,* DeMarco told himself. *That's where to do it.* He knew exactly where the machete was, thought he could grab it even in the darkness. On a long plank shelf behind the car, he had long ago laid out every tool he owned, always returned each tool to the same place after its use. Nearest to him now were the power tools, the circular saw and the portable jigsaw, the sander and power drill in its plastic case. Then the hammers, the ball-peen and claw and the rubber mallet and the roofing hammer. Then, organized in boxes of various kinds, all of the smaller items, nails and screws and tapes and cords.

On the far edge of the shelf he had mounted a vise clamp, and below it, hanging by a leather thong, was the machete he infrequently used to hack down the weeds that grew alongside the garage. The weeds were three feet high now and bent double by their own weight, but if he could get to the machete, he would put it to use tonight. When he made the turn around the rear fender, he would have his only chance. Three powerful hops — not pretty but maybe effective — then he could yank the machete off its nail with his bound hands, spin and swing with all his strength and, with luck, disembowel Inman with a single stroke. Then, since Inman would probably have just enough juice left to lash out with his own knife, DeMarco would more than likely drop beside him, and they could lie there looking at each other until the lights went out.

DeMarco shuffled toward the rear of the car. He remembered Bonnie suddenly and for a moment wondered where she was, but then he let the question go and only thought about the machete. He was calm now but looking forward to the explosion of crimson rage that would occur when his hands seized the machete and he pivoted and swung. He could see it all clearly now, and even the thought of his unavoidable death filled him with a deep peace.

He let the back of his hands brush against the cool side of the fender. One step around the rear of the car and then he would go.

Inman's hand clamped down on his left

shoulder and suddenly the blade was against his throat. "Easy now," Inman told him.

DeMarco's sense of peace dissolved. He had no options now. He had thought that he wouldn't mind dying, but he wanted to die while doing something productive, such as eviscerating Carl Inman. Now Inman was shoved up against him, pushing him sideways against the rear bumper, back in control.

Inman put a hand on his shoulder and drove DeMarco headfirst into the trunk. It all happened in an instant, and even as DeMarco tried to roll over to kick at Inman, his legs were seized and crammed into the trunk, the trunk lid came down hard and fast, and the darkness was complete.

DeMarco lay very still. Kicking against the trunk lid was useless. His only chance now was to somehow get the tape off his mouth, then somehow chew through the tape binding his wrists. He had four hours to accomplish it. No doubt Inman had searched the duffel bag DeMarco kept in the trunk, found only the sneakers, socks, chinos, and sweatshirt. But had he searched the little compartment on the side of the trunk, where DeMarco kept his father's old Harrington & Richardson .22? The cylinder held only three good bullets, the first three loaded with birdshot. But three loads of birdshot in the face would work nicely to improve Inman's countenance, then three .22 longs to the heart would improve his demeanor. DeMarco's only regret was that he would have to wait four hours to pull the trigger.

He heard the driver's side door open. Next he expected to feel Inman's weight settling onto the seat, then he would hear the engine turn over. Instead there was a soft thud and a grunt, then another thud. Then silence for ten seconds or so. De-Marco held his breath and listened.

The scrape of a key at the trunk. The lid popped up and was lifted open. A man was standing there looking in at DeMarco. Smaller than Inman, slender, smiling, the rubber mallet in his hand.

"You okay?" Thomas Huston asked.

DeMarco cocked his head.

"I'm glad," Huston said and closed the trunk lid atop him.

FIFTY-NINE

All DeMarco could do was listen. Scraping and clinking noises, something metal knocked off the shelf to clatter on the floor. More scraping noises. Then silence. Five full minutes of it. Then the tick of the key going into the trunk lock again, the click of the lock springing open. The squeak of the hinges as the lid was raised.

"I'm sorry I had to do that," Huston said. He spoke softly, half leaning into the trunk. "And I'm sorry that I'll have to leave you like this for a while. I just need to talk to you now. Can we do that? Can I trust you to just stay where you are for a minute and talk to me?"

After a moment, DeMarco nodded.

"Thank you," Huston said. "Just lie still for a second." Gently, he peeled the tape off DeMarco's mouth.

"Now you listen to me," DeMarco began. Huston leaned back, raised both hands to the trunk lid.

"Okay, okay," DeMarco said. "I'll listen to you."

Even in the darkness, Huston's smile looked sad to DeMarco — so tired and sad. Huston nodded toward the floor. "What's this piece of shit want with you?"

"He's down there?" DeMarco asked.

"Hog-tied. With a big, ugly bump on the side of his big, ugly head."

"I like the sound of that."

Huston said, "I don't understand why he came after you."

"I don't either. I also don't understand what you're doing here."

Huston smiled. "I've been staying upstairs in the little apartment you're making. Ever since the night at the lighthouse."

"You've been out here all this time?"

"You believed me. I thought I'd be safe here."

"Jesus," DeMarco said. "How did you get here?"

"After the lighthouse, I just walked along the shore for a while. I came across three kids sitting there drinking beer, two boys and a girl. They had a pickup truck, so I offered them sixty dollars to drive me to my friend's house."

"The sixty I gave you."

"Originally I thought I might just knock on your door. But then I saw this little barn and . . . I used to sleep in my grandfather's barn when I was a boy. In the summer, when I'd help him make hay. A couple times in college, before my grandmother passed away and the place was sold, Claire and I sneaked in for a while. I can still smell the hay, the night air . . . the way she always . . . always made me feel."

There was a quality to Huston's voice now that made DeMarco uneasy, a timbre of melancholy, of longing resigned to loss. De-Marco said. "No hay in my barn, though."

"No, but . . . it was very comforting to look out and see a light on in your house, you know? I watched you come and go to your car. Then tonight I looked out and saw you standing on your back porch. Then not long ago I heard your car being pulled inside, and then I watched this asshole marching you across the yard. It wasn't hard to put two and two together."

"I'm glad you're good at arithmetic."

Huston smiled.

"So how about you cut me free now? Let me take care of things from here on in. I guarantee he's going to suffer a long time for what he's done."

"Time is short, my friend," Huston said.

He continued to smile, "So I think I'll take care of the cleanup myself. No use getting your hands bloody."

DeMarco knew that kind of smile. He knew it held no happiness, only a peculiar feeling of calm and the pleasant strangeness of knowing that the end is near. He said, "You can't do what you're thinking, Thomas. You can't go down that road."

"It's the only road there is now."

"Thomas, please, you have to trust me on this. I have some experience with what you're feeling. I lost a child too."

"I lost all of them. Everything and everyone."

"I know you did. I did too. And yet I managed to go on. I've been doing it now for a dozen years."

"You have to want to," Huston said. "And I don't."

"No, I never wanted to. I just did it."

Huston smiled awhile longer. Then he said, "I found your handgun in the house."

"My service weapon? In the bedroom?"

"I'm going to have to take it with me. I'm sorry."

"You're a writer, Thomas. You're not a killer."

"I am and I want to be. The writer is dead. The husband and the father are dead. All that's left is the other guy."

DeMarco lifted his legs, hooked his heels over the edge of the trunk, and pulled himself into a sitting position. Huston stepped back toward the shelf. He reached behind his back then, pulled DeMarco's handgun from his waistband, and aimed it at DeMarco's chest. He said, "Keep doing what you're doing. Just do it very slowly now."

"You're not going to shoot me," DeMarco said.

"Him, you, me . . . In the end, what difference does any of it make?"

"It makes a difference and you know it."

Huston said nothing. Then he stood to the side until DeMarco managed to crawl out of the trunk and stand. He placed a hand against the back of DeMarco's shoulder and directed him to the passenger side of the car. There, to an eyehook screwed into the garage wall at waist level, Huston had tied a six-foot length of nylon rope. He turned DeMarco to stand facing the eyehook, then tied the free end of the rope around the sergeant's wrists.

"You're just going to leave me like this?" DeMarco said.

"You'll get yourself loose."

Huston returned to the car, laid the

service weapon on the shelf, and retrieved from the trunk the strip of tape he had peeled off DeMarco's mouth. "I'm afraid this has to go back," he told DeMarco.

"Even if I promise to be quiet?"

Huston smiled and pressed the tape into place. He remained standing close. "I wouldn't have shot you," he said.

"I know that," DeMarco mumbled.

What Huston did next seemed a strange thing to DeMarco. Huston laid his hand atop the sergeant's head; he leaned against him, their bodies touching, heads touching side to side. He remained motionless, eyes closed, for several seconds. DeMarco felt like a little boy again, and his breath caught in his chest. Then Huston moved away from him and returned to the rear of the car.

For the better part of five minutes, Huston struggled with Inman's body, dragging and lifting and pushing until he had it crammed into the trunk. There was plenty of slack in DeMarco's rope so he was able to turn and watch the struggle. Inman had regained consciousness but was far from fully alert. He squirmed against Huston's efforts but with his legs bent back at the knee and tied to his wrists with nylon rope, his mouth taped shut, his resistance accomplished little more than to slow Huston down.

Next, Huston went to the opposite side of the garage where a dozen cement blocks were stacked underneath the stairs leading to the apartment. He laid two of these blocks on the floor behind the driver's seat. Then he picked Inman's knife off the floor and stuck it under his belt. When he returned to the shelf, he picked up the handgun and stuffed it into his waistband, then faced the car and closed the trunk lid. DeMarco grunted and moaned as loudly as he could to get Huston's attention.

Huston peeled the tape off DeMarco's lips but left one end attached to his cheek.

"Don't take my service weapon, please," DeMarco said.

"I'm sorry. I need it."

"Thomas, c'mon. I'm too old to be demoted again."

"I have no choice," Huston said. He started to press the tape in place again.

"Wait, wait, wait. In the compartment for the jack on the side of the trunk. Take that weapon instead. It's unregistered."

Huston popped open the trunk again. With the service weapon now aimed at Inman and keeping him cowered to the side, Huston recovered the other handgun. Then he slammed shut the trunk.

"Thank you," he said and pressed the tape

over DeMarco's mouth. "I'll leave your service weapon on the shelf for you. Out of reach for now."

He smiled one more time. Then he climbed into the car and drove away.

SIXTY

Through the barn's open door, the early morning mist was cool and as gray as a shadow. For the first few moments after Huston's departure, DeMarco did nothing but inhale the morning in one deep breath after another. He was clearheaded and unhurt except for a dull throb at the base of his skull. *It looks like you're probably not going to die today,* he thought and was a little disappointed in himself because of the shiver of pleasure the realization brought.

Even more pleasurable was the realization that Inman would die soon. DeMarco would do his best to prevent that because it was his duty to do so, but he knew he had small chance of success, and he considered his first priority keeping Huston alive despite the man's obvious intent to subvert that duty.

DeMarco stood close to the wall and surveyed the possibilities. No nails within reach that he might employ as a scraping tool against the duct tape and nylon rope. But he soon discovered that if he moved as far from the wall as the rope allowed, held the rope taut, and rotated his hands downward, he could, with small, quick movements, saw the edge of the tape against the rope. Three minutes later, the tape around his wrists broke free. Now he could peel the tape off his mouth and pick at the knot on the rope. The latter was not easy with his upper arms down to the elbow taped to his body, but by bending forward, he could raise the knot to his mouth now, pull on it blindly with his teeth, lower it to check on his progress, then repeat the process until the knot finally gave way.

No longer tethered to the wall, he shuffled to the corner of the tool shelf, lifted the machete from its hook, and very carefully held the cutting edge against the layers of tape circling his chest. The tape split easily against the sharpness of the blade. With his arms free, he quickly unshackled his ankles.

He knew he should call in for backup, get an alert out on his car. But if he did that, he would have to report that Huston was armed. Any police officers encountered would be inclined to disarm him by whatever means necessary. And how would

Huston react to that?

DeMarco felt certain he could track his friend down without such a confrontation. "You better be certain," he told himself. "Because either way, you're going to pay for this." He recovered his service weapon and headed for the house.

In his living room he grabbed his cell phone off the floor, scrolled through the list of recently dialed numbers, found the one he needed, and hit the dial button. The clock on the DVR read 4:54.

He was grateful to hear Rosemary O'Patchen's sleepy voice answer. "It's Sergeant DeMarco," he told her, "and I'm sorry to call you so early but I need your help, Rosemary, I really do."

"What can I do?" she said.

"I need to know if there's a place at the lake that has some special significance for Thomas. Some place private and secluded that he knows very well."

"There is, yes. Is that where he is now?"

"It may be. I'm not sure. But I have reason to believe that I can find him there. How do I get to it?"

"It's on the north shore," she said.

"In Canada?"

"Excuse me?"

"The north shore of Lake Erie is in Canada, right?"

"Oh," she said, and he heard the disappointment in her voice. "Then no, I'm sorry. I don't know of any place along Lake Erie that was special to him. I mean, the kids loved the beaches; they usually went to Beach 7. But there's nothing private or secluded about it."

"I'm confused," DeMarco told her. "What lake are you talking about?"

"Lake Wilhelm. Where we all went camping every summer."

"Of course," he said. "I should have thought of that first. This camping place is private?"

"Very private. In fact, each time we went there, he insisted we follow a slightly different path to the campsite. So we didn't leave a permanent trail."

"I need to know how to get there, Rosemary."

"The easiest way is to go north on 19."

"How far north?"

"About halfway between Sheakleyville and Black Run."

"Okay, that's good. But here's the thing, Rosemary. GPS is useless for this. Can you give me landmarks? Tell me exactly where to make my turns?"

"Let me think for a minute," she said.

He waited.

She said, "Just after 19 crosses over the headwaters, you'll see an old logging road going off to the right. It starts off parallel to Black Run, but then it heads south again. It ends in a clearing maybe a hundred or so yards from Schofield Run. Kids have parties there, so you'll see lots of litter and old campfires and such."

"You're doing fine. Just keep going." As he talked he crossed toward the back door. His car was gone but he knew that Inman had not arrived at his house by taxi. Bonnie's car, maybe with an unsuspecting Bonnie still waiting patiently inside, was parked somewhere nearby, probably within a couple blocks of DeMarco's garage.

Rosemary O'Patchen told him, "You can't see Schofield Run from the clearing but if you stand very quietly you can hear it. Just make your way to it as best you can. There's no path to speak of but it's mostly red pines, so the brush isn't heavy. Then just follow the run downstream to where it feeds into Lake Wilhelm, a couple tenths of a mile maybe. Then you have to cross over the run — it's only a few feet wide and a foot or so deep — and pick your way along the lakeshore another fifty yards or so. That's where the campsite is."

DeMarco was standing behind his barn now, squinting through the darkness as he surveyed Lawson Street in one direction and then the other. He told Rosemary, "That sounds like a difficult place to get to," and thought, *Especially frog-marching Inman and carrying two cement blocks.*

"That's why Thomas liked it so much. He wouldn't allow so much as an MP3 player along on those campouts. He took one cell phone just for emergencies, but otherwise it was family only. No outside world allowed."

"And there's no easier way to get to it?" A dark shape that was either a vehicle or a couple of garbage bins was visible a block and a half to his right. DeMarco started toward it.

"None," she said. "But if he's hiding somewhere near the lake, that will be the place."

"Thank you," he told her. "I'm sorry to have wakened you like this."

"You won't hurt him, will you?" she said.

"Never."

"Please promise me that you won't let him be hurt."

"I swear to God," he said. Then, "He didn't do it, Rosemary. You can tell your husband that for me. Thomas would never harm his family in any way. I know that now."

"Oh God," she said and started to sob. "Thank you. Thank you so much."

And now he recognized the distinctive shape of the Mustang's backend, the taillights and spoiler. Bonnie's car. "I'm sorry, Rosemary, I have to go now," he said. And he shut off his phone.

Sixty-One

DeMarco held the handgun against his leg as he approached the Mustang. There were no streetlamps along Lawson and all the houses were still dark. He doubted that Bonnie would draw a gun on him, but on the other hand, he would not have believed she would participate in a multiple homicide. He told himself that love makes fools of us all and moved quickly from one front lawn to the next, staying far enough to the right that he could not be seen in the Mustang's side mirror.

Only when he was nearly parallel to the car could he distinguish a silhouette in the passenger seat. Bonnie was sitting with her head laid back against the headrest. *Awfully relaxed for a murderer,* he thought. *Maybe she doesn't know what her boyfriend was up to.*

He raised his weapon to a ready position and moved forward. She did not turn his way. He moved closer and looked at her through the passenger window. Still she did not move. *She's sleeping,* he told himself. He tapped the barrel against the glass. No response. He tapped again, harder. No movement from within.

With his weapon aimed at her now, De-Marco put his free hand on the door handle, then swung the door open. The dome light had been turned off, and in the predawn darkness she remained no more visible than a shadow, but he was able to see that she did not move in any way. He leaned forward and put a finger to her cheek. Her skin was not cold, but it was cool enough that he felt something catch in his chest. "Oh fuck," he said.

He slid his hand down the jawline to her carotid artery. Instead of a pulse, he felt the sticky smear of blood that had flowed over her blouse, and immediately the coppery scent reached him too.

He leaned away from her, softly closed the door, stood there breathing deeply. "What a fucking mess," he told the last dim stars overhead. He hunkered down low to rub his fingers clean in the wet grass.

He knew he should not proceed on his own now, knew that if he did he could end up manning a radar gun the rest of his career, or putting in long hours doing traffic control at a construction site, sitting on his hemorrhoids and trying to stay awake. But he also thought he knew what Huston had planned. The cement blocks were probably to slow Inman down should he attempt to run. In all likelihood, Huston intended to take Inman's life exactly as that psychopath had taken away Huston's family. And then to use DeMarco's revolver on himself.

What Huston did not know was that the first three shells in the .22's cylinder were filled with birdshot. What would a load of birdshot do to the inside of a man's head? DeMarco didn't want to think about it.

He hurried around the car and climbed into the driver's seat. Inman had not locked the car because he'd had no intention of returning to it. The keys were in the ignition. The smell of blood was thick, its scent of rusty metal. DeMarco turned on the dome light and looked at Bonnie. The front of her white blouse was soaked with drying blood. The blood had run over the top of her jeans and soaked her to the thighs. Her hands were bloody and there were bloody handprints on the dashboard.

DeMarco leaned over her body, pulled the seat belt harness across her chest, and buckled her in.

■ ■ ■ ■

Twenty minutes, he told himself. Twenty minutes to the clearing near Schofield Run. Huston had a twenty-minute jump on him. But Huston would be driving cautiously. He wouldn't want to get pulled over in a stolen car with a man in the trunk. De-Marco, on the other hand, had no such concern. He drove through the graying morning as fast as the turns allowed. He knew there would be no troopers hiding along the highway for another two hours. So maybe he could make up a few minutes on Huston by speeding.

"Then the hike to the campsite," he told Bonnie. "He'll have to cut Inman's legs free. Then he'll either make a second trip back to the car for the cement blocks or he'll make your boyfriend carry them. That's what I would do."

The seat belt straps across Bonnie's chest and lap kept her upper body tight against the seat, but her head jounced forward and back, side to side. Her feet slid over the floor mat, sometimes kicking out violently in re-action to a hard turn. She was wearing a pair of straw-colored mules but soon both feet were bare. DeMarco wished he could stop long enough to put her shoes back on, but he could not.

"Why did he kill you?" he asked. "Did you balk when you realized he was coming for me? Did you try to talk him out of it?"

He wondered if she had even known about the Huston murders before the fact. Probably not. Hard-timers like Inman learn to trust no one. They impart information on a need-to-know basis only, and even then it's usually a lie.

"Why did he come after me?" he asked. "Why not just get away as far and as fast as you could?"

Her head rolled side to side with the movements of the car. Her bare feet scraped the floor.

SIXTY-TWO

In gray light, DeMarco pushed his way through the stand of red pines, his left arm raised to bat the branches away from his face, his forearm already scratched and bleeding. He moved toward the burbling of water over rocks. The needle-matted ground was soft and fragrant, and if he ran stooped low, he could pass under most of the branches. Behind him in the clearing, his car and Bonnie's Mustang sat side by side, both hoods lightly steaming from the engine heat. He thought maybe he could get to the campsite in time. Maybe he could prevent what he knew was going to happen there.

The first shot echoed through the tops of the trees and over the misted lake like the crack of a bullwhip. It threw DeMarco off stride for a moment, then he was running again, harder now, listening to the silence, the pause, and praying that it continued. Huston would have been surprised by the effects of that first shot, the spray of tiny pellets, the sudden bloody pockmarks all over Inman's face and chest. It would be a killing shot only if delivered point-blank, and he doubted Huston's ability to do that. So now maybe Huston was checking the cylinder, seeing the two remaining rounds of birdshot, the three .22 longs. Maybe he would take some delight in the birdshot, see it as a way of prolonging Inman's pain. But certainly he planned to save the last round for himself.

A less attractive scenario was that the little shell full of birdshot had been emptied inside Huston's own mouth or against his temple. In which case, Huston would have already used the knife to dispatch Inman. Both images made DeMarco cringe.

Only ten more yards and he would be into the white beyond the trees, the mist along the shore and over the lake. He ran full speed now, chest aching. Praying for more silence.

He broke out of the trees and onto the pebbly shore and swung left. Then he was splashing with long strides across Schofield Run, the water icy against his shins. He slipped and went down and banged his elbow hard against the rocks but was quickly on his feet again, splashing onto dry ground.

He put a hand to his jacket pocket, made sure his service weapon was still there, though he felt no need to take it in hand. He had already decided that he was not going to pull a gun on Huston, no matter what.

DeMarco could make out two dark figures through the mist now, two faceless silhouettes, one standing in the water, one lower, possibly sitting on shore. Then the second shot cracked. The sound slapped DeMarco full in the face. "Thomas, don't!" he yelled. But with the words came the splintering crack of four more shots in rapid succession, and the figure on the shore fell onto his back, and DeMarco slowed, blinked, and as his focus on the figure in the water sharpened, the ache in his chest swelled and pulsed, and he reached into his pocket and withdrew his weapon and walked toward Inman. The man was standing beside a small boulder that protruded from the water, his hands taped at the wrist and clasped hard around DeMarco's father's revolver.

Huston's face and neck and chest were riddled with bloody splotches from the first three shots. The last three, all to his chest, had made slightly larger wounds, and around them, the blood was bright and flowing, emerging with the slow, shallow pulses of his heart.

DeMarco knelt beside him. He kept his right hand extended toward the lake, held Inman ankle-deep in the water. He placed his left hand atop Huston's head. Huston lay with his eyes wide open, staring into the high, deep whiteness. His hands were clenched against the pain but a small smile creased his mouth. "You're a very clever man," DeMarco told him.

Huston gave no indication that he had heard. *He's somewhere else,* DeMarco told himself. Maybe he was with Claire and the children already. Maybe he was watching as they approached him hand in hand.

"I'm fucking bleeding to death, man," Inman said, but DeMarco had no interest in him at the moment. He was interested only in the art of dying as practiced by a former writer he admired, so he sat very quietly with his hand atop Huston's head until Huston's labored breathing ceased and he lay still and smiling and far away from the pebbly shore.

Now DeMarco turned his attention to other matters. Beside his knee lay Inman's heavy-handled knife, where Huston had placed it. Inman was leaning forward from the edge of the water, shivering violently.

There was a cut down each of his thick arms, running from the armpit to elbow, and a long cut down the inside of each thigh. His jeans and gray T-shirt bore Rorschach images in blood. Lashed to each ankle was a cement block from DeMarco's garage.

DeMarco smiled. Something of Huston's calmness had passed into him and he was in no hurry now; he had nothing important to do.

"That fucker got what he deserved," Inman said. "He's a fucking lunatic."

"Is he?" DeMarco said.

"Look what he did to me!"

DeMarco studied the situation. Inman's clothes were wet to his chest. Huston's clothes were too. A thick ribbon of mud swirled through the green water behind Inman. But there were no drag marks leading into the water.

DeMarco said, "Check me out on this, Carl. He held the gun on you and marched you out into deeper water, right?"

"I'm fucking freezing here!"

"Answer my questions and you can come out."

"All right, yeah, that's what he did."

"Did he tie the cement blocks to you in the water?"

491

"No, before. Then he made me carry them until I was out there farther."

"And that's when he cut you?"

"While holding this fucking gun to my head!"

"Then he walked back, laid the revolver on that little boulder there, came back here, and sat down on the shore. Do I have that right?"

"I told you he was fucking nuts, didn't I? What did he think, I wouldn't go for the gun? Dumb fuck just sat there grinning at me."

DeMarco smiled. "He even left your knife here so you could cut yourself free afterward. He knew your only hope would be to get back out to the road. But the harder you ran, the faster you'd bleed out. He wanted you to experience your death. Every terrified moment of it."

Inman shivered. "And you think that's fucking funny?" He made an attempt to hurl the empty revolver at DeMarco, but with his wrists still bound, the handgun barely cleared the water and clattered against the rocks.

The urge was strong in DeMarco to pick up the revolver, clean it off, take it home where it belonged, the only thing he had left of his father. But it had to stay.

DeMarco looked away from Inman then, down the lake and across the water to the trees. They were still dark in the rising mist, but behind them the soft orange light of morning glowed.

"Hey, asshole," Inman said. His voice was softer now, pleading. "You just going to sit there and let me die?"

"I would never do that," DeMarco answered. "Come ashore."

Inman dragged one foot forward, then the other. The cement blocks scraped over the lake bottom and churned up the mud. Finally he stood shivering and hugging himself only a few feet from DeMarco. He said, "You going to get these fucking blocks off my feet or what?"

"Of course," DeMarco said. He then laid his left hand atop Huston's head a final time, raised his right hand toward Inman, and put a bullet through Inman's heart.

SIXTY-THREE

Bowen laid the slender sheaf of papers down on his blotter, then looked across the desk at DeMarco, who was gazing out the window. Early afternoon sunlight gave the air beyond the glass a stunning clarity. The few remaining leaves on the twin maples in the barrack's front lawn trembled like brown flames in a guttering breeze. Bowen said, "It's nicely written, I'll say that much for it."

DeMarco smiled. "I've been taking a crash course."

"How about we go through it together. I'm still puzzled about a thing or two."

"Have at it," DeMarco said.

"Last night at your place. So Huston just showed up out of the blue. Knocked on the back door. You let him in. You take him into your living room. But you don't remember much about your ensuing conversation."

"Only what's there in the report. And for

494

that I have your little white pills to thank. I was spacy from the time he woke me pounding on the door until Inman coldcocked me."

"In the kitchen."

"Correct."

"Where you went to get a couple of beers."

"Get some beer, make some sandwiches . . . Huston hadn't eaten since I saw him at the lighthouse."

"So you go out to the kitchen, just you, and there's Inman standing."

"Big, bald, and ugly."

"And how did he know where to find Huston?"

"Are you asking me to guess?"

"I'm asking you to surmise. Speculate. Ah what the hell; take a guess."

"Maybe he was watching my place, hoping I would lead him to Huston."

"If he wanted to kill Huston, why didn't he do it when he had the chance last week?"

"I guess I should have asked him that. My bad."

"What do you fucking *think*?"

"I think maybe he initially thought Huston would be arrested, convicted, disgraced, put away where Inman's buddies could have some fun with him. Obviously Inman likes to play with his victims. Problem was, we couldn't find Huston, and I was starting to make Inman nervous. So he decided he'd better take out the one remaining person who could pull him out of a lineup."

Bowen rubbed a hand over his cheek. Then he ran both hands through his hair. Then he said, "So you go into the kitchen to get Huston something to eat, and there's Inman, and he decks you. Just like that."

"I was still groggy, remember? Reflexes were slow. Thanks to you. In a fair fight, I would have kicked his ass in six seconds flat."

"Okay, sure. Next thing you recall is looking up from the kitchen floor to see him dragging Huston out the door."

"I also recall this little dream I had. Something about mermaids on the linoleum. Should I have put that in the report?"

Bowen leaned back in his chair. "So you pull yourself together, make your way outside, and you're just in time to see your car going down the alley behind your barn."

"You're an attentive reader, Kyle. It's nice to know you take my writing seriously."

"How about if you take this conversation seriously?"

"Absolutely."

"Every question I'm asking you, the press is going to ask me. I'd like to not come off as a complete moron."

"It's a little late in life to be making that decision, isn't it?"

Bowen sighed audibly. "Our history together will carry you only so far. You need to understand that."

DeMarco smiled. "History used to be my favorite subject. Those who cannot learn from history are doomed to repeat it. Or something like that. George Santayana."

"Santayana the guitar player said that? The guy who wrote that devil woman song?"

"The song is 'Black Magic Woman' and the guitar player is Carlos Santana. And he didn't write the song. In fact, it was recorded by Fleetwood Mac two years before Santana covered it. You really suck at just about everything, don't you?"

Bowen smiled in spite of himself, then was startled by the buzzing of his cell phone. He looked at the number. "Channel Four," he said before silencing the phone. "So back to the matter at hand. You make it outside just in time to see your car leaving. But instead of picking up the phone and calling for assistance, you go running after the car."

"Staggering is more like it. I wrote *staggering*, didn't I?"

"You go staggering away in pursuit."

"I wasn't in pursuit so much as I was hoping to ascertain the perp's probable flight path. So that I could then call for assistance."

"You didn't say that in here," Bowen said and tapped a finger to the report.

"I just now thought of it. I mean that was probably my intent."

"Probably."

"Listen, you're the guy who forced the pills on me. Threatened me, in fact, with something awful — I forget what exactly — if I didn't take them. So if there are some holes in my memory, you put them there."

"It was twenty milligrams of Valium, for Chrissakes. A mild relaxant."

DeMarco shrugged. "Maybe it was the right to the jaw. I think Inman might have banged my head on the floor a couple times while he was at it."

"Are you making this up as you go along?"

"Certain details are coming back to me. I wasn't fucking chasing the car. Do I look like a Labrador retriever to you? I wanted to see which way it turned at the corner."

"But you also saw and recognized Bonnie's vehicle parked along the street."

"I did."

"So you approached that vehicle with your weapon drawn."

"As I recall."

"So you were wearing your weapon when Inman coldcocked you in the kitchen."

"That doesn't seem likely," DeMarco said.

"Yet you had it when you went outside."

"Now there's another hole in my memory. At some point I must have retrieved it from the bedroom. Then I staggered outside."

"Is that how you now recall it?"

"I'm just trying to fill in the gaps. Not much is certain."

"So it would seem."

"Seeing Bonnie with her throat slit kind of slapped me awake though. You know what I mean?"

"Except that you still failed to call in for assistance."

"I thought you read my report carefully."

"Okay, you attempted to make the call once you were in pursuit in Bonnie's vehicle. But your cell phone battery was dead."

"You ever notice how technology always lets you down when you need it most?"

"You're fucking driving me nuts. I'm trying to make some sense of this . . . this . . ."

"Report?"

"This assemblage of inconsistencies. And if I didn't know you better, I would say that you're making every effort to subvert my understanding."

DeMarco chuckled.

499

"What's so damn funny?"

"Sorry, I just thought of this line from Raymond Chandler's *The Big Sleep*. 'I test very high on insubordination.' Not that it has any application here, you understand."

"We're talking about a multiple homicide, Ryan."

"Which I've been beating out my brains over ever since day one. Look, I'm not attempting to subvert your understanding in any way, shape, or form. I'm just feeling a little giddy, I guess, because it's over. At long fucking last, this ugly, horrendous episode is finally over. And yes, I am also more than a little bit testy about how it went down. It cost us a good man. A very good man."

Several moments passed. "All right," Bowen said. "You can't make a call because your cell phone's dead. You continue in pursuit. Where did you catch up with them?"

"I never really caught up. I would see a pair of taillights every now and then, enough that I could stay with them. Where I really lost some time was after Inman abandoned the car in the clearing."

"Right," Bowen said. "It's what, maybe six in the morning by then? Still fairly dark. Yet somehow you managed to track them to a campsite you didn't even know existed."

"I followed my ears. After the first gunshot, it wasn't all that difficult."

"And what you saw there strikes me as very bizarre indeed."

"Indeed," DeMarco said.

"Why would Inman use birdshot?"

DeMarco shrugged. "He's a sadist. If anything should be clear by now, it's that."

"He shot Huston three times with birdshot just to make him suffer?"

"That's all I can figure."

"Then he finishes him off with three .22 longs to the chest. Using a fifty-year-old revolver."

"The word *weird* doesn't even scratch the surface of a guy like him."

"I would say not. Because then he apparently wades into the water and starts cutting himself. Why would he do that?"

"You're asking me to explain irrational actions."

"I'm asking you to speculate."

"He's a sadist *and* a masochist. He was seriously *insane.*"

Bowen scowled and shook his head. "So you arrive on scene. You check on Huston. See it's too late for him. And you order Inman out of the water."

"At which point he comes at me with that

long mofo of a knife."

"End of story."

"End of his anyway."

"He falls back into the water; you wade in and drag the body out."

"And that water was *cold.*"

"But wait, now it's time for a miracle. Suddenly your cell phone works!"

"I went back to the clearing, plugged in the charger in my car, and made the call. I guess I forgot to put that part in my report."

"Still groggy?" Bowen said.

"Nope. Right now I feel as clear as this beautiful autumn day. A little tired though. Hungry and tired."

"Let's talk about the crime scene for just a minute. Apparently there's some evidence of rope burns around Inman's wrists and ankles. But you didn't find any rope?"

"At the campsite? Nothing but rocks."

"Any idea then where those rope burns might have come from?"

"Maybe he and Bonnie had a little rough sex before coming to my place."

"Culminating, apparently, in the slitting of her throat."

"Let me refresh your memory, Kyle. Carl Inman? *Insane.*"

Bowen blew out another heavy breath. "And while you waited for the units to arrive, you built yourself a nice big fire. Kind of a signal fire, was that your intent?"

"My intent was to keep my cold, frozen balls from falling off."

"You know, you've always been a bit of a loose cannon, but this time . . . There are a hell of a lot of holes in your story this time."

"So I'm not a natural storyteller. Just another one of the many deficits I'm learning to live with."

"There are no suspicions whatsoever on your part that maybe, being so groggy and all, you got a few things wrong?"

"For instance?" DeMarco said.

"Like maybe it was Huston doing the cutting on Inman? That would explain the rope burns at least."

"Seems quite a stretch to me," DeMarco said.

"You're not even willing to consider the possibility?"

"That scenario would require that Huston somehow overpowered Inman, tied him up . . . with rope he found where? There was no rope in my car, I can tell you that. He then somehow was able to convince Inman to stand chest deep in freezing water so that Huston could slice away at him? And then what? Knowing that Inman would freeze and or bleed to death before he could get back to civilization, he then handed him an unregistered weapon, loaded with birdshot, for fuck's sake, then sat on the shore and said, 'Okay, your turn, shoot me.' You think that's the more plausible story?"

"What I think is that it's not outside the realm of possibility that you might be hoping to rewrite a bit of history. For Huston's sake."

DeMarco said nothing. After a few seconds, he turned in his chair and gazed out the window again. The bareness of the trees made his chest ache. The sky was heartbreakingly blue.

Finally he faced Bowen again. "Are you asking me if it's possible that a good, decent, and compassionate man could resort to torture?"

"That's what I'm asking."

"You tell me," DeMarco said. "You have a wife and a little girl who mean the world to you. Let's say you come home one night and find them butchered. What would you do to the man responsible? What would you consider a suitable punishment?"

Bowen stared down at DeMarco's report. He sat very still for half a minute. Then he pulled open a drawer, removed a manila folder, slipped the report inside the folder, and closed the cover. "Do me a favor," he said. "Take your frozen balls and get out of here."

DeMarco stood. "Oh, they're both nicely thawed by now. You wanna check?"

SIXTY-FOUR

Before returning home in the afternoon, DeMarco drove to the village of Oniontown. From the O'Patchens' driveway, he could see Rosemary in her backyard. On her hands and knees, she was moving down the rows of withered tomato plants in her garden, pulling them up by the roots and stuffing them into a plastic bucket. As De-Marco approached, she looked up at him. Her eyes were red and swollen, cheeks slick with tears and streaked with the dirt from her hands.

"Where's Ed?" DeMarco asked.

"Sitting by the TV," she said. "I think he's hoping the news will change somehow. But it's not going to. 'Last member of Huston family brutally slain before killer is brought down by state police.'"

She yanked a tomato plant from the ground and shook the dirt from its roots. "At least you got the son of a bitch," she said. "At least you got him."

DeMarco knelt beside her. He picked up the bucket and held it while she stuffed the dead plant inside. "How are you at keeping secrets?" he said.

SIXTY-FIVE

The day of Huston's funeral was appropriately gray and chilled. Now that his innocence had been proclaimed over the Internet and beamed from one broadcasting tower to the next across several continents, his colleagues and neighbors were quick to claim him again as a close friend whose innocence they had never doubted. The jealousy they had felt for Huston alive became a personal sense of loss for Huston dead. On the day of the announcement of his death, every bookstore in the country sold out every copy of his work in stock, and tens of thousands of copies were back-ordered.

At the crowded gravesite, coeds hugged copies of Huston's novels to their Halston stadium jackets, sobbed, and shivered while thin, sensitive boys looked on longingly and plotted ways to turn grief into sexual conquest. The poet Denton, in a charcoal cashmere overcoat, a lavender wool scarf wrapped twice around his throat, spoke for fifteen minutes about the special relationship he and Thomas Huston had shared. "Colleagues, friends, and even collaborators," he said, "laborers toiling side by side in the vineyards of truth," "brother soldiers . . . warrior poets." Afterward, he threw back his head and recited Poe's "Lenore" and "Annabel Lee." His shaggy chestnut hair lifted in the gusty breeze, his eyes glimmered with tears, and his voice quavered just enough to be heard.

DeMarco stood well behind the deep half-moon of mourners. Only occasional snatches of Denton's recitation reached his ears. DeMarco had meant to remain at the ceremony only briefly, then to return to the silence of home and the thoughts that nagged at him, but he lingered on until shortly after the coffin was lowered into the ground and the feature-length histrionics of sobbing and keening began. Rosemary and Ed O'Patchen were the first to lean over the grave for a final good-bye. They stood side by side, motionless for half a minute, Ed's ungloved hand resting in the middle of his wife's back. When the couple turned away to make room for the others queuing up behind them, Rosemary's eyes found De-

Marco at the rear of the crowd, and with a whispered word, she directed her husband's gaze to him. Though their cheeks were red with cold and shiny with tears, both O'Patchens greeted DeMarco with a subtle smile only he understood. He nodded once, then turned and walked the long, winding asphalt pathway back to his car alone.

What had been troubling DeMarco was the nagging question of why Inman had shown up at DeMarco's house three nights earlier. Why would he risk capture by confronting DeMarco? The two men shared no history. DeMarco had never busted him, had had no role in any of Inman's previous arrests. All DeMarco could figure was that, at some point, Bonnie had mentioned the sergeant to her boyfriend, and something in her tone of voice had tripped Inman's jealousy trigger again, so he made a slight detour in his escape route, slit Bonnie's throat, and came after DeMarco. Given the convolutions of the criminal psyche, De-Marco considered this a plausible explanation, yet it failed to quiet the mumblings in his brain. For that reason he had ordered that Bonnie's vehicle be impounded and scrutinized, but it produced no further rationale for Inman's behavior. The small trunk was crammed with their clothing in two suitcases and three duffels, the glove box held road maps for Pennsylvania, West Virginia, Kentucky, Arkansas, and Texas, and in Bonnie's purse was their traveling money, two packets of three thousand dollars each in Citizen Bank wrappers. None of it spoke to DeMarco, not a word of insinuation. It left him only with a vague uneasiness that refused to gel.

And now footsteps intruded on the uneasiness, long strides coming up from the rear — brisk movement, the solid slap of soles growing louder by the second. *A man,* DeMarco thought, *or a tall, athletic woman in flats, not heels.* Slowing only a little he turned at the waist.

"Hey," Nathan Briessen said. His black overcoat hung open, black cable-stitched turtleneck sweater and jeans. His cheeks were red from the cold, eyes red rimmed from a deeper chill.

"Hey," DeMarco answered.

The young man came alongside and matched his stride to DeMarco's. For a while they walked in silence. Then DeMarco told him, "I'm sorry, Nathan. I know he was a good friend to you."

The young man nodded. His gaze held the distance. "How did you like the show?" he asked.

"Touching," said DeMarco.

"I'm surprised he didn't set up a table and do a book signing while he was at it."

"Denton?"

"Fucking self-promoting son of a bitch. I wanted to strangle him."

DeMarco cut a glance at the young man's face, the grim set of jaw. And now he understood Nathan's need for company, the anger, outrage mixed with grief.

Nathan said, "To use a man's funeral like that. Especially a man like Thomas. He'd have been disgusted by that, you know."

"Maybe," DeMarco said. "Or maybe just amused. Able to forgive his friends their excesses."

"Friends?" Nathan said, then shook his head.

They walked in silence awhile longer. They reached the sidewalk finally and turned right, continued beside the long line of cars parked at the curb.

DeMarco said, "So Thomas didn't consider Denton a friend? You know this for a fact?"

"He would never come right out and bash somebody, you know? He just wasn't like that. But Denton's constant self-promoting . . . Thomas found it distasteful, to say the least."

DeMarco said, "Tell me about the self-promoting."

"He never passed up a chance to put himself in the spotlight. The man was constantly angling for the department chair, full professorship . . . or just to be the center of attention. He was obsessed with it. Just like today. Insisting on giving the eulogy. And then turning it into the Robert Denton show."

DeMarco thought he recognized the young man's car as they passed it, a blue BMW coupe. But Nathan continued walking. DeMarco remained silent.

Nathan said, "Every time he published a poem in some obscure literary journal, he'd send out a press release, for Chrissakes. To the local papers, the campus paper, the alumni newsletter. He'd even send out emails to the entire student and faculty lists."

"And Thomas didn't approve of that?"

"To him it was all about the work, you know?"

DeMarco nodded. "He was a special man, all right."

They came to DeMarco's car then. Both men paused beside the right rear fender. DeMarco turned to face the young man and waited.

Nathan stared past him. "Even that thing up in Albion," he said. "He even sent out press releases on that. That one really got Thomas's hackles up."

At the mention of Albion, something pinched at a corner of DeMarco's brain, in the same brain wrinkle that had been twitching with uneasiness. "What thing in Albion?"

"At the correctional facility. The poetry class for the inmates."

"Denton taught a class at the prison?"

"From what I hear he's been teaching a class there every semester for the past couple of years at least. He sends out a new announcement every semester."

All of a sudden DeMarco felt a heaviness in his chest, a tightness that made his heart beat fast and his breathing come quick and shallow. "I take it you weren't aware that Carl Inman did his time in Albion. Until a few weeks ago."

The young man locked his eyes on DeMarco's. "Are you serious?" he said. "Fuck, you are serious."

"You really didn't know?"

"I swear to God I didn't."

SIXTY-SIX

DeMarco could have contacted the correctional center by telephone, but then he would have had no excuse for not going home. Home was as gray as the sky and as stagnant as a grave. The thirty-minute drive to Albion would provide not only a sense of movement, some kind of forward progress, but would also allow him time to consider all the implications of this latest bit of news. Nathan's tip about the poet might in fact be a dead end, but DeMarco doubted it. The pinch in his brain that had been harassing him since Huston's death had not only subsided now but had been replaced by a kind of lightness, a decrease in intercranium pressure. The day seemed brighter by a lumen or two, the air fresher. Something had been changed by Nathan's revelation. The fog of ignorance was lifting.

The new deputy superintendent for the facility was a slight man of medium height named Gallagher. DeMarco had hoped to be received by Superintendent Woods himself, as soft jowled and sturdy looking as a bloodhound. Gallagher, on the other hand, reminded DeMarco of a robotic Chihuahua, his every movement small and quick and preceded by at least five motionless seconds while his brain whirred through the binary code. Unfortunately, today was the superintendent's day off. But DeMarco's request was little more than a clerical matter and hardly required a blue tick's temperament. He sat beside a potted ficus and watched Gallagher pull up the information on his computer.

Gallagher said, "Professor Denton has taught a two-week course in writing poetry five times so far. One every June, one every January. Scheduled to teach for us again at the first of the year."

"How about the class rosters?" DeMarco said.

Gallagher stared at the computer screen, motionless but for two finger taps to scroll down the page. Finally he said, "Carl Inman, no."

"Never? Not even one of the five times?"

"Correct," Gallagher said.

DeMarco leaned back in his chair. He leaned away from a ficus leaf that was tickling his ear. "Would you know if Professor Denton had any other association with the inmates? Any opportunity for individual meetings, that kind of thing?"

"It's unlikely," Gallagher said. "Two guards are present at every class meeting. Class sizes ranged from . . . seven to twelve."

"Are your visitation records computerized?"

"Yes, sir, they are."

"Could you check to see if Denton signed in to visit Inman at any time?"

"Two years sufficient?"

"That should be fine."

Again DeMarco waited. He wondered if Gallagher was so stiff and mechanical at home. Wondered if he was married, had children, owned a real live dog and if so what kind.

"Negative," Gallagher told him.

DeMarco said, "No visits, no class contact. No direct contact as far as you can ascertain."

"As far as we can ascertain. That's correct."

After a few seconds, DeMarco put his hands on his knees and pushed himself to his feet. He approached the deputy superintendent's desk and held out his hand. "Thank you. I appreciate your help."

Gallagher sat motionless for a few seconds, then stood and thrust out his hand.

DeMarco was surprised by its warmth and the firmness of the grip. He said, "So how do you like the job? You've been here what, five months now?"

"Five months shy a week, yes, sir. And the job is fine."

"Two thousand inmates more or less. That's a lot of responsibility."

"It is," Gallagher said. Then added, as if it were expected of him, "But not an unwelcome one."

And suddenly DeMarco knew why Gallagher was so stiff. *He's scared,* DeMarco thought. *Scared to death he's going to fuck up somehow.*

"You and I should probably split a pitcher of beer some time," DeMarco told him. "What do you think?"

Gallagher blinked. "That would be fine, sir."

"I'm Ryan, by the way. Save the sirs for the guy who signs your checks."

"Oh," Gallagher said. Then, a moment later, "Nelson."

"Is that what your friends call you?"

Another pause. Then, "J. J."

"How the hell do you get J. J. out of Nelson Gallagher?"

Gallagher smiled and blushed. "Nelson Jamison Jerome Gallagher. My mother's brothers."

"Lucky for you she only had two."

"Don't I know it."

The pinch in DeMarco's cerebellum came back around midnight. After talking with the deputy superintendent earlier in the evening, DeMarco had managed to convince himself that the prison poetry classes were a red herring; they had no relevance to anything Inman had done. DeMarco's remark in Bowen's office was the only relevance. *Carl Inman? Insane.* There was no sense trying to apply logic to the workings of an irrational mind. The frustration would only end up driving the logical mind crazy.

Six ounces of room-temperature Tennessee whiskey helped. The mindless drone of the television in a darkened room helped. But not long after DeMarco crawled off to bed, only to lie there staring into the darkness above him, the pinch began again. It felt to DeMarco as if somebody were tugging on a single hair a couple of inches behind the crown of his head, and the hair extended maybe three inches into his brain. He scratched the area, rubbed it with his

519

knuckles, probed it with his fingers. Every ten or fifteen seconds the pinch came again. The longer DeMarco studied it, the more certain he was that the pinch was less physical and more linguistic, that the deep-rooted hair being tugged was his unwillingness to accept his own explanation for Inman's behavior. DeMarco even questioned his own reluctance to accept that explanation. *Do I feel personally insulted because Inman came after me?* he wondered. *Is that why I can't accept it?* He didn't regret putting a bullet in Inman at the lake, but he did regret having done so too soon. *Why did you come after me?* he should have asked. *Why did you kill Bonnie?*

The darkness offered no answers and no respite. After a while, he went back to the living room and climbed into his recliner. He refilled his glass and turned the television on. On channel 262 he found *Touch of Evil,* an old black-and-white movie, Charlton Heston as a Mexican, Orson Welles as a crooked cop, Marlene Dietrich as a hooker. He turned the volume low, audible but not understandable, and let the noir wash over him. Just enough noise and light to numb the pinch. Just enough whiskey to finally lull it to sleep.

SIXTY-SEVEN

He awoke to another gray dawn and an infomercial about a penis enhancement pill. Two very busty women in low-cut tops and high-cut hems were praising the product for its effect on their boyfriends' penises. De-Marco looked at the women until he was sufficiently awake to get depressed again. Then he took his unenhanced penis into the bathroom, where he urinated, stripped, and stood in a steaming shower with his forehead pressed to the tile. He was toweling dry when the telephone rang.

He caught it on the fourth ring, stood naked and dripping on the living room carpet.

"DeMarco," he said.

"Didn't catch you on the can, did I?"

He recognized the warm, gravelly voice of Delbert Woods, superintendent of the Albion Correctional Facility. It was a voice that always reminded him of the fifties character actor Broderick Crawford.

"Hate to disappoint you, Del, but no, you didn't."

"Just now haulin' your lazy ass out of bed?"

"A few minutes ago. What's up?"

"My blood pressure. Numbnuts here tells me you stopped by yesterday for some information."

"That I did."

"He didn't give you what you came for, am I right?"

"He gave me what he had. It just wasn't what I had hoped for."

"That's because he's a literal-minded half brain. You asked if Inman had taken any poetry classes. So Nelson pulled the poetry class rosters."

"And?" DeMarco said.

"He should have searched using Inman's name instead of the type of class. We offer lots of classes here. Most everybody takes one from time to time. We encourage it."

DeMarco took a long, slow breath. "Quit fucking with me, Del. What did you find?"

"Adult literacy class. January through May of this year."

"Last spring?"

"Yep."

"I thought Denton only taught poetry."

"You got a hard-on for Denton or what?"

"Who taught the fucking class?"

"Conescu. Looks like Roman Polanski with a thyroid problem?"

"You're shitting me."

"I shit you not."

For a few moments DeMarco was unable to speak. His brain was whirring, spinning like a rock tumbler. But the pinch in his cerebellum was gone.

Woods said, "They have you on leave for a few days?"

"Yeah," DeMarco said. "SOP."

"Sure. You doing okay?"

"I'm fine. Even better now."

"You better be fine. Nobody deserves a bullet more than Inman did."

"So why'd you let him go?"

"Model prisoner, I had no choice. Parole board says cut 'em loose, I cut 'em loose. But Inman. I always thought of him as a kind of pet shark, you know? Just keeps grinning and showing you his pearly whites. Thing is, you know sooner or later he's going to bite off your fucking arm."

"Unfortunately he did a hell of a lot more than that."

"That's what I'm saying. About time somebody aerated his chest."

DeMarco nodded. He considered the

goose bumps pimpling his arms, the chill of excitement playing down his spine. "I got to get dressed now," he said.

"Would it do any good for me to remind you that you're on temporary suspension?"

"I think it just got canceled."

"Knowing you, it never went into effect."

DeMarco made a move to hang up, then he remembered something. "Hey. About J. J."

"About who?"

"Your deputy. That's his nickname."

"Numbnuts? Since when?"

"Since he told me."

"First I ever heard of it."

"I think he prefers it to Nelson. And to Numbnuts."

"Christ, who wouldn't?"

"Don't chew him out over this, okay?"

"Why the hell not? It's not the first mistake he's made, I can tell you that."

"He's scared shitless, that's why."

"With good reason."

"Well, I'm going to take him out some night and get him hammered. See if I can't shake some of that stiffness out of him. Maybe you should join us."

"You buying?"

"Listen, your expense account is four times the size of mine."

"That's not the only thing that's four times the size of yours."

DeMarco laughed. "Hey, I appreciate the phone call. This is good information you gave me. I'll let you know how it plays out. Say hi to J. J. for me."

"You kind of like the kid, don't you? Think he's pretty cute?"

"You still driving that green Cherokee Laredo? I'll be sure to tell the boys out on the interstate to keep the radar guns ready."

"And I'll tell J. J. how much you miss him. Have a good day, Ry."

"You too, sport. I'll call you about that pitcher of beer."

SIXTY-EIGHT

The first thing DeMarco had to do was to clear the morning's events with his station commander.

"You are officially on suspension," Bowen told him. He had not yet removed the plastic lid from the extra large crème brûlée cappuccino DeMarco had purchased for him at the convenience store. Bowen sat at his desk, hands in his lap as he looked up at DeMarco. The sweetness of the drink wafted up through the sipping hole in the lid and was discernible with every breath.

"Don't even think about denying me this," DeMarco said.

"I don't know how to justify it. I'm the one who's going to have to answer for it."

"How about if you just tell everybody to kiss your rosy red ass."

"You have no idea what color my ass is. Don't pretend you do."

"I want this, Kyle. I fucking need this."

Bowen thought about it for thirty seconds. He peeled the lid off the coffee. A thin layer of foam still floated atop the liquid. The rising steam was sweet and heavy. He said, "Your presence is sure to rattle him. There's some value in that."

"You better believe there is."

"Or we could just bring him in for questioning. Let you stand in the corner and watch."

"You don't know this guy. He feels safe in his little cubicle. It's his fucking cave. We need to do it there."

"I could get my rosy red ass in a sling over this."

DeMarco smiled. "Trooper Morgan can do it all. I'll just be a spectator."

Bowen raised the paper cup to his lips. He allowed the foam to touch the tip of his tongue. The smoky caramel warmth filled his mouth. Then he said, "Yeah. Like that's really going to happen."

Sixty-Nine

DeMarco and Trooper Morgan strode softly down the corridor of Campbell Hall. At the appropriate door, DeMarco inserted the floor key he had persuaded the department secretary to lend him, then put his hand to the knob, turned it, swung the door open, and strode inside. Morgan followed but stayed hidden behind the row of filing cabinets.

Conescu jerked his head around. For just an instant, his eyes were bright with anger, his mouth coming open to castigate the interloper. Instead, he went motionless but for a tiny snort of air. "Good morning, Professor," DeMarco said.

Conescu told him, "I am making revisions to my book," and swept a hand toward the computer monitor. "I have no time for you."

DeMarco crossed behind him and stood just off Conescu's left shoulder, which required that the professor swivel to his left.

Now he glared up at DeMarco, but the brightness in his eyes was no longer due to anger.

DeMarco continued to smile. "I take it you found Carl Inman to be an apt student?"

Conescu blinked. "I do not recognize that name. I have no such student."

"Is that why you withdrew five thousand dollars from your account at Citizens Bank, sir? Five thousand just four days ago, plus another five thousand two weeks ago."

Now DeMarco could hear the man's breathing, the shallow, quick breaths, the rapid rise and fall of his chest. "I sent that money to family. My uncle and aunt in Romania."

"Why didn't you send them a check? Or make a wire transfer? Instead you withdrew it in cash. Because you gave it to Carl Inman. Most of it was found in his vehicle, still in the dated bank wrappers."

Conescu stared at DeMarco for another ten seconds. Then he closed his eyes. His chest rose and fell, rose and fell through a dozen short breaths. Eventually his shoulders sagged. He opened his eyes and turned slightly to his right, gazed past DeMarco to the window, and there, fixed his gaze on the four inches of dirty glass visible beneath the faded canvas blind.

"He was not supposed to kill anyone," Conescu said. "To discredit him only. As he deserved to be discredited."

"Except that Professor Huston didn't deserve discrediting, did he? Because he never touched any of the dancers. All he did was talk to them."

Conescu said nothing.

"How did you find out he was visiting Whispers? Did Inman contact you?"

"I only wanted to be left alone. He would never leave me alone to do my work."

Because he hated frauds, DeMarco thought. "So you cooked up this plan to have him videotaped at Whispers. You get tenure, promotion, whatever it was you wanted. Except that Professor Huston fooled you, didn't he? He was a better man than either of you."

"What that man did . . . Inman. What he did to that family. I had no part in any of it."

"How about the money you paid him to take care of me? Did you have any part in that?"

When Conescu failed to respond, DeMarco crossed to the window and raised the blind, filled the room with bright morning light. Conescu blinked and squinted, lowered his gaze to the floor.

"It was only for him to go away," he said. "He threatened me."

"You didn't pay him to get rid of me? Because maybe I had you worried?"

"I did not know the things he would do. He was . . . not a civilized man."

"I guess maybe you bit off a little more than you could chew, didn't you?"

Conescu slowly rotated his chair until he faced the computer screen again. He saved the document he had been working on, then closed it. He then shut down the computer. When the screen was black, he said, "My mother had a saying. If you lie down in shit, don't complain about the stink."

"Smart woman," DeMarco said. Ten seconds later, he cleared his throat, his signal to Trooper Morgan. The trooper came into the room and unsnapped the handcuffs from his belt. To Conescu he said, "You need to stand up now."

But Conescu did not move. He seemed about to slump forward in his chair. DeMarco put both hands on the back of the chair and slowly rotated it a half turn. Conescu looked up at him. "He did not like you," Conescu said.

"Are you speaking of Mr. Inman now?"

"He did not like you at all."

DeMarco gave Morgan a look of astonishment. "Imagine that," he said. "And me so adorable."

SEVENTY

DeMarco did not attend Bonnie's funeral, which had been organized, he assumed, either by her brother or some of the dancers. But two days later, just after seven in the morning, he stopped by the cemetery. The grave was marked only by a small bronze plaque on a metal stake and a small pile of frost-withered flowers atop the low mound of dirt, yellow and white calla lilies with their fluted petals shriveled and brown, wrinkled like old skin. He didn't know what he wanted to say to Bonnie, couldn't think of anything that, uttered aloud on such a gray still morning, would not sound foolish. He stood there for several minutes with his ungloved hands tucked into his armpits, stood there looking out across the leaf-strewn grounds, and thought to himself, *So many dead.* The air on his freshly shaved cheeks felt sharp against his skin, and the cold made even his good eye tear up. The sky was a muddy watercolor, a child's smear. A quarter mile away, an eighteen-wheeler Jake-braked as it approached the first traffic light in town, and the sudden roar of released air set DeMarco's teeth on edge. He waited until the truck had rumbled through town and could no longer be heard. Then he looked at the grave a final time.

"Okay," he finally said. "I'll see you later maybe."

A half hour later, DeMarco's car rolled to a stop beside Moby's little trailer. There were no lights on inside, no signs of habitation. He shut off the engine, then peered through his windshield at the layer of frost atop the trailer's tarred roof. He popped open his door and lifted the two paper cups of convenience store coffee out of the cup holders.

There was no response when he knocked on Moby's front door. He set one cup down on the concrete step and turned the knob. The door opened easily and released a chilled, sour scent into DeMarco's face. He picked up the second cup of coffee, stepped inside, and closed the door with his hip.

Moby lay on the short vinyl sofa, knees drawn against his chest, hands shoved between his legs. He was wearing a too-large black suit, probably a recent purchase from the Goodwill store, and a pair of scuffed brown loafers with white wool socks. Close to the sofa, a gallon bottle of Rhine wine sat on the floor beside a plastic coffee mug. The mug was empty; the bottle held only a puddle of wine.

DeMarco stood over him for a moment, motionless and listening. The coffee was hot against his hands, but the room was so cold that he could see his own exhalations in evanescing puffs of ghostly white. He leaned closer to Moby, watched the man's chest for a rise and fall. Satisfied then but beginning to shiver, DeMarco looked around for the thermostat, found it in the corner of the room, leaned close, and squinted. Fifty-four degrees. He slid the plastic lever to seventy-two and heard the pop of the oil burner's flame kicking on.

With the back of his hand, he nudged Moby's shoulder. Two more nudges, each more forceful than the last. Finally a low grunt and a slit-eyed squint. DeMarco said, "How about you sit up for a minute and have some coffee."

Another ten seconds passed before Moby responded. Instead of sitting up, he squeezed himself together even more tightly. "It's fucking cold in here," he said.

DeMarco took a seat at the little dinette

table across from him. He set both cups of coffee atop the table. "You had your heater turned off," he said. "You should feel things warming up in a minute or two."

Moby lay there and blinked at him.

DeMarco said, "I brought one coffee black, one with cream and sugar. Take your pick."

Moby gave a little nod at the bottle on the floor. "There anything left in there?"

DeMarco emptied the dregs from the bottle into the plastic mug, but instead of handing it to Moby, he set the mug on the table. He said, "I need you to sit up for me."

Moby brought a hand to his cheek, rubbed his face for a while, then scratched his forehead. His movements fell into a slow repetition, fingernails tracing a slow loop from the top of his forehead to his eyebrows and back around again, over and over. Finally DeMarco leaned forward and pushed the hand away. "You're scratching the hell out of yourself, Moby. Sit up and talk to me."

By slow degrees, Moby dragged himself into a lopsided sitting position. DeMarco handed him the mug of wine. Moby took a long swallow, then shivered. DeMarco told him, "You'd be better off with the coffee."

Moby said, "I disagree."

DeMarco peeled the lid off the cup of black coffee, took a sip, held the paper cup between his knees. "I need you to help me figure something out," he said. "Why would Inman kill your sister?"

With both hands, Moby clutched the mug of wine against his chest, just below his chin. Every now and then, he raised the mug to his lips. His gaze never left the floor.

"Why, Moby? You're the only one who might know."

Moby's head moved back and forth, a slow negation. *But,* DeMarco wondered, *a negation of what?*

Moby said, "She wasn't in on any of that shit he did. She wasn't like that."

"That's the way I see it too," DeMarco told him. "But afterward. When it came out in the news what had happened at the Huston place. She must have had her suspicions, right? She must have asked him a question or two."

"You ever notice that little limp she's got? That was from asking him a question he didn't want to answer."

"What about the abortion?"

Moby sat motionless, said nothing, held himself unnaturally still.

"You knew about it, right?"

Moby pursed his lips, thought for a moment, and nodded.

DeMarco said, "Huston claimed he never touched her."

"Far as I know he didn't."

"So the baby was Inman's?"

Moby said nothing. He stared at the floor.

"Moby?" DeMarco said. "She doesn't need you to keep her secrets anymore."

Moby raised the mug to his lips, held it there for a moment, smiled a small smile. Then he tilted the cup up and took a swallow. Then he closed his eyes and sat motionless for a while, the cup against his chest. Finally he sucked in a noisy, glutinous breath, then opened his eyes, leaned back against the cushions, and fixed his gaze on the door.

He said, "She had a couple of regular customers, you know? I don't mean at Whispers. Private customers. Longtime friends. All she knew was that somebody's stuff must have slipped past her diaphragm. She's forty-two years old, runs a strip club, for Chrissakes. You think she was going to let herself bring a baby into this world, no matter how much she might have wanted one?"

"So how did Inman find out about the abortion? Why would she tell him?"

"That abortion place did a thing on her.

Before they gave her the pill and whatever. Like an X-ray or something. On her belly."

"A sonogram."

Moby nodded. "They put the picture of it on a computer disk for her. She said it looked like a fuzzy dot is all. But she just kept telling me about it, you know; she got all teary-eyed. Over a fuzzy little dot. I guess that's why she held on to it. That computer disk, I mean."

"And Inman found it?"

"She already knows he's going to beat the shit out of her, right? I mean, that's a given. But if she admits that the baby might not be his . . ."

"So she did what she had to do."

"All her life," Moby said.

"Okay. So you think that's maybe why Inman killed her that night he came for me?"

Moby shrugged. "All I know is she thought you were a decent guy. A decent guy for a cop is what she said. And when she packed up to leave her place, she just thought they were clearing out for a while. Getting away from all the mess. He was taking her someplace warm, she said. Sit out the winter. She hated the fucking winters here. Always did want to get away from the cold."

"So it probably surprised her when he

pulled the car over on the street behind my house."

"I figure he would have reached for that big knife of his, you know? He kept it under the seat when he was driving. She would've said something then for sure."

DeMarco nodded. "She knew where I lived. From the old days. Back when she had that little place on West Venango."

Moby sipped his wine. Then, "She didn't often stand up to him, but she would have over that. I even know what she would've said. She'd've said, 'You do this, and I won't be here when you get back.' "

DeMarco nodded and considered the possibilities. *So Inman had planned to kidnap me, steal my car, transfer his clothes and traveling money out of the Mustang, then drive north. The maps were probably a ruse to fool Bonnie into believing they were headed for Mexico. Maybe he had intended from the beginning to kill her too. As punishment for destroying what he thought of as his, for depriving him of another poor creature to bully and beat. He was a nutcase, but not an idiot; he knew I'd be hauling him in sooner or later. Maybe he thought that by kidnapping me, then killing me, making it difficult for anybody to find my body for a while, he could short-circuit the investigation long enough to find a safe place to hide. Maybe he thought I could lead him to Thomas.*

"The thing about Bonnie," Moby said. "She didn't often go off, you know? But when she did, she let it fly in all directions."

"Go off how? I don't get what you're saying."

"It took a lot for her to snap. Usually it only happened when she was really, really scared about something."

"Like what?" DeMarco asked.

Moby said, "You know why she gave me that job at Whispers?"

"How about you tell me."

"Up till three years or so ago, she always hired some college kid as a bouncer. Somebody with more muscles than brains."

"So what happened three years ago?"

"I had a little too much to drink one night. Borrowed somebody's car. Sliced a telephone pole in half. The top half came right down through the roof of the car. Missed me by half a splinter or so."

"That's when she lost her temper?"

"At the hospital that night. I was just banged up a little is all. Till she started laying into me. Called me every name in the book at the top of her lungs. It got so bad, they wanted to give her a shot of something and strap her down. I told them to leave her alone, 'cause I had it coming. And I knew she was just scared because of what I almost done to myself."

"And you think she might have lost her temper like that with Inman?"

"I think she could've. He was always pushing, always digging. Always accusing her of this and that. For all I know, they really were off to someplace warm and then he started in on her. Calling her a slut, a whore. Saying she fucked this guy, she fucked that guy. Maybe she just lost it. With him, she was damn close to the edge most of the time. And she could cut you when she wanted to. She'd say shit that'd make you bleed like a stuck pig, whether it was true or not."

"So what do you think she might have said that night?"

"His big thing was . . . I mean, the thing he was always throwing in her face was the sex stuff. It was like, 'How many dirty cocks did you suck today, bitch? Who'd you fuck today, slut?' If he wasn't accusing her of fucking, he was telling her she was too ugly to fuck, she was all used up. She was just a fuckbag is all. That was his nickname for her. Fuckbag. That really used to piss me off."

"And you think she might have finally had all she could take of it."

"I can hear her, man. I mean, I didn't; I don't know for sure. But I can hear what she might have said. It would've been like, 'You want to know what I did today? I sucked some stranger's dick, then Huston fucked me three times, then DeMarco came in my ass. Then after lunch, I sucked De-Marco's cock and licked out Huston's asshole.' And on and on and on. She could be as crude as they come, I'll tell you that. But she was no whore. She did Inman because she was afraid of him, plus she had a couple of private customers who treated her right. But she was no goddamn whore. And I am glad as hell that sick, twisted motherfucker is dead. I just wish I'd had the balls to be the one who took him out."

By now, Moby was sitting huddled over, scrunched up in misery with the plastic coffee mug pressed to his chest.

DeMarco sipped his coffee for a while. It was only his second of the morning, but it tasted bitter already. It tasted like his fifth cup, when his stomach would start to sour and a tight astringency would rise into his throat. He set the half-empty cup on the table beside the full one. *I need to start treating my stomach better,* he thought.

Then he looked at Moby again. A small man in a too-large suit, stubbly cheeked, hopeless and alone, wet eyes blinking back tears.

DeMarco told him, "You can't be falling asleep in here with the heat turned off, Moby. Have you been like this since the funeral?" He was answered with a look from baleful eyes, a look that asked him, *What difference does it make?*

DeMarco told him, "I could get you into a place in Erie if you'd let me. Sort of a community house. You'd have your own room probably, but there'd be a few other people around. It's a place where everybody sort of watches out for each other."

"You're saying I can't take care of myself. Maybe I don't want to."

"Fine. Turn the heat off and fall asleep. The kind of sleep you don't wake up from, is that what you want? If so, I hope you like the idea of rats crawling around in your stomach, because that's what's going to happen in a day or so. The minute you start to stink. You'll be a rat smorgasbord in no time at all. They start out anywhere they can find an opening — eyes, nose, asshole, you name it. Eat their way inside, invite the family and all the neighbors in, then they just slurp and chomp away. You end up as rat shit scattered all over your own floor. It's a very efficient process."

Moby hugged himself and shivered. After a while he said, "They going to let me drink in that place?"

"You know better than that."

Another minute of silence. Then, "Am I going to get Bonnie's car back at least?"

"When you're ready for it, I'll see that you get it. Same thing with Bonnie's house."

"Is there blood all over it? The car, I mean. Where she was sitting."

"You can have the seats replaced. There'll probably be some money coming to you as well. Did she own Whispers or rent the building?"

"Rented."

"So that's one thing you won't have to worry about. You get yourself right, and I'll see that everything of hers goes to you. But not unless you get yourself right."

"If it's mine, you can't keep it from me."

"You'd be surprised what I can do, Moby."

"I thought you were supposed to be a decent guy."

"You think Bonnie wants you to be rat shit? I'm doing this for her, whether you like it or not."

Moby sniffed a couple of times. "What about him?"

"Who? Inman?"

"Where'd they bury him?"

545

"He was cremated."

"Where's his ashes?"

"We'll hold them for a while to see if anybody claims them. Then we'll dispose of them."

"Can I claim them?"

"Why would you want them?"

"So I can dump them in a toilet somewhere and piss all over them."

DeMarco thought for a few moments. "You going to let me drive you up to Erie?"

"I don't know," Moby said. "I might."

"In that case . . . In a way, you're sort of the brother-in-law, right?"

Something like a smile came to Moby's lips. "Seems to me."

"So we give it thirty days," DeMarco told him. "If nobody has claimed the ashes by then, they're all yours."

SEVENTY-ONE

Now came the emptiness. A deep hole that if not soon filled would make a perfect home for the birds of sorrow. DeMarco could sense them circling already, twittering shrilly, eager to move in. But DeMarco did not want to accommodate them this time. Why must his heart be always a nest of sadness? Unfortunately he had little talent for making it otherwise. He lacked Thomas Huston's gifts for creation, for imagining himself as something other than he was.

So he sat on the back porch a long while that afternoon. For a long while, he stared at the unkempt yard and the unfinished path, but they registered on his optic nerve only as backdrop to what could not be seen. He understood the cause of his sadness. The source of all sadness. The loss of what had once been but was now irretrievable. The loss of what had never been and could never be.

For the past many years, he had filled that emptiness with his work. One case of tragedy after another, puzzle after morbid puzzle to solve. *Is that all you have to look forward to?* he asked himself now. *Just sit here and stare at the grass until another catastrophe occurs? Live a life that can find meaning only in other people's mistakes and misfortune?*

The air was crisp and clean and cool as only a day in November can be. Three weeks before Thanksgiving. Seven weeks before winter. He did not want the birds of sorrow taking up residence in his heart again. They were small, black, noisy birds, and they would add nothing but darkness to the dark days and long dark nights ahead. But he did not know how to keep them out. Work silenced them only during the daylight hours. No amount of whiskey could drown them.

At the end of Thomas Huston's novel, the one Huston had signed and presented to DeMarco in appreciation of the lunches they had shared, the novel's protagonist says, "What I have to do now is that which is not easy. That which I most fear. If I keep accommodating my fears, I can only move in reverse. That would be fine if by moving in reverse I could move back through time, but the past is a wall, a solid and impermeable wall. The past is a fortress that cannot be stormed."

DeMarco remembered the first time he had read that passage, and how, when he'd read the first line, he had thought it a grammatical error. Years earlier, back when Laraine was pregnant and he had decided to try for a promotion to station commander, he had asked her to proofread the short essay he had been required to submit. What he remembered most about her critique was the lesson on the difference between *that* and *which*. The difference between nonrestrictive and restrictive modifying phrases. A comma preceding *which,* no comma before *that.* Then, years later, alone in a quiet house, with no wife or teacher or proofreader to explain things to him, there on the final page of Huston's second novel was *that which is not easy.* No comma. What had initially puzzled De-Marco was that the error was repeated in the next sentence too. *That which I most fear.* So, he had concluded, Huston must have had a reason for that awkward construction. DeMarco studied those two lines. He read them out loud. Listened to them. And finally heard the hesitancy couched in an awkward formality. The hint of exhortation. *Yes, of course,* DeMarco had thought back then. Huston wants the sentences to be awkward. Because the narrator is screwing up his nerve here, trying to talk himself into something. Trying to force down his terror of what he knows he has to do. Of that very difficult thing he knows he must do.

Now, in a house whose silence he had grown accustomed to, DeMarco reread the paragraph in full. Then he laid the book against his chest as he leaned back in his recliner and stared at the ceiling and asked himself, *And what do* you *fear, DeMarco? What is that which you must do?*

He thought about it a very long time. Despite his efforts to do otherwise, he could come up with only one answer.

SEVENTY-TWO

It was later than usual when Laraine finally pulled into her driveway. This time her car was followed by a black SUV. The man who climbed out of it appeared to be several years younger than her. He walked with a cockier step than most, swung a bottle of beer from his left hand, even paused outside his car to survey the neighborhood and take a long look at the pale gibbous moon. It seemed to DeMarco that the man actually wanted to be seen standing there on the edge of an older woman's midnight lawn, that he conveyed none of the furtiveness of his paunchier predecessors, maybe even wanted Laraine to take note of his insouciance, consider herself that much more fortunate for his attention. Laraine was already inside her house, the front door standing open, before the man deigned to cross the yard.

This time, DeMarco did not wait for the

usual signals that she and her new friend were on their way upstairs. He climbed out of his car and walked briskly to the front door and knocked. Soon she opened the door and stood there looking at him with the same practiced expression on her face, the same clouded eyes.

He told her, "You know the kind of man I am. When I make up my mind to do something, I do it."

Her face remained a blank, a cold and beautiful stone.

"So I just want you to know. I'm done letting you do this to me. And I'm done watching you do it to yourself."

For just a moment, her brow furrowed.

"I really don't know if you think you're punishing me or yourself or both of us. All I know is that I'm not going to participate in it anymore."

She kept her mouth tight but he could hear her breathing now, the sibilance of controlled inhalations. He believed too that he could hear her heart beating, a soft thrumming in the night.

He touched her cheek. Its warmth startled him and drove a long splinter of heat through his chest. "Good-bye, sweetheart," he told her. "I'm sorry for all the pain."

He walked away then and struggled

against the urge to look back. If he looked back and she was still standing there, he would return to her. But he did not look back after he had climbed into the car and he did not look back as he drove away.

A few minutes later, on the interstate and heading south, with no music playing and the only sounds the hum of metal speeding over concrete through the chill black air, he pulled to the side of the road and sat with his foot on the brake as he tried to catch his breath.

When his breath finally slowed, he reached for the pack of antiseptic baby wipes in the console, took one out, and cleaned his palms, then wiped each finger one by one. Then he crumpled up the little towel and tossed it to the floor. He stared into the darkness ahead.

Then, acting on impulse, he pulled his cell phone from his pocket. *About that rain check . . .* he typed, and hit Send, and sat waiting.

And just when he began to wish he could pull the text back, erase it, go home and be alone, and live alone with all his misery just as he deserved, his screen lit up with Jayme Matson's text: *Saturday night. Bring flowers. Wear a jacket and tie. You're taking me to the most expensive restaurant in town. Try not to be an ass.*

Twenty seconds later, he pulled back onto the highway and brought his vehicle up to speed. Only then did he give in to the need to take a long look in the rearview mirror. Behind him, the lights of Erie appeared to be underwater now, a twinkling city sinking into an indigo sea.

READING GROUP GUIDE

1. The character of Thomas Huston, a writer, was named as an homage to Hemingway and his novel *Islands in the Stream,* whose main character is Thomas Hudson, a painter. Can you discern any other Hemingway influences in *Two Days Gone?*

2. The novel is divided into four sections, just as Thomas Huston's novel-in-progress was intended to be. Why did Silvis structure *Two Days Gone* this way?

3. Are there any other ways in which *Two Days Gone* parallels Thomas Huston's proposed novel *D?*

4. Many of the characters in Silvis's novels are, as the *Washington Times* noted of his first mystery, "extraordinarily literate." Is it necessary to be familiar with all the literary allusions in *Two Days Gone* to be

engaged by the novel?

5. At what point did you become certain of Huston's innocence or guilt?

6. Silvis has said that one of the themes of this novel is what happens to men when they lack, in Thomas Huston's words, "the annealing effect of women." Did the absence of a prominent female character detract from your enjoyment of this novel?

7. What other themes and motifs do you see at work in this novel?

8. Hemingway wrote that a story's end must be inevitable but unpredictable. Does the ending of *Two Days Gone* achieve those qualities?

9. In a review of Silvis's novel *The Boy Who Shoots Crows*, *New York Times* bestselling author John Lescroart wrote that "Randall Silvis gets to the hearts and souls of his characters like few other, if any, novelists." Did the author succeed in getting to the hearts and souls of his major characters in *Two Days Gone*?

10. Randall Silvis tells his writing students

that the two most important pages in a story are the first and the last. He says, "The first page brings the reader in, and the last page brings the reader back." Does *Two Days Gone* succeed in doing that?

A CONVERSATION
WITH THE AUTHOR

What are your influences as a writer?
There are many. More, probably, than I'm
even aware of. I'll start with my next-door
neighbor when I was a boy, Sara McNaugh-
ton. I have no idea how old she was when I
was little, but she looked ancient to me, a
small, shriveled, hunched over, and hooked-
nosed spinster — very Wicked Witch of the
West–like, for those who chose to see her
that way, as did most of the older boys in
the village, especially when an errant softball
flew into her yard, was grabbed by her, and
was tossed under her porch. Summer or
winter she wore long gingham dresses and a
wide-brimmed sunbonnet. She lived in a
tiny white cottage with an ivy-covered front
porch, almost never had visitors, and seldom
volunteered to talk to anybody. She had no
television, maybe no radio, and, as far as I
could tell, spent her days baking bread,
making jams, gardening, and tossing errant

balls under her porch.

For some reason I found myself knocking on her door nearly every day, especially before I was old enough for school. She would look out at me and scowl through her screen, and I would ask, "Got any jelly bread?" She always did. Thick, yeasty, crusty, homemade bread spread with home-made strawberry or plum preserves. And we would sit at her little kitchen table playing Old Maid until my mother started calling for me.

When I was seven or so, Sara gave me my first hardcover book. An illustrated copy of *The Swiss Family Robinson.* I can still see the bright greens and yellows of the cover art. I felt like a millionaire. And I was hooked. Sara and books and jelly bread. To a lonely little boy in a hardscrabble village, they were the closest thing to comfort and salvation I had back then.

Later there was Hemingway with his deceptive simplicity and masterful subtext. Faulkner with his lush prolixity and steamy, shadow-shrouded settings. Garcia Marquez with his ghosts and bedraggled angels and his startling, idiosyncratic way of seeing a world that seemed so like my own.

And I continue to be influenced and taught: by my sons' openness and tolerance and big-hearted love; by the many brilliant women and men who write so beautifully and insightfully; by my eager and determined students; by my dreams, the music I love, the night sky at three a.m., a smile from a stranger. Everywhere I look there's another inspiration.

If you hadn't become a writer, what would you be doing now?
Before I decided to become a writer, around the age of twenty-one, what I really wanted was to be a songwriter. I wanted to be the next Paul Simon. When I wasn't reading I was banging away on the family piano, writing song after song after song. I taught myself to play piano and guitar and to do musical notation, but I was too shy and insecure to ever share the songs with anyone.

During my first two years in college, where, for lack of any semblance of true ambition, I was studying to be an accountant, I spent all my spare time hanging out in the music rooms, sometimes tinkling away at a piano but mostly just sitting there with the door open so I could eavesdrop on all the real student musicians. I envied them and was intimidated by their talent and technical knowledge. I ached to be a music major. Music has the power, like no other force on earth, to fill us with emotion and to connect us with one another in some mysterious alchemical transcendence of even our basest human shortcomings.

Fortunately, in my junior year, two professors, during the same week, took me aside to comment positively on a couple of writing assignments. Both told me I had talent and asked if I had ever considered being a writer. I grabbed that suggestion like a drowning man grabbing a chunk of Styrofoam. And so began my self-education as a writer. And I learned, through Hemingway and others, that the written word can possess music too.

So, in answer to the question *What would I be doing if I hadn't become a writer?* I honestly don't know. I only know that everything I've done of any importance derives from two activities — trying to be the best father I can, and trying to be the best writer I can.

How would you define or characterize your writing?

I've written in several genres of fiction, and I also love creative nonfiction. But I suspect you're asking a bigger question than that — one that asks me to account for what and how I write, especially in regards to fiction. In order to answer that, a couple points of reference are required. At one end of the contemporary fiction spectrum, let's say we have commercial, mass market, plot-driven genre fiction. At the other end we have plot-less literary fiction. I see my own work as being smack dab in the middle of that spectrum.

I'll explain. I started out as a literary writer. My first book was awarded the Drue Heinz Literature Prize by Joyce Carol Oates. So what does it mean to be a literary writer? It means that theme and character development, the character's inner journey, are the most important elements to the story. Prior to the arrival of minimalism, it also meant that distinctive language was important, as were setting and mood and tone. Minimalism, to my mind, came into vogue in the late seventies and sucked all the lifeblood out of American fiction by employing pedestrian prose, vague settings, and a universal theme that life is bleak and meaningless. Fortunately, true minimalism died an early death, and in general contemporary literary fiction has gravitated away from that stark end of the spectrum. But literary fiction has still not yet fully reembraced the importance of plot.

And that is the most apparent difference between a genre novel and a literary novel. In the genre novel, plot is king; the story is typically driven by the need to resolve an external problem, such as saving the world from an asteroid, banishing an evil wizard to another dimension, or identifying and capturing a serial killer. The protagonist is often one-dimensional and does not change from the beginning of the novel to the end. In a literary novel, there often is no external problem to resolve; the story is driven by the protagonist's emotional or psychological need — for love, for acceptance, for understanding, and so forth.

I wrote my first mystery novel in the early nineties. My agent's response was that the novel was too well written to market as a mystery, and the plot was too strong to market as a literary novel. I said, "It's a literary mystery." He said, "There's no such thing." I said, "That's why I wrote one."

I ended up marketing that novel on my own, and that's the kind of crime novel I've been writing ever since: one that pays attention to theme, deep characterization and character growth, dialogue with subtext, imagistic description, some interesting twist on structure when possible, and prose that, when applicable, reaches for the musical and poetic. *And* a fully developed plot.

Earlier in my career I described myself as a literary writer who never abandoned plot, and I think that definition still holds. Even in my noncrime novels I aim for a beginning, a middle, and an end, though the plot in those stories focuses on the character's inner journey and not on some external goal.

Readers who prefer commercial mass market mysteries, which emphasize plot over any other element, might find my descriptions of setting and my characters' introspections and inner struggles distracting from the external goal. But for me, the resolution of the external problem is not of primary importance, but serves to reveal and test character and drive it toward a changed state of awareness. For me, character growth is the most important part of a novel. The addition of a compelling plot with an external goal helps to bring about that inner growth.

It's probably fair to say that I'm a throwback to the generation of writers preceding my own generation. I continue to reread Hemingway (who was not a minimalist, by the way, no matter what the minimalists claim), Steinbeck, Eudora Welty, and other masters of the twentieth century. I also read a few of today's younger literary writers, but generally only their short stories. Like most readers, I need something to happen in a novel, but I also need those events to have meaning and application to the soul of humanity.

ACKNOWLEDGMENTS

All the solitary hours a writer pours into a novel would avail little if not for the solitary hours poured into it by many unseen others. Anyway I assume those others also do their work in solitude; maybe they work in pairs or crews or tag teams, but I'd rather imagine them slaving over my words in a poorly lit and otherwise unoccupied room, just as I do. Maybe they will have a little music for company, but nothing too upbeat, something along the lines of Mozart's *Requiem,* for example, because as everybody who has ever worked on a book knows, this work can be as grueling in its way as crawling on your knees through ten acres of ground-hugging plants to pick potato beetles off one at a time and flick them into a galvanized bucket filled with soapy water. But it can also be as transcendent as the *Requiem* — or as picking potato beetles when you are in the right frame of mind for it.

Knowing other people are engaged in the same underappreciated labor and squeezing a perverse kind of joy out of it is what keeps me writing, especially if it's my field of potatoes they are picking over. Sometimes I like to picture each of my collaborators working their way down a row, their backs aching, hands filthy with beetle juice, finger-nails broken, eyes going cross-eyed in the faltering light. It's inspirational.

Thirty years ago, I would have written (and did) a dull-as-dirt acknowledgment to thank each of my collaborators. It would have had all the excitement of a divorce decree. Back then I had no idea how difficult and precarious a job it is to turn out a novel every couple of years. It gets more difficult and precarious every year. So does living. To me, they're pretty much the same thing.

So this time, I'm putting some honest-to-God gratitude into it. I want each of these thank-yous to be the equivalent of a bear hug and a big, sloppy kiss. I want to scoop each one of my collaborators up out of the dirt and clutch them to my bosom. (And yes, men do have bosoms. I Googled it just to be sure: *the breast, conceived of as the center of feelings or emotions.* If you can't trust Google, who can you trust?)

And I am using the term *collaborators* because that's exactly what these individuals do: *to collude, join, assist, abet, usually willingly.* I also enjoy the subversive connotations of the word *collaborator.* If you don't think the making of a novel is a subversive act, you've never made one. The sole purpose of the work involved is to undermine society as we currently know it.

My most ardent big, sloppy kiss goes out to my first and probably most exhausted collaborator, my literary agent, the wonderful Sandy Lu. This otherwise intelligent and perspicacious young woman is unfortunately saddled with a literary aesthetic nearly as ancient as my own, which is to say she does not love anemic prose any more than I do, despite a literary culture that cries out for it like an overweight infant bawling for another bowl of mashed peas. I cannot tell you how long and hard she searched for just the right editor for this novel — but not until she had run the manuscript under the microscope time after time, dye-staining every flawed cell and organelle. Without her collaboration, this novel would not be a novel; it would be a stack of slowly yellowing pages, if, indeed, it escaped the flames long enough to become one.

Also essential to the success of this collaboration was that just-right editor, my Goldilocks editor, the wonderful Anna Michels, another lover of the dark and brooding and irreverent and literary, of the academic and grisly and the grisliness of academe. Not only does she possess the consummate good taste to like this novel (insert smiley face emoticon), but also the consummate good sense to tell me all the ways the story could be improved. And then she championed the novel through a gauntlet of good reasons to simply let it fall from the vine and die, not least of which is that an editor's own career, like an agent's, lives or dies by the books she chooses to champion.

Agents and editors perform similar functions in that they employ their own talents to elevate both the book and its author. If they choose their acquisitions wisely, they also elevate readers and, in the best of scenarios, the culture as a whole. As literary gatekeepers, they can either pander to and perpetuate the lowest common denominator of taste, or they can exercise a delicate manipulation by challenging both the writer and society as a whole to be better than they are.

I could spend another page or so here accentuating my indebtedness to both Sandy and Anna by comparing them to other agents and editors I've been acquainted with over the past thirty years. But there is no comparison. I feel blessed to have these two young women on my side. I've always known that if I am ever to be saved, it will be by a woman. Little did I know it would take two of them, working together, to do the job.

And to the entire team at Landmark, I am humbled and deeply grateful not only for what each of you does, but that you have chosen to do it, to care so deeply about books and the fools who write them that you willingly spend your days (and, I imagine, many nights) copyediting, fact-checking, packaging and promoting, formatting and illustrating, and adorning and otherwise beautifying those books. Without unseen toilers like you, there would be no books, and therefore little dissemination of information and wisdom, little chance to explore distant places and cultures, little chance to be stirred by another's courage or despair or joy or triumph, little balm for the aching soul. Without you, we fools might still be wandering the land to tell our stories from campfire to campfire. Without you, we would leave small trace of ourselves when the wind of time blows our dust far and wide.

And what can I say of those individuals who, without pay or other pocketable recompense, will consent to read a raw manuscript so as to intercept its flaws and infirmities before a reader can? Their time and expertise is present in this novel too. I owe much to writer/editor Michael Dell for pointing out at least two dozen typos and misspellings my forty readings of the manuscript missed, and for his keen editorial insights illuminating textual moments when the clarity I thought existed did not exist. My thanks also go out to Trooper Jason Urbani of the Pennsylvania State Police, who patiently and generously responded to all of my questions regarding behavior and protocol among those guardians in gray and black.

Gentlemen, I thank you. I hope that your contributions to this novel will win each of you a few extra credits in the karma column, though I doubt you have need for them.

And no acknowledgment page would be complete if it ignores those who make the rest of us possible. Without Readers, those essential and beloved Readers, we would all be six shades of bereft.

A writer without readers is like a man adrift on the ocean in a very small boat. In that small boat, he might float from island to island, from one strange and exciting place to the next. He might make wondrous observations and discoveries, might be thrilled to the marrow by the revelations that come to him out there in the vastness of a star-speckled night when the seam disappears between earth and sky, God and sailor.

But because he is alone in that boat, he will have no one to share his discoveries with, no way to test the soundness of his insights. Is he an explorer or just a madman? The wonders he carries will lie rotting in the bottom of his boat until he gets tired of the way they smell in solitude and tosses them overboard, himself along with them.

The irony of this business is that most writers are solitary and misanthropic, but to be of any value, they must also be the garrulous captains who stand at the bows of their ships and cry out, "Iceberg over there! Whale sounding there! Sea serpent dead ahead!" The writer's cargo is a human one, and he must pilot his passengers up and down the swells of human emotion, through the sargasso of grief and over the jagged reefs of despair.

His job is to lead his passengers, not by the mind, but by the heart and the gut, to chaperone them into a white-knuckling storm or down through an ear-popping dive or into a cove of sweet relief. A writer's job is to love his readers and to want nothing more than to pilot them from experience to experience, emotion to emotion. The best fiction is a voyage of feeling, and the writer's job is to generate *sentipensante* for his readers, those feelings that give rise not to an intellectual kind of knowledge but an emotional knowledge, a deeper connection with what Faulkner called "the old verities and truths of the heart."

Another way of looking at this relationship between writer and readers is through its intimacy: the reader comes to a story wanting to be wooed, desirous of seduction. If the writer's inducements are successful, the voice sufficiently tempting, the promises sufficiently alluring, the reader gives herself over to the story not for minutes but hours and, for days at a time, melding her own imagination with the writer's while falling into step with the characters, hoping for the best, giving them her heart. What greater gift can a writer receive than this?

At its best, the making of a novel, from the original thought to the reader's bookshelf, is a long and tenuous journey of unselfish love. Each of us gives to the story what we have to give. Maybe that's a romantic notion that seldom holds true today, but it's the notion I cling to.

Writers survive and endure only because of all of you, collaborators one and all. To misquote the Beatles, we get by with a lot of help from our friends. And so, to each and every one of you, I can say only this:

Thank you, my collaborator. Thank you, my friend.

ABOUT THE AUTHOR

Randall Silvis's fifteen books of fiction and nonfiction have appeared on Best of the Year lists from the *New York Times,* the Toronto *Globe & Mail,* SfSite.com, and the International Association of Crime Writers, as well as on several editors' and booksellers' pick lists. His multigenre work has been hailed as masterful, not only by the *New York Times Book Review,* but also by *Publishers Weekly, Booklist,* and *Mystery Scene* magazine.

The author's short fiction has twice been nominated for a Pushcart Prize and has been included in the *Best of the Net* anthology and Houghton Mifflin Harcourt's *Best American Mystery Stories* series.

As a former contributing writer for the Discovery Channel magazines, Silvis authored numerous cover and feature stories on subjects of history, natural history, biography, and science and technology. His nonfiction narrative about the exploration of Labrador, *Heart So Hungry,* was a Best of the Year pick by the Toronto *Globe & Mail.* His many articles and essays have appeared in the *Chronicle of Higher Education,* the *Christian Science Monitor, The Writer, Writer's Digest, Pittsburgh Magazine,* and elsewhere.

Also a prize-winning playwright and produced screenwriter, Randall Silvis's literary awards include the Drue Heinz Literature Prize; two literature fellowships from the National Endowment for the Arts; a Fulbright Senior Scholar Research Award; six writing fellowship awards from the Pennsylvania Council on the Arts for his fiction, drama, and screenwriting; and a doctor of letters degree from Indiana University of Pennsylvania for "distinguished literary achievement."

Cohost of the popular podcast series *The Writer's Hangout* (www.thewritershangout .com), Silvis lives in western Pennsylvania, the setting for much of his work.